GILBERT DE VILERS
Defrocked Brother Gregory took his bride at swordpoint, and stole her love with his passionate embrace. But not even Margaret could keep him from his perilous crusade.

MARGARET OF ASHBURY
She had found her destiny in Gregory. Now she would risk her life to save him from unspeakable danger, calling upon the powers of heaven and earth for aid in her daring plan.

IN PURSUIT OF THE GREEN LION

"EVEN MORE DELIGHTFUL THAN RILEY'S *A VISION OF LIGHT* . . . GRAND ADVENTURES AT A JOLLY CLIP."
                                        —*Kirkus Reviews*

"A CUNNINGLY CONTRIVED, CONVINCING, THOROUGHLY GOOD BOOK."
                                        —*The Macon Beacon*

"A MARVELOUS, FULL-BLOODED PICTURE OF THE MEDIEVAL WORLD—AND OF AN UNFORGETTABLE WOMAN WHO LIVED LIFE TO THE HILT."
                                        Book-of-the-Month Club News

By the author

A VISION OF LIGHT

IN PURSUIT
OF THE
GREEN LION

JUDITH MERKLE RILEY

A DELL BOOK

Published by
Dell Publishing
a division of
Bantam Doubleday Dell Publishing Group, Inc.
666 Fifth Avenue
New York, New York 10103

The trademark Dell® is registered in the U.S. Patent and Trademark Office.

ISBN: 0-440-21103-4

Reprinted by arrangement with Delacorte Press

Printed in the United States of America

Published simultaneously in Canada

April 1992

10 9 8 7 6 5 4 3 2 1

RAD

for
Marlow
with love

ACKNOWLEDGMENTS

I am grateful for the loving support of my husband, Parkes, my son Marlow, and my daughter Elizabeth, who read the manuscript and offered valuable criticism. I also owe much to the intelligent insight of my editor, Carole Baron, and the encouragement and wisdom of my agent, Jean Naggar.

As always, among the great pleasures of working on a book with a wide range of historical sources are the hours spent in splendid libraries. I am particularly appreciative of the outstanding medieval resources of the Henry E. Huntington Library of San Marino, California, where a large part of the background research for this book was completed. I would also like to thank the Honnold Library of the Claremont Colleges and the Pomona City Library. But most especially, I wish to acknowledge the contribution of the Francis Bacon Foundation Library, for it is from the pages of its alchemical collection that the Green Lion leapt whole one sunny fall morning.

PROLOGUE

It was in the Year of Our Lord 1358, in the summertime, just two days before the Feast of Saint Barnabas, that a Voice spoke out of heaven into the ear of my understanding.

"Margaret," said the Voice, "just what are you doing there?" My pen stopped, and I looked up.

"Surely, You know already," I said to the still air.

"Of course I do, but I want you to tell Me, and that is entirely different," the Voice answered.

But to begin in the right place, I must begin with God's gift of daughters, which is made to mothers as a test and trial. For on the Day of Judgment when we must answer for all things, what shall we answer if our daughters be too stubborn and impatient for the needle? Thus does God try our souls, and likewise cast out vanity, for the mothers of ungovernable children must be always humble.

Now the day on which the Voice spoke was all fair and warm, and everything was blooming and growing. We had removed our household from London for the summer once again; the disorder in the kitchens at Whithill Manor had at last been put right, and there remained only the never-ending clatter of the carpenters rebuilding the burnt stables and outbuildings. The air was so fresh, and the green fields so inviting, only a fool would imagine that two little girls as willful as Cecily and Alison would remember their duty. And only twice a fool could think that two children so wily could not, like the serpent, beguile their nursemaid into the bargain. Still, as I climbed the long outside stairs to peep into the bower up under the eaves, I did not foresee what I would find. Empty! It was clear enough what had happened—two little pairs of shoes tumbled underneath the embroidery frame, a few dozen halfhearted stitches added to the work of months, and on the windowsill, Mother Sarah's abandoned distaff.

"And she's no better than they are! How could they?" I called out the window, "Cecily! Alison!" and thought I could hear the answering shriek of children's laughter from a far-off place. Oh, failed again, I brooded. How ever will I make them into ladies? And then God will say at the end of the world, "Margaret, you allowed your daughters to become hoydens. Their French knots unravel. And those daisies. Ugh. Exactly like toadstools. Pass on My left, unworthy woman."

But the silence of the abandoned bower was so inviting, I could feel the wonderful possibilities rising from the floor like mist. Mine, all mine, rejoiced my careless heart. Space, room, and quiet! And before I knew it, I had my paper and ink from the chest, and my writings about housewifery spread about me.

Now you must know that long ago I made a plan to write down all the wisdom Mother Hilde taught me, so that it would not be lost. And my girls shall have it after me and so become celebrated for their mastery of the arts of healing and cookery and housewifery. And it is very well that it all be written, even though these are all true secrets, for suppose some grief should come to me—how would they manage then? And this I must say of them, though they are slow at the needle, they are swift at the art of reading, which is most rare among females.

I set the pen at the place I had left off. "To keep the moth from woolens . . ." I had written, all those months ago, in London. How much had happened since then! Their father dead, so much changed. A bright shaft of sunshine from the little window above made a warm puddle of light on the page. Moths. How can keeping the moths off make my girls happy?

"Oh, bother moths! What do I care about moths? What ever possessed me to write about moths anyway?"

"Certainly not Me, Margaret." The Voice sounded warm and comfortable, as if it were somehow inside the sunlight. I looked up from the paper and inspected the sunbeam carefully. The only thing I could see were thousands of dancing dust motes, all shimmering golden.

"It seemed like such a good idea at the time," I addressed the sunbeam. "But now it's all turned into moths and recipes for fish. And I don't even like fish."

"Why write about them, then?"

"I thought it was proper."

"What is proper is what you understand best, Margaret."

So of course it was all clear. It wasn't fish and moths I needed to write about after all. It was about something much more important. And certainly something my girls should know about, for the world tells them nothing but lies, leaving them entirely deluded on the subject.

"Why so busy, and so inky?" asked my lord husband that very evening. "Have you taken up that recipe book again? Write about those tasty little fruit things in pastry—they would definitely be a loss to posterity. My future sons-in-law will bless me."

"I'm writing a love story."

"Another tale of courtly love to add to the world's stock of lies? Surely you lead mankind astray. Pastries would be far better."

"No, I'm not writing about that false, flowery stuff. Jousts, and favors, and lute playing in rose-covered bowers. I'm writing the happily-ever-after part. I'm writing about real love."

3

"Real love? Oh, worse and worse, Margaret. Nobody writes about that. For one thing, it's not decent. For another, it's impossibly dull. No, if you wish to write about love, you must respect the conventions. What interests people is the trying to get, not the getting. Look at Tristan! Look at Lancelot! What kind of romance would it be if they could have had what they wanted? Tristan marries Yseult, and they produce a dozen moon-faced brats! Lancelot and Guinevere run off and set up housekeeping, and she yells at him for tracking mud inside! Where's the romance in that? Absolutely none! There's no story there at all. That's why the trouvères, who understand better than you that married people do nothing but get fat, always leave off before the wedding. You must face facts, Margaret. You don't understand anything about writing love stories. Stick to recipes."

So of course I set to work right away. After all, my lord husband considers himself a great expert on the topic of love, because he has written a number of poems on the subject. But I, I have loved the most greatly.

CHAPTER
1

Most love stories begin in May sunshine, with secret glances at a dance or feast, or stolen conversations in a hidden garden. But mine begins in winter, with a funeral, when my heart's love was sealed into the tomb forever. It was only duty then that kept my soul from following Master Kendall's into that long sleep. Nothing but the tears of the two little daughters he had left me bound my unwilling heart to the earth. So I resolved to stay yet a while for Cecily's and Alison's sakes, but to give myself only to their upbringing, and never to another man. For having once been wed to Master Kendall, who would be the spouse of a lesser man? There were others who were lords in rank, but who more lordly in manner than Roger Kendall, mercer of London? And who could ever be his equal in kindness, or greatness of spirit? His memory strengthened my resolve against the ever growing numbers of badgering suitors who hoped to obtain his fortune by marrying his widow.

But what men cannot achieve by cozening or guile they will have by force. Master Kendall's memorial was scarcely set into the wall at St. Botolphe's when I found myself stolen from a house spattered with the blood of failed contenders and would-be heirs by the most shameless, fortune-hunting family in the entire realm: the impoverished, quarrelsome, pretentious tribe of the de Vilerses. And worst of all, it was I myself who had foolishly let the first of them into my house, in the form of a scapegrace younger son, a failed monk and poetic scribbler who went about town under the name of Brother Gregory. For it was through my intervention that he'd got himself retained by my husband as a clerk. And now, grief, self-pity, and rage at my own weakness contended for first place in my heart when I found myself wedded to him by the sword in the chapel of his father's house.

It was one of those gray, drizzling days in early spring, when the sky seems that it might almost touch the ground. Here and there the snow, standing in unhappy piles crusted by slippery ice, broke apart to reveal a bit of dead grass or frozen mud. Along a rutted track that wound across a frozen meadow and through a village of thatched huts, a party of riders approached their destination: Brokesford Manor, a fortified house built in the old Norman fashion, half hidden behind a tumbledown wall at the end of an avenue of bare-branched trees. At the village, a dozen peasants, barefooted in the icy mud, stood in a cluster by the road, while children peeped out of the windows to see the spectacle. It was mid-February in the Year of Our Lord 1356, and the Sieur de Vilers was returning home from an adventure to which he had ridden out at full canter less than a week before, followed by his sons, squires, grooms, and an arms-laden packhorse.

A murmur went up from the group as the party came closer. It was not the same group that had set out. At its head, it is true, rode old Sir Hubert himself, straight and arrogant, on his tall red palfrey, followed by his eldest son, Sir Hugo, on the bay. Then a groom, leading the packhorse. But—after that— something different altogether. Robert and Damien, the two esquires, were riding double. Before their saddles were the small figures of two children. Girls, by the look of them, though they were heavily bundled. Behind them, in a shapeless gown and sheepskin cloak, rode Sir Hubert's younger son, the one who'd been seized by a religious mania and run off heaven knows where for years, causing his father untold trouble. But the most delicious scandal of all was that he'd got a young, pretty woman riding pillion behind him. A frail-looking, pale-faced woman, with red, swollen eyes, wearing a rich, deep black cloak and gown. Even before the grooms at the end of the party were within the gates, the gossip had spread that the woman was a wealthy widow, an authentic heiress from the City, rescued from certain death by the bold lords of Brokesford.

But the best part, the part that set up clucking speculation around every hearth in the village, was that she was to be married on the instant, without even publishing the banns. And not to old Sir Hubert, who had long been a widower, or even to Sir Hugo, who really ought to be producing a legitimate heir by now, but to Gilbert, the lunatic who wasn't fit for anything better than looking in books. How had he found her anyway? Perhaps Gilbert was more his father's son than they'd thought. Imagine the opportunity for a man of religion to slip into married women's houses by the back door. Exactly like the rascally friar in the ballad! And everyone knows that the women who live in London have no morals. To think he'd been loose in a whole city full of shameless women. After all, the old lord and his eldest between them had at least a score of unacknowledged bastards spread all the way from the Cinque Ports to the Scottish border. It was a great joke that the runt of the litter might have outdone both his father and elder brother.

But in the bustle of the return, the widow had seemed to have been forgotten. She'd been fussy about setting her fancy slippers in the mud, so they'd lifted her off at the stair before the horses had been led off to the stable through the churned-up muck of the courtyard. There she stood, a black bundle silhouetted against the low, arched door, her little girls clutching her skirts.

Not until he'd seen that the horses were off and sent for the chaplain did the old lord remember to offer her his arm, and the hospitality of his house, leading her into his hall with a flourish. She sat shivering in her damp cloak on a bench by the fire, while the squires cleaned up the bloodstained breastplates and chain mail and went to stow them upstairs. The old knight called for drink and turned to eye his younger son up and down. The young man was nearly a head taller than his father, rawboned and dark-headed, with arched eyebrows over brown eyes that glittered with intelligence. With a shrewd, appraising blue eye, the old man took in the sandals with ragged leggings wadded beneath, the worn, ankle-length gray gown with the blood splashes dried all down the front, and the atrocious, matted sheepskin.

"You're not getting married in *that*," the old man said.

"There's nothing wrong with it. Getting married was your idea," said the younger.

"Insolent as ever. Don't any of those books you read tell you 'honor thy father'? I'm telling you now, you're not getting married in that. You're in my house now. Remember that, and quit acting disgracefully."

The young man looked truculent. His father called for a bath to be drawn in the kitchen that lay behind the screen at the end of the hall. Then he sent one of the lounging housegrooms to look up a suit of clothes in the solar upstairs. The stone walls of the hall were twelve feet thick, and as damp and cold as a cave. Puffs of frosty air could be seen coming from the old lord's mouth as he spoke.

"I don't want a bath."

"You've gone soft, living in the City." The old man prowled around his son, looking at him from all angles, as if to assess which side had grown softest. The widow turned her head to watch, her face impassive.

"I don't need one. I don't want one. Getting married ought to be enough to satisfy you."

"There are four times in a man's life when he should wash—in your case three. When he is born, when he is knighted, when he dies, and—WHEN HE'S MARRIED! And if you don't yet know your duty, I'll call six men to show it to you, even at the risk of your drowning!" The old man's voice was thunderous. The son drew himself up to his full height with a graceful, catlike dignity.

"As usual, father, your command of logic has convinced me."

"Serpent's tooth," growled the old man as he followed him into the kitchen.

The widow had looked about her, where she sat by the great fire in the center of the room. She was still clutching the cup she'd been given, but the ale didn't look touched. She had wrinkled up her nose when she first smelled it, but luckily no one had seen her do it.

Beyond the screen, in the tall, rain barrel–shaped bath by the kitchen fire, things had proceeded as the old man had commanded. The widow could hear the splash as the manservant poured cold water over the standing occupant of the tub. The old man's voice, never a soft one, carried beyond the screen.

"Don't you dare turn your back on your father. . . . Turn around and look me in the eye.—Hmm, who laid *those* on? He had an even hand. A priest? That accounts for it then. —What for? A book? You went and wrote a book? Damn fool thing to do. That's what you get for messing with books. And they burned it, too, you say?—Well, knowing you, it's probably better off burned. I've never known you to have a sensible idea yet. You should have listened to me. If you'd done the respectable thing and stayed in the military, instead of giving yourself over to this ridiculous God-chasing and scribbling, you'd be carrying your scars on the front, like an honorable man, instead of on your back. . . ."

Margaret sighed, put down the cup, and clutched Cecily and

Alison to her. It didn't seem like a very auspicious way to begin a marriage.

It was early in Lent, on the eve of the Feast of Saint Matthias the Apostle, and scarcely more than a fortnight after my hasty and dreary wedding, that I began to suspect I was being followed by something that was—well, not entirely natural. Sorrow and loneliness can play tricks on us. And sometimes, too, God makes wonders for our consolation, as when a friend of Robert le Tambourer received, in the midst of remorse over a great sin, a visitation of Saint Bartholomew that was fully twenty-five feet high and glowed with a color like flame.

But this visitation was no handiwork of God's; it was an eerie unsettling feeling, very like being watched in an empty room. It followed me in the day and lay with me in the dark. When I sat, all wakeful in bed beside the stiff, stubborn form of my sleeping husband, who, in his rage against his father, still refused to consummate the marriage the old lord had ordered, I could hear a strange whistling sound, soft, like the blowing of wind in the night stillness of the room. So I fell into despair that the Evil One might be watching me secretly, and redoubled my prayers in the cold, ill-furnished little chapel of the new father-in-law's house. What did I pray for, besides my deliverance? Most of all, I prayed for the soul of my lost husband, good Master Roger Kendall, who had died so swiftly, he had not been shriven.

The fearful watching began after my new husband and his relations returned from that first trip they made to London after the wedding. For no sooner had the vows been said than they were off again to get their hands on the property that had been left to me, and on my girls' dower-funds, if they could. There was other necessary business too: seeing lawyers and bribing the judges in the case concerning the murder of my stepsons, which they claimed was entirely justified as self-defense. I suppose in a way it was, depending on how you look at it, since my stepsons had tried to kill a member of the de Vilers family first. Of course, as Master Kendall's sons by his first marriage, they had expected to inherit everything until, in his old age, he had married me and produced new children to suck away what they thought was their due.

Now Master Kendall was very fond of me and always interested in my improvement, so he hired Madame for my French teacher and Brother Gregory for my reading tutor. That's what gave them their chance. First they tried to get him to put me away by telling him I had disgraced his name with Brother Gregory. But Master Kendall just laughed at them and then disowned them entirely for their insolence. Everyone in the household knew Brother Gregory was too prickly for that; he was touchy because his family had come down in the world and women were nearly as high on his list of dislikes as merchants, money changers, lawyers, purchased knighthoods, and forged genealogies. But what no one knew at the time was that because he had needed the work, he hadn't bothered to tell anyone that his abbot had thrown him out for his unbearable quarrelsomeness, and he wasn't a Brother anymore, or a Gregory either, though I still call him that when I forget.

But then when Master Kendall died, his sons plotted to be rid of me again, and when Brother Gregory discovered the plot and tried to help me, they would have been rid of us both if his family hadn't finished them off. So you see I counted Gilbert de Vilers as a friend, at least until his family decided they would reward themselves for their pains with Master Kendall's fortune and make off with me as if I were a bride in a story. After that he wouldn't talk to me, and every glance was full of resentment for the marriage his father had forced on him. And as for me, the more I saw of his family, the more I counted him as one of *them*—a hypocrite, a shameless tomb robber in a false monk's gown.

Then in the midst of this bitterness came the watching, the strange flitting chill that left me with a feeling I was on the verge of madness itself. It was a week after the wedding—the

11

day they came back from London with my things—I remember that very clearly.

"Well, sister," said Hugo, striding into the room ahead of two churls carrying a chest, "we've brought your things from the City. Father says he doesn't want to see a new bride moping around the house in black, so he says you are to wear color to supper tonight." I can't tell you how much Hugo irritates me. I have yet to decide whether it's his stupidity or his vanity that offends me most. Or perhaps it's because he thinks no woman on earth can resist him. At any rate, there he stood in his travel-stained surcoat, hands on his hips, with his vulgar ballocks-knife slung low down at midwaist. When he talks to women, he caresses the long handle and eyes them suggestively. It's hard to imagine he and my husband are brothers, they're so different. Gilbert is dark and tall, but Hugo is medium in height and rather square-looking, like his father, and light-haired like him too. Or rather, his father must have been blond once, for his hair and beard are quite white. But where his father is fierce, with ferocious white eyebrows and piercing blue eyes, Hugo travels about instead in a cloud of self-conceit that irritates my husband nearly as much as it offends me.

"I'm wearing what I want to wear," I told him.

"Be careful how you refuse me, you stubborn little she-ass," he replied. Hugo was coming much too close. I glared at him.

"If you were mine, you'd be better disciplined," he said, stroking the long, leather-bound hilt of his knife. "I'd tear that dress off and beat you until you begged to wear whatever I told you. Gilbert's a fool. Unbedded women always get shrewish." He leered and then turned on his heel. The chest had been set down in the corner of the solar, and Cecily and Alison were digging in it, looking for their things. Suddenly Cecily shouted and held up her amber beads. How could I help it? When I saw them, I thought of how her father had given them to her that last, beautiful Christmastide, and started to cry. Then Alison, who is still a baby, started to bawl, and Cecily to wail.

I could hear Hugo's "Women! Ridiculous!" as he thumped

down the narrow, coiled stone stair to the Great Hall, leaving both the stair doors open. The stair is not designed for convenience, but for the defense of the upper part of the house—only one person at a time can go up its slippery stones, directly under the murder-holes, and the heavy oak doors at the top and bottom can stop a battle-ax. But when the doors are open, the sound from the hall rises up just like smoke through a chimney, and the goings on can be heard as clearly as if you were in the hall yourself.

As I knelt on the matted rushes to look through my chest, I could hear the rising sounds of the quarrel downstairs.

"You DAMNED fool! I tell you, if they find out it's not consummated, they'll try to get it annulled! Then where will I be?"

"Out of purse, which you deserve for being greedy."

"Out of purse for your sake, you miserable whelp! Bribes for the judges, bribes for the bishop, an entire tribe of lawyers, and God knows who else will turn up! How was I to know he'd left her so much that half of London would be ready to cut my throat for it?"

"You could have asked, before you made off with her."

"It was you that wanted it. It was all for your sake."

"My sake? MY sake? Who wanted the roof mended? You saw the money and you grabbed her! I was HAPPY the way I was! It's YOU that couldn't resist meddling, and got us into this mess!"

"Mess? There'd be no mess if you'd do your duty and put a baby in that woman's belly. What's wrong with you anyway? Hugo could put twins in any woman! Look at him—bastards here, bastards there! Now THAT'S a man! HE doesn't roll his eyes up at the sky and gabble about God all the time!" There was the noise of blows, before Hugo's voice sounded cheerfully above the scuffle.

"Come now, father, he won't be able to do anything if you keep bashing him like that."

"Then—just—have—him tell me," said old Sir Hubert, catching his breath, "what excuse he has this time."

"It's Lent. What's more, it's a Friday." I could hear Gregory's voice. It sounded prim and righteous. I knew him well. He'd have turned up his nose and looked at his father with that priggish look that drives the old man crazy. Just thinking of it made me smile. I sat back on my heels to listen better. In all the time I'd known Gregory, thorny-tempered as he is, I'd never imagined he had a family like this. That's the problem with marriage. You don't just marry a person, really, you marry a whole family.

"What has *that* to do with you failing your family?"

"All the Authorities agree, that if a man dedicated to religion finds it necessary to marry, he should foreswear carnal relations on holy days."

"Just what *sort* of holy days, you holy imbecile?" rose up the staircase in a low growl. There was a crashing and a rustling in the rushes below, as if someone had leapt aside to escape a blow. I could hear Hugo laugh.

"Lent, Advent, Sundays, feast days, the eve of feast days, Wednesdays, and—also"—another crashing and rustling, and the sound of a bench hitting the wall—"Fridays."

"Mama, they're smashing the furniture," whispered Alison, her eyes big.

"Don't you *think* to go down there, Cecily, get away from the stairs at once." When I saw her reluctantly pull her tousled red head in from the doorway, I looked again in the chest. Beneath a pair of little shoes and the folds of my blue wool kirtle, the spine of a book peeped out. I felt a brief start of joy. Gregory must have slipped it in when they'd gone through the London house. I pulled it out and ran my hand over the initials embossed on the binding. *M. K.*—Margaret Kendall. My Psalter. Maybe God hadn't abandoned me after all. Voices echoed up the stair.

"I tell you, father, I intend to see God whether or not I've left Witham, and you're not going to stop me."

"See God? SEE GOD? Didn't the abbot knock that idea out of you for once and for all? What makes you think God has time to see *you*? God's a busy man! He doesn't waste his time seeing younger sons who disobey their fathers! I tell you, you take care of your family's business, and God will take care of you!"

"Try all you want, I refuse to let you distract me. My conscience belongs to me, and I've got plans. . . ."

"To spend your time listening for voices in the air? Quit trying to distract me with moonshine and play the man, or I tell you, I'll lay on stripes that make that priest's look like a baby's handiwork. . . ."

I picked up the book, opened the pages, and ran my finger along the neatly written lines marked off with the red capitals. All English. Beneath them, the lines marked by blue capitals were in Latin, and a mystery to me. My good dead husband had had the idea of the book, and he had commissioned Gregory to do the translation, because he said he knew a first-class scholar when he saw one, even if he was as prickly as an entire basketful of nettles. Who had ever loved me as much as Master Kendall, to think of something as a gift that meant the whole world to me? It was at that very moment that I felt the eyes watching me, and a sort of cold breath on the back of my neck.

"Who's there?" I whirled around in a panic, but I didn't see a soul. Except for the two girls, who were now standing on their toes at one end of the long window seat, trying to peep out the window, there wasn't anyone in the room. It was a big room, the entire second story over the kitchen, buttery, and pantry, and a "solar" only by courtesy, since it didn't catch that much sun. The walls were eight feet of solid stone, pierced by high, narrow, unglazed and shutterless windows that let in thin columns of pale sunlight when the weather was good. Long stone window seats, devoid of cushions or comfort, were set perpendicular to the windows in the wall openings. Nothing could hide there. Was there something in the shadows? I looked along the walls and checked the corners. The long perches on

15

the walls above the beds were still hung with clothes, chain mail, and sheathed longswords. At the squires' bed, a falcon napped, head under his wing, while another paced up and down the perch beside his companion, jingling his bells.

Maybe it was a person, someone hiding under the beds. Well, he wasn't going to catch me unaware. I got up and pulled down a heavy longsword, and poked it under the nearest bed. "Get out of there, you," I whispered fiercely. Nothing under the bed where the squires slept. Nothing under the rumpled, pulled-out straw truckle bed where their bodyservants slept—it lay directly on the floor. The chests were against the wall. No room for anyone behind them. On the opposite wall stood the sagging little bed where the pages had once slept, when there had been pages in the house. Now it was Cecily and Alison's. Suppose he were hiding under there? I strode across the room, carrying the heavy sword in both hands. But behind me, I heard something like airy footsteps rustling in the rushes, just behind my own.

"Get out of there!" I said, prodding fiercely under the little bed. But there was nobody beneath it. I sat down on the bed to think. The big door that led from the solar to the tower was shut—nobody could have left that way. The stair door was open, but no one had come in. That left only the big bed, Sir Hubert's second best, standing against the wall. Our wedding bed, such as it was. The sagging curtains were pulled aside, so no one could be hiding behind them. But underneath—well, underneath it was very wide. Too wide for the sword to reach. I'd look first, no matter how much it frightened me. I crept quietly to the bed, crossed myself, turned up the hanging covers, and knelt to peek underneath. I need to be strong, I told myself. My girls are here, and I won't let anything get at them. I peered into the musty darkness, half expecting to see the white shine of a pair of evil eyes in the shadow.

"Get out at once or I'll call the men up and have you killed," I hissed, and whipped the sword in a semicircle, as far as I could reach. I thought I heard a soft sigh behind my ear.

"No use," it said. And that is when I knew for a certainty that it wasn't human. I turned and leaned against the bed, still kneeling, and clutched at the cross I always wear at my neck. It is a famous talisman, not, perhaps, as famous as the Cross of Rouen, which has a fragment of Christ's shroud in it and has been known to raise the dead, but almost as famous. It has protected me ever since I got it, though I haven't the time to tell you how just now. "In the name of God, begone and trouble me no more," I whispered, so the children would not hear. But the only answer I had was like an icy puff of wind that passed through me and made my spine crawl.

Downstairs, the quarrel had not abated one whit, but I was no longer interested in it. I could hear Hugo's voice announcing, "When I wed, I'm certainly not going to hunt up any skinny, sharp-tongued, snobbish London widow. I don't blame you a bit, Gilbert. She's too long in the tooth to give pleasure anymore. You might as well use her money and be holy. *I'll* find something fresh and new to bear me plenty of sons." There was the clatter of more furniture being overturned. I could feel the tears running down my face. Old, old. That was it. I was old. Not young and fresh anymore. Twenty-three, and tired of trying so hard, and too old ever to be truly loved again.

"Oh, Master Kendall, why did you have to die?" I cried. "You always loved me and were good to me. You weren't all that old—not too old for me—you could have lived longer, and spared me this." I could feel the cold thing wrapping around my shoulders, but I was too sad even to shiver. The girls had tired of climbing on the window seats, and seeing me so sorrowful, they came to sit on my lap and console me. In the air behind us there was a thin sound—sad, like a sigh.

But soon it was suppertime, and after that, drinking time, which is the chief entertainment in this house, which hasn't even got a minstrel. The big fire blazed at the center of the hall, its only light, setting an orange glow on the faces at the trestle tables. At the head table they always spoke in French, just to remind anyone who was listening—including God—that the de

17

Vilerses are a very old family, and not tainted with a lot of English peasant blood. On our right was a long wall entirely forested with antlers, still clinging in pairs to the bits of white skull-bone from which they had sprouted. The wall on the left of the dais was decorated with captured pennants from Sir Hubert's recent campaign against the French, with old Scottish and Welsh battle-axes, and a large, dented shield displaying a badly peeled version of the three cockleshells and red lion of the de Vilers arms. Not a single tapestry. They were too "soft." If he'd ever had one, Sir Hubert would have traded it for a horse.

"I pray you, drink, madame my sister," said Hugo, passing the ale cup. "You've picked at so many meals, you shrink daily. You need to pad out your bones to please my brother." Chivalry: just meanness in fancy dress, I thought.

"Dear brother, I thank you for your concern, but I am not yet thirsty," I replied also in French. It's hard to get thirsty in a house where they draw the water for the ale from the same moat they throw the garbage into. Not that I would ever tell them, but I could brew ale ten times better than this. I never use anything but sweet spring water; that's one of my secrets. The other secret is a special prayer I use when it's fermenting, but I'm not going to write that down for just anybody to know. Master Kendall loved my ale; so did Gregory—that's one of the reasons he hung around the house so much, picking quarrels about theology with Master Kendall.

"Ha, listen to that wool-in-the-mouth accent. Convent bred, I'll wager," said old Sir Hubert, wiping his beard on the tablecloth. Gregory, who knows more about my family than is decent, composed his face in a sardonic look. At the lower table, we could hear the jokes and insults traded in English getting louder. Sir Hubert drained the cup. Ale, even this ale, made him mellower—but not mellow enough. I inspected their faces as they sat there, wondering if Gregory would ever become as impossible as his father. The old man belched and wiped a drop of gravy from his raggedy white beard with the tablecloth.

18

He was dressed with a kind of shabby arrogance in a well-worn old-fashioned knight's gown of heavy wool cut below the knee topped with a long brown embroidered surcoat lined in squirrel's fur. Beside him in the place of honor sat Sir Hugo, whose new knighthood had exhausted the family's resources. He's even worse, I thought, watching him tilt the cup to his lips. Gregory is at least much better looking.

Sir Hubert's younger son was at least a head taller than his father and older brother, with a heavy mop of dark brown curls, dark eyes, and savage eyebrows that he could arch up in ironic detachment, an expression he favored, especially when among his family, fools, and strangers. I ought to know, he used it often enough on me when first we met. He had a mind, too, and that made him different from the others in his family. He could write poetry in three languages and argue about theology well enough to make a bishop weep, neither of which counted for anything under his father's roof. Here at his father's hearth his witty, malicious tongue was stilled, and a habitual look of sullen rage had transformed his handsome features. His father had trapped him into coming home again, trapped him by using me, and he was furious.

But Sir Hubert had seen me inspecting them. As his squire knelt to present the next dish, he put down the cup and addressed me:

"Madame my new daughter-in-law, what do you think of our ancient family seat?" He raised a white eyebrow and gazed at me as if he'd seen a louse crawl up my neck. Oh, table manners, I thought, I'm tired of you. Your only virtue is to give me relief from all the shouting. I spoke in my politest court French.

"Most honored lord and father-in-law, your esteemed manor is a source of infinite interest and novelty for myself, who had previously to content herself with a simple life in the City."

With a silky growl, he replied, "It would delight me to hear you enumerate these novelties that interest you so much."

19

Even as he spoke, I knew it might have been unwise to have anything to drink on an empty stomach.

"It is my duty to obey your every wish," I said, looking down regretfully at the dark green surcoat I had put over my black kirtle. "So I will now tell you that your delightful house has rats in the rushes, fleas in all the beds, and a Weeping Lady in the chapel." I saw him start with rage, and put his hand on the dog whip he always wears stuck in his belt when he's at home. The hounds under the table shifted and growled. I set my chin. Just let him break courtesy at table.

Suddenly, he sat back and chuckled in English, "Sharptongued, but at least you've got backbone. Not bad—this is no house for limp women." He leaned toward me. "I suppose you've been gossiping with the chaplain, and he told you about the Weeping Lady. Don't you know you've swallowed a fool's tale? It's his excuse for saying Mass drunk."

"No," I answered, "I've never found him sober enough for conversation. In fact, it's a wonder he ever got through the wedding service without falling down. I heard the Weeping Lady myself."

"Yourself? Now there's a tale. Pray tell, what's she weeping about?"

"I wondered that myself for quite a while, but as I pray alone in the chapel quite a lot, I hear her weeping quite frequently. Then one night just before vespers, I heard words in the weeping. She sobbed, 'All my children, all dead,' and then went on weeping a while more before she vanished." At these words, Hugo started and crossed himself, and Gilbert looked grave and quiet.

But the old man thumped on the table with his fist and shouted, "Wouldn't you know it? She's gone and found another way to annoy me! Just when I thought I was free of it! There's no end to the trouble women give a man!" His voice was so loud that people looked up from the lower tables to see what was going on. But when the evening was ended and we were all going upstairs, Sir Hubert grabbed his oldest son by the sleeve.

"Stay with me, Hugo. I'm going to get very, very drunk to-night," he said, and together father and son and all their rowdy retainers sat at the fixed table, among the rubble of dismounted trestles and sleeping hounds, and began a whole new hogshead of ale.

I could hear the sound of doleful singing below as I sat on the bed, took off my veil, and combed out my braids. They hadn't even found a maid for me, or a nursemaid either. They were incapable of imagining how anything female ever got done, and they'd never bothered to ask me either. Not that they'd listen if they thought to ask. Gregory, as usual, had stripped to his underdrawers and knelt before his crucifix, which he had hung by the bed. Monkish habits die hard. You could still see a bit of a dent in the curls at the back of his head where the tonsure had grown out. He was furious his father wouldn't let him reshave it, at least in the scholar's tonsure to which he had a right, and had burned his long gown. But looking at him now, I wasn't so sure it wasn't an improvement. I'd never noticed when I first met him how attractive his unruly dark curls were. And who would ever have guessed what a well-made figure had been hidden beneath the shapeless old gown? But he'd kept his hair shirt. And he wore it every day now, underneath his father's second-best hunting tunic, as if to punish himself for having returned home.

Sometimes I wished so hard things were back the way they were: that I was his student and he was Brother Gregory again. It was easier when I thought of him only as a mind, and not a man. I know people say that there was something nasty going on between us, but that really wasn't true at all. That's why it was such a good thing. I loved Master Kendall best, and I loved learning next best. And Brother Gregory, even if he was a trial, was my gate to learning, and helped me open my mind to the sunshine. How could I not admire him for that? It was all an innocent distraction, watching his moods, fits and fancies, like watching cloud pictures form and re-form in the sky.

To this day I remember how his long, muscular hands

looked, so curiously delicate as they held the stylus, elegantly tracing letters in wax for me to copy, and his sour face when he saw the first letter I spelled all by myself. Then there was the disgusted look he'd get when my old mongrel dog would lie on his feet under the writing table, falling asleep with loud snores just as he was trying to explain what Aristotle said about aesthetics. Or his standing quarrel with Cook's bird, who chattered rudely at him when he entered the kitchen unannounced. And when Master Kendall, with gracious good humor, would offer Gregory a dinner or a new gown, the whole household would crowd around to watch with amusement the conflicting emotions on the tutor's face as he tried to decide whether he could accept such an offer from a man who made his living in trade. Brother Gregory was the only man I had ever seen who could accept his wages as if he were doing you a favor.

So of course I couldn't have been more surprised—or more grateful—than that day after the funeral when he turned up, sword in hand, to rescue me from my murderous grown stepsons. But after that it was only bitter gall. He wasn't made to be married, nor I to marry again.

Now, without even looking at me, he laid the hair shirt on the bed beside me and fumbled for his discipline in the bundle he had taken from the chest. The more I saw of that nasty little stick with the sharp leather thongs, the more I hated it. Maybe I'm simple, but I don't see what beating yourself has to do with pleasing God. And every night, the same. Didn't he think I was even worth a courteous "good night"? Was I too ill-favored, or too ill-born, to deserve a look or a decent word, now that we were wed?

As I watched Gregory set up once again for his devotions, I got angrier and angrier—so angry, my face felt hot and my heart beat harder and harder. Was I so old, so plain, that I deserved this? He had faced the wall, now, kneeling silently before the crucifix that hung beside the bed. I looked at my shift, which hung nearly to my bare feet. It had a nice embroidered hem. It's not a hag's garment, I thought, and there's no old woman underneath it. I picked up one of the long, pale ash-brown locks that lay in waves all the way down to my waist. What's wrong with this? It's still pretty, even if it's not blond. I put down the comb. He paused, and as the blood dripped down his back, I could hear him say, "Blessed be God . . ." God indeed! Doesn't God say that men who marry have an obligation to their wives? What was so wrong with me that he should act as if I were invisible?

I could feel myself getting angrier and angrier. I've had two babies, strong ones that still live, and only one little stretch mark that hardly even shows. Some people would count themselves fortunate to have a wife like that. And I've brought him money, too, so he can do anything he likes—even feed his stuck-up, greedy family. And he never says a kind word to me, even though I'm all alone here among strangers. What would God say to that?

The anger came and stuck like a knot in my throat. I was so very angry, I didn't even think. My eyes felt all bloody inside. Suddenly, my mind just broke with the rage. I snatched up the hair shirt from the bed, and before he could even realize what I'd done, I leapt up, grabbed the whip from his hand, and ran like a madwoman for the door. I flew down the stairs so fast, my feet didn't even feel the stones. I didn't listen to his shout of rage as he tore after me, or the drunken cheers of the men downstairs as I raced to the fire in nothing but my shift. Shaking with rage, my face all hot and red, I threw his hair shirt and discipline into the fire, grabbed the poker, and shoved them to the very hottest part, where they began to burn merrily. There was a chorus of guffaws as the drinkers realized what I was burning.

Then I felt a heavy hand spin me around—his other was holding up his underdrawers, the points, freed from their moorings on his hose, flapping behind.

"What have you DONE, you shameless, wanton—*woman*!" he roared at me.

"I've burned them, and it serves you right!" I shouted right back, oblivious to the fire dancing perilously close behind my loose hair.

"My God, what a woman!" I could hear his father exclaim. Gilbert turned his head to see the old man leaning on the table, thumping it repeatedly with his fist, tears of laughter rolling down his flushed face.

"I'll have her anytime, if you don't want her!" shouted a man's drunken voice.

Gregory turned back to me in a fury, and I was fortunate that one of his hands was already occupied, or he might have strangled me.

"Look what you've done. You've disgraced me. You've disgraced me in front of everyone." I didn't care if I died. Just let him push me into the fire.

"Go ahead and kill me! I'm *tired* of you!" I shrieked.

Gregory's father had ceased holding his sides, and had walked up beside him. Silently, he took the dog-whip from his belt and held it out to his son. "It's high time you broke her to your hand," he said calmly.

"Don't you *dare* beat me, don't you *dare* touch me!" I shouted, looking frantically at the crowd of grinning red faces taking in the scene. Gregory looked at them too. God, it's going to be bad, I thought. He hates being humiliated worse than anything.

Gregory let go of my shoulder and took the whip without a word. He looked down at his other hand, and then, with as much dignity as he could manage under the circumstances, said to his father, "But not down here in front of everyone. Leave us alone, and I'll take her upstairs and do it right."

"Of course," said his father.

"If you touch me, I'll throw myself out the window," I hissed at him. I hated them all: heartless, repulsive men.

"Margaret," he said in a hard voice, "you've gone too far, and it's time you paid. Now march upstairs, or there's plenty of people down here who'll be delighted to assist me." They were all silent, and those who could stand had formed a circle around us. There was no escape.

As Gregory walked up the stairs behind me, I heard someone hiccup, "I always *said* that woman needed a good beating." I could feel my eyes burning. As I got to the top of the stairs, I turned. His face looked grim.

"For God's sake, don't kill me. Think of my babies. Please." But his face never changed. With a single harsh move he threw me down on the bed. Savagely pulling the curtain behind him, he climbed up beside me, and I screamed and put my hands up to protect my face as I saw him raise the dog-whip high above my head. There was a horrifying *whack*, but I didn't feel the blow. Had the madness made me lose my senses? I peeked out between my fingers, and my eyes opened wide. He'd missed; he'd hit the bolster.

"For goodness' sake, Margaret, keep on screaming, or they'll be up here to do the job properly," he hissed. I was shaking all over.

"Then—then you're not—not going to . . . ?"

"Did you truly think so little of me? Can't you see I couldn't ever bear to hurt you? Do you want to break my heart, looking as if you fear me so?" Biting his lip, he raised the whip again. "Scream again, you ninny." Then he brought the whip down savagely on the pillow. "It's them I hate, I hate them!" and he gave the pillow cut after cut.

"Oh, God, don't break my bones!" I screeched, getting into the spirit of the thing.

"I'll break every bone in your body, wife; it's my right!" he thundered. "Never disobey me again!" We could hear them cheering downstairs. I howled horribly. Somehow it felt good— I don't know why. Then he howled too. Another few cracks, and the bolster split. A cloud of feathers flew into the air, and I began to cough. It sounded just like sobbing. More cheers from below, and a rising wail from the children's bed.

"Wait a moment," I said, and slipped out from the curtains

to shush the children. "Mama's fine," I told them. "You're just having a dream."

"Pretty loud dream," said Cecily, sitting up.

"I don't like dreams. Can we get into bed with you, mama?" queried Alison, half asleep still.

"No, you can't. We're playing a game. We make the noise, and you be still as mice and go back to sleep, and—and I'll let you ride the donkey tomorrow." I tucked them in again.

"All day?" whispered Cecily.

"All day, but only if you go to sleep right away, and no cheating." They made an elaborate pretense of sleeping, but as it is with children, pretense soon became reality. Before long I could hear them breathing softly, sound asleep in each other's arms. I turned back to see Gilbert sitting glumly on the bed, the dog-whip drooping from his hand. A beam from the full moon shone in the window, laying a streak of light across the place where he sat. He had feathers stuck in his hair and beard. I went to sit beside him.

"You've got feathers all over," I whispered.

"So do you," he whispered back. Downstairs, they were singing again. Something about an old man who beat his scolding wife all around the town-o.

"Do I look as silly as you do?" I asked.

"Sillier," he said, blowing away a feather about to land on my nose. I tucked my feet up onto the bed, and he pulled the curtain.

"It's been horrible," he said. "I thought you didn't like me anymore—you've been so sharp."

"I thought it was you who didn't like me," I said. "You never said a kind word—never even looked at me. You didn't even lecture me about Aristotle, like in the old days."

"It's father," sighed Gilbert. "He drives me crazy. And now he's tangled me up with lawyers and land claims—your estates are a hopeless tangle, you know, and there are at least a half-dozen spurious claimants—so I haven't got a moment to call my own."

"I never understood about your father, before, when you told me," I whispered into the dark. "But now I know that's because words are inadequate to describe him."

"Too true." He sighed again. "It's because he's always wanted me to be just like Hugo. You don't admire Hugo, by any chance, do you? Most women do."

"No, I think he's awful. His head looks just like a plucked chicken to me, and he's not very smart."

"A plucked chicken, eh? You know, you're right. I never thought of that." I took his hand, and for once he did not pull it away.

"Oh, Gregory, Gregory, I'm so sorry I embarrassed you in front of them. Just be my friend, and I won't ask for anything more."

"You ought to be sorry," he said ruefully. "We must have made a sight." I couldn't see him, there in the dark behind the curtains, but I could feel his warm breath. Something about it made me feel strange all over. "It's my fault. It made me angry to see you hurt."

"It did? Was that really it?" I could feel his body tremble slightly.

"Gregory, have you ever done it before?" I asked into the dark.

"You know I've been saving myself for God, Margaret. I've never sinned. Well—not sinned that way, at any rate."

"It's not sin, if you're married, and if you—like—the person, and if you—want to," I answered him.

"It's not just that, you know—it's them too. Always prowling around, checking up. This is the first night they haven't all been up here, ready to count how many times—just like one of father's stud horses. I couldn't bear it." I reached out and put my hand on his arm. I could feel him shaking all over.

"Oh, God, you're so beautiful," he said, just before I kissed him, pulling him down on me. I didn't need to show him much. Somehow he seemed to know already. It was I, I who had known everything who knew nothing. What could I ever have understood of a lifetime of passion, all locked behind high walls, until the moment I had opened the gate to be drowned in the flood of it? I could feel the heat of his body blazing on mine, my skin all damp and flickering with the strange shivering glow of the lightning that leapt within us and between us. I don't even know what to call what we did that night. The heart of a fire, the eye of the sun—it consumed us to leave only a whisper of white ash behind. And somewhere in the midst of it I realized that this must be the passion of the body that the bards sing of: the stuff of dreams and damnation, that only leaves you the hungrier for the having of it. Mindless and mad, it kindled itself and belonged to itself. A thought, like the drift of a sinking ship, swirled to the surface: Is this death? Die here then. Then we were pulled under again by the maelstrom.

It was nearly dawn before we fell asleep, racked and exhausted by lovemaking. It wasn't until several days later I remembered that in the last moment before I closed my eyes, I heard something like the sighing breeze, and felt the Cold Thing, even though the curtains were pulled tight.

CHAPTER
2

As dawn poked through the bed curtains, I could hear stirring and groaning in the room outside. The world, the ordinary world, was out there again, as if nothing had happened. Someone had been sick in the rushes, and it didn't smell nice. The tower door was open—somehow they must have dragged the old man up to his great bed in the tower room. But most of those who'd got upstairs at all, hadn't got farther than the solar. I could make out Hugo's head and one arm among the tangled bodies in the bed opposite. There were more bodies, still clothed, strewn about on the floor. It looked as if the plague had been through the house. Gregory opened one eye, pulled me back from the open curtain, and looked out himself.

"Hmm. The battlefield of Bacchus," he said, and brought his head in again. Then he leaned back in the feathery mess and put both his hands behind his head. He looked speculatively up at the sagging canopy, and a slow smile spread across his face. A thin beam of light through the open bed curtains picked out the line of his arm, and the dark hairs glistened, as if they still glowed with the fast-fading night blaze.

"Haven't we had a time, though? I never expected it to turn out like this. I mean, being married and all." His voice had a contented ring. Oh, morning, morning, why must you come? Why must we be so plain by day? I hugged the last of the fading glow to me, as if I could save all of last night to feed on through the cold day.

"I'm hungry, Gregory."

"Me too. Remember when you used to make me eat breakfast before you'd have your lesson? You said I wasn't fit to be spoken to without breakfast." How could he be just the same, after what had happened? How could everything be just the same?

"I could go downstairs, and see if anyone's in the kitchen." Suddenly I was starving.

"You had good breakfasts at your house. Of course, father says breakfasts are for sick people, and anyone who isn't a weakling can wait until eleven for a proper dinner." I couldn't believe it. Was this the same man that had set my body aflame with unquenchable fire? "I wonder what God thinks about breakfast?" he rambled on cheerfully. "Now, since He doesn't eat, with Him it would be purely a theoretical issue, but . . ."

"Help me brush the feathers off my back, and I'll get dressed and find something."

"Actually, Margaret, you can't get out of bed today. If you did, they'd think I hadn't a heavy enough hand."

"But I can't stay in bed. I haven't a nursemaid, and I promised the girls they could ride the donkey."

"For once, they can wait. You can't get out of bed until after everyone else, and if anyone speaks to you, moan a bit."

"But it's all feathery in here. I don't want to stay in bed."

"Too bad, that's an order. After all, who's master?" He raised a sardonic eyebrow.

"I'm still hungry. Are you going to starve me up here all morning?"

"Don't worry, I'll send somebody up—if there's anybody to send." And he went downstairs whistling.

Pretty soon there was a clatter of footsteps up the stairs, and a girl in wooden clogs made her way through the bodies to the bed. The noise of her footgear elicited groans, and I could hear her say, "My, what a stink!" before she appeared at the bedside with a tray. It was Cis, the laundress. The sleeves of her old gray wool gown were rolled up and tucked above the elbows. Her butter-yellow hair, damp from steam, was hanging in limp curls around her round face. I had noticed her before, the only woman in a womanless house, a plump, busy little figure who never seemed to be much occupied with laundry. But now that I saw her closer, I saw she was not so much plump as big busted, and short for her age, which must have been around sixteen. She was staring so hard, you'd have thought I was a unicorn.

"Just look at all them feathers, will you? He must have really done you."

I could barely understand her thick country accent. But since I couldn't honestly bring myself to groan, I just said, "Is that breakfast? Can I have it?"

She looked down at the tray in surprise, as if she'd forgotten it momentarily. "Yes. *He* sent it up. I'm sure he's sorry. You're lucky. The others are never sorry."

What a tactless girl. I wondered how she knew. I started to eat, but she didn't go away. She just kept staring. Finally I swallowed what I was chewing and asked: "Why are you staring?"

"Ooo. I've never seen a lady before, and I have to remember everything, to tell the others." Her gaze wandered to the perch. "Them your clothes?" she asked, fingering my shift. "Nice. That's linen, ain't it?" Then she saw the surcoat hung beneath. Her eyes widened, and she ran her hands over the embroidery. "My, my. That's gold—and green velvet too. Is it from London?"

"It was made there, but the material's from Genoa."

31

"That's far, isn't it?"

"Very far. My former husband brought it on a ship. But tell me, is anyone up downstairs?"

"Hardly anyone. The inside grooms are still lying in the hall, but Cook's up, though his head hurts. The outside grooms have taken the horses out, and mam and me was boiling the table-cloths in the courtyard when Master Gilbert came out. Mam told me all about ladies: she saw Lady Bertrande almost every day. But I don't remember her at all. She died when I was very little. Everybody says she was the greatest lady in the whole world. When *she* came here after her wedding, she brought chests and chests and chests from her father's house. And falcons, and hounds, and a white mare, and a lapdog, and two grooms, and a chaplain, and three maids." Then she looked me over. "You don't have any maids, do you?"

"Not here." I was beginning to be annoyed.

"But you have got all the rest, haven't you? The chests and the lapdog and all, somewhere else?"

"Yes, of course I do." How horrid. Judged by my lapdog. I certainly wouldn't want to disappoint her by telling her I wasn't a real lady at all. Just a merchant's widow with money. And what will happen to me when the money's gone? I wondered. I could be trapped here forever, doing other people's mending—the useless younger son's useless wife.

Now if only the property claims could be settled, then Gregory could take me away, I mused. Without his relatives, everything would be better. After all, a man and a woman don't have to love each other to live well together. Look at last night. It's good, that part of it. And he does care for me, in his own way. And he's clever—we'd have things to talk about. We could be happy. We could visit his family twice—oh, maybe once a year. Yes, once—that was about right. Just until the furniture started flying. That wouldn't be many days at all. Living with relatives, that's what makes things bad in a marriage. Not that just about everyone doesn't do it, especially the landed gentry. But usually it's only the older son who has to live in his father's manor until he inherits, and often enough it drives him crazy. So if I can get Gregory to see it right, he'll understand that we're fortunate, we have possibilities.

By this time Cis had remembered herself enough to make a curtsey, before clattering off through the groaning and stirring bodies. I pulled the curtains and had just settled back to eating when I heard rustling outside the bed.

"Mama, can we get in?"

"Mama, I need you to tie the lace at the back of my dress."

"Mama, have you got breakfast in there? We're hungry too." They had dressed themselves in the eccentric fashion that children have: Cecily had put Alison's dress on her inside out in the bargain. They clambered up into the bed.

"Look at the feathers! Mama, you've spoiled the *whole* bed, and nobody's here to fix it." They were right—I hadn't even a needle to sew up the pillow again. They'd not thought to bring away a single useful item from the London house. Men. They'd brought the carved chest with Master Kendall's astrolabe, his books, and the Saracen scimitar, but they hadn't brought a needle, or a distaff, or anything a woman might need. Well, surely, I thought, if they've got clothes here, there must be a needle and thread. I'll wait a decent interval to satisfy Gregory, then get dressed and go hunting. Somebody has to be doing the mending. Maybe I can get that laundress to put the feathers back and tidy things up. By this time, the girls had eaten most of the breakfast and begged to go downstairs.

"Now you go straight to John in the stable, and you are to ride the donkey only in the courtyard. Be sure to share. Cecily, don't be greedy and take all the turns. And look after Alison, because she's little and could get hurt. Do you promise?" They looked so sweet as they promised. Cecily, tall and thin for a girl not so far from six, bobbed her unruly mass of red curls. She never could keep them properly combed; they were as troublesome as the splash of freckles across her nose that simply would come out every summer, even when I rubbed cucumber on them. Alison, even though she's not yet four, so it's a little early to tell, will probably never have a freckle problem. She's as pink and white as a rose. The sweet little thing put two fingers in her mouth as she looked solemnly out of her great blue eyes at me.

"Iss, mama. I pwomise," she said. The waves of her strawberry blond hair glistened in a ray of early morning sun that fell through the narrow slit of the window. An angel, I thought. She looks just like an angel. God protect them both. But I guess I'll never learn. There are only two times when the girls look like angels. One is when they're sick; the other is when they're planning something. It is a good thing I couldn't see the something they had in mind. It was the beginning of events that changed everything.

The Sieur de Vilers had risen at dawn, heard prayers in his chapel, and was now preparing to ride out and inspect his pasture, where a number of his mares were in foal. It was not too far to walk, but a knight does not set foot on the ground when it's possible to ride, so he was standing at the top of the stair before the low, carved arch of the door to his Great Hall, waiting for the groom to bring him the freshly saddled roan. Not a bad horse—a good fifteen and a half hands, tall enough for a man who would never shame his ancestors by being seen on a short horse—and the creature did have a pleasant amble. But he also had three white feet, and that's a great flaw. The feet had bred true, and the amble hadn't, so Sir Hubert had had him gelded. And while he wouldn't have been seen among gentlemen on him subsequently, the animal's gait was well suited to a man whose head was still throbbing as if Beelzebub himself had sat on it all night.

Looking at the mares would help him make his decision. It was early in the season, too early, really, and he would have liked to see even some of the foals before he made his decision, but it couldn't wait. The Duke was leaving for France again, and he was sworn to go with him. So something had to be done to slash through, at a single stroke, the knots that those damned lawyers had tied all about him to deny him his due. After all, who'd taken the risk, and borne off the prize? Him, not them. And he was damned well going to keep every penny and every square inch. It was fair spoils, and his due. Those imps of hell and their papers and Latin gibble-gabble should all be sent back to their vile maker, the Father of Lies. The only sort of people who are worse are the judges—especially the kind who take gifts from land thieves and false claimants. People of no proper blood, who talk through lawyers' mouths, instead of man to man, and think the backing of an earl will win their case. Well, they'd find out Sir Hubert de Vilers was not a man to be trifled with; he'd apply counterpressure.

As usual, the sight of his mares, all but one placidly and heavily in foal, soothed him. The cold wind ruffled their shaggy winter coats as they lifted their heads to stare at him. Walking gold, all of them. Yes, he'd do it. A duke outweighs an earl anytime—especially his duke, who was the greatest warlord in England. He'd take him the French stud, the famous French stud that he'd brought back from the wars, and the court cases would swing his way. A sacrifice, of course, but not as bad as it might be if enough mares weren't in foal, or if the stud hadn't been getting older. A great horse, still a real man's destrier: gray, nearly seventeen hands, and as wide as he was tall. A good sire, too, even on the wretched English mares he'd started out with. Now he'd crossed the line back and got something worth looking at. Not quite deep enough in the chest, though. If he could somehow get the black's chest and height, and the gray's hindquarters and disposition, he'd be close—so very close. Of course, there was the black's temperament. High, too high, but it might improve with age. There's no reason, no reason at all, mused the old knight through his headache, that the French should breed the best destriers. Someday, if it all worked out, he'd have it: the perfect English destrier.

For a moment there, standing in the brown, ice-mottled pasture beneath the wide, brooding dark sky, he could almost see the dream stallion before him. Eighteen hands, as broad as a house, with iron shod feet as big as trenchers barely visible beneath heavy feathering. Gray, of course, the best color, with a deep black velvety muzzle, and no ugly china eye. The de Vilers breed, they'd call them, and a man wouldn't count himself properly mounted unless he had one.

But his reverie was interrupted by the sound of shrill little voices, and the snorting, rumbling sound of a stallion that has been disturbed. Peasant brats in the stallion pens? No, by God, the widow's brats.

"Bring the oat pan and stick it through the gate, Alison, and when he comes near the wall and puts his head down, I'll get on. Then you open the gate. All right?" It was the bigger one speaking. How old was she? All children looked the same age: small. Hadn't her mother said she was nearly six? She had clambered up to the top of the stone wall of the black stud's pen like a monkey, sticking her toes in the cracks, and now he could see her curly red head emerging at the top of the wall as she got ready to drop on the stallion's back. The little figure stood out against the morning sky, cloakless and barefooted, as she crouched like a cat getting ready to pounce. Damn her, Urgan was roused up; he might fling himself against the wall and take an injury. The little one, bundled up in a cloak with a pointed hood, stood in the mud before the gate.

"Now, Alison, open the latch and run back!" the thin little voice called. The stallion snorted, threw his head up, and rolled his eyes wildly as the tiny creature dropped on his back. He was preparing to smash her against the wall when the gate clicked open, and instead he smashed his heavy chest into it, banging it open so that it crushed Alison into the mud.

"Cecily, no-o-o-o-o!" he heard the belated cry from the distant upstairs window. For some reason the high, thin cry spooked the stallion, who changed his strategy of dealing death to one of flight.

"Head him off!" Sir Hubert shouted to the groom, and clapped spurs to the wretched gelding. The boldness of the brat was extraordinary: she hadn't a hope of clinging to the huge barrel with her short legs. It was all balance and hands—she'd tangled them deep in the stallion's mane and was holding on for dear life. But it couldn't last long. At every stride, she was thrown in the air; the slightest mishap and she'd be under the slashing hooves. She looked straight ahead, her eyes glassy with determination and terror. The black was headed for the wide, stony-bottomed brook that meandered across the meadow and gave Brokesford its name. At this speed, and with the slippery snow patches still on the ground, the horse would fall and break his neck, and very likely kill the little rider into the bargain. Sir Hubert came in at a full gallop from the stallion's left side, and for a moment pulled even with the frantic stud. The stallion's frothy flanks were heaving; his eyes rolled crazily. Great conformation, rotten temperament, was the old knight's thought, at the very moment when he snatched the brat off by the back of her gown and threw her across the withers of his roan. And as his prize stud ran insanely on toward the brook, the ungrateful little bundle lying in front of him squeaked,

"Put me *down*! I was doing *fine*!"

"Fine indeed, you little monster, you've killed my stud. And if you weren't worth eight hundred pounds to me, I'd wring your neck right here!"

It was prophecy. The stallion careened crazily into the water, slipped and fell, and didn't rise again. He was thrashing and squealing in the water, raising his head up frantically, his eyes terrified. Cries could be heard as people ran from the house, and when the groom pulled up, Sir Hubert was already dismounted. He was deep in the muddy brook, all mucked up with mud and blood, trying to hold the immense horse's slippery, wet thrashing head.

"Leg's broken," he shouted to the groom. "Hand me your knife; I have to cut his throat." It was something he'd done often enough on the battlefield—in fact, it was the only time anyone had ever seen him weep. But to put down a destrier at home, the best he'd ever put good money on, why, that filled him with an explosion of rage and grief. He was crazy with the loss and the stupidity of it, so crazy there was no telling just what he'd do. The groom hesitated a moment at the order. The stud was the best-looking thing Sir Hubert had ever brought onto the place. Even though he knew better, the groom said, "Are you sure, sir?"

"Goddamn it, I know a broken leg when I see one. Hand me that knife." This morning, the best-looking horse in twenty miles. This afternoon, dog meat. Sir Hubert felt something running down his face, and that sign of weakness made him angrier than ever. The groom waded out into the water, trying to avoid slipping on the rocks beside nearly a ton of thrashing, bloody horseflesh, and slashing hooves that could crush a man's rib cage at a single blow. Whatever madness had possessed the old knight, that he could not wait for the great horse to exhaust himself before he dispatched him? Still, it was not his job to question. But as the groom finally managed to extend the knife, handle first, to his master, the horse threw his head and knocked it spinning irretrievably into the water.

With an oath, the old man tried to grab the slippery neck with one hand while he reached for his own knife with the other: the very move he'd tried to avoid by getting the groom's knife ready to hand. He lost both, for when the creature felt the grip on his head slacken, he gave a heave that half lifted his whole body out of the water, and somehow threw Sir Hubert off balance so that he slid partly beneath the destrier in the icy water, where the animal's vast, writhing bulk threatened to pin him and drown him.

"Sir, sir!" cried the groom, and grabbed at the old knight's shoulders, trying to pull him loose and out of danger. "Help me, help me! My lord is pinned down!" Two more grooms, who had run to the scene, splashed into the brook to retrieve their master. Dark figures could be seen in the distance, hurrying to the brook. Cecily stood silently by the bank, not moving, gazing with awestruck fascination at the catastrophe she had set in motion. Then Gregory's voice barked over the commotion:

"Get him out on the bank! Wrap him in my cloak!"

"Wrap *who*? You're not wrapping me in anything yet, you whelp!" shouted the old man through his chattering teeth.

"For God's sake, dry off, father, before you get sick. I'll put the stud down."

"You'll put him down? YOU? I won't give you the PLEASURE! Bookworm! I do my own dirty work. That's a knight's horse, and a knight will put him down!"

By this time Margaret, hastily dressed, head bare and her hair wild behind her, had run to see to her children. She reached the brook dragging a mud-caked, sobbing little girl behind her. When she had seen Alison's face, crimson and swollen with rage, and heard her howl: "I didn't get *my* turn! Cecily cheated!" she had known immediately that the child was entirely whole. Now she briefly inspected her oldest child before she assessed the chaotic scene at the edge of the brook. Well, all too well, was Margaret's thought, as her narrowed eyes looked shrewdly at the pensive, barefooted little figure taking in the scene with wide eyes. The little girl was stiff with delight at the complex train of events she had set in motion. Gregory and his father were fighting on the bank, the grooms stood immobilized, and at the center of the brook, in two and a half feet of muddy, churning water, the bleeding, heaving flanks of the pride of Brokesford Manor were laid sidewise on the sharp stones of the brook. Margaret took in at a glance the rolling, hysterical eyes of the terrified stallion, and waded unhesitatingly into the freezing water.

"Get away, Margaret, you'll be killed!" Gregory shouted, now distracted from the battle with his father.

"He's hurt," called Margaret, without stopping.

"Of course he's hurt, you idiot woman. Your brat has broken his leg and cost him his life," cried Sir Hubert.

"Maybe not broken . . ." Margaret's voice was carried away by the wind. She had got to his head, and made a low, chirruping sound as she grabbed the creature's long muzzle.

"What the hell do YOU know about horses? I've seen you

39

ride—like a peasant on top of his grain sacks, poking along on his nag to market. Get away and let me do my job." The Sieur de Vilers had got another knife, and was wading back into the water. The destrier's eyes had quit rolling, as she stroked his head and spoke quietly to him. But the massive black flanks were still quivering in terror. Margaret gingerly worked her way around the huge chest, and her hand slipped under the water, carefully feeling the length of the deadly forelegs. "Now, now," she crooned as her hand felt for the injury. Her lips were turning blue with cold. "Here it is. Both bones," she said softly to herself. "And caught—here."

She bent over, and an arm went nearly to the shoulder into the water. The horse hadn't moved. Neither had anyone else, for fear he would take fright, lash out, and split her head open. Even the Sieur de Vilers stood, frozen still, the knife in his hand, as the water rushed around his legs. She was doing something under the water, he couldn't quite see what, and then heaving with both hands, gritting her teeth with the effort. Suddenly she turned her face toward him. Her hair was blowing crazily about her shoulders, and the way her hazel eyes caught the light, they glistened yellow for a moment. Like a falcon's, thought Sir Hubert, and he tried to remember just where it was long ago, in a distant place, on another face, that he had seen that look before.

"Help me get him to his feet," she said to the old lord. And with that quiet, precise movement that all great horsemen have, he sheathed the knife and stepped to her side. Together they threw their weight against the stallion and lifted his head. With a kind of groaning squeal he heaved up and righted himself, as they drew back. Sir Hubert threw his belt over the stallion's neck and led him, badly limping with each step, to the bank.

"Get back, the lot of you." The Sieur de Viler's voice was hoarse and quiet. "Go home, make up the fire, and get those brats out of here. I'm taking him to the stable myself." He gritted his teeth against the cold. The woman, he saw, was blue around the mouth, but wouldn't leave the stallion's head. Her long, wet kirtle clung about her knees, and its long sleeves dripped. Another time, and he'd have ordered her beaten for appearing half naked like that, without a surcoat and a decent head-covering, the laces of her heavy wool gown showing indecently up her back. But this time he looked at her, shaking with cold, and said, "You go home too. You're frozen."

"No," she said quietly, "he's still frightened."

Together they walked him back and shut him in his big stall. Sir Hubert himself found his halter and tied his head, then called for the grooms to check his wounds and clean off the mud. He stood back and looked at the bad leg. The destrier was holding it so only a tip of the huge hoof touched the ground.

"He's ruined," said the old lord, shaking his head. "No foot, no horse. And I've no guarantee he'll breed well."

"I can stay, and look to the leg."

"You'll stay nowhere. You're frozen through. Let John look to him." Gregory's cloak was still over the old knight's shoulders. It was only damp at the hem. He took it off and put it over her shivering figure. "City bred. No sticking power," he said.

The fire in the hall was piled high with new wood and smoking heavily when they entered at last. Two grooms stripped the old lord naked, right there before the fire, and dressed him in a heavy wool gown and fur lined *robe de chambre* of an unusual richness for this austere place. Warmed and seated, he looked curiously at Margaret. Suddenly she remembered her hair wasn't properly covered, and she was dressed only in her long, dark kirtle, and in spite of the cold she blushed crimson.

"You haven't a maid," he said, looking at her clutching Gregory's old cloak over her soaking dress. She looked at the floor. "And you're not in bed. Gilbert has a weak hand, evidently." He called his steward and spoke to him. The man went upstairs and returned with another *robe de chambre,* a woman's. It was heavy crimson, stiff with gold and silver embroidery, and lined with sable. Sir Hubert pointed to her wordlessly, and the steward lifted off the cloak and put it on her. The old lord could see her fingering the embroidery.

"French," he said. "Spoils of war. It's yours. Haven't made you a wedding present yet. Cold in here."

"Merci, beau-père," she said. He stared at the fire awhile.

"And now, madame, there is the question of your daughters." She looked at his huge hands.

"Don't hit them; you'll kill them," she said.

"I assure you, madame, I have no intention of causing them permanent damage. It would mar their marriageability and delay their exit from my house." She looked silently at the floor.

"I suppose you've never struck them. It's a problem that weak-minded women have. My late wife, for example, who was as weak-minded as they come. 'Don't hit the baby,' she'd wail, 'what if he died?' 'But what, madame, if he lives, and you raise a little monster?' Then every time the baby takes ill, they moan that it's because you hit him. That, woman, is how brats are made. Women, children, dogs, and fruit trees all need regular beatings." He looked fiercely at her.

"My girls are good girls." She looked fiercely back, and he could see the flicker of gold in her eyes again.

"The signs are plain, madame. Your children lack discipline." It was so quiet in the room, he could hear her breathing.

"Children are not unknown to pay with their lives for their failure to heed their elders," he added, and he saw the flicker weaken.

"Not too many."

"Five for the big one, three for the little one."

"She didn't do anything—she's only a baby." By this time the girls had been brought in and stood before the old lord. They were listening to everything.

"I distinctly saw her holding the oat pan, madame."

"Not so many, then. She doesn't understand what she did."

"Three and one. And there I stick." Everyone in the hall was listening. They'd never heard of such a thing before. A villein's child who'd done such a thing would be beaten to death by the grooms in the courtyard. Even a son of the house might expect a great deal more. And here was this woman, with eyes unlowered, facing down the old lord's justice. It was something to be talked about for many years after at the firesides of the little houses in the village.

"Stand the little one in front of me, and hand me my riding crop," he directed the grooms. Margaret gripped her seat until her knuckles turned white. The old lord looked fiercely at Alison. She looked innocently up at him through her long lashes, her eyes large and blue.

"Do you understand what you did?"

"I didn't do it. Cecily made me."

"You understand then. For holding the oat pan, one stroke. For trying to shift the blame—cowardice and slyness, one stroke. For lying, one stroke." They weren't easy blows, and left deep welts under her heavy wool dress. The grooms had gathered in the hall to watch the administration of justice.

"This is my house. I won't have lying, slyness, or cowardice in it. Not ever," he addressed the howling child. "Now the big one." Cecily looked entirely unrepentant and, if anything, rather pleased at her sister's treatment. It was no less than what she had thought of her all along.

"It will be at least six years until I can sell your marriage, and they will be very long ones for you unless you learn obedience." He looked at her; she stared right back. Suddenly he thrust his heavy head forward and glowered at her from beneath his bushy white eyebrows.

"Why?" he asked.

"He was the best. The biggest of all. I didn't know he'd fall."

"You've crippled the best stud in twenty miles."

"I'm sorry." Sorry, sorry. Sorry she couldn't ride him again. It had been perfect. For a little space of time she had been the ruler of the world. No one could take it back.

"The laws of this house are—first—girls do not ride stallions, not ever. Second—no one rides anything without permission.

Third—no one takes or uses anything without permission." As he spoke he delivered the blows. Cecily never wept, though her eyes filled with tears and she bit her lip so hard it bled.

"God help the fool who marries you," said the old man. He handed back the whip to one of his grooms to put away, and looked at Margaret where she sat. Her face was white, and tears were running down it. He motioned, and the idling grooms ceased watching and went to set up the trestle tables for dinner.

"You'll sit on my right at dinner," he said calmly to Margaret. The place of honor. He'd never offered it to her before, not even on her wedding day.

At supper, he offered her the best part of the dish with his own hand. She stared at the trencher and shook her head slightly.

"Again you don't eat? You dishonor my house."

"I'm sorry. It's not that," she said, looking worried. "It's just that I don't eat *them*."

"Salt herring? It is Lent, madame. I can offer you nothing better." She turned her pale face to him, frightened and apologetic at the same time.

"I'm truly sorry. I'm not trying to dishonor your table. It's—just—just that I can't eat anything with eyes."

"Is that all? I'll take them off."

"No, not that—I mean that ever came with eyes on."

"And why is that?" Gregory stiffened as he watched the exchange. The old man was capable of anything. With a sudden blow to the head, he could smash a peasant's skull. He had been eerily controlled for too long—at any moment something might set him off and he'd lash out, God knows how. Margaret was too small, too frail, too crazy for his father's house. He needed to take her away. If only the inheritance could be freed up, he could keep her someplace safer. A moment gone wrong, and it could turn out very badly for Margaret.

But the old lord looked authentically curious this time. Margaret saw that, and answered simply: "I'd see the eyes in my sleep. They'd all be looking at me, and they'd give me night-mares." The answer didn't seem to surprise the old man a bit. When Damien knelt before him to offer him the next dish, the Sieur de Vilers broke the order of service and sent for a cheese. He observed her all the while she ate, stroking his beard with his left hand and thinking. He knew horses very well, and he knew he wasn't wrong. He had seen what he had seen. A woman who could raise a fallen destrier was no ordinary woman. But a woman who raised a horse with a broken leg, who saw eyes and didn't eat fish, and who stared at him with a frightened face when she realized he'd seen what the others had missed—that was something else entirely. It might very well be a problem.

Had Gilbert known all along? It certainly would go far to explain the look on the pup's face when he'd announced that as long as they'd taken the trouble to rescue her they might as well carry her off. He inspected his second son's face. No, it would be entirely in keeping with his character never to notice what was right under his nose. But then again, it was Gilbert who had burst out and said that he should have asked before he'd made off with her, and the old lord was never going to admit that Gilbert might have been right, even this once.

In the days after the strange dinner when the Sieur de Vilers gave me the wedding present, things were better, or at least quieter. But Cecily and Alison were in disgrace. After they'd gone and nearly killed his destrier, Sir Hubert had confined them to the solar in the care of a ferocious fellow named Broad Wat, a onetime pikeman who had followed him through all the Scottish wars. This worthy had instructions not to let them out of his sight until a nursemaid of sufficiently dragonlike qualities should be located.

"You should count them lucky," said Gregory after supper one day, "he used to lock me in the cellar on bread and water for far less. And there's a veritable legion of spiders down there."

"He's very hard. He's frightened me since the first day I laid eyes on him."

"Oh, do cheer up, Margaret. At least he's never heaved a bench at you. But whatever made you wade in after Urgan, feeling the way you do about father? It's a miracle you weren't killed."

"I just saw him rolling and squealing there, all bloody, and I felt so sorry for him. That's all. So I had to. I never thought about it. I might not have, otherwise."

"Sorry? For a horse? You are strange sometimes. You had better save your sympathy in the future—warhorses are trained to maul humans, and I'd really like you to stay away from them. He could have smashed your head like an eggshell, and then where would I be, Margaret? And Urgan's famous all around the shire for his bad temper. Father got him at a bargain after he killed a man, and he's lost his head groom to him since, as well. Father's just too stubborn to get rid of him. He's convinced he can breed the height into his line, and breed out the bad temper. Oh, well, I suppose you'd have seen Urgan's eyes too."

"How did your father know how I learned how to ride? I've never even told you that I always sat on the grain sacks when father led the horse to the mill—that is, when we had a horse." Gregory winced. I knew it was something I shouldn't ever mention again, at least while we were in his father's house.

"Father knows everything, when it comes to horses. He's never wrong." He looked at mè speculatively. "You're afraid of them, too, aren't you? Horses, I mean. Father knew that too. He told me the first time he saw you mounted. How did you ever get to your country place in the summer?"

"You saw the little white mule in the stable? That's mine. Master Kendall got it for me."

"And it sits there still, eating its head off, until the country property is settled. Father says it's a total waste, and ought to be sold."

"He won't sell it, will he? He won't sell my mule or my

house? Don't let him, Gregory. It all comes to you, not him. Remember that we were happy there, and can be happy still."

"Father's the head of the family, and I owe him obedience—but if there's enough for the upkeep, after all these lawyers get through, I will. But you know, in this family, you can't be seen mounted on a mule. It would irritate father, and there's no telling what he'll do when he's irritated."

"But—but—"

"No buts," he said gently. "You're on his good side now, and I won't see you lose it. Don't look so worried. You're brave enough, in other ways. You just sit a horse like a coward. I can fix that." His voice sounded warm and strong. It would have convinced anyone that the thing was easy.

So, much to my mortification, that is how I found myself the very next day atop a dreadful mountain of a beast, mud flying from beneath its hooves as it cantered in circles at the end of a lunge line.

"Sit up straight, Margaret! Quit clutching like that!" Gregory held the line in his left hand, flicking the long whip in his right whenever the horrid creature faltered. And, of course, I couldn't help noticing how tall and well made he was, and how strong his hands looked as he paid out the line, and this sort of distraction came close to costing me dearly more than once.

"So what are you going to be doing now?" he asked as we walked from the stables.

"Sitting quietly for the next week until I quit aching," I answered, brushing the mud off my sleeve. The acid in my voice made him laugh.

"You're a hard case, Margaret. But don't think I give up all that easily. Whether you like it or not, I'll have you riding like a de Vilers. After all, I haven't the least intention of ever giving Hugo the satisfaction of paying him off."

"What? You have a wager?" I was furious. Gregory didn't seem bothered at all.

"Father put him up to it, I'm sure. He thinks he's sly, but I know he did it—it's got his mark on it, that idea. Hugo's too dense to have noticed without father's prodding." I was so livid, I couldn't decide which one of them enraged me the most. Making sport of my misery! I could just see Hugo gloating, with that stupid smile of his.

"We'll ride again tomorrow," I snapped.

"That's what I thought you'd say," he said serenely.

And so I went to nurse my wounded spirit in the solar, where I had in mind to spend the rest of the afternoon teaching my girls their stitches, as a way of keeping their fingers out of trouble. There I found Broad Wat bemoaning his fate. A formidable widow was being acquired from a neighboring hamlet for his relief, but it was not soon enough, in his opinion. He had worn himself out giving rides and telling lies. When threats and bribery no longer had any effect, he had resorted to numbing his senses with a plentiful supply of ale, brought up by a parade of kitchen boys eager to hear his lurid complaints. When I emerged from the narrow stair, he was lying on the straw bed before an audience of kitchen boys, half dead by his own account, while Cecily and Alison ran rampage through the solar.

"It's punishment for my sins, that I'm trapped with them for another three days," he was complaining. And while he talked, the kitchen boys laughed behind their hands. For they could see what he could not—that as he spoke the girls were engaged in pouring an unknown liquid out of Wat's great mug onto the head of some unwary soul beneath the window. Clearly, it was time for female intervention.

The girls left off their activities to crowd around me while I hunted through the ornate little chest where I'd been told the sewing things were.

At the bottom of the chest was what I wanted: a strange-looking box, all bound in carved brass that was badly in need of polishing. In it was an embroidery hoop with a bit of unfinished work in it, looking a bit as if it were destined for a priest's vestments. There was also a distaff, richly set with silver, and under it a pile of neatly folded baby clothes. I lifted up the first. A little girl's smock, unfinished, too small for Alison. Then a little gown for a newborn, half-sewn, pretty linen but no hem. A tiny cap, with heavy quilting set in rolls about the crown, so a baby learning to walk wouldn't split his head on the hearthstone. No strings, and the rolls not all stitched down. What kind of woman was this, so rich she could afford to leave good stuff unworked—so many things unfinished?

As I held the dusty, darkened little things, I could feel something very sad about the chest. In my mind I could sense what had happened. It was a rich woman's box, yes—a woman whose embroidery surpassed mine, for she had learned on silk and velvet, and I had learned on coarse stuff. But it was a poor woman's too. A woman whose fine stitches and piety and silver hadn't been able to save her children. I could feel it like a certainty inside me—each little garment was for a child, unfinished at the time of death, and put away because she couldn't bear to complete the work. And then she put away her embroidery, too, and died. A woman's life, all shut up in a box, was what I saw there. Maybe it would be my box, too, in the end. I put my hand on my heart, to keep it from hurting me. And while I was still, kneeling in the rushes beside the box, the Cold Thing came back and surrounded me, and made me shudder.

But there was more. Beneath the little box with the needles, all pressed flat, was a tiny pair of baby's shoes, all made out of some very thin leather, as soft as silk, with holes worn through the little quilted soles. This one lived, I thought, and she loved it best, so she saved the shoes.

"Mama, doll clothes! Can we have them?"

"We need them, mama, Martha is *naked*!" The girls tried to pull the box out of the chest. Broad Wat retreated to take another drink.

"They're not yours," I said, removing their hands and shutting the big chest tight. But the girls hadn't even time to whine before they were entirely distracted by a dreadful commotion on the stairs.

"Who poured ale on me? I'll thrash him to death!" Furious shouts were echoing up the stairway. It was Damien, the squire. He and Robert had been hard at work in the courtyard, hot in mock combat, when Damien had stopped to lean against the wall, with unfortunate results. The girls jumped up and ran to hide beneath the big bed, giggling.

"It *was* you then! I tell you, I'll paddle you properly! Get out from under there, you little devils!" He grabbed a protruding arm from beneath the bed, and pulled hard. He had Cecily half out, when she bit his finger and he let go suddenly. She scuttled back under the bed, and he sat on the floor, sucking on his sore finger and trying to spy the glitter of her eyes in the dark. Suddenly he saw the humor of it, and started to laugh. He was just sixteen, a year younger than Robert, the other squire, and he looked charming, sitting there and laughing. His cheerful blond curls were all wet and matted, but the new beard on his chin shone like gold. He had not a prospect in the world, except that everybody liked him, and that's worth something. And he was used to children; I'd heard him say once that he had eight living younger brothers and sisters eating his father out of his living. He was the hope of his whole impoverished tribe, and they'd somehow scraped up enough to get him nourished as a page in the Sieur de Vilers's house, back when there was still a Lady de Vilers.

"I hate you," he said to the shadow beneath the bed.

"I hate you too," Cecily's voice came out from under the bed.

"Me too," said Alison, from where she hid behind her sister. It was love.

From then on, the girls were as orderly as is possible for them. If Damien asked anything, it was as good as done. They followed him about until he was entirely distracted, begging to carry his things for him, or run his errands. Even the villagers laughed at it. Of course, the girls still fought.

"When I'm big, I'm going to marry Damien."

"No you're not, he'll marry *me*!"

"No, he's going to go away, and get rich in France, and then he'll come back and take me away on his horse—ow! Quit kicking! Mama, Alison kicked me!"

"I didn't. Besides, she made an *ugly* face, mama. Tell her it will stick that way!"

"Nya, nya, it won't."

"It will *so*! You'll be all wrinkled up that way forever, and then he'll marry *me*!"

CHAPTER
3

It was more than a month from the time we'd married. March was nearly over, and the first green points of April's daffodils could be seen poking up through the mud. And yet I'd seen less of Gregory alone than before the priest had raised his hand in benediction. I began to wonder whether he really liked me at all; I felt as if I had just been taken for granted, like a new piece of furniture that one has got used to. And not only that, let me tell you that for sheer irritation, there's hardly anything worse than being the sole source of novelty and amusement in a household of strangers.

"You'll be wantin' that kirtle cleaned up, won't you, mistress, as well as the surcoat, now?" Cis grinned as she held up the muddy garments to the light. "Mmm. Nice embroidery on that."

"Just sponge the mud off, and then soak it in cold water. I don't want the colors to run. Remember now; I don't want to see it boiling with the dirty linen when I come downstairs."

"Oh, I know better now. I can get it just like new—and you'll be wanting another poultice? That's a wicked bruise you've got there."

"That's only the one you can see," I said morosely, pulling the warm *robe de chambre* tighter about my poor huddled, sore, undressed body as I sat on the edge of the bed.

"My now, that's too bad. You'll be wearing this one for dinner, won't you?" she queried, picking a garment off the perch. She stroked a sleeve with her cracked, work-reddened hands. "Now—what's this kind of cloth called?"

"Sarcenet. Hold it sideways to the light so you can see the weave. No, the threads, this way. And see the glimmer? That's how you can tell it's genuine." After all, I hadn't been married to a mercer for nothing.

"My, wouldn't it be fine, touching soft things like this all the time. Sarcenet. I won't forget." The mood of reverie vanished as quickly as it had come. "Goodness, I'm learning all the time," she announced cheerfully as she knelt to rummage in the chest for the proper set of hose to replace the muddy mass so recently peeled from my legs. As she held them up for my approval, she said,

"If you won't think it bold, mistress, you'd be spending less time in the mud and more time on Blanchette if you'd lengthen your stirrups a bit and brace back against the cantle when you take the jump. Old John's agreed with me, and so are Wat and Simkin."

A public amusement, that's what I'd become. And that's the difference between learning to write and learning to ride: You can't fall off the page when you've got it wrong. I could still feel my face burning.

"So what makes you know so much about it?" My bruises made me ask in a more sarcastic tone than was proper.

"Me? Oh, I've ridden pretty near everything on the place. I never had a brother, so when I was little, my dad would sit me on the foals. The first weight they ever felt, you know, and they don't always like it. He'd lead them around, then drive them, walking behind with the long reins, with me in the saddle. He was important here—head groom of my lord's stables, and none better—but that was before your time. And before that big ugly black thing broke his neck for him."

I started, but before I could question her further, she took advantage of my shock to add, "And let me tell you, mistress, angels got their hands on them little girls of yours—and so says mam and Simkin too. Though *he* says he can't imagine why."

Entertainment for saucy laundresses and kitchen boys, I said to myself, as I listened to her clogs clattering down the solar stairs. I've been brought low in this house.

Sometimes I'd find my heart bursting with longing to be alone with Gregory. I knew he'd like me better if he were away from his prying, noisy relatives. As it was, he thought more of annoying them than pleasing me. Before his father, he still pretended he was totally indifferent to me, just to set the old man raging about holy idiots and a man's right to progeny. I guess being the second son, Gregory had never enjoyed so much attention before. But we both knew he wasn't really like that, and I wanted the real Gregory back again.

I could just imagine us all by ourselves somewhere, in a bower of roses, perhaps, or on a mountainside by a waterfall, with the whole world spread before us. Instead, what did we have? A cold, dark solar floored with smelly old rushes and crowded with retainers, all of whom were charged to report the very minute anything went on between us. But whenever the family left on business, they'd take Gregory with them. And when he came back, he was always as sour as spoiled ale. So much for the bower of roses.

I still remember the drizzling gray March afternoon when at last I was by myself for a moment, mending Alison's hose on the window seat at the far end of the solar. Widow Sarah had taken the girls to see the new kittens in the stable, the laundresses had come through and gone off, lugging a large basket of filthy linens between them, and Hugo, the squires, and the groom had gone to join in the hunt that Sir Hubert never missed on the days that he was home. It was dark and dank inside, and I was brooding about the difference between a marriage of the body and a marriage of hearts. The dismal sound of dripping water on stone sounded like tears. My own, maybe, except that mine were secret.

I couldn't help but think of Master Kendall, that day, and the way he had of chasing off sadness by saying something wise and funny that would distract your mind. How I missed his generous soul, and the web of kindness we had knitted between us! I wish you were here, I said to myself. In return, I heard a soft puffing sound like breathing, and felt a gust of cold air prickle the back of my neck. The Cold Thing was back again. I was beginning to get used to it. I blessed myself, and it passed by, making a sound like rustling.

As I looked in the direction of the vanishing sound, I saw a tall figure silhouetted in the doorway, and my heart gave a leap. Gregory! But then it sank when I saw the expression on his face. More bad news.

"Gregory? Have you come to sit with me? I never see you anymore."

"Oh, Margaret," he said, still standing. "I don't know whether to be pleased or not that you still call me that." He looked tired, but I could see his heart in his eyes.

"Would you prefer Master de Vilers? That's the proper way. I always called Master Kendall 'Master Kendall' like a proper wife."

He shook his head, and smiled. "I'd like to tell you that you're as silly as ever, but I know that you know what I mean." He came closer. I couldn't help admiring the way he looked. It wasn't just that he had such a fine figure, once he wasn't wearing that shabby gray robe he used to go about in. It was the elegant way he walked, all even and connected, without even knowing it, and the way he looked at things, and the light of intelligence on his face that showed he really saw them, and understood everything that was going on. Some women admire clothes and jewels on a man, or the way they turn a pretty compliment, but I've never thought much of that. Those things can wear out, but a wonderful mind never does.

"Margaret," he said, and looking as though he could see what I was thinking, his voice changed ever so slightly. "I'm afraid we'll be leaving day after tomorrow. The Duke holds court at Kenilworth, and father's got to see him."

"See the Duke now? Whatever for? Can't you just stay with me and let them go alone?"

"It can't be done, Margaret, because it's about your lands, you see. It has to be settled before father leaves on campaign, and the Duke's the only one to do it. There's some friar who's laid suit on the manor at Thorpe, claiming he's the legitimate heir, and it was sold to Master Kendall illegally. He's left his order to take up residence there, and your steward's driven him off twice. But the worst is the estate at Withill. The very day he heard Master Kendall was dead, the Earl drove off your cattle and began trying to collect your rents. When we filed suit against him, he sent his men to occupy the manor. Not only is he too powerful for anyone in the area to say no, but he's bribed the local magistrate, who backs him on it. So you see, only the Duke can handle it, and it may very well take more than the law. We haven't enough men here to smoke him out, even if we could outbribe him in the courts."

"Still, couldn't you stay for just a day—a half day—even just an hour—and join them later? It would be lovely with you here and them gone."

"Really, Margaret, for a woman who ought to be clever, you do act dense sometimes. We're mired in deep, and sink deeper every day. We've borrowed on the estate to pay the lawyers, and if I can't defend your lands they'll be shorn away until there's nothing left but a mass of debt. You don't want to live here forever, do you?"

I shook my head silently, and he went on. "I'm not a rich merchant like Master Kendall, you know, and we haven't a hope of supporting the London house you care for so much unless money is coming in from somewhere. The only hope I have for bringing in that much is in the field—or with the rents of his manors, if we can keep them in the family. But I know your heart is set on keeping that house, and I intend to try for your sake. You ought to know what father thinks of town houses. Even less than he does of men who can't hold on to inheritances. He'd have sold it a dozen times over if I hadn't fought him every step of the way."

"Oh, who'd have thought it. Master Kendall never had all these problems with his manors. He just bought them and there they were. I never thought it would be so hard for you."

Gregory sat down on the opposite window seat. "Humph. There's a cold spot here," he said, getting up quickly and reseating himself next to me. "Did you notice that?" he added. "It's very odd. It made the back of my neck prickle." Who'd have thought the Cold Thing was still hanging about? Well, this wasn't the time to tell him about it, not with all the worries he already had.

"Margaret," he said, taking my hand. "I'm sorry I haven't been able to do it all for you as well as Master Kendall did. But he was a man with influence at court and half the world, to whom he'd doubtless loaned money. But the Earl thinks your lands have fallen to a little family, without influence, and that he can bully us out of what the law says is ours. You can't believe how wrathy he's made father! He even sent father's messenger back with a rude letter about it, and kept his horse in the bargain. I tell you, I've never seen father on such a rampage. He won't rest until he's got his own back."

"Why didn't he tell me, instead of being so horrible?"

"Tell a woman? That's not his way. He'll be angry even if he finds out that I told you. 'The more women know, the more trouble they can make' is what he always says."

"Trouble? When have I made trouble for him? It's him that's made trouble for me. He storms about, and says rude things, and beats on my children! He's never been anything but trouble!"

"Margaret," said Gregory firmly, "you should be grateful for what father's done for you."

"Grateful? I knew he was horrid the minute I first set eyes on him!" I could feel the Cold Thing stirring.

"Don't you speak against my father!" Gregory stood up suddenly. "Just because I can't stand him doesn't mean you can say things about him! Besides, the whole thing's your fault anyway!"

I could feel myself getting angry. After all I'd put up with, and all I'd done, and all I'd waited, I had to hear this.

"My fault? *My* fault? So now it's my fault, is it? What makes it my fault, pray tell?" I could see him shudder briefly and shift places—he'd gone and stepped directly into the middle of the Cold Thing.

Then he waved his hands in the air as he said, "So tell me, when did I ever have troubles like this before I married you? Stupid lands! Stupid houses! Stupid furniture! Everything I owned could be carried in one bundle, and I was *free*! Free of father, free of Hugo's envy, free of lawyers, free of petitions and testimony, free of stewards and bailiffs, and free of brats! It's women who do this to men, and it's all your fault!" Gregory had turned all red and taken on an increasingly injured look as he worked his self-pity up to even more splendid heights. "I tell you, I was much happier contemplating God! God doesn't make all this trouble for a person!"

I was so angry, I didn't even know where to begin to tell him off. I wanted to say, If you were so busy contemplating God, then why didn't you just stay in your order? Or, why don't you blame your father? He's the one who had the bright idea of grabbing my inheritance by carrying me off. But all the mean things I wanted to say got all jammed up together, trying to come out at the same time, so I just stood up to confront him there with my mouth open and my face all hot, completely speechless. That's what men bring you every time! Trouble! What did he know about trouble? He wasn't sorry a bit! All the while I stared and turned red, he just stood there counting up his injuries in front of me, as if I didn't have any myself. I felt like choking, or maybe sobbing, I couldn't tell which.

"—so maybe it's about time someone informed you, Margaret, you are a very selfish woman—"

"—so who do you say is selfish? You ought to know, you're selfish yourself! That's all you think about—you, you, you—you and your stupid father, and it's me that makes all the sacrifices —do you think I like this horrible house one little bit? Just tell me one way I'm selfish—just one, I dare you!"

"Selfish? You're so selfish you're even selfish when you're asleep—just look at how you roll up in all the covers at night— you don't even leave the corner of a sheet. I tell you, any man who sleeps with Margaret freezes to death, that's what!"

"You—you—" I didn't even have any words left. How could I have ever gotten myself tied up in something so ridiculous? God, I was a fool! And this man a worse one! I could feel it all coming up, all bitter and wild. Laughter. Crazy laughter at Margaret the fool. This is how it all ends—this is what happens with all these stupid hopes and plans. I doubled over with it, and the spasms made me sick with pain.

Gregory stopped in the midst of his catalogue of woes, his face all red with resentment. "That proves it, proves it entirely —everything I've said! You see? You know it's true, so now you laugh at me—after all I've been through! How can you?"

"I'm—not—I'm not—" I managed to choke out, hiccuping and clutching at my sides.

"Then just what do you think you're doing?" The look on his face, all puzzled and self-righteous at the same time, just set me off again, and I couldn't explain.

"You're hysterical. I always knew you were the hysterical type. I could tell when I first saw you. All women are hysterical. I ought to dump a bucket of water on you."

"Not—yet," I managed to gasp. The spasms were beginning to slow down. I started to wipe my eyes.

"You see? That's just what you needed. Even the threat of

cold water works wonders." Feeling clever made him start to cool down.

"No, no," I gasped. "That's not it at all. It's my side. It hurts. I need you to help me rub it—here, where it hurts." God, I needed him.

"You're an idiot," he said, putting his big hand on the sore place under my ribs that I showed him, and rubbing it for me.

"And you're not?" I couldn't resist asking. I felt weak all over, as if I'd just been through a disease.

"Of course not. I'm never an idiot."

"You're very fortunate, to be always right." I sat down on the window seat, still trying to get my breath.

"It's a burden I've worked hard at getting used to." He smiled ruefully. I was still sore in the ribs, but the look on his face made my heart feel better.

"Sit by me," I begged, "I've been having a terrible time. I need you. I need you to hold my hand."

"This being-married stuff," he said, dropping down beside me. "It's more complicated than I thought."

"It's always that way," I said. "If it isn't money, it's family, or a thousand other things."

"I guess that's why perfect lovers are never married," sighed Gregory.

"You think you can't be in love if you're married?"

"Of course not; it isn't proper." Gregory looked all schoolmasterish.

"Proper?"

"So say all the scholarly Authorities."

"How do they know? Were they married, these scholars?"

"Naturally not; it's not proper for scholars to marry." Gregory looked suddenly sad; I was so sorry for him. I put my hand on his arm. The rough wool of his sleeve was somehow comforting, even if it was his father's old hunting tunic, and too short at the wrists. He started, as he had so long ago, when I'd inadvertently touched his hand. But then he looked at me, grateful for the solace.

"Being married doesn't make you not a scholar, you know. The learning is still in your head—it doesn't just vanish."

"Oh, Margaret, if it were only that easy. You can't be married and be a scholar; it mixes up the mind."

"Are you sorry then you married me, after all?"

"No, I'm not sorry at all," he said, and looked at me in such a curious manner. "That's my problem. I'm not sorry at all. I've never known anyone like you before." My goodness, his face looked handsome. I waited for him to say what I was hoping for.

"You—look so nice. And you're fun to talk to. And—and—" He looked as if he were trying to find some word that eluded him, and then he colored, and blurted out "—you bake the most amazing rolls!" Oh, merciful heaven, how can men say women have trivial minds, when theirs work like this!

"Then if we can't be perfect lovers, couldn't we be imperfect lovers?" I smiled.

"Actually, Margaret, I'd had something in mind like that myself," he said, looking around the room to see if it was still empty.

"They'll be gone for a while, if you're thinking what I'm thinking . . ." I said.

"I think I was," he said, and his face shone with sudden joy as he scooped me up in his arms so quickly, I didn't even have time to be surprised.

"Gilbert! . . . GILbert! Where is that mooncalf?" The raucous bellowing echoed up the stairwell, shattering the silence in the solar. A noisy cluster of hounds and humans centered on Sir Hubert clattered through the door and passed by the curtained bed, as the Lord of Brokesford went to his own room to have the grooms change his muddy, wet hunting clothes for his traveling attire.

"Aha! There you are, Gilbert, lurking about indoors like a woman—or"—and here his expression changed to a knowing, conspiratorial one—"possibly *with* a woman?" He watched his son stiffen. Gregory could see his father's shrewd eye taking in the room: the abandoned sewing on the window seat, the hastily neatened bed. The old man looked as if he were calculating for a moment. Then he inspected his troublesome son's face. The air of contentment was well concealed, but not to the old man's well-practiced eye.

His face relaxed only for an instant before he growled, "And where's that wife of yours anyway? What good is a woman who isn't around when it's convenient? I have something I want to talk to her about."

Gregory looked down on his father from his full height and responded with aloof dignity: "If you are looking for Margaret, she's in the chapel, praying. It is her habit at this hour."

"In the chapel? Another weeping, praying woman in the house? Pah, they're all alike."

"She prays for the soul of Roger Kendall."

"That old merchant? He has perpetual Masses sung for him. He doesn't need all that extra praying."

"She says he does. She says he died unshriven, and she's not going to quit praying until she's sure he's in heaven."

"Unshriven?" The old man sounded serious. "Then that's entirely proper. Leave her alone." Sir Hubert ruminated uncomfortably a moment, then paused as if something had occurred to him suddenly, and asked: "But how's she going to know when to stop? Is she expecting God to tell her personally when he's saved?"

"That's what she says."

The old man shrugged and shook his head. City women were all crazy anyway. It's the bad air—it softens their brains. Well, her brain wasn't any softer than Gilbert's—they certainly were well matched in that respect. But, of course, despite his every effort, Gilbert's had remained in a state of mushy inadequacy for as long as he could remember. Backbone! Discipline! It was as if he'd never heard the words. It was enough to drive any father mad.

The old man strode up and down and stroked his beard with

one hand, his head bowed. It had to be bad blood—doubtless from his wife's side. It's a thankless task, dealing with bad blood. It had been a bit of luck, getting this chance to marry him off. But if marriage couldn't steady him, it was time to give up. Sometimes you just have to face facts. Thank God, Hugo was normal. He'd have to be damned careful checking the bloodlines on any wife he got for him. It wouldn't do to have an heir with bad blood off Hugo. "One line tainted already," he grumbled to himself, inspecting his second son as he stood at attention, waiting to be dismissed. That was one thing he liked, seeing his sons standing at attention every time he entered a room. It was one of the few decent habits he managed to have beaten into that sullen brat before he'd gotten too old to defy him.

"You may go now," he said. As he watched him depart, he thought, as soon as this business is settled, I'll start negotiations for a proper bride for Hugo. It's high time this family had a houseful of grandsons. Suddenly a vision of rank upon rank of grandsons, all obedient little soldiers, all standing at attention for their grandsire's inspection, filled his mind. At the thought, a rare wave of contentment rolled over him. It was almost perfect.

I think I haven't yet mentioned the chapel of my father-in-law's house. It was cold and damp, and there wasn't even a proper coat of whitewash on the gray stones, let alone some colored holy pictures. It's because Gregory's father was stingy, and never wanted to pay when one of those wandering painters would come between towns in the summer to make lovely pictures of the holy Madonna and the saints in churches and chapels, or whatever else you like. There was nothing much in the Brokesford chapel but a little altar, some very cheap candlesticks, and an old altarcloth that had once been beautifully embroidered by someone, but was now grown grayish and raggedy about the edges. There was a ghost, too, though she wasn't much trouble, really, except for sobbing and weeping in the

night. In my experience, it's always the damp, sad, stony places that have ghosts. A warm, well-painted place full of children and music hasn't any room for them.

Now, when a chapel is cozy and well furnished, I must admit it is a lovely convenience to have right in the house. Master Wengrave, next door to us in London, who is Cecily and Alison's godfather, has a little one right downstairs, where the family could hear Mass every morning without going down the street in all weathers to St. Botolphe's. But there is the bother of including a chaplain in the household, which is not the expense, but the fact that they do nothing but eat and drink and carry gossip. It is bad enough when they tell your mother-in-law the flaws in your child-raising. But sometimes they do more, and you find the kitchen maid pregnant, and then it is a great problem. Then, too, they can get nasty if roused, and little things upset them, like getting the wrong place at table when there's company, and then there's no end to what they can do.

So in our London house we didn't have a chapel, although no one could understand why we did without something that added such splendor and comfort to a house. Master Kendall often had guests from far-off places in his house, and he also had me, and he didn't want to run the risk that a loose word might bring the bishop's officers to the door.

But in the country, where it's far from the bishop, they can do the same thing in other ways. And my father-in-law's way was very simple: He had found a priest who hadn't a sober moment in the day. Of course, no one could tell if he sang Mass right, but most people can't do that anyway, since it's all in Latin. But you could hear *Deus* and *Paternoster* and *benedictus* in lots of places in the service, and he rang the little bell nicely. Father Simeon was willing to take a drink in exchange for many things—a secret baptism, the sale of the Host to put in the first furrow for good crops, or even a wedding without banns. He was a useful fellow at confession, too, which is how he got his nickname of "Father Three Aves." You see, he usually wasn't in a state to remember what you said, so he'd just give feather-light penances, which suited my new relatives perfectly.

"Killed two fellas last night," my father-in-law would puff and grunt as he got to his knees.

"Do you repent?"

"Of course, I never would have done it if they hadn't come after me first."

"*Ego te absolvo.* Three aves."

It was a method that worked far better than Master Kendall's, for even he couldn't entirely protect me from the sternness of my confessor. Of course, that one knew I'd signed a confession and abjuration of heresy, and was under orders from the bishop to prevent my relapse. It was all because I'd been in the faith-healing business—that's how I met Master Kendall— I'd fixed his gout, and after my troubles he decided to marry me so I could go on fixing it. They said I was a witch and a heretic and a sinner and a lot of other rude things, and then I was in so much trouble, I almost didn't get out of it. I was lucky to get off with just a confession, instead of getting burned up, which would have been even more painful.

But ever since then I haven't done any faith healing, except for a very tiny bit at home, though I'm still very good at it. It even turns out to work on horses, though I must say I wouldn't have run the risk if it hadn't been for Cecily and Alison. And when the Gift works outside, you can't see the light it makes, so I don't think anyone noticed, though sometimes I worry about that sharp-eyed old man. It all came to me in a vision that I am sure was straight from God, and if God wants you to do something, then you really ought to go ahead with it. Of course, sometimes it goes away, when I'm sick or when I'm pregnant, but after all, what on this earth works perfectly every time anyway? But now I'm very careful, because the inquisitors promised to burn me all to cinders if they caught me at it again, and that is a great discouragement, even if God did tell me to do it.

I used to worry that I might have done something bad that I

didn't understand, because I really did not want to be wrong with God. But now I know it's just a question of monopoly of trade. I learned that from Master Kendall, who was a great trader, and ever so wise about the world. He was always so interested in my improvement and education, which is why he always told me so many important things and hired tutors to make my thoughts higher. Master Kendall always said that most things boil down to a question of money. And when I understood at last that if Margaret got a dozen eggs for taking off warts, they didn't go to the priest at some shrine for praying for the same purpose, then I saw it all more clearly. It is a great blessing to have an intelligent husband, who can explain things like that. I've always admired men with good minds.

Now I had two reasons for visiting the chapel that day—three, if you count hiding from Gregory's father. The first was to pray for Master Kendall, which I'm very careful to do every day, even now. The second was not a very nice one, so I planned to do it after I'd prayed, so my conscience wouldn't interrupt me. I'd found out where Father Simeon kept his paper and ink. And since I needed it and he never used it but once or twice a year, when a letter needs to be written, I felt that God would prefer me to have it.

But when I got to the chapel, there he was. And if I'd been thinking about God more and the paper and ink less, I suppose I wouldn't have minded, but as it was it seemed very annoying that he was there. He was noisy, too, so a body couldn't concentrate. He was hopping and dancing about, trying to brush something off his robe.

"Come to confess, eh?—get off! Get *off*, I say!"

"Father—"

"Couldn't be much. I absolve you. Get *off*! Three aves." Then he brushed some more, and hopped about a bit. "They're all *over*. Can't seem to get them off."

"What are they? Bedbugs?"

"No—can't you *see* them? Nasty things, off!"

"No, I can't see anything there."

"Devils! Damned little devils! Green, like big spiders, but with such nasty little faces. Off, off! They make my skin burn and crawl. Oh, God, my sins—forgive—get them *off*!"

"I can brush those bugs off, I think—quit jumping around so much and let me try." I knew right away where those bugs were from. But the problem is, if you heal a person who drinks too much, then they remember why they were drinking, and get much more upset than they were before. I did it only once, and the man jumped out of the window to try to kill himself, but only broke both legs—and that was a much bigger healing job.

Just a little bit, for the bugs, so he can sit still, but not so much he gets sober, I thought to myself. Then he'll go off to bed. And I quieted my mind and called just the tiniest bit of the healing light, which God sent to me in my vision. When I could feel it in my hands, I knelt down and brushed his robe all about the hem, until he sighed,

"Oh, gone, gone at last. Those little faces! Ugh! I'll see them in my dreams. However did you manage?"

"You just didn't brush hard enough, Father Simeon, and you couldn't get round to the back, where they were hiding."

"Where? The back?" and he whirled around. "No, none there, God be praised. You seem to have got them all. If you'll pardon me now, I must withdraw to—meditate." He looked about him unsteadily. "You're staying?" he asked.

"I haven't yet said my prayers for Roger Kendall."

"Very good, very good. I'm glad to see a pious soul in this house at last." I couldn't help feeling just a little guilty as I watched him stagger off. A wisp of fog whirled across the room behind him sobbing dolefully. The Weeping Lady. I knelt down anyway, and as I started, the sobbing stopped. Then, just as I was especially explaining to God that Roger Kendall's good deeds must be taken into account, I heard a soft little voice in my ear.

"I saw you," it said. Goodness, the Weeping Lady could speak. Most of them aren't clever enough.

"I saw you. Your hands and face glowed, and the light made me feel warm. Have you any idea how cold this chapel is? That's how I died, you know. I got a chill, and now I'll never be warm again."

"I'm terribly sorry," I said. One should always be polite to Weeping Ladies. They're usually the ghosts of women who died in childbirth, come back searching for the baby. They deserve respect, especially from us women. Then she moaned a bit, just to keep in form, and bewailed her dead babies awhile.

"Doesn't that frighten you?" she asked, a little maliciously.

"If you were evil, it would frighten me, but I don't think you're evil," I answered stoutly.

"How do you know that? After all, I'm here for vengeance. That's what our sort of being exists for. Why," she added, rather haughtily, I thought, "I could go to heaven anytime I wished, but I just chose to wait here until I've got even— something I never got a chance for, when I was alive. I had to petition, and get all sorts of special permissions," she went on rather pridefully. "Not just *everyone* gets to be a Weeping Lady. You have to have a *special* mission."

"Why, that's very impressive," I answered humbly. A snobbish ghost. There's something new all the time, isn't there? "Could you tell me what it is?"

"Of course not. It's a secret. But I'll tell you this much. It's men I'm getting even with. They're nothing but a trouble and a bother. Take my word for it, and don't waste your life on loving any of them. Or it's soon enough you'll be a Weeping Lady. There. Wasn't that impressive? Not many people get advice from a Weeping Lady." The wisp of fog swirled around me.

"And by the way, if you want to do any more glowing, come in here. I like the way it feels. All warm again. It's very nice. And tell the Cold Thing that followed you here not to bother me anymore. This chapel's only big enough for one apparition." The wisp of fog thinned and vanished, leaving me vexed and curious, instead of peaceful, as I expect to be when I'm in a chapel. It took me no end of time to compose my mind again and resume my prayers.

When I'd gone on a proper long time, long enough to secure Master Kendall's soul for another day, I finished up and went to rummage in the big chest of books and vestments that was kept in the corner behind the altar. But after I'd folded the sheet of paper I'd found and tucked it into the bosom of my surcoat, I heard the sobbing resume. I looked up to see a wisp of fog whirling up above the crucifix. The Weeping Lady was still there. But where was the ink? Ah, there in the bottom of the chest, well stoppered. I poured it off into the little jar that used to hold my rose water, leaving just enough so Father Simeon would think he'd forgotten that he'd used it himself. The weeping stopped. A long column of mist was forming in front of me, and I thought for a moment that I could make out in the vapor the tall figure of an elegant-looking lady with a long, straight nose, and hair that might once in life have been darkish, all tucked up under a fancy French headdress. She had a large number of rings on her long, slender fingers, which interested me at the time, since I wondered how jewelry, which is so hard and lumpy, could become all misty like that. She was peering intently at me.

"I saw you," she said. "You took paper and ink." I blushed.

"Did you take them for yourself?"

"Yes, I did," I confessed.

"Then you can write?"

"I can," I answered.

"I can write too," she said rather haughtily. "I can write my name. Not many can, but I am exceptional. Why do you need a whole sheet of paper? Are you having a letter written?"

"I'm writing for myself. I write things I learned from Mother Hilde, so they won't be lost. Recipes and secret charms for childbirth, and things like that. Also I write my thoughts, because everyone tells me I talk too much and I'm trying to reform, but if I can't talk to someone about the things I think, then I might die."

The Weeping Lady looked rather sympathetic at this last. She swirled a bit, so I couldn't see her face. Then she formed up again and said firmly, "Then you're a nun. Mother Hilde is your abbess. Why aren't you wearing a habit, and what are you doing here anyway?"

"I'm not a nun. Master Kendall hired someone to teach me to write, because I begged him. Mother Hilde is the wisest woman in the whole world, but she's not an abbess. She is a healer, and a wisewoman, and a midwife, and she taught me all of her secrets, long ago. I am writing them in a book for my daughters."

"A midwife? I don't trust midwives. I'm sorry she wasn't an abbess, though I don't trust them either—they're always hunting for endowments." The shape separated and wavered at the edges, as if she were finding it difficult to concentrate herself. "Do you know I had eleven babies?" She rippled and swayed. "All but two are dead. They weren't even a year old. It was my husband's sins that killed them. I couldn't pray enough to keep his sins away. Oh, it was cold, cold, so cold. And then I died. Are you sure Mother Hilde isn't an abbess?"

She sounded so disappointed that I said, "She really isn't, but I have a brother who's a priest."

"A priest? Oh, that's nice." She sounded approving. Good, I thought. It's important to humor spectres. "I've a son who's a priest," she added. "Probably much more important than your brother by now. My, he was a pretty little boy. Just like me. I had my confessor teach him reading and Latin when he was just a tiny thing. He was ever so quick—not thickheaded, like my first. Bad blood, that one had. That's what comes when you marry beneath yourself. My father would never have stood for it if he'd lived. 'Never marry beneath yourself, my little chick,' he'd say. 'It's better to be a nun.' Now, my little boy, he must be very large by now, but he's gone away to be a priest and I've never seen him since the day I died. He was too little to be left; I heard his weeping even on the other side. But I'm sure he remembered what I'd told him. 'Be a priest,' I said, 'not a sinner like that creature I married. Stay pure. Remember, you're not like them.' Oh, the pity of it, that I married beneath myself, and was brought to all this grief."

As she spoke I began to have a curious suspicion. It grew and grew in me, and made my skin crawl.

"You must have very fine blood," I said very carefully. "Even now you look very elegant." The Weeping Lady swirled a gracious acknowledgment. "Just who was it you wed? Would you care to tell me his name?"

"Oh, what a crude young man. Mother was quite taken in. A true chevalier, she said, come to rescue us in our distress. Well, he did look nice in his armor, I must confess, and he carried my favor to victory in the tournament, which did turn my head at the time. But can you imagine? The moment we were wed he spent my dowry to repair his tower and didn't even have the chapel painted. Oh, father, how right you were!" She became agitated and rose to the ceiling awhile, and then billowed down. "The only thing he ever spent a penny on was his horses!" she hissed spitefully in my ear. "A new saddle blanket? Spare no expense! A new dress for his poor wife, who'd married beneath herself? Never! I wore out my wedding clothes, I tell you, and then I died. A woman can't live without a decent dress. But I tell you, I've come back to haunt him, haunt him, haunt him, until he's ashamed to show his face in public! Take my advice! Never marry beneath yourself!"

"And the name, just so I'll know how to follow your sage advice?"

"Sir Hubert de Vilers, may the Devil fly off with him! A horrid blond young man, a bit on the square side—very vain about his swordsmanship. You can't mistake him, no, not at all!" Her anger had swirled her all up again, so I couldn't see her, but it didn't matter. Even after she was gone, I had to put my hand over my heart, it thumped so. There was absolutely no mistaking it. I had a Weeping Lady for a mother-in-law. It was really altogether too much.

Now, Mother Anne, who was not my real mother but my

stepmother who raised me up, was a woman of great practical sense, and she always warned me about mothers-in-law.

"Now, Margaret," she always said, "when you get married, be very careful of your mother-in-law. Remember, they are always angry at the girl who marries their son, so be respectful! Don't give them any cause to get peevish! Give them the best of everything at table, and make sure their bed's warmed before they get in it. Call them 'Madame my mother' even if they're no lady at all, and kneel before them in respect. I've had several mothers-in-law, and believe me, I know. That's the only good thing I can say about your father—he didn't come attached to a mother-in-law, and for that I'm grateful."

Oh, Mother Anne, I miss you now! Surely, surely someday we'll meet again. And when we do, I'll tell you about my first mother-in-law, because Master Kendall was so old, he didn't come with one either. You'll be amazed! And I certainly never needed your advice more than now, in this very delicate situation I've found myself in.

The nights that followed were hard, hard. I'd turn restlessly in bed, sitting up suddenly in a cold sweat, worrying about the Cold Thing, and listening to the breathing all around me. The circles grew underneath my eyes, but I never told anyone why —that I was worried by Cold Things, by ghosts that swirled and boded no good, especially if that foolish Weeping Lady ever managed to catch up with the changes in the house and find out that her little boy wasn't a priest after all, and it was partly my fault.

Sometimes, if there was a moon, I'd get up and tiptoe across the rushes, around the sleeping dogs, and go to stare out the window at the stars, I was so torn with hidden fears and secret anguish. They were so cold and sparkling, all set up there on the dome of the sky. How did God ever manage to stick them up there, so they could move about without falling down? I'd put my elbows on the windowsill, even though I was half frozen, and watch the clouds scudding across the moon until my numbing feet sent me back under the covers. Gregory's lucky. He can sleep through anything. Then I'd hear his soft breathing in the dark, and feel the warmth of his body, and my heart would melt inside me, in spite of everything—because of everything. Who knows?

My greatest fear was of the Cold Thing, however. I feared— no, I knew—that one day it would come between us. It would come in the night, and reveal its beastly, unnatural self. It would shake its huge, shaggy head and seize me in its slavering jaws. Or maybe it was a devil, and in the morning, they'd be able to find nothing but a faint stain on the sheets, where I'd lain, and smell a whiff of brimstone. Oh, it was coming to get me, all right. I could feel it near. It was just biding its time.

A little longer, please. Leave me a little longer, Cold Thing. Let me have him just a few more nights. I know what you're waiting for, Cold Thing. You're counting my sins, and when you've got the last one, which is wanting him too much, then you'll take it all away. Oh, yes—it was at night that the thought of the Cold Thing frightened me. When the sun is up, I can manage anything—even the formidable task of placating a Weeping Lady. But night makes even common things eerie. The shadows of the clothing on the perches looks like monsters' faces, and the sound of rustling insects like ghosts' footsteps.

So now, whenever I heard a rustle in the night, my eyes would fly open with fear, and sleep would vanish until I recognized the sound of mice scampering in the rushes, the *whuff*, *whuff* of a dog having dreams, or even the sound of someone using the chamber pot. But then, late one night, I woke to a rustling sound that did not turn itself into something ordinary. It sounded like the feet of a large animal, most probably a hound of hell, or some other awful monster, shuffling slowly toward the bed to fetch me at last. Gregory was rolled into a ball, the pillow over his head, sound asleep but grinding his teeth with worry. He'd never tell me what the worry was, but I knew anyway. He'd lost his life's calling, and being married isn't a calling, and coming into money isn't a calling either. And farthest of all from a calling is having to come home and be shouted at instead of being free and a scholar, and in search of God. So I didn't wake him up. I just got up my courage to pull aside the bed curtains and peep out. Maybe all they'd find in the morning would be some greenish slime in one slipper, but that's the way it was going to be.

It was terrible, the thing, as it inched along in the pitch black. A shapeless mass, about three feet high, it shambled slowly toward my side of the bed. I could barely make it out. But I could feel it coming closer, ever so slowly and inexorably. So I gathered my courage and whispered at it, "What do you want, and why are you here?" The moundlike thing shifted, and a tiny, indignant voice issued forth from its depths, "Mama, Alison *peed* in the bed!"

Then another indignant little whisper replied, "Did *not*, you did it!"

"I never did that, it was *you*, baby, baby, baby!"

"I never did it either."

"Then why's it all wet in there, so we can't sleep?"

"The Devil did it."

I was relieved and annoyed all at once. "Both of you stop that this minute," I whispered fiercely to the mound of blankets they had put over their heads and wrapped about them, to keep out the cold. "You'll wake everyone up."

"Then let us in with you, mama, it's warm and dry in your bed."

There was a shifting in the bed, and a low, growling voice said, "Don't you *dare*." I could hear an indignant voice from beneath the pillow. "There are things no man should ever put up with, and wet children head the list," came the threatening whisper.

So I got up and herded the mound back to its own bed. Fleas bit my ankles as I crossed the floor, and I nearly stepped on one of the dogs in the dark. Then I turned their mattress over and tucked them up in a dry blanket. And as I kissed them Alison said, "It wasn't my fault, mama; papa didn't come to tuck us in and kiss us good night."

"He's forgotten us and gone away," added Cecily forlornly. My heart felt so heavy for them. I'd been selfish, thinking of my own grief.

"Dear hearts," I answered. "Papa's been in heaven for more than two months now. He didn't forget you. He's thinking about you both in heaven."

"No, mama, he never went to heaven at all. He stayed with us. He sits on the bed at night, and sometimes tells a good story. But now he's forgotten us. Alison's just a big baby, and thinks he won't come back at all. But *I* know he will. He promised."

I can't deal with children's fantasies at night. I have enough trouble with my own. I told them not to wake anyone, and we'd talk about it in the morning. Besides, I was freezing. But before I fell asleep, I marveled at how children change things in their minds. Their father had been a busy man. He'd have never once considered putting them to bed, even though he was a veritable wellspring of good stories.

The morning after, of course, I forgot all about what Cecily and Alison had said. Children can't be held responsible for their nighttime doings. Besides, things are always different in the morning. The sun comes up and makes the earth new, and it's just possible that something good might happen. This morning the squires were exercising by cleaning chain mail in the hall, for Sir Hubert wanted all the armor glittering white for his trip to petition the Duke. Cecily and Alison had trailed behind the two young men to admire the process, for with them it was a kind of sport. They stitched the mail with a coarse needle into a sack full of sand, making a kind of heavy ball, which they pitched about, shouting and leaping, until the sand had quite worn away the rust on the links.

I had plans for the morning. Special plans, all for me. I'd said I was going to do mending, and that's what they thought they'd seen me go alone upstairs to do. Now I tiptoed quietly to the stair door, and shut it ever so silently. Then I piled the girls' spare clothes beside me on the long window seat, in case anyone came through. But beneath the clothes was my new ink, reed pens, and two big sheets of paper, one half written. I'd been so careful to be quiet for the last two days, I was just bursting at the seams, and had to tell the paper what I thought of them all. So first I wrote what I thought of lords, and then I wrote what I thought of love, and then I wrote what I thought of the housekeeping in this place, and how much better I could have done it, if I could give the orders to the steward and bring in some women from the village to dig out this den.

How different it was with Master Kendall! He let me run anything, as long as it was well run. And he always liked how pleasant I'd made his house, and praised me when it smelled of lavender, and nothing jumped out of the corners and bit him as he passed by. Nobody, he said, had ever made his house so comfortable and proper—not his steward or even his first wife, though she was a blessed woman, and he'd cross himself at her memory. And then he'd kiss me and say, "Margaret, you're such a dear girl, I can't imagine how I ever lived a day without you." My goodness, things like that make it possible to undertake anything.

So there I was, with my feet tucked up under me on the window seat. The first pale spring sun was full on the page, and outside the birds were chirping and the first leaf buds forming on the bare branches of the trees. I was all lost in writing, and so full of happiness that I barely heard the ferocious voice calling from the tower passage, "GILbert! I want you here! Search in the chapel, he may well be wallowing about on the floor in there. I'm off for the stable, have him meet me there." But as the hawk's shadow makes the coney scuttle for his hole, the first footsteps caused the paper to disappear under my skirts as I looked up to see who it was.

"What's that you've hidden so quickly, sister? A lover's favor, perhaps?" Hugo's sharp eyes never missed details, especially when spying traces of the prey at the hunt or when there was anything to do with what might be a woman's intrigues. "A fine bag of surprises my addle-headed brother has here—a sly woman with secrets hidden beneath her skirts. Hand it here." He stuck his left hand on his hip and extended the right. If only I were a man, I'd write in the open, on a table, and shout at people who disturbed me, "How dare you!" But Hugo was twice my size and perfectly capable of breaking a bone or two. I couldn't keep it from him. By this time his father had come up behind him. He waited silently behind Hugo, his arms folded, looking grim and stern.

"Hand it over, madame," repeated Hugo. I reached beneath my skirts, which I'd spread out on the window seat over the paper, and handed him one of the sheets, without moving from my place.

"Worse than a favor. It's writing." Hugo took the sheet and squinted at it, holding it at different angles to the light. "A lover's letter, no doubt." He looked hard and cold. It was, after all, a matter of the family's honor. Then he held the sheet out to the old man: Sir Hubert scrutinized the page, drawing his white, bushy eyebrows together.

"Hmm. Nasty handwriting, this. Can't make out a single letter. Call the priest." A boy was sent off and soon returned with Father Simeon in tow. They sat him down on the other window seat opposite me, and watched gravely as he peered at the sheet and read, " 'To restore the color of faded garments, soak them in verjuice and hang them out of the sun. I do not know if this works, but Mistress Wengrave swears it's a sure remedy.'

" 'To rid the hall of flies, hang branches of fern upside down from the ceiling. When the flies have settled, throw the branches away. . . .' "

He squinted further at the paper. "These are recipes, my lord. Women's recipes. Not a love letter in here anywhere. Perhaps she wrote them herself. The handwriting's most unscholarly."

Did you think I was so stupid as to give my writing over to

the enemy? The real sheet that I'd been writing on was still hidden under my skirts. I always keep a false one, just for surprises like this. It's a good thing I'm in black, I thought, or I might have got a nasty ink spot on my dress from all of this paper shifting. Sir Hubert looked at my hands, clutched together on my lap.

"Hold them out," he said quietly. "As I thought. Inkstains. Whatever you are, madame, it's plain you're no lady. But in this house, you're to act like one. Hand the ink and pen over to the priest. If you've any more recipes you wish recorded, you're to dictate to him before witnesses. I won't have even the suspicion of dishonor on my house. And as for reading, do as the queens of France and England and the great ladies of the court do. If any writing comes to them, they make a great show of how they do not know how to read it, and have the paper unsealed and read to them by a clerk, before witnesses. That is how a lady preserves the honor of her house. And that is how I expect you to conduct yourself under my roof, no matter what that feather-brained second son of mine says. Do you understand?"

What could I do but bow my head and hand over the ink and the pen, sitting ever so still to preserve the sheet of writing still hidden beneath my skirts? For, of course, if they ever saw that, I don't know what would become of me.

Margaret waited until she saw the broad backs of the two men pass the upper door of the stairs before she furtively folded the sheet of paper that remained to her. She scurried across the room and knelt to hide it in the ornate chest that had been brought from her old house. The chest was foreign, and cunningly made to conceal a secret compartment beneath a false bottom. Master Kendall's house had been full of odd things like that, for he had been very fond of rarities and curiosities. Margaret had been one of his curiosities, too, although she had never really suspected it. Kendall had a rival in Germany who possessed a jeweled statue of Saint George and the dragon so finely made that it fit in the palm of his hand. Then there was that Italian who had the fabulously made table-clock that depicted not only the hours but the planetary epicycles; he'd refused to sell it to Kendall at any price. But Margaret was the ultimate possession; in a stroke, he'd outdone them all. Her presence in the house had filled him with a kind of complex and exquisite joy; her acquisition was his crowning achievement.

He had known what she was from the first time he spied her. He had seen it several times on his travels before, and was too shrewd to mistake it, even concealed beneath a threadbare russet gown and a worn hand-me-down cloak. First the look of her eyes, when they shone all tawny in a stray beam of light, and then the curious repose of her face had caught his eye. Then there was the way she walked—a fluid motion perfectly centered, a kind of balanced straightness without stiffness, and the graceful, competent look of her hands. There was no doubt at all; she was one of Them, even if she didn't know it herself. How deliciously ironic, to find one in the back alleys of the City, in the form of a girl not yet twenty.

He'd snatched her up, of course, and been repaid with countless hours of enjoyment, watching her antics as she tried to appear exactly like everyone else. The greatest amusement he had was indulging her completely, just to see what she'd do: she wouldn't wear the jewels, they were "too cold," but she gobbled the sweets like a street urchin. Unless he forbade it, she'd give away the clothes. She had to see what was in this, or how that went, so he'd hired Madame just to watch the funny faces she made, trying to learn to pronounce French vowels. He'd even indulged her freak to want to learn reading. And just when things were getting altogether too stuffy with his business and associates, she'd find some eccentric in the street who'd move into the house and refuse to be dislodged, turning everything charmingly topsy-turvy. The Cold Thing sighed. His treasure thrown among the weeds. And not a thing to be done about it. Bitter. Bitter.

The Cold Thing followed Margaret down the stairs, and criticized the sloppy way the indoor grooms laid out the trestle tables in the hall for dinner. It bobbed about the room, frightening one of the hounds, who suddenly howled and bolted, to everyone's surprise. It drifted into the kitchen to criticize the food as it was being laid in the serving dishes. One of the kitchen boys, who was dipping a crust of bread into the potjuice on the sly, felt a cold draft on the back of his neck that made his scalp prickle. Then the Cold Thing floated out to see how well the squires carved—Robert was deft, but Damien would always look like a bumpkin—and finally settled itself across the table to observe the face that Margaret would make when she bit into the bread and found it bitter and heavy with bad leaven. That girl could certainly bake; it was something in her touch. The bread always rose high and sweet. And her brewing—ah, that alone would have been worth marrying her for, even if she hadn't been as pretty as a little wild thing met unexpectedly in the woods.

Aha, now she was breaking the bread—now she'd bit it. The Cold Thing laughed—a series of silent gusts of icy air. It was a wonderful face she made, and well worth waiting for. She was pretending she hadn't tasted anything amiss, but her nostrils flared, and an instant of shocked distaste flickered in her eyes. Now the old man had bitten it. He growled, "A man could break a tooth on this," and pitched the remainder of the piece he'd bitten under the table for the dogs. "A bakehouse that can't turn out a decent loaf. Damned disgrace. Ought to flog them all, and see if it improves their style," he grumbled vaguely in the direction of his daughter-in-law.

"It's the water," she said unexpectedly, breaking her usual silence.

"Umpf?" he raised an eyebrow at her. The brothers turned their heads.

"The well water is sour. It spoils the leaven. I've watched them—the well's near, and the spring is far, so they don't bother to spend the effort to get sweet water. It spoils the brewing too. I think your well is too close to the moat. The sour water seeps into it underneath the ground."

"If you've done criticizing my table and my well, madame, I challenge you to prove the truth of what you've said."

"And if I do?" The old knight scrutinized her face a long time. Damned impertinent woman, he thought. Another beating would go far to improve her humility.

But the notion of better ale corrupted his knowledge of right, just for a moment, and he said, "I'll give you back your pens and ink." Hugo looked shocked, and Gilbert's mouth twitched and his eyes glittered with amusement. The Cold Thing chuckled, but no one could hear it.

By the morning after the Feast of Saint Benedict, when the Lord of Brokesford, flanked by his sons and retainers, rode forth to the Duke's court at Kenilworth, he had become a man of many worries. First, there was the question of the petition to the Duke, but almost next in importance was the fact that in a moment of weakness, before witnesses, he'd given his son's mad wife a chance to turn the house upside down in his absence. A lord cannot break his word, and the story had now become a living thing, traveling about on its own swift feet through the shire, causing derision, speculation, and even the placement of a few wagers. Then there were the negotiations for Mother Sarah, who belonged to a village on Sir John's neighboring demesne. He'd had to trade a pretty wench for the old dragon, who was famous for nagging three husbands to death, just to acquire someone fierce enough to keep those beastly little girls under control. That had caused considerable merriment among the neighbors, as well. It's women who bring this kind of ruin on a man, he thought to himself in a rare moment of meditation. They don't have to do anything but be, and they destroy the correct ordering of the world.

It had been unspeakably vexing, the last two days. The woman could be seen everywhere, usually bundled up in a big apron, giving orders. He'd ridden out on a vermin-hunt with the neighbors, and there she was, having commandeered an oxcart, tasting the water in its load of barrels with a big ladle. On their return, he could hear over the terriers' jingling bells the sound of her voice coming from the bakehouse: "This flour's not bolted right. It's fit only for coarse bread, not table bread." Women's voices in general annoyed him. They were too high and shrill. Especially when they gave orders. All women should be required to whisper, he thought grumpily. And then he'd spotted a pair of redheads racing unattended toward the bakehouse. One of them ran close enough to risk tripping up the horses.

"Not so fast," he growled. With a single movement he leaned from the saddle and scooped up the struggling creature by the back of its garment. "Where is Mother Sarah?"

"Under the stair with Little Will. Now put me down, will you? We're helping mama." And the neighbors had laughed so heartily that he had dropped the offending creature on the spot. For it seemed that he was the very last in the shire to discover that Mother Sarah was as famous for her ability to acquire husbands as to survive them. So rather than bringing order, he had loosed another of these horrendous creatures into his well-constructed male world. It was a dreadful feeling, the feeling that his universe was falling into uncontrolled chaos, and that women were the cause. They were almost as bad as lawyers.

Now when Sir Hubert left with Gregory and with Sir Hugo, I felt altogether like that woman in the story who is supposed to spin straw into gold overnight. New leaven is not something that can be made in a day, or even several days, and although the brewing went well, the leaven was a worry. First you must make the starter just right and leave it in the air, and then I have a way of burying the crocks just so that is my secret, while the leaven makes itself all lovely smelling and bubbly. Or it may rot; it's quite a worry. You never know till it's out what has happened, and I didn't think I'd get a second chance to prove myself and win our wager. So I was very busy and forgot entirely about the Cold Thing, which would have been healthy except that when you forget about things like that, that's when they come and grab you.

So that's just what happened. I was by myself in the tower passage when I suddenly stepped right into it. I shuddered and leapt back. The Cold Thing followed, hanging on to me like a clammy mist. Oh, Jesu, it's finally decided to get me, I thought. I began to panic, but as I started to run I tripped and fell flat.

"Wait, wait!" sighed the Cold Thing, as I tried to scramble up and flee. I'd hurt my knee and couldn't get up fast.

"Hear me, hear me." It surrounded me as I sat, rubbing my bruised knee. It was so cold, it made me shudder. But it had me now, so I might as well speak to it.

"I'm sorry, but I can't stay here if you keep freezing me."

"Is that why you run whenever I come near? Can't you see me?"

"No, I just feel you; you're like an icy cloud."

"Then you can't tell it's me?"

"Who—or what are you?"

"Oh, Margaret, Margaret, don't you know me? I'm between heaven and earth, Margaret, here in the shadows," the Cold Thing sighed. Suddenly, beneath the soft windy sound, the voice seemed familiar.

"Is it really you? How did you get here?"

"Oh, it wasn't easy. At first I sat with you all the time, but you didn't seem to notice me. Then I lost you. Couldn't find you anywhere. I tried hunting for your little light, but instead I found other people with lights: a fishmonger's wife, an ostler, and an anchorite. The anchorite had an interesting one—bluish white. I'd supposed they were all orangish pink, like yours. I knew you weren't dead, because I see all the dead people come by here—even saw my son, Lionel, with his head tucked under his arm, on his way—umm—downstairs. Then I thought, wherever you were, you'd find a way to get your Psalter, so I followed it out here. Where is here, by the way?"

"Brokesford Manor, in Hertfordshire."

"Broken Down Manor is more like it," huffed Master Kendall's ghost. "I certainly kept my places in better trim than this."

"I couldn't agree more," I said. "But I still don't understand how you got here—I mean, between heaven and earth."

"Oh, Margaret, you have no idea how unpleasant it was. At first I floated above my body—it was very nice of you to wash it yourself, by the way—most women would have hired someone —but then, you always were special. They usually let you stay until the funeral, if it's a nice one. But then I found out that— well, it was a question of the infernal regions—if you see what I mean."

"I was so afraid of that," I cried, wringing my hands. "It's because you died unshriven. I started praying right away. I set a schedule, and do some extra in between."

"Yes, that's what did it. The praying, I mean. You bothered them so much, they couldn't decide what to do with me. So here I wander, neither up nor down, and most people can't see me, but I can see everybody. It's a poor kind of company, here in the shadows, and I've missed you dreadfully. That, and of course I dislike seeing that dreadful fellow Perkin Greene taking over my trade."

"Oh, Master Kendall, I've missed you so much, and our house that we made so beautiful—and it's not fair at all that you should suffer so, just from having died so suddenly." I put my hands over my face and wept.

"Now, now, don't cry so. You know I never want to see you cry. It's not at all painful, this existence—just dull. No one to talk to until now, except that ridiculous Weeping Lady—I had to put her in her place—told her I knew His Majesty and also the late king personally, and then I didn't hear any more about social-climbing merchants trying to take over her chapel. And a damned dismal place it is, too, as if I'd ever want it. No, the buttery and under the stairs are far more interesting."

"Master Kendall!" I was shocked. He laughed, that cold,

gusty laugh that was like an echo of the laugh I loved so. Oh, he always knew how to put everything right with that laugh.

"Don't think they're unfair up there, Margaret. That wouldn't be right. There were just a few things I never told you about—the piracy, for example. I was much younger then, and thought they'd forgotten. Also I thought I had a very good excuse. And there were one or two other things I'd still be embarrassed to tell you about. You were always such a lovely little thing, Margaret, and I wanted you to think the best of me."

"But I did, and I do. I will always love you."

"Ah, Margaret, you seem to be getting very fond of that troublemaking Brother Gregory—or should I say Gilbert?— these days. I must say, I never thought he had it in him, running off with you that way. Though now I've seen his family, I understand a good deal more."

"Are you angry at me then?"

"For what? For not weeping at my tomb perpetually? Or burying yourself in a convent, young and lively though you are? Oh, no, Margaret. I only want your happiness above all. I loved you more than anything on earth when I was warm and living, and now that I am cloudy and cold, I know you need youth and warmth beside you. Just promise you won't forget me, that's all."

"Oh, how could I not promise that? You know I loved you with my whole heart, when you were living, and I love you still."

"There's only one thing . . ."

"What's that?"

"I can't go until I'm sure you're well looked after. And in all the time I've been watching that tempestuous young man who's married you, there's one thing I've never heard him say."

"I know," I said, bowing my head. "Maybe it's not in his nature."

"If it's not in his nature, then his nature's not for you, no matter how much fun you have between the sheets." Goodness, Master Kendall could be blunt. But then, we'd always been honest with each other.

"I know you too well, Margaret. You can't live without a warm heart next to yours. So remember, I'm waiting to hear it as much as you are. Then I can go up or down or wherever it is I'm bound—though I must say I hope your prayers work and it's the glorious region and not the hot place. But no matter where, I'm not moving until I hear it. Even they can't make me."

What was it we were both waiting for? It wasn't much, but they were words that had never actually come out of Gregory's mouth in my presence. In all the time he'd known me, he'd never said, "I love you."

CHAPTER
4

"And so, like a greedy greyhound, you swallowed it whole?" Sir Henry of Grosmont, Duke of Lancaster and Earl of Derby, Lincoln, and Leicester, Steward of England and Lord of Bergerac and Beaufort across the seas, had received his petitioners, as was his habit, in his bedchamber in his immense fortress at Kenilworth. Still a vigorous man, although already well into middle age, England's greatest warlord radiated an almost visible aura of power even in repose. And well he might: lord of over a score of castles in England alone, he possessed the powers of the crown within his own vast dominions. He had his own seal, his own courts, his own diplomatic missions. His wide lands supported not only their own administrators, but the immense and busy household that moved with the Duke himself from castle to castle when he was not in the field.

The Duke was sitting erect on the richly embroidered counterpane of a vast, silk-hung bed, his gouty foot, newly inflamed by yesterday's banquet, propped on a little stool before him. These were the last petitioners of a morning's long business, begun at dawn. The case was a bit different. Amusing, even. A man the Duke usually saw more of in the field than at home, when the fellow visited only annually to do formal homage for his estate. The knights and clerks that stood about him ready to take care of anything he ordered had grown restive thinking about the noontime dinner that would be waiting for them.

"I'm afraid that is so, my lord," answered the Sieur de Vilers, head bowed, hat in hand, on his knees among the rushes on the floor. His two sons, each in a similar posture, flanked him.

"I knew old Kendall," said the Duke, letting his gaze wander out the window. Outside, a brisk wind was pushing clouds across the blue spring sky. Crocuses were poking up through the dead earth in search of the sun, and you could hear through the unglazed window the lapping of the water in the wide artificial lake that surrounded the castle on three sides. "He sold me a number of rarities. And, of course, no one was a better judge of a length of crimson than he." It was one of the Duke's weaknesses, the smell of the fabulously expensive dye on a length of new crimson as it was unfolded. And Kendall had made a great deal of money catering to it. "A shrewd eye he had, a collector's eye. And no finer piece than his little dolly. I saw her dancing last winter at my masque, when I opened the Savoy to the London merchants. Did you know that? A lively little thing she was, who seemed to know all the most fashionable new steps."

"No, my lord, I had no idea."

"She turned down every go-between in the City," he said, the distant look still on his face. Including mine, he thought. And quite ungracious of the little wretch, considering that I expect gratitude when I stoop to a merchant's wife. He paused a moment, as if thinking things over. Then he stopped. He inspected Gilbert at leisure. It had been nearly a decade since he had seen him last, the maddest of an impetuous lot of new-made squires nourished in his household at Leicester. It was hard to believe that the tall, austere figure kneeling there in the threadbare, mended brown velvet surcoat was the same one who featured in the raucous new ballad that was sweeping London. It was something about how the old merchant's walls were high, high, high, but his wife was young, young, young, and a bold young squire, dressed as a humble friar, had sneaked in by the kitchen door, kitchen door. He'd have to have his minstrel sing it again tomorrow night, after they were gone. The melody wasn't much, but there were several quite lurid verses describing goings-on in the chambers while the old man slept. If they hadn't been borrowed wholesale from another ballad, they might have seemed more serious. But Gilbert?

It wasn't something he'd have ever suspected of Gilbert, and he believed he was a good judge of men. How could anyone ever forget that prank where the other squires had substituted a pair of naked laundresses in place of themselves in the bed that two of them shared with Gilbert, just to see the horrified expression on his face when he woke up and found them there? Just what was it he'd shouted as he'd snatched up the sheet and run off? He'd forgotten, but it had been very funny, even at the retelling over dinner all that long time ago. Even then, Gilbert had acquired a reputation for being a bit more priggishly holy than is proper in a military man. Of course, that had never bothered the Duke much. As long as a man fought like a fanatic on the battlefield, he could do whatever he liked with the rest of his time. Even pray and scourge himself, if that was his preference.

"So it's your son Gilbert who snatched her up, is it?"

"Yes, my lord. But he hadn't the slightest suspicion that Master Kendall had left·everything to her. It's unseemly. An allowance maybe, or a lifetime interest in the house. But everything? None of us thought it possible. But now, you see, our honor requires that we keep it."

The situation had its entertaining side. A faint smile crossed the Duke's face. A little thought flitted across his mind: It's a good thing they can't see my face in that posture.

"Sir Hubert, rise, and your sons also. The honor of the de Vilerses is dear to me. Just what was it the Earl said?"

"About the shabby cadet branch of the de Vilerses?" said Sir Hubert, rising. The veins stood out in his temples just thinking about it. Sir Hugo's nostrils flared. And Gilbert, looking tall and somber, clenched his jaw.

"No, the other bit—"

"Oh, the part about the palsied claws of an aging patron?"

"The Earl is young, and needs to be put in his place. How many men do you need?"

"We could do with thirty. He can't mount nearly as many."

"I'll send fifty. Sir John"—and he gestured to the aide who stood beside the bed—"go and see that two score and ten men at arms are prepared to depart for Sussex on the morrow. I assure you, I am wrathy that the Earl should interfere with my knights' livings on the very eve of my new campaign in France. Brother Athanasius"—and he gestured to one of the two clerks that always stood by him, wax tablet and stylus in hand, when he heard petitions—"I will need a letter written to the magistrate, informing him that the de Vilers matter concerns me, and another one to my lawyers in London." The clerk bowed and left with a swift step. Sir John left, giving orders, as men moved in and out of the bedchamber.

"The new destrier, Sir Hubert. I'll try him when my foot permits." The Duke was at his best when he was at the center of a hive of activity. He sounded positively mellow, now that the formalities were over.

"Beautiful mouth, my lord. You'll never find a better anywhere."

"Of that I'm sure. You're getting quite a reputation for your horses." Sir Hubert turned red with pleasure. The Duke had the key to his heart. "And you've brought me two fine sons, as well." Sir Hubert seemed a little taken aback, and glanced at Gilbert furtively. He still looked exactly the same. Less than he ought to be.

The Duke shone the light of his charm on Hugo in turn.

"Sir Hugo, your father's courage in my service has been measureless, and you look to be like him. I've had my eye on you for quite a while. I expect great deeds of you." It was Hugo's turn to look content beyond words. The Duke could charm the birds out of trees when he wished, or men to their deaths in the mud of foreign places, all for glory.

"And you, Gilbert. At long last you will be joining us." Gregory looked surprised. "Better you than these fishmongers and soap-sellers' sons I'm plagued with." Gilbert looked puzzled. "Surely, Kendall's manors, once secured in your name, will bring an income over fifteen pounds a year, will they not?"

"Why, yes—that is, once the debts are paid off," responded Gregory, still puzzled. He had been over the accounts himself. The income, though considerably more than a poor knight's fifteen or twenty pounds a year, was irreparably mortgaged for many years in the future to lawyers and to the Bishop. For having a university degree had meant that he was automatically in minor orders, and marriage to a widow would have brought penalties for bigamy except that the Bishop, for a tidy sum, had exempted him. Then there were the loans to cover the bribes for getting murder charges dismissed as self-defense, and for the repair of the roof of the hall at Brokesford Manor, which his father had said he was owed for his trouble. Then there were all the curious inheritance taxes, which included the best beasts on each estate being driven off by the overlord and the priest. Even elopement isn't simple, he'd found: a web of indebtedness and financial ruin stretched like a nightmare before him. All at a stroke, by becoming rich, he had become poor.

"You are aware of the new law, surely? It has been in force for the last three years. Not, of course, that a man of honor would require a law to point out the right course of action." Gregory still looked puzzled. He had become addled with laws lately, and couldn't tell what was meant.

"My lord, I need to be informed. I was in the Carthusian monastery at Witham for most of that time, and heard nothing of the outside world."

The Duke absorbed this piece of information, paused, and spoke again: "For the past three years His Majesty has required that every landholder with rents over fifteen pounds a year take up the obligations of knighthood and required military service. Our next ceremony will be at Whitsunday." The Duke looked contentedly at Sir Hubert's exultant face. "It is a good thing when lands are removed from the hands of the merchants and bankers. Gilbert de Vilers, you'll mount many a good man from these lands of Kendall's. I have made a good bargain for the King this day." When he did not see the appropriate look of gratitude on Gregory's face, but rather one of shock, he continued suavely, his canny eyes never leaving Gregory: "Gilbert, they tell me you're a scholar. It's a curious activity for a scholar, carrying off a woman at sword's point. But then, how many soldiers are scholars?" Gregory never moved, but looked unspeakably embarrassed.

"Did you know that even I have given thought to my soul's health? I am composing a book of meditations that might well interest a scholar's eye. One like yourself, who is something more than a scholar." The Duke watched with satisfaction as Gregory's curiosity stirred, and showed itself on his face.

"I often think, perhaps a scholarly mind, one that has given deep thought to the sacred, of course, would be able to offer comments to improve my little work."

"It's all in the composition. If you have a felicitous arrangement, you have everything, my lord," Gregory blurted out, being unable to contain himself.

"That is what I thought—what do you think of ordering the bewailment of sins according to the parts of the body?"

"Why, that's brilliant," said Gregory, and he really meant it. The Duke looked pleased with himself. Sir Hubert and his eldest looked uncomprehendingly at each other.

"I suppose I should tell you," said the Duke, as if the thought had not just occurred to him the previous day, when he'd been told the de Vilerses were here, "I have need for a man in my personal suite in France. Someone who's a scholar, but not a useless one. A soldier, a gentleman of good family. I've been thinking that a chronicle of my campaign—written right there, not by some sleepy monk who's never seen anything of life and understands nothing about chivalry—would be a worthy thing to have." He watched as Gregory's mind started working over the idea. He knew it was not the princeliness of the offer—the glory of the Duke's service, or the handsome rewards that a great patron makes to a chronicler—that would turn Gilbert's head, but the fact that it touched his weakest spot, his vanity about his intellect. And while, for amusement, the Duke collected women, his serious work in life was collecting men. He had made it his study and his art, and he understood the wellsprings of men's actions perfectly. It was why he had grown great, when others remained small. And now that he was growing older, he would sometimes awaken in the night, when not on campaign, and think what a fine thing it would be to have his greatness all recorded in black, red, and gold. Illuminated, of course, at least in the final version. It was not quite as great an idea as the one he'd had about charming God Himself with a book of meditations, but it was very nearly so.

"Would you—"

"My lord!" exclaimed Gregory with unfeigned joy.

It was Watkin the herdsman's middle boy, standing barefoot beneath the new-leafed willow at the brook's edge among his woolly charges, who first spied the mounted party. A row of dark shapes in the distance, silhouetted against the rolling first green of the spring meadows, they toiled slowly along the narrow track to Brokesford Manor. As they approached you could make out the figures of Sir Hubert and his two sons in the lead of a half-dozen mounted retainers, two laden sumpter horses, and a clear dozen hounds, including the old spotted bitch that never left the old lord's side.

The child ran across the field shouting, "They're back! They're back!" to tell the manor folk to open the main gate. The Lords of Brokesford did not look like men who had come home empty-handed, though even the hounds that ran beside the packhorses looked wearier than when they'd departed.

Margaret had left the low, thatch-roofed malthouse well content with the progress of the reforms there. She was wrapped from neck to ankle in a big borrowed apron, and had now settled into the bakehouse to sniff the new leaven in the crocks that had just been lifted from the cool earth of the floor. The wide brick ovens stood cold this morning, the ashes newly raked out of them. Tomorrow would be baking day. She wrinkled her nose at the acrid, sweetish smell of the yeasty brew in the last crock. It was good, all good. And what's more, she'd taken advantage of everyone's absence to browbeat the steward with the proximity of Easter and the need to placate a particularly demanding Lord, whose eye was not only on the sparrow but on the dirt in the corners. Several old layers of rushes had been dug out of the manor house and thrown on the compost heap, and new ones laid on the scrubbed stone. Even the chapel was whitewashed in a manner that the Weeping Lady pronounced to be adequate, but still beneath her.

"What the—?" said Sir Hubert as he rode through the great gate. The kitchen midden and attendant pigs had been banished from the forecourt. As he dismounted and saw the horses led off, he noticed that the piles of muck in front of the stable, which somehow never managed to be removed, but instead grew higher all winter, had been carted off, with a subsequent diminution of flies. Well, that at least is not an altogether bad idea, he thought, though I wouldn't want her to know it—it might make her think she had a right to shift everything around.

"Where is that wife of yours, Gilbert? Don't City women know how to greet a returning lord?" At that very moment Sir Hubert was gratified to see a figure streaking from the bakehouse to the kitchen door at the end of the hall, stripping an apron off as she ran. By the time the bowing steward had welcomed him back to his hall, Margaret, still breathless, stood beside him, holding out a large cup of ale from her own brewing. Greeting the old lord in the accepted fashion, she offered him the cup. Only Gregory spied the vague air of well-controlled sarcasm in the elaborate gesture. His father took it as his due. She's coming along, the old man thought. That beating Gilbert gave her did her no end of good. A few more and she'll be entirely trained to the family standard.

Sir Hubert lifted the cup to his lips and drank deep; the look on his face changed to astonishment. He passed the cup silently to Hugo, who drank and said, "Better than the Duke's," looking with surprise at his father. Then, remembering himself, he passed the remainder to Gregory, who finished it off without any surprise at all. After all, everyone in London knew about the ale at Master Kendall's house. It had been one of the attractions of his tutoring job there, back when he had been a free soul meditating on the Godhead. In a way, you could almost say that everything had been caused by that ale; it had kept him coming back despite every annoyance caused by Margaret's daftness. Margaret remained kneeling in front of them, waiting for the answer to be witnessed by the entire household, which had crowded silently into the low, arched curve of the open door to watch. They backed into the hall, and one or two of them even held infants on their shoulders to let them have a better view. There wasn't a soul in the shire who didn't know about the strange bargain the lord had made in a moment of weakness. And when news that the new ale was stronger and sweeter than any in Christendom had spread to the neighboring manors, interest had mounted daily in anticipation of his return. How would he keep his promise? How could he keep such a promise?

"It is good," he said.

"Better than yours, as I swore," reminded Margaret.

"Yes, better," he said. He didn't want to puff her up. Puffed-up women are one of the original sources of trouble in the world. If anyone knew that, it was he. He counted it as one of his duties to mankind to keep women from puffing themselves up, though it had been a most monumental duty in his own marriage. A job requiring a hero. It was one of those things that God, being male, questioned you about before you were let into heaven, and he was proud to say that he hadn't neglected it.

"Hear how a knight keeps a bargain, even one made in a moment of weakness," Sir Hubert addressed the assembled crowd in a lordly fashion.

"Dame Margaret"—he addressed her in the polite form—"you may have pen and paper when you wish them, if your duties are fulfilled, and you may read books." Shocking. The people looked at each other. "But only when a man of this household is present, preferably Father Simeon." Oh, admirable. A lordly judgment. Heads nodded in agreement at the old knight's wisdom—a Solomon, fit to chop a baby in half anytime.

Margaret thanked him and rose. Her face was totally expressionless. The old lord looked benignant as he thought he detected a look of humble gratitude in her eyes. But he was deceived: Margaret was suppressing a powerful urge to tell him exactly what she thought of him. Now, tongue, she was telling herself, just stay out of trouble this once, and I'll write down what I think of him later, that pompous, ignorant, rapacious old hypocrite.

"And now, dinner," boomed Sir Hubert, breaking the silence. "A celebration is in order, for the retaking of the estate at Withill. And I shall keep Saint Edward's Day with a great feast, for justice has triumphed in a world full of iniquity."

"Your father is very mellow," said Margaret in greeting Gregory as the milling knot of retainers and gossips dissolved to see to the laying of the tables.

"We've got it all, Margaret, except for the law cases that are pending. And those should go our way too, now. We did sap the walls of Withill Manor and burn part of the roof, so the hall will have to be rebuilt. The stables went up, too—the thatch was just like tinder. But we pried every one of the Earl's men out of the place, and sent them packing. Didn't lose a man, either, although old John took a swordstroke. And can you believe, after it was all done, the Earl sent a message that his steward had overreached himself against his orders, and he'd never meant to offend the Duke? It just goes to show, winning is everything." They were standing now beneath the wall forested with antlers. A shaft of light from the high window caught the rich green folds of wool of Gregory's heavy fur-lined cloak.

"That's a new cloak, isn't it?"

"From the Duke. Hugo's got a velvet gown, and father a new brace of hounds—those brindled ones, over there. Margaret, you've no idea how gracious, how admirable he is—how far-sighted and noble! The greatest and most perfect leader of men in all of England, save only for the Prince, and of course King Edward himself."

"Gregory, what happened there?" Margaret sounded suspicious. Gregory had thought the Duke too stern, too unbending, and too undevoted to matters of the mind and soul previously.

"You've no idea what a spiritual force he is. . . ."

"Gregory, what's made him a spiritual force, since he's just as he always was?"

"And his insight . . ."

"For God's sake, tell me what he has done."

"Why, Margaret," said Gregory happily, "he's made me a gift —enough to pay off all the debts on the property."

"A gift? What on earth for? Great men don't give gifts for nothing."

"Of course not. I'm entering his service. I'll be going to France in his personal suite. Can you believe the good fortune? I tell you, there's many a good family that can do nothing but dream of an honor like that. He's arranged for me to be knighted, Margaret, knighted! It was never in my future, you know, father couldn't afford the fees. Why, you'll be a lady— aren't you pleased? He knights twelve of us on Whitsunday next. And that's not the end of the honors he's granted me. I'll be personally writing down his noble and courageous acts in preparation of the greatest chronicle of our times. Just think, a chronicle of action and chivalry, not the stale maunderings of some dried-up cleric. My name will be celebrated forever! He said there weren't many capable of doing it—a scholar who was also a soldier—"

Margaret's eyes widened in horror.

"—a man of ancient family, who understood chivalry as well as letters—"

Margaret turned pale.

"A noble commission, nobly granted—"

"Not France," she said. "Sweet Jesu, not France."

"But Margaret, it's an honor," Gregory said gently.

"I'm all alone here. I haven't anyone but you, Gregory. Don't you see, if anything happened—doesn't our marriage mean anything?" she asked, putting her hand on her heart.

"The greatest honor of my life—"

"Couldn't you just talk to people when they got back, and write it down that way?"

"That's not what the Duke has in mind, Margaret. Don't you see I'm a new man? Why, I could go on to anything. We might even be at court someday. Aren't you even grateful? He's secured your inheritance and cleared the debts on the property, all with one princely gesture. And now—why, I've got a patron for my poems, the work on meditation that I plan to write—"

"Oh God, oh God," said Margaret, clutching his sleeve. She was shaking all over. Gregory put his arm around her and gently led her to one of the benches along the wall of his father's hall, directly opposite the fire. They sat there in the midst of the noise and confusion as if they were entirely alone.

"You have to understand, Margaret. I've got my life's work back."

"I know," said Margaret, snuffling into her sleeve, "I only want what's best for you." He's caught you, that old hunter, she thought. Caught you like a hare in a net, and you don't even understand it's been done.

Hugo strode by the little scene.

"You really have a town woman there, don't you, brother? A true lady's heart beats with fierce joy when her lord rides forth to smite his enemies," he announced. And he passed on without waiting for an answer to see that his breastplate was being properly cleaned up after the battle for Withill Manor. Margaret lifted her head from her arm and stared after him, red-eyed.

"That's because if he's anything like you, she's glad to be rid of him," she said spitefully.

"Margaret!" Gregory was shocked.

Margaret bit her lip as she sniffed. She'd had a number of conversations with the Weeping Lady on this topic, and knew exactly what she was talking about.

I couldn't believe what he told me that day. My God! I've never heard of a more harebrained idea in my life. That's how it is with the great ones: They get a touch of brain fever and everyone else has to run off and get killed for their half-baked schemes. And all the while bowing and saying, "Yes, my lord! Brilliant, my lord!"

It's one thing to go off to a nasty, dangerous place like France, where everybody hates the English goddams, if you enjoy killing and raping and looting. It's much more difficult to enjoy these occupations at home, where it makes the neighbors mad. Whereas in a foreign country, you can have your sport and come home rich—if you don't come home dead. Or rather, part of you comes home. Usually your heart in a sealed casket, since it's easier to ship. I tell you, you can always tell when something's too unpleasant for a sensible person to get involved in: they call it an honor, every time.

But what business is it of a man who plans to write a book of meditations going to France? It's not as if he's going to come home either rich or happy. In fact, you can pretty well bet it won't work out. But who asks a woman? Now, given the way old soldiers like to brag and lie around the fireside, I'd say, if you have in mind to write a chronicle, write it all when you can stay cozily at home. You'll only get into trouble if you write the truth, anyway, since it might contradict all the tall tales they want to tell.

But do men hear good sense when they're all puffed up with deeds of chivalry and *courtoisie*? Oh, no. It's their upbringing, I think. It makes them gullible. And especially they don't want to hear good sense from their wife. Myself, if I were a man, I'd pay the fine, avoid the knighthood, live comfortably as a squire in the country, and keep my arms and legs in the bargain. There's plenty who do. In the City, they think it's a sign of cleverness, not cowardice, to pay off one's service. The fine is just part of the price of doing business, and a sensible investment. Master Kendall explained that to me when he paid off the fee himself, being "too old for the honor," as he put it in his letter to the King. But, of course, Gregory couldn't get away with it—not with his family, and not if he hoped to win his court cases and collect his rents someday and pay off his debts. So glory and honor sweetened the agreement, and turned his head in the bargain.

Still, I could see the temptation to believe it was all for the best. That night at supper his father and older brother kept staring surreptitiously at him, as if he'd done something really unexpected and admirable. Every so often Gregory's father would look him up and down, thoughtfully—the way you'd inspect a colt with bad conformation that has outrun the best stallion in the district. Silently, marvelingly. And he'd mutter, "The Duke's personal suite. Imagine!" as if no one could hear. Gregory didn't say a thing, but gloried in it. And you know, when men decide to box one of their number into a corner with some "honor," the victim can't usually back out, no matter how much he wants to. It's like having a marriage arranged that you don't care for. You can't just run off. You have to go through with it and hope it works out for the best. But in my experience, it usually doesn't.

But they do love the trappings of war, men do. Even Gregory got that serious, self-absorbed look about him as he announced he needed a new cuirass and helm, more suited to his new dignity, and went off to the London armorer's to equip himself. He returned with all sorts of this and that, including a long military surcoat with the three cockleshells and the red lion of the de Vilers arms embroidered on it, cut fore and aft to the waist for the saddle. It was as if he'd caught a disease. I missed his sense of irony, the easy self-mockery with which he'd catch himself in a particularly pompous moment, the sharp way he could see through the shams of the world. Now he was all caught up in the glory of the things he'd once poked fun at: who sat where, who got served first, how many retainers should he engage, how would he modify the family coat of arms to serve as his personal one, how many horses should he go into debt for, and should he order a pavilion, and what kind? And, of course, he started treating me the same way. One day he came in all hot from exercise with the identical rolling horseman's gait his father and brother had, and addressed me as "my lady wife," in all seriousness.

"Gregory!" I was shocked.

"Please respect my station," he said, and in vain I searched his face for a trace of his old sardonic smile. "You may call me my lord husband, or, after Whitsunday, Sir Gilbert. You should get used to it, so you won't lower my dignity before others." I turned and fled. By our Blessed Lady, I thought, it won't take much more of this before he's turned into his father. I needed to hide, I needed to think, but everyplace was aswarm with family or grooms. So I ended on the cellar steps, with the spiders, wiping the tears off my face and the grime onto it.

"Good Lord God, how are we to deliver men from their folly?" I wept. But God, who is often so talkative about some things, was entirely silent about this point. I waited a long time, until the tears were worn out. "A lot of use *You* are," I said, picking myself up and dusting off my skirts. "I'd think if *You* were considerate, You'd be offering Divine Guidance when I'm needing it so much." I smoothed my surcoat down and found a clean bit of sleeve to wipe the smudges off my face. "So," I said to myself, "that's how it is. Well, women have been married to fools since the world began, and they've never yet managed to change the situation. I'll just have to do my best, there's no more I can do."

And so we went to Leicester to see Gregory knighted in a mass ceremony on Whitsunday. There were a few spindly young sons of great families—too great to speak to anyone, of course. But for the most part, I felt right at home in the crowd of rich wool-packers and vintners and soap-sellers who'd put down good hard money for themselves or their sons for the honor and celebration of it. I even knew a couple of them who were from the City, and one had the gall to jostle me before the entrance to the church service and say, "So, Mistress Margaret, we do bring ourselves up in the world, don't we?"

All freshly bathed and looking somewhat hollow-eyed from their all-night vigil before the altar, the candidates went up one by one in church, then knelt to take the blow from the Duke before receiving the belt and sword. Gregory's father and brother buckled on his spurs themselves, and he was so set up that he unhorsed three men in the tourney afterward and was never unseated himself, though he took a hit very nearly at the center of his shield.

But at night, after all the feasting was done and the great dancing chamber at Leicester castle emptied, instead of rejoicing, he looked haunted. We sat up together in the big guest bed and I put my hand on his lean, scarred arm.

"What's wrong, Gregory?"

He started. "Don't call me that anymore, I've already told you."

"My lord husband, I never do in public. Can't I save some little bit of our first feeling for private?"

"It reminds me of—of what I've done. And of what I am, instead of what I should be." I took his big, rawboned hand into my two small ones and held it tight. Even in the shadows beneath the curtains I could sense the trouble and the worry in his dark eyes.

"And what have you done, but save my life and give me hope again?"

"All this honor, on a dead man's grave," he muttered to himself. "I wanted to dedicate myself to God, and then I sinned, and instead of being flung into the fiery pit, I was rewarded with the honor I'd never dared dream of."

"Oh, husband, put it from your mind. How else do heirs get titles but on another's grave? So how is it different, that Master Kendall should die, and that you should be lifted by his inheritance to a life of ease?"

"But Margaret, I didn't inherit you, I stole you."

"But not while he lived. You always acted with honor. You had his trust and friendship. That was more than his sons ever had."

"Trust—my God, that's worse. My mind is eaten up by what we've done together—he trusted me; I took his wife. I've violated God's commandments for this sweet, sweet sin. I can't pray with a clean heart. . . ." I could feel him shudder. "If it weren't a sin to marry a widow, then why would the Church forbid it to me?"

"Calm your conscience, Gregory. It's in the wrong place, entirely. There's a hundred men quick enough to snatch up a widow for her money without the tiniest fragment of your guilt. They'd do nothing but rejoice, as you should be doing."

He sounded horrified. "Even you—you think I did it for the money—for this"—he swept his arm around to gesture to his new world—"and for—oh, God, for—"

"Gregory, I know you didn't. Doesn't that count for anything?"

"I suppose it does. It must," he muttered feverishly.

We returned to Brokesford for the last days of preparation before the ride to the coast to sail for France. Everything was in a turmoil: Sir Hubert rode through the village, making his final selection of those who were to go with him, and there was much weeping and wailing in the little cottages by the muddy lane. Gregory had acquired two boys to mind his horses and a stolid, spotty-faced squire named Piers, who complicated my life by claiming he was in love with me as with the untouchable stars. When I told him to stop, he said it was a holy passion that burned with unquenchable zeal and beat on his breast, before he went off in pursuit of Cis, who pushed him into a watering trough. The girls sat awestruck while Damien tried on his armor and polished the horse gear. They asked to feel how sharp the edge of his sword was, and he told them they didn't dare— and besides, the grease on their hands would spoil the blade. So of course Cecily managed to cut her finger.

In short, everyone rushed about, posing and putting on airs in the way that is common before a military campaign. All except Gregory. After the morning's exercise, he would sit silently at Father Simeon's little octagonal writing table in the corner of the chapel, writing without cease from late afternoon into the night. Finally I couldn't stand it any longer. Why wasn't he out bustling and boasting, and getting drunk with the rest of them?

The sun was already setting, and most of the household in bed already, when I sought him out in the chapel. By the light of a single flickering candle, a feeble replacement for the vanishing daylight, he was deeply engrossed in his writing. The pen traversed the page in his right hand, followed a few inches behind by the little knife for scraping out mistakes in his left. I called quietly to him, so that I wouldn't startle him. If he were startled, he might make a blot, and Gregory is a great perfectionist about his writing. If he makes a blot, there's no speaking to him for hours sometimes.

"Margaret?" He looked up from his writing. "What are you doing here?"

"Come to ask the same of you," I answered. And when the ink was safely put away, I stood behind him and embraced him, kissing him on the neck.

"Oh, Margaret," he said in mock reproach. "Truly it is written that women's appetites are unquenchable. Doesn't any other thought ever cross your mind?"

"Yes, it does—I want to know why you're writing all the time. After all, the Duke hasn't done the great deeds you're supposed to write about yet."

"Oh, yes, he has, Margaret, and I've got to put down the already has been before I write the will be."

I looked over his shoulder at the writing. It was in Latin, but I could make out some words. "But I just see writing with *angeli* and *Deus* and—that looks like *Adam* and *Eve* down there, and—that thing, there, that looks like the Tower of Babel."

"You know, Margaret, it may be a mistake to teach women how to read, if they're not going to have an education."

"That's mean, I must say. So why don't you remedy the defect by explaining it all to me?"

He sighed, and explained very slowly and clearly, as if to a simpleton or a deaf person.

"All proper chronicles start at the beginning of the world, Margaret—and I have a long way to go to catch up to now. I'd hoped to do it all before we leave, but things have been so disorderly around here lately."

"Why don't you just write about the Duke, and leave out the Tower of Babel?"

"Margaret, if you were educated, you'd understand that a chronicle that just starts now is nothing but gossip. It lacks substance." The room had grown dark as we spoke, and the flickering candle threw his handsome features into relief, as he raised one dark eyebrow and smiled that faintly mocking smile of his.

"I'm sorry I don't know all about the Classics and the Authorities the way you do—I just thought it would save time." I still think it's a good idea, no matter what men think.

"I suppose I shouldn't fault you, Margaret. But writing is not a matter of common sense, like buying fish in the market. It's a matter of adherence to a proper discipline and form. It's like that notion you once had that everything should be written in English, because more people speak English than Latin. Sensible, except that people who speak only English can't read, and nobody who can read respects a work that isn't in Latin. By adherence to correct form, one avoids foolish mistakes and embarrassment. That's why the standards of civilization are absolute and universal. It's like truth: you can't have two kinds."

I still think that idea of mine was a good one, too, even if it does have a few little rough spots to work out of it. But I've never told him that either. Besides, he's so charming when he gets didactic. His face grows all serious, and his eyes shine, and then he'll tell you all about Saint Augustine or Aristotle or somebody else who's been dead a long time.

"So you see," he went on, "just as Latin adds substance to a work, so does starting at the beginning of the world."

"Did Aristotle start at the beginning of the world?" I asked.

He smiled. "Oh, Margaret. You're a ninny, but a dear one. Aristotle didn't write chronicles. But I assure you, he always began at the beginning."

So that was the end of it. But there were certain advantages. I'd lie in bed with my eyes open and staring, waiting for him because I couldn't sleep without him. And when I saw the candle nodding and bobbing through the dark, as he picked his way around the dogs on his way to bed, I'd rejoice that everyone else was sound asleep. Because then, oh then, we set the sweet darkness on fire.

But our time together was too short, and as the hour of departure arrived, we grew more feverish, as if we might never again see one another in this life. And more and more we realized what it was that we might be losing; yet something kept us from saying it out loud, perhaps it was the fear of loss itself. In this frantic time, even the beginning of the world had been abandoned. Only iron constitutions had kept Sir Hubert and his neighbors from collapse during the frantic round of drunken dinner parties that accompanied their parting. It was busy under the stairs and in the tower bedrooms, too, for this was a time when women could deny nothing to heroes who might never return.

"So, Margaret, we ride for Dover, encamp until the men and horses are enrolled, and then it's overseas to Normandy and glory." I was sitting on the window seat in the solar, doing mending, while Gregory was explaining things to me to allay my fears; it was all easy, he said. He had spread several packets on the seat opposite, and was checking over their contents. The girls were listening quietly for once.

"You enroll horses? They're paid too?"

"No, not that. Just men are paid—and I might add my military pay's gone up considerably now that I'm no longer just an esquire. But note is made of the value of each horse we bring with us, to compensate us if one of them's lost."

"But who will compensate me if you're lost?"

"Don't be silly, Margaret. I'm not a horse. Besides, I get a third of my pay for the entire campaign in a lump sum in advance. I'll send it to you from Dover, to pay the Lombards. All right? Don't look so pale. I'll be back. It's only a few months, after all. It would be different if I were riding with father. He sticks at nothing, and damn the consequences. There's a reason I don't tell you stories about when I was in France with him the last time. But a commander's staff is different. You get only as much glory as you wish for. —Piers, could you go see if they've finished packing my sumpter horses yet?"

Gregory looked over his last packet, and checked it once again, before he wrapped it himself and sealed it against the damp in a rawhide cover. It was the box of pens, paper, and a well-sealed inkhorn that would not part company with him until he returned home again. Damien was finishing the last of his packing, too, on the floor of the solar. We all turned to look as Robert the squire sauntered by him, a flower from some lady tucked in his hat, whistling casually.

"Sir Hugo says you're to hurry," he said, inspecting Damien's work. Then he smoothed down one of his eyebrows with a forefinger, and teased, "So, Damien, you're wearing no favor? You haven't any lady?"

"I certainly do," said Damien cheerfully, strapping up his pack. "My lady mother."

"Your lady mother?" Robert repeated with some sarcasm. "Then she's given you her favor?"

"Why, yes indeed. Her kiss when I went away into service, and I've never had a better favor."

"Damien, you will always be a bumpkin. You need a proper lady, not your mother. I myself"—and he smiled a wicked smile —"have Sir John's wife, the lady Genevieve." Robert, you sly-boots, I thought, that's the only reason you bothered to come up here. Kiss and tell; they're all alike, men are, old or young. With a very few exceptions—so few as to hardly count at all.

"And so have half the world," said Damien cheerfully. "When I choose a lady, she will be chaste, and not pass out favors the way a priest sprinkles benedictions. Then I'll worship her from afar and gain a noble reputation, long after everyone's forgotten who you wallowed in the mud with."

"Tall words, tall words for a man who's as slow as you are," answered Robert, who was not much annoyed, since he'd made his point.

"Damien, Damien." Cecily had left my side, and gone to stand by him where he sat on the floor. Her sister trailed after her. Cecily had untied the ribbon that held her tousled red curls, and held it out to him.

"What's this?" he said, looking up.

"My favor," she said, extending the limp, soiled object. Robert laughed sarcastically. Alison's face turned red and swelled up, and she burst into tears.

"No fair, Cecily, you're always first!" she howled.

"You haven't a lady," Cecily insisted.

"Alison, Cecily! You behave!" I was shocked at how forward they'd become. Cecily set her chin in that stubborn way she has. It was going to be a scene.

"Don't worry, Dame Margaret. I won't hold her to it."
Damien was always sweet-tempered.

"You said you haven't got a lady," Cecily repeated.

"Mine too, mine too! Cecily can't be anybody's lady. She's
too mean!" Alison's fat little fingers undid her own hair ribbon.

"Well, it seems that I do now," said Damien, looking be-
mused. "Two little ladies, in fact. When you grow up, you'll
choose finer knights than me by far, but for now, I'm honored."
That was one of the things that made Damien so winning. He
always took children seriously, at their word. Taking the two
hair ribbons, he twined them into an elaborate lover's knot, and
tied the ends about his sleeve.

"There," he said. "Now I can do battle with dragons—with
ogres—and even with the French." He smiled his wide smile,
which was just like sunshine. Robert looked disgusted. Gregory, who had watched the entire proceedings with a look of
austere disapproval, just shook his head as if to say, Women,
shameless as soon as they're out of the cradle.

"My lord husband," I said, "you've asked for nothing from
me."

"From a wife? France is no tourney; besides, this time I'm
packing pens."

"And a sword. But you will take my blessing, won't you?" He
looked amused at my presumption. After all, who'd studied
theology?

"Of course," he answered. "Always."

I couldn't help it. As he knelt before me where I sat on the
window seat, I could feel the light surging up inside. As I put
my hands on him, I could feel it springing and seeking. It shone
through the bones of my hands, and flowed between us like a
thin sheet of flame. It trickled through all the places in both
our bodies, healing as it went—an old bruise, a muscle strain, a
little kitchen cut. It was like being in the presence of a living
thing. And when it was done, it spread to illuminate the room
—pale orangish pink, before it glimmered and vanished.

"Goodness, Margaret, you have such cool hands," said Gregory. He wriggled his shoulder. "Hmm. Odd. That bruise I took at the quintain feels much better. Did you see how the sun came from behind a cloud just now? Quite lit up the room."

Damien and Robert were totally silent. They had stopped what they were doing and stood stock-still.

"Why are you staring?" asked Alison. "It's just what mama does for bumped knees."

"My lady Margaret," said Damien, and his voice was shaky, "may I have your blessing too?" Robert followed silently behind him, and each knelt in turn. How could I refuse them what they needed, even if it revealed me?

But as they stood, awestruck, Gregory whispered in my ear: "Margaret, it's not kind to trick the gullible." I didn't answer. I suppose sometime husbands are the last of all people to recognize a wife's qualities. But you'd think, since he knew the whole story of my adventures with the light, he'd have recognized it when he saw it.

"What's going on here? You're slow! Too slow! The men are in the courtyard and the horses waiting! Enough of touching farewells!" Hugo had come up the stair unnoticed, and his shout broke into the strange silence of the room.

"Damien, that pack should have been loaded long ago!" he barked. Damien swung it onto his back. With Cecily and Alison holding my hands, we followed the men down the stair through the hall and into the courtyard.

The pink of dawn had faded, and the morning was fresh and fine. Birds sang in the orchard, where the blossoms had already given way to the new green fruit. Grooms held the great destriers, which the squires, mounted on their palfreys, would lead on the long trip to the coast. The armor was already loaded on the sumpter horses, and the last of the baggage was being strapped up. The men from the villages, with no armor but leather breastplates and helmets, stood, some holding pikes and others with longbows on their backs, while their women embraced them and wept.

Gregory had already informed me that as the only lady present, I must set an example. I stood, sick and forlorn in the arch of the door, clutching his big sword. He was the last of the family to mount. As his horse was led to him at the foot of the stair, he mounted solemnly, and I handed up the sword to him with an impassive face, as the villagers turned to watch the little drama. With the gentry, staging is everything. I've seen players at work, and I know. Then the gates were thrown open, and Sir Hubert, dressed in his finest, gave the signal to go. They were a brave-looking lot, even for a little manor, with pennons flying and gold-embroidered surcoats glistening with the de Vilers coat of arms. And no family was better mounted. Sir Hubert had stripped his stables for the venture—and his stables, even then, were notable.

As the last of the party passed through the gate, I could feel a terrible lumpy thing moving inside me. It got bigger, and pushed into my heart, which pounded violently, and then to my throat, where it nearly choked me. They were well down the long avenue of trees when the thing seized my whole body. It was panic. Raw panic.

"Wait, wait!" I screamed after them. The women in the courtyard stared at me.

"Don't go!" I cried, and I began to run like a madwoman after them. People drew aside to let me run through the court-yard and frantically past the still-open gates. The departing men proceeded as they had begun, at a dignified walk, the unmounted soldiers marching behind the mounted party. My breath was tearing through me, my chest was bursting as I ran —ran past the marchers, who turned to stare, the grooms, the packhorses, the squires with the destriers dancing beside them on their halters, to where the family rode, staring impassively ahead. Gregory rode just behind his father and brother. As I drew even with him and grabbed his stirrup, I was panting so desperately that I couldn't speak. He pulled out of the line of march as I dragged at his stirrup, looking down at me reprovingly the while.

111

"Margaret, what is it? You're making a fool of me," he hissed, reining in his tall black palfrey by the side of the road.

I still clutched at his stirrup, which was all that kept me from falling, as I managed to say in between gasps, "Wait—oh, wait."

"For God's sake, for what?" he said, looking down into my panicked, tear-stained face.

"Say it, in God's name—say it. Don't go without saying it."

"Say what?" He looked utterly puzzled now.

"Say 'I love you.' You have to say 'I love you' before you go."

"Oh, Margaret, you idiot," he said, and his face looked all tender. "You know that's true already." He leaned down and gently detached my hands from his stirrup, and kissed my up-turned face as you would a baby's.

"Now don't you make any more fuss, and do act like a lady," he admonished, turning his horse, which was dancing with impatience. "God bless you, Margaret," I could hear him say as he spurred his palfrey to canter back to the vanishing column.

"Oh, Jesu," I whispered to myself. "We didn't—" My knees grew so weak, I had to sit down, right there in the dust by the side of the road. "I'm lost."

Now let me write down this true thing: there is something that changes about a manor when none but old men and boys are left. It is the women. Women who sit silent speak out, women who are weak plant and sow and reap; women who are simpletons make hard judgments, and women who faint at the sight of blood defend great houses with arrows and boiling oil. It is as if a spell is lifted: when the men return, the spell does, too, and we all become stupid and weak again. It is a mystery, how it happens. And, of course, the men don't think it does, for they were gone during the transformation. Though how did they suppose their world was there for their return if we were as incapable as they believe?

So it was at Brokesford, where the first sign of change was in the village brewster's house. Without husbands to forbid women's gathering, drinking, and gossiping, the benches were full of chattering women who ended a hard day's labor as any man would. And then, with the lords gone, poaching increased, for the women were as fierce hunters as any men. The steward turned a blind eye to peasant vermin hunting in this season, for it protected the harvest and the chicken coops in the absence of more genteel sport.

Often as not, I'd find the bakehouse, the malthouse, or the dairy abandoned and have to go myself to retrieve their wayward occupants. There they'd be, surrounded by a crowd of other screaming peasant women, clubbing coneys as the little creatures fled the muzzled ferret let loose within their burrow. As they came to the surface, they'd be entangled in the nets spread over the entrances, and thence it was but a brief time before they were converted into stew and mittens. But I can't bear coney hunting. The only time a coney utters a sound is in mortal terror, as it sees the club descend. It's a thin, high scream that tears through the mind. It would take me all my strength to penetrate the eerie wailing to order the manor folk back to their duties.

And, of course, since I was the lady of the place, at least for the time being, I found myself constantly accosted by petitioners, mostly appeals for reversals of judgments of the steward's court, or, increasingly, women with familiar-looking little blond children in their arms, asking for alms. I suppose they thought I'd be more compassionate than the old lord, who always said, "If I support one, they'll all be at my door; and who's to say they're mine, anyway? These women who can't keep their skirts down—pah! They'll all claim anything for a handout."

But I've never yet been able to turn away a child in need, and even though the old lord had left me without a penny of ready money, I found meals and gleanings and old garments and lengths of coarse wool from somewhere so that they did not leave as naked and hungry as they came. But the steward complained that I gave away too much, and each time we clashed it was fiercer, so that I dreaded each confrontation more than the last. And, of course, it was embarrassing explaining to the girls, who were curious. But I suppose it's my fault for telling them that the way you get babies is by being married. I thought at the time it was a better story than saying that God sent them from heaven in a basket on a rope, but I hadn't anticipated the difficulties.

"Mama, why do those women with babies come here to ask for bread?" asked Cecily, who was always observant. "Why don't they just bake it in their own houses, or buy some from the bakers?"

"Umm. Well, they don't have houses or money, Cecily."

"Did their houses burn down?"

"Not quite. You see, they—ah—aren't married."

"Oh. But where did the babies come from? Did God make a mistake when He lowered the basket?"

"Where did you hear about the basket, Cecily?"

"Oh, from Mother Sarah. She told me all about it. The basket is gold, and God takes it back afterward—otherwise the world would be much too full of gold baskets. I think those women should shout up at God when they see the basket coming, 'You made a mistake, God. I haven't stood at the church door. Send the basket back after I'm married.'"

"Well, that's a good idea, Cecily." I sighed.

"Cecily's a dummy," said Alison. "God never makes mistakes. Those women are all married, and the papas died. Now they haven't got any house anymore, or any money, just like us."

"You shut up, Alison," said Cecily, and gave her sister a ferocious cuff. "I told you not to tell mama that." As Alison howled I could see Cecily's anxious face seeking out the worry in my own. "That won't ever happen to us, will it, mama?" she asked.

"No, sweetheart, never. You'll always be looked after. Your papa left you a dowry for marrying." If I can keep hold of it, I thought silently. Cecily was silent, working it over in her mind.

"Mama," she said suddenly, "aren't knights supposed to protect widows and orphans?" I hesitated a moment, thinking of the widows and orphans being made abroad.

"Why, yes, they are, Cecily," I answered.

"Stepgrandfather is a knight. Why doesn't he give them anything?" Oh, deeper and deeper. I sighed again.

"People forget, sometimes, what they've intended."

A woman's voice broke in from behind us: "You do put things in the kindest way, don't you?" It was Cis, the brazen, with a basket of wet laundry on her head, on her way to hang it out.

"Cis, you forget yourself before children," I remonstrated.

"Sorry, mistress. But I'm an orphan, and look how they took care of me," she said, smoothing her old gown over her stomach with the hand that wasn't balancing the laundry basket.

"Cis, not you too?"

"And what do you think comes from all that tumbling? If they were here instead of you, I'd be out in a ditch like a dog—and they'd have another laundress." She didn't sound bitter, just matter-of-fact.

"Cis, I'll help."

"With what? A loaf of bread? An old raggedy blanket? I tell you, lady, that good as you are, no one can live on that. But I got faith. God means better for me, and I'm going to take that better when it comes."

But I hadn't even time to shush her when the welcome distraction of a gaggle of shrieking women and children was upon us. Mother Sarah, old Malkyn, Peg the dairymaid, and a half-dozen others.

"Mistress, come quick! The steward's got a thief in the dairy!"

"And where were you when he got in? At the brewster's?" I hurried off to investigate with the whole crowd of them, even Cis and her basket, on my heels. I gritted my teeth for battle when I saw the scrawny-looking fellow the steward had by the ear. Both hands were bound behind his back, and he was pleading for mercy. A scrubby mongrel, completely overlooked, was finishing the remains of a new green cheese, lying on the ground entangled in the cheesecloth in which it had so recently been hanging.

"I tell you, we chop the hands off thieves here." The steward showed his yellow teeth in a malicious grimace. "If you're so innocent, why didn't you ask for hospitality at the gate?"

"I found no one here—"

"And you'd heard the lord was gone, and the mistress is soft in the head—"

"You stop that now!" I shouted, trying to sound as fierce as the old lord, which isn't easy. "How dare you speak against me in my presence!"

"Will you hang him here, or let him go without his hand, my lady?" the steward snarled. "Or do you intend to fill the place with thieves as well as beggars?"

"I tell you, there is not a word of this Sir Hubert will not hear when he returns. You insult me, and you bring shame on his house by denying justice. I tell you, I'll see you beaten in the courtyard like a dog if you make one move against me. I want to hear this man." The steward let go of his ear.

"Speak up the truth, you knave, or I swear I'll have your tongue," the steward hissed at him.

"It was all a misunderstanding. I can pay you back," said the man. His face could have used considerable fattening, but I liked his gray eyes, and he spoke well.

"How do you propose to pay, since if you had a penny, you'd have been at the brewster's, dining better than this—" I pointed to the remains of the dog's dinner.

"She wouldn't take what I had in trade," he said. You could practically see through his threadbare russet gown. His moth-eaten hose reached to the ankles, and his feet, like so many others in this season, were shoeless. He chattered on, desperate to make his point. " 'A bush is fine enough for me,' is what she said to me, 'I don't need any fancy picture.' But for you, I could do something splendid. A nice coat of arms in the hall, per-haps? I tell you, I've done for the best. Why, the only reason

I'm crossing this godforsaken shire is that I've a big commission waiting for me at the cathedral at York." A painter! What a piece of luck!

"Are your paints in that bundle there? Malkyn—" I nodded in the direction of the bundle, and the old woman opened it up. There were jars, little boxes, a big board splashed with all sorts of colors, and brushes of every size and description.

"That much at least is true, my lady." The steward looked furious at having his prey snatched from him. "Though I much misdoubt they'd be wanting a beggarly fellow like this at a great cathedral like York. And don't imagine you won't pay for this when I tell Sir Hubert on his return," he grumbled sourly as the fellow, now loosed, hastily gathered up his paints. Have I told you the steward is some sort of cousin to the family? The kind of cousin with no inheritance. It gives him airs and makes him nasty. It also made him difficult to get around.

"Our chapel is newly whitewashed, and looks very bare," I told him, and the painter was quick to overhear and interrupt.

"Why, I could paint a holy Madonna, Our Lady of Mercy, with your own beautiful face on it, most gracious lady."

Goodness, the stranger seemed to recover in a flash. There's something charming about a fast-working mind.

"I had in mind a Last Judgment, to go over the altar." I turned to address the painter. The steward stood silent, his long face still sour as year-old vinegar.

"A Last Judgment?" The painter sounded calculating. "There's a lot of figures in a Last Judgment. A lovely Madonna is much better for a chapel—it's a question of artistic harmony, you know." The steward turned his hard little eyes on the painter.

"A Last Judgment's what's best—after all, you took the cheese first. Besides, you should consider the alternatives," I pointed out.

"Not a nice Holy Family?"

"*She* wouldn't like a Holy Family, and she told me herself

that she'd like a Last Judgment, just like there was in her grandfather's castle in Brittany."

"*She* wants it?" said the steward, and all of a sudden he seemed shaken. He blessed himself. "She told you?"

"Oh, yes—and just think of the opportunity. If you hadn't been so swift about catching this fellow, she'd be bothering us all summer. I do believe you've saved this house from her wailing for a good long time. This ought to please her no end." Long ago, I wished with all my heart to be as clever as Mother Hilde in dealing with people. Well, I'm getting better all the time, though I'm nowhere near her yet.

"Well, if it's for *her* . . ."

The painter looked puzzled—he inspected first one and then the other of our faces during this exchange.

"*She? Who's 'She'?*"

"Oh, that's our Weeping Lady. She considers the chapel hers, though she does get about on occasion. Last year she dried up the milk, and the summer before, she put a rust on the rye."

"A Weeping Lady? You expect me to paint an entire Last Judgment in a chapel with a ghost in it?"

"Shh! Don't call her that," cautioned Mother Sarah, looking shocked.

"Yes, don't ever call her that," I told him. "She considers ghosts common, you see, and will be terribly offended. She calls herself a manifestation. She can get very nasty if she hears you call her a ghost. You should be very careful when you're working there."

"Working there? Working there?" He seemed aghast.

"Yes, working there," I said, folding my arms. He looked about. Everyone else had folded their arms, too, even the steward. It seemed entirely fair. "Besides, you'll have a bed in the hall and a place at the board until you've done. And you can keep your dog too."

It worked out very well. I don't suppose a Last Judgment has ever been more quickly painted, though it did take several weeks even so, and I don't think he did the faces all that well. But just think how he probably dragged out his jobs for more luxurious patrons—so it all worked out to be even, I think. And he provided entertainment for everyone as they stopped by to check on his progress. The girls especially liked to sit and bother him as he stood on the ladder, his dog lying at the foot of it while he painted devils and saints.

"How do you know devils are green?" Cecily would ask.

"God sends me the vision in my mind that they're green," he'd answer calmly, brushing color on a forked tail.

"I think they're red," said Cecily.

"Then go paint your own," he'd say, without ever turning his head. But from him she got the idea of using charcoal to draw devils and fanciful creatures on the flat stones of the hearth. And he seemed to know when I had it in mind to scold her for getting dirty, because he came up behind me where I was inspecting the eccentric figures and said: "They're really not bad for a child. She's got an eye. Too bad she's not a boy."

But whenever he saw me coming as he worked up there, he'd turn away and look all injured. So, of course, I had to ask him: "Now what's wrong? You eat, you drink, and all your limbs are still attached. You should be grateful to me—at least grateful enough to greet me properly."

"I make entertainment for the whole world here—I should at least get jongleur's wages," he sulked.

"You might as well know, the Sieur de Vilers did not leave a penny of money in my care. He's the tightest man in the shire, except for his horses—and he took most of them with him." The summer foals were already racing about their dams in the meadow. All beauties, and we hadn't lost a one. I'd seen to it myself. I knew it would set him in a good mood when he got home.

"Well, then, at least you should have warned me."

"Warned you? About what?"

"You drive a hard bargain, madame. You didn't tell me there were two."

"Two? Two what?"

"Two gh—manifestations."

"Oh, really?" I said. This was a shock. No one had ever seen Master Kendall but me—and his little girls, of course.

"Yes—there's a smoky fellow in a merchant's gown, forms up in a corner when *She's* gone—now, she's really not bad—quite gracious, actually. But *him*! He bothers me to death! 'Why do you paint halos like that? They don't look like platters at all. You should put points on them, like real light, not do them up like a set of dishes. Now, that vat of boiling oil—it looks just like a chamber pot. In Rome, I saw a much better Last Judgment, where the Blessed floated on clouds . . .' Chatter, chatter! As if I hadn't anything better to do! 'So why don't you just go back to Rome, now?' I says, and he gets all miffed and tells me ghosts can't cross the water, and he's going to make sure I never sleep again unless I apologize—"

"Master Kendall? You're back again? Why didn't you come to see me? I've missed you." I spoke into the air.

"So you know him then! You did deceive me. Imagine! Two of them! And they don't even get along. Who is he, anyway?"

"My husband. Or rather, my former husband. He has wonderful taste. You should take his advice. But how did you see him, anyway?"

"Me? I'm a painter. That's because I have very good eyes. I see *Her*, I see your Master Kendall, I see the odd light around you that no one else sees, and I see that you are always weeping even when your eyes are dry—as you are now, in fact. A lot of women do. Now, if you were really holy, your light would be all round and golden, like a platter, no matter what that meddlesome ghost—er, pardon—manifestation says, so I'm not sure what you are. But I've stayed to memorize your features. I was going to York, to paint for the canons of the cathedral, before I was so rudely interrupted, and I intend to make use of your face. Why else do you think I'd bother with all these figures, my lady of the hard bargains?"

"You see too much," I said, suddenly annoyed with him.

"A lot of people tell me that," he answered. "Oh—here he is again." Sure enough, it was Master Kendall's smoky form, wearing the New Year's gown in which he died.

"Master Kendall? Where have you been so long?"

"Oh, I went to Bedford to watch the money changers cheat people. I've learned some very pretty pieces of sleight of hand. I'll show you sometime. How's that ridiculous painting coming along?"

"Ridiculous, pah!" exclaimed the painter.

"But I've missed you."

"Missed me? I thought you were too busy for me—all that bustling about you've been doing. And really—delivering foals and bastards—that's not very ladylike. You should be more careful of your reputation here, with these rustics. . . ."

"I'm happy you still care so—but let me tell you about the girls—"

"Love! It's everywhere!" exclaimed the painter sarcastically as he put the finishing touches on God's beard.

But when he was done, everyone pronounced the painting the most splendid thing that had ever been seen in the district, and I was very ashamed that I didn't have any money to give him. It wasn't like that when I was married to Master Kendall, I'll tell you. He was never stingy with artists and intellectuals. But I had an idea.

"If you'll carry a letter for me to Father Bartholomew at the cathedral, for him to send with a captain to Normandy for me, he'll reward you on my behalf. He's my husband's father's second cousin, once removed, and he thinks well of my husband."

"Which husband, the ghost?" responded the painter wryly.

"No, my real husband, who is alive with the Duke's army in France," I said somewhat impatiently, for I'd been feeling rather cross and tired lately.

"Oh, I see," said the painter, and he looked at me and through me, with those curious gray eyes, as if, somehow, everything were explained.

So I sat down and wrote, with Father Simeon at my side, a

letter that I sealed with wax three times, even though I was careful not to put anything too embarrassing to be revealed in it.

To my most well beloved husband, the Sieur Gilbert de Vilers, knight, in France:
Most dear lord, I have missed you day and night. Your steward sends word that the harvest on your lands is good this year, but the rain has split the cherries. The girls are well and so are the cattle. Tell my lord your father that we have eight new foals at Brokesford Manor since you left. I live for the day of your return. When the wind cries, I hear your voice. When it rains, I weep sore for wanting you here. I kiss this dear paper, since it will take you my words.
I pray God and His angels keep you safe and bring you home to me.

Your loving wife, Margaret

Dear God, I love him, I thought. Just let him know that, at least, no matter what. I am too weary with waiting and wanting him to ask for anything more.

The painter watched the entire process with some curiosity, and then put the sealed letter in his bosom.

That evening, watching the moon rise, I realized why I had been so tired lately. I was pregnant. It must have been the very last night he was here, I thought, for the light hadn't begun to sink inside me yet, where I couldn't call it up. The next morning at dawn, they found Cis in the kitchen in a pool of vomit and blood. I knew right away what it was, for I have seen it before. She'd taken a remedy to rid herself of the child, and had very nearly ridded herself of her life as well. I had her cleaned up and carried to her straw bed in the crowded little servants' room behind the kitchen and there, before dozens of prying eyes, delivered a tiny baby no bigger than the palm of my hand. I baptized it Child-of-God with water from the cistern as it emerged, and held her hand as she lay sobbing into the long afternoon. God knows how little separates us, we women. A bit of money. Some words. A piece of paper. A man's life.

It was in mid-August, on the eve of the Feast of the Assumption of the Virgin, that a mounted messenger rode through the village, demanding admittance at the manor gate. He wore well-used leather and scale mail; his horse was foaming, and his face stained with the dust and sweat of the fast ride. Margaret herself saw him brought into the hall and offered drink. Between sips of ale, taken slowly to avoid cramps from the exertion, he told the assembled company that the old lord was returning home with a wound that was enfevered.

"The lance splinters remain embedded deep within it, madame, and he can neither walk nor ride. But he comes with his son, to see him married and the succession assured, before he gives up the ghost. He has done mighty deeds of chivalry; he will be remembered forever."

"But what news of Sir Gilbert, who is with the Duke's suite?" said Margaret anxiously. "When will he be coming home?"

"Sir Gilbert?" The man was silent a long time. Then he spoke again. "His son, Sir Hugo, is accompanying him. He's gone mad with fever, the old man has. You'll need to make everything ready for him here. Some say it's the loss of his other son that's done it. He's lost the will to live. Though why, I don't know. He still has the one, and that his heir, which is more than many have—"

Margaret couldn't help it; she began to scream. It was like the eerie, thin, high scream that a coney utters only at the moment of death. It echoed among the dark arches of the hall again and again, until they led her away upstairs.

CHAPTER
5

It was a melancholy procession that wound its way through the village and up to the gate of the manor. The ragged column of foot soldiers dissolved as it met the crowd of villagers that stood by the road, and the sounds of joyful reunion mingled with the howls of those who had just discovered their loss. Sir Hugo rode on ahead, impassive on his gray palfrey, Robert leading his destrier on his right hand. Behind them a horse litter bore the lord of Brokesford Manor, heavily swaddled in fur rugs against the bone-shaking chills that had overcome him. Beside the litter rode Damien, bearing his master's sword and shield and leading his saddled destrier, for all the world as if he might mount it once again.

Behind them a train of heavily laden sumpter horses guarded by mounted archers testified to the success of their expedition. Within the bundles lay tapestries and rugs, silver goblets and chests of gold coin, swords and mail, the spoils of the French lords and burgesses who had had the mischance of meeting up with them. The most fabulous piece, a great gold nef, had already been sold to the King for ready cash, along with the ransoms of three French squires and a knight banneret. The winds of politics had brought them home; they'd found a place on the ship bearing the turncoat Philip of Navarre to England to pledge homage to the English king as the rightful King of France; with any luck, the wind would bear a new lord of Brokesford back into France with an heir on the way. It was the old lord's dying dream.

When the horn sounded and the gate was thrown open, Margaret could be seen in the low arch of the hall doorway, at the head of the manor folk who waited to receive the returning party. Wan and thin, she had resumed her deep black gown and surcoat. She looked barely strong enough to stand upright as her gaze scanned the returning horsemen, hoping that it was all a mistake and she'd see Gregory's tall, familiar form somewhere there.

As the grooms ran forward to assist, Hugo gave curt orders to the horse soldiers, who dismounted to unhitch the horses from each end of the heavy litter.

"Don't jar him, now," he snapped as the soldiers hoisted the litter. The old lord's face was gray with pain. The only sound he uttered was an involuntary groan as the litter was borne up the steps and deposited across two benches in the hall.

"Is everything in readiness?" Sir Hugo asked the steward.

"Yes, my lord."

"He cannot be moved up the stairs. Have the great bed dismantled and reassembled here in the hall, behind a screen."

"Immediately, my lord." And six men were dispatched to bring the cumbersome object, piece by piece, through the narrow passage from the tower and down the steep corkscrew stairs, barely the width of a man, into the hall.

"So, father, you shall soon be comfortable again," Sir Hugo addressed the still figure on the litter. The poisoned wound had shriveled the old man's body to the bone. His teeth, now prominent in the skull-like face, parted, and his shriveled lips stirred in a hint of a ghastly smile.

"Thus did the ancient lords of Brokesford dwell, in the hall, amid their people. It was a good custom. I am home again."

"Yes, father, home. And a hero."

The horrible lips parted, and the old man's voice was barely audible. "The box, Hugo. Don't forget to give Dame Margaret the box."

"No, father, I won't"

"And Hugo, I will die happy if you fulfill the arrangements I have made with Sir Walter. Bring home his daughter as your noble bride, to get this house fair sons again."

"Yes, father, I will fulfill my duty and your wishes." Was the father deceived, or had the humble tone that Sir Hugo habitually used with his sire faded, if just a little, to be replaced by a note of triumph? The old man was so weak, he found it hard to tell. Still, Hugo had attended to everything with great care. The sea voyage, the dreadful trip home. But the wound, which had seemed so small at the beginning, was draining his life away. At first slowly, and now swiftly.

Then, as he watched the dark arches of the hall swaying and shivering, high above the litter, he thought he heard something through the dreadful clattering and banging of the great bed being put together. It was a clear voice, thin and strong, that said: "I am here."

"Thirsty—" his lips said, almost without sound.

"Yes," she said, and he could feel wine, all cool from the cellar, make its way across his tongue. She laid his head back on the pillow, and he could feel the heavy fur coverlets being turned back.

"Get away, you, the surgeon's been summoned from Bedford, and one of the Duke's personal physicians is coming from London."

"It will take the physician many days to get here, and I trust Mother Hilde's wisdom better than any surgeon on earth. Step back, I say, and let me see it." There was something authoritative in the voice, and he could feel the shifting and grumbling men move and give way and the voice move closer to him again. He began to shake again with the chill as the covers were pulled away, for he was clad in nothing but the heavy bandage around his side.

"Filthy," the voice said, and he screamed as the bandage was pulled away.

"Malkyn, the pot in the kitchen, and the fresh cloths."

"What are you doing—are you so vengeful that you want to kill him like this? I tell you, I'll run you through if you harm him."

"A hot poultice," said the woman's voice. "It draws the poison." The heat and the pain mingled with the sound of hammers. For a coffin? So soon, a coffin? How long could he bear it, this pressure, and this pain, like a knight?

"See?" he heard her say, and he screamed again as the poultice was stripped away, and something dreadful burst inside, draining and stinking, and giving unspeakable relief.

"By God, there's pints of it in there. How much can a man hold, and live?"

She spoke again. "That, I do not know. Look—here's something black poking out."

"Splinters. Splinters from the lance tip. I saw it from afar. He took the blow badly on his shield. Unlike him—so unlike him. The lance shattered here, at the edge of the breastplate—and the splinters went through the links of the mail beneath. He was unhorsed—Damien and Robert captured the French knight—but who would have thought all this could come from so small a wound?"

"Small, but deep—aha! I have it out."

"Four inches, at least. There's another."

"I have it," she said. And the infinite blackness sucked him down.

"Jesu!" The cry was terrible.

"Dead. You've killed him," said Hugo to Margaret as the grooms clustered around them.

"No, he's fainted, and he'll live," said Margaret, looking at

Hugo with a curiously detached, cold, calm expression as she rebandaged the wound. "You can put him in the bed now," she announced. And Broad Wat lifted the shrunken figure as carefully as he would a baby and laid him beneath the great canopy.

"How do you know he'll live?" asked Hugo in a suspicious voice, his eyes narrow as he shifted them back and forth to take in the whole scene.

"I can feel it. Also, that's one of the things I can see. The black shadow around him is thinning."

Hugo stepped back and looked her up and down. The black gown gave her a pallor like a corpse. Her hollow, red-rimmed eyes looked at him as if he were an insect. He thought for a moment of hitting her, but backed up a step and crossed himself instead. She could see death. A witch. A witch between himself and the lordship. And arrogant as the Devil himself. She would sing a different song once he'd collected Gilbert's property—his property now—and brought home his beautiful young bride. There wasn't room for something like this in the house—not with a tender young girl, and his own sons. First he'd sequester her, then have her burned—no, that would mar his sons with scandal. He'd have her strangled secretly—that was neater and quieter.

And if the old man insisted on living now, why, he could just fade away later, the way God had intended him to do. After all, it was God's will, the way he took that lance. In all the years he'd watched him, he'd never done anything like that. Of course, he'd had no sleep for days. He'd ridden all over the place like a madman, when the word came about Gilbert, searching and searching, as if that would do any good. No, it was all God's work. God intended to pay Hugo back for his years and years of dutifulness to his grasping, dictatorial sire. It was entirely fair. God meant him at last to be rich, as befitted a man of his honor and lineage.

Then there were her brats, of course. It would be four or five years before he could sell their marriages. Yes, it was a good plan not to taint them by burning the mother, even if she was a witch. But wait—what good were a few hundred pounds compared to taking their whole inheritance? Ah, better and better—Hugo, you clever fellow, your brain is really working now. Get rid of her, and shut them up in a convent as soon as possible. How soon? After the wedding might be best. Might as well get it all settled quickly, while the old man was unconscious. Brilliant. And all part of God's plan. Thou shalt not suffer a witch to live.

He looked at the old man on the bed. He could hear his heavy breathing. Too bad, he thought. Do you know how I've hated you all these years? All the while I was bowing and scraping and laughing at your stupid jokes, I was hating you. You were too damned cheap with me—kept me on short rations—took all the best women for yourself first—kept me rotting here in the country, instead of letting me winter in London, where the fun is. Everything for the horses, nothing for Hugo. I've waited a long time for this. Now I've got a town house, Gilbert got it for me from that little witch. It was wrong for a commoner, a merchant, to own anything that good anyway. Well, it's in the right hands now.

He looked away from the gray, shrunken form on the bed, and saw that Margaret was waiting for him. He was all politeness. There were many witnesses, and he was never less than a model of *courtoisie*.

"Robert, get the box." Robert removed himself and went to search in the baggage.

"Dame Margaret, I must inform you that your husband died a hero. He saved the Duke's encampment, and possibly his life as well. It was at the siege of Verneuil; we burned the suburbs and divided into three parties, surrounding the town, to begin the assault on the walls the following morning. That night there was a counterattack through the walls by stealth, on the Duke's own party. They strangled the sentries so silently that no one was roused. But they had not counted on Gilbert—he was up alone at night, writing with a little candle in a hooded lanthorn to conceal the light. The first thing that anyone heard was the de Vilers war cry, and as the camp roused, they saw him half clad, swinging his great two-handed sword in pursuit of the fleeing rogues. The Duke's men pursued, and after the melee six corpses were found—all French—but not his. The following day we breached the city wall and slew every living thing in it. One tower held out another day, but fell at last. But Sir Gilbert was gone. His last words, they say, were 'For God and King Edward!' A noble death. Robert, what was it that Piers said he heard him cry out that night? I ask you to confirm that they were most admirable words."

Robert seemed to hesitate; a debate was going on within him. Piers had been lost in the taking of the tower on the third day, but not before he had told Robert everything. It posed a bit of a problem. Should things be as they had been, or as they ought to have been?

"So?" prompted Sir Hugo.

"Well, um—actually, um—what I heard—or I thought I heard—I may not have remembered it all entirely—but—"

"Yes?"

"What he cried out was said to have sounded very like 'You bastards, my manuscript!' "

And that is how Margaret knew, all of a sudden, that it wasn't a mistake after all. He was really gone. She'd been hoping they'd made a mistake. And she'd been really sure they'd mixed him up with someone else—surer and surer as Sir Hugo told his story. But Robert—no, that was Gregory to the life, or rather, to the death. She put her hand over her heart to still its terrible pounding.

Hugo broke in quickly to cover this lapse of Robert's. "The Duke has commended Gilbert's courage and service, and says he will not forget. He sends you this remembrance of him. You'll understand, he's kept the notes of the campaign that Gilbert was writing. We've brought back his armor and personal effects."

Robert had retrieved the little box, and silently handed it to Hugo. Hugo in turn proffered it to Margaret. Margaret was terrified to open it. For all she knew, it might be the dried and shriveled remains of a human heart, the great severed arteries gaping like toads' mouths. Gregory's heart, a loveless, unloving object of horror. The end of everything.

She opened the box a little and peeked in very carefully. So far, nothing horrible. Then a glimpse of white—paper. She opened it farther.

"It was the paper he was writing that night," explained Robert, sensible of the drama of the moment.

Margaret unfolded it. It was a poem, or rather, the beginning of one. It was written in French.

"Margaret of the white hands," it went, "you are queen of my heart—" And then there was a blot. A great big oblong blot, where the pen had been laid down in haste. And she suddenly saw everything, how it all must have been on that night, for there was hardly anything in the world that would make Gregory leave a blot, except Death himself.

He did love me, he really did, she thought as she began to sway. He couldn't say it, so he was writing it. And my letter—it didn't get there in time, and he never knew how I— As her knees crumpled Robert bore her up, while Hugo called for someone to attend her.

That night, when Margaret knelt in the chapel with her customary prayers for Master Kendall's soul, she added to them prayers for Gilbert de Vilers's as well. She was heavy from within from unspeakable grief, and dizzy from a nameless fear of a dreadful future. So few months for such terrible changes. So far from friends and home. So alone. And her girls—who would protect them now? And Gregory, her love, her great love, lost and gone, and his bones rotting in a foreign place. And she'd never been able to tell him what he'd come to mean to her. Regret twisted her heart.

"Oh, God help me," she said to herself. The formless sobbing that perpetually echoed among the stones of the chapel ceased.

"Well, now you have something to weep about, too," whispered the spiteful voice of the Weeping Lady.

The next morning Sir Hugo dispatched Robert, all bathed and shining in new clothes, with two attendants in livery to Poultney Manor in Leicestershire, where Sir Walter de Broc had deposited his three unmarried daughters and youngest son for the summer. There they were to inspect the eldest, and best dowered, and if they found her suitable in visage and figure, to announce that Sir Hugo de Vilers was coming to arrange the terms of his marriage with her as soon as her father should return. They were to inform the family that should the financial arrangements prove satisfactory, Sir Hugo wished to proceed immediately with the betrothal and wedding, in accordance with his dying father's wishes and his prior negotiations with Sir Walter last spring in Calais.

"Only fifteen and as pure as a lily, Robert, just think of it." Hugo was acting love-smitten; he'd tucked a flower behind his ear, and was ordering up new hangings for the wedding bed.

"And beautiful, they say, too," agreed Robert, who was always anxious to see what was new and female.

"Yes, and with a hundred acres settled on her, and bloodlines that can be traced for three centuries on both sides. Make no mistake about it, Robert: It's a high marriage—one that might have escaped me, if not for our recent good fortune."

Robert nodded agreeably. He thought Hugo meant the capture of the French knight, whose ransom he had sold to the King for an immense sum. He and Damien could settle down on it, even with the third they'd had to give to Hugo. The poor bastard had been hauled off in a cart with a half-dozen others in the same fix, stripped of his armor and stiff with the disgrace of it all. The King, of course, would resell the ransom to the man's family at a steep markup. It was how he managed to live so well. War, after all, is just business carried on by other means.

"And just think, Margaret," said Master Kendall's ghost that evening, after the children were asleep. "Here I am, between heaven and earth for a bit of piracy and a few adventures between the sheets—long before I knew you, of course—and these fellows practice on a much larger scale than I ever dreamed of, and get blessed by the bishop for it into the bargain!" He was sitting on the edge of the bed, all smoky in a shaft of moonlight, while Margaret sobbed into her pillow.

"Quit being so gloomy, Margaret, and sit up. I want to show you the trick the money changers use—it'll make you laugh."

"How can you be so cheery when Gregory's dead? You're not nice at all," came a muffled voice from the pillow.

"Dead? Who says he's dead? Do sit up and let me show you the trick—I have to get you to do it, because I can't lift anything—even a pebble, these days."

"What do you mean, not dead?" and one eye turned up from the pillow to inspect the smoky form.

"Not dead is what I mean. He may be gone, but he's not dead. I see everybody who comes through here, you know, on their way up or down, and he's not among them. You were so concerned, I made inquiries—met a number of the fellows he went over with—all butchered quite awfully, trailing limbs, heads, that sort of thing. They haven't seen him. Wherever he is, Margaret, he's not dead. So now, sit up and try my game to please me."

Margaret could feel the heaviness begin to lighten.

"You swear?" she said, sitting up.

"On my love for you," said Master Kendall, and he looked so like his jaunty old self that Margaret had to smile.

"Now," he said, "take that little bit of plaster, there on the floor, and pretend that it's a false gold piece, and the little pebble there is real money. Slip the first up your sleeve—no, no, not that way, this way—yes, that's it." And as Margaret tried the trick out, she began to smile. How like Roger Kendall, who, live or dead, had the gift of being able to make people smile. I'll never stop loving you, she thought as Master Kendall pronounced her fit to go into the money-changing trade, if she ever needed to.

"Pity you can't get to London," he said. "You could make inquiries of the returning knights and find out where he is."

"But even if I knew, how would I raise a ransom? I haven't a penny anymore."

"Ha! And you won't ever get it from Sir Hugo," announced Roger Kendall. "He stands to inherit, the greedy dog, so he'd rather have things as they are. No, Margaret, you get to London, and I'll show you where I have a bit laid by."

"Laid by? It's all with the Lombards, or spent on those nasty horses."

"Oh no it's not. What kind of merchant would I be if I trusted the world? Our house, the central part at any rate, is quite old. Built by a fellow called Aaron fil Isaac well over a hundred years ago, before the Jews were driven out of England. There's an escape tunnel to the river no one knows about. And panels! Oh my, yes. A number of secret ones, and hidden hollow stones beneath the hearth, and all sorts of things like that. I've got gold and silver cached in them all. I died before I could tell you about them, though I always meant to. Get to London, and I'll show you where it all is. After all, it won't do me a spot of good anymore. And why should it be Hugo's? He doesn't deserve a penny."

"That's true. Just think, when Gregory told me what he thought of Hugo, long ago, I didn't even understand him. Now I understand entirely too much."

"Now I'll just whisk off—I want to see if anything's doing at Bedford. I never sleep anymore. Just imagine, bored in the day and all night as well! Now, you sleep properly so you can get your mind to working. You can get that ridiculous young man back, if you want him."

"Want him, oh, God, want him!" Margaret leapt up for joy to embrace Master Kendall, temporarily forgetting his incorporeal state, and wound up freezing her face and arms.

"Oh, Margaret," he said, looking at her tenderly as she shuddered and wiped off the spectral dampness, "you have no idea how much I regret not being warm anymore."

Certain kinds of things I can't write down. One kind is the things that are too horrible to talk about, and the other is things I don't remember. Now, when I lost Gregory, it was too horrible to talk about, and also I can't remember much, either, because my mind was gone and I had dreams, waking and sleeping—dreadful dreams. I think I dreamed that Sir Hugo rode forth as a groom on a white steed, wearing new clothes and a hat with a peacock feather, after kneeling before his dying father for his blessing. He took with him hounds, attendants and gifts, and a snow-white mare with a gilt sidesaddle on which to bring back his bride. I dreamed that a great feast was prepared for her reception, not as great as if the house had not been in mourning, but great enough. As the pigs and sheep were brought in from the country and, with terrible screaming, made to give their lives for sausage and meat pies, I dreamed that I tended the shrunken shell of the old man that Hugo had left behind, and that he screamed as I changed the dressings. There was a time that I'd hated him, but it had passed by.

"God," he whispered. "I scream like a woman. It's the pain. It's worn me down, and I die like this, instead of on the battlefield. Like a dog. In bed."

"Lie still, and drink this," I'd say, and he'd answer, "Horrible stuff. Tastes like the devils in hell brewed it," in gasps, between sips.

Then, one time he looked at me with his eyes, his once terrible blue eyes, now all sunken in and rimmed with black, as if he were staring out of a cave.

"Save me," he whispered.

"I'm doing my best. I've come with another poultice," I said.

"No," he answered. "Save me. Save me with the light in your hands, as you did Urgan." Sweet Jesu, he'd seen. He'd known all along, and said nothing.

"The bone. You mended the bone and lifted the destrier.

Mend me, mend me like that," he whispered desperately, so that no one else in the hall could hear.

"The power's not with me now," I answered.

"You mean that you hate me," he said with resignation. "It is fair. I did too much. I ask too much," and he turned his face to the wall.

"No, no," I said, pitying him so much that I could no longer hold back my secret. "The power can't be used. I can't call it up. It's gone within, as it always does with me, to aid the child."

He turned his face back and looked at me a long time.

"It's true then. He did sleep with you after all. I thought he had, but he'd never say."

"I love him, and I have his child."

"Loved him, you mean."

"No. Love. He's not dead. I know it. He will come home to his child, and to me."

"You are a fool; I misjudged you. Misjudged badly. I never took you for a lady, when I first saw you there in that rich man's house. But now I see that you love nobly. Hopelessly, and without recourse. It proves your blood."

I tell you, there are times even a pitiful half-dead man can make a woman furious. But it's not nice to shout at sick people. So I said, "I swear it to you; he lives."

"You've gone mad," he answered, "but I wish to heaven it were true. Madness is more merciful than what I must suffer. If only God would take my life, instead of letting me know what I know." And he moaned as I changed the poultice. "He's gone; he's dead. Are you too crazy to believe the truth?"

"You didn't look hard enough. He's alive."

"Look? I didn't look? You fool woman! What do you know? I tell you, I searched for days and nights. I went out with the heralds by torchlight, and turned over every corpse as they took down the coats of arms for the death-roll. Every face, every dark head, looking for his. I went through the smoking ruins of that city searching—searching and calling."

"He's captured then."

"We've never had a ransom message. No man of rank can disappear without a corpse or a ransom notice."

"He's wounded then, and hiding."

"Hiding? With the French? They'd as soon cut his throat, after what we did there. Make up your mind to it, woman. He's dead and that child you carry is an orphan, God help it."

"Never, I say."

"Mad, completely mad. As I wish I were. My God, my God, he was the good son, and I never knew it until it was too late." He clutched at my sleeve with his feeble hand. "Whatever you do," he whispered, "don't tell Hugo you're pregnant. If I die, get away—get away from here before the child is born. Hide it. Hugo has become a wolf. The thought of money has turned his head. I know. I see everything clearly now. Too clearly, now that it is too late for anything but bitter repentance."

"Bitter repentance, eh?" said Master Kendall's ghost at midnight. "That's cheap stuff. Pretty plentiful where I am now." His airy voice drifted above the bed in the dark room. He chuckled softly. "In a way, I'm grateful God let me live long enough to mend my life. I met you, Margaret, and I've never repented of anything that came since—except that I had so little time at your side. Ah, me, so I do repent, after all. I repent for my greed at wanting you forever. But you need a live man, Margaret. You can't make a life with only a cold ghost. Let us lay plans for your search."

"Oh, Master Kendall, I've always been so grateful for your intelligence." The filmy thing acted pleased—even in the darkness I could sense the movement.

"I may be dead," he answered happily, "but I'm not stupid."

But in the days that followed, while we awaited the bridal pair, old Sir Hubert did not die of his bitter regrets, but got better in spite of himself. His color turned from gray to a kind of pale ivory, and sometimes when the fever was up, you could see two hectic spots of red on his cheeks. When the horn sounded from the gate, he demanded to be propped up on pillows to greet the new bride, to the great joy of his steward and Broad Wat, as well as all the other folk of the manor. There was never a more beautiful pair, as they knelt before him for his blessing: Sir Hugo, radiant in strength and youth, beside his graceful, honey-haired young bride, the lady Petronilla.

I looked her over closely when we were introduced. Not a day of sorrow had ever marred her face. Her hair was bound up in thick coils under an exquisite translucent silk veil, held in place by a circlet of gold. She had blue-gray eyes with pale lashes; her nose was straight, with a bit of a turned up tip. Her features were even, and she had a hint of brown in her silky complexion, for she loved the hunt and all out-of-door sports. Her riding was legendary, as was her prowess with the short bow and arrow. Gossip had it that she could sing and play the psaltery. I do admire the sound of the psaltery. Perhaps we'd get along. After all, it was a lonely business, being the sole lady. Two can do a lot more than one.

Her hands were covered with rings, sometimes two on a finger, and she fluttered them when she talked, so that the stones would catch the light. Her kirtle was of deep blue silk, bound at the edge with gold, and her surcoat a rich crimson, embroidered with flowers and curious beasts in gold and silver thread. She knew how to walk with mincing steps in that special way that showed off her trailing train and the tiny slippers that peeped from beneath her hem.

I had seen her lean to Hugo and heard her whisper, "Who is that?" as she looked across the room at me, where I stood with Cecily and Alison in the crowd of well-wishers and retainers. Somehow her glance told me that I was too old, too plain, and too thin with grief.

"May I introduce you, dear one, to Dame Margaret, my brother's widow," said Hugo, leading her forward by a single finger held high. The silk in her gown rustled as she moved gracefully toward me. She wore a lot of jewels. She had a great gold cross, set with rubies, and a gold chain, and yet another chain of worked gold set with pearls. I don't care to wear jewels, myself. They're cold and hard and get in the way—even if they do look elegant. I wear just two rings. The narrow, plain band of gold engraved with the de Vilers arms that was my wedding ring from Gregory, and Master Kendall's wide one, which is worked in flowers and leaves, and has *Omnia vincit amor* engraved on the inside. They're both from somewhere else. Gregory's was from his mother, and when his father produced it at the wedding, Gregory shouted at him for robbing his mother's corpse, and it delayed the proceedings considerably. Master Kendall's was made up for some mistress, I suspect, but either he thought better of it or she threw him over— because there it was, all fancy and ready made when he proposed to me unexpectedly. I've shifted it to the other hand, but I'd never take it off. And then there's my cross, of course. It's very old and comes from beyond the sea, and has very strange properties.

She looked me up and down.

"Dear sister," she said. "What a lovely cross. May I touch it?" I was going to say no, for the Burning Cross has a peculiar property. Master John of Leicestershire who gave it to me years ago, said if I could wear it I could have it, because it burned all those who did not walk closely with God. Of course, I didn't believe him; I thought it was a graceful way of offering me payment for saving his daughter's life, when I told him I'd take no money for it. But it's done some odd things since then that make me suspect that maybe John might have been right. But as the word formed on my lips I saw the look in my new sister-in-law's lovely eyes. It was greed. She expected me to say, "Beloved sister, it's yours."

"Of course you may touch it," I said. "It's an old relic, from the time of the Crusades." She reached out her beautiful hand to fondle it and her eyes said, "Don't wait so long, dear sister, to offer it to me as a wedding present. It's not gracious."

"Lovely—ah!" she cried. "My finger's burnt." She put her finger in her pouting, exquisite little mouth and sucked on it. "There's something wrong with it."

"I am so terrible sorry, dear sister. It must have been an

insect. See? Little Alison touches it without harm." And I leaned over to demonstrate. As she looked down at Alison, a cold look flashed across her face.

"My dear lord, do introduce me to the rest of your guests and family." She smiled, and he led her away to meet the neighbors and their wives, their two hands held high, joined only by his index finger crossing hers, in that elegant gesture of the French court.

"A lady, a real lady," I heard the servants murmur behind me.

"How elegant, how courteous, how beautiful!" I could hear the guests whisper as the beautiful couple circled the room. As soon as I was unnoticed, I ran upstairs to weep. The solar was full of guest beds, as was every room in the house. The chapel, all shining in its new paint, was hung with flowers, and Father Simeon was already arguing in there with the little Franciscan that Lady Petronilla had brought with her as her confessor. So I was reduced to hiding under the tower stairs with the rats, and weeping there until there wasn't a tear left in my body.

That night, lying in bed alone in the dark, I was waked up by a terrible pain in my belly. Was it a dream or not a dream? I opened my eyes to find a dreadful serpent peering at me with horrible red eyes.

"Get off!" I said.

"Off?" it said, with that dreadful smile serpents have, and its forked tongue flicked in and out. "You mean out, don't you?" I looked down the length of its shining green and red scales, to where its coils lay. No wonder it hurt so—it had gnawed a great hole in my belly, and coil after coil of it oozed endlessly out of the deep wound.

"God save me!" I cried—or didn't cry, for no one in the room waked up.

"God? You want God? He's very far from wherever *I* am," hissed the odious monster, and writhed so that the pain nearly tore me apart.

"Who, or what, are you?"

"I am Envy, dear sister, and I have eaten out your guts. When I am finished with them, I will eat out your heart, and you'll die." I screamed, screamed soundlessly again and again. How had I given myself over to this evil monster? I knew. It was when the chests upon chests were carried in, until the servants marveled. It was when the beautiful greyhounds she'd brought were admired by everyone, even the old lord. And when her chaplain had sprinkled holy water on the great new marriage bed her father had sent, and her old nursemaid had exclaimed, "My little rose! My precious beauty! So soon we are a woman, a great lady, a mistress in our own house!"

Yes, that's when I'd let the thing in. And dream or no dream, it was eating me alive. How could I get rid of the awful thing? I leaned over the side of the bed and vomited into the chamber pot, and the bitter taste of it reminded me I was awake. I stood up in the dark, and felt on the perch for the great, soft *robe de chambre* that the old lord had given me, and wrapped it around my naked body. A bit of moonlight came from behind a cloud. My girls—who would protect them from Hugo's greed if Envy ate up my heart? Who would save the baby? Who would find Gregory? I tiptoed to my sleeping girls, to hear their breath in the dark—half drowned as the faint sound was by the snores of Mother Sarah, who slept in the straw bed on the floor beside them. Silently, I crossed to the tower door, and pushed it open ever so slowly, so it wouldn't squeak. I'd go to the chapel, and beg God to take away the terrible serpent—I must before I died here in this dreadful house. The cold air in the tower passage took away all the sleep that remained in me as I felt along the wall.

The chapel, too, was dark, but moonlight came faintly through the windows and made the new whitewash glisten darkly. The Last Judgment, with "all those figures," was a dark shadow above the altar. Through the narrow, arched windows, you could glimpse the cold stars trembling high on the dome of the sky. The world seemed so empty and cold.

I stood on tiptoe at the high stone windowsill and looked out at the dark, silent world. "God, God," I whispered out into the silence. "Where are You now? You've abandoned me here alone, and I'm lost." I suppose I expected God to answer. Sometimes He does, you know. But you never know when. It has to do with logic—His logic, which is too deep for me to follow. Half the time when He speaks, I don't understand a word of it anyway. But this night, nobody answered. The shadows of the trees below rustled in the night breeze, and I remained utterly alone.

"You want to run away, don't you?" Oh, just what I needed. To be bothered by the Weeping Lady in the midst of a spiritual crisis. I tell you, there's no privacy anywhere.

"I know you want to run away. I can tell by the way you stare out of windows and count over the things in your chests. I used to do that too. 'I'm going home to my mother,' I'd say, and he'd say, 'I'll beat you so badly you'll never step over that threshold again.' You have no idea how I've enjoyed watching him scream and suffer down there in the hall. If you run away, he'll die and go to hell, which would please me greatly—except that his little image, Hugo the knightly, will take his place, and I don't want him to have the pleasure."

It's very tiresome to hear someone so narrow-minded when one is pondering great issues, like why God is silent, and also trying to get rid of a large personal problem.

"You're planning to leave with that smoky old merchant. I've been listening. Well, I want to go too. It won't be interesting when *he's* in hell and Hugo is lording it over everyone, so I'd like to be gone, as well. London might suit me. It's interesting there. I'm going to look into cradles, as all the other Weeping Ladies do."

This was the last thing I needed.

"You don't want me, do you? Pretty snippy, for a daughter-in-law. Oh, don't be shocked. You thought I was stupid like all those other Weeping Ladies. You ought to know he gets his brains from *me*—not from that shriveled old mummy on the bed downstairs. I knew perfectly well that he grew up. Of course, boys are like kittens. Very cute when little, ugly when they grow up. It took me a while to recognize him—not much of the kitten left. But you couldn't mistake the nose. Very elegant. A long, Norman nose just like mine and father's. And all mixed up in his mind, and ungrateful for good things—just like a *man*—you're welcome to him. I had him when he was pretty. Besides, he needs someone with sense to look after him. He hasn't got much, not that I didn't try. No, you need me to go with you. Especially if you decide to go hunting for him."

"This is not what I need—not tonight. Can't you see I'm suffering? Bother me tomorrow, won't you?"

"Tomorrow? Tomorrow's too late. No. Tomorrow morning I want you to take the little badger skin shoes, the ones with the holes in them, and put them in a sack about your neck. They're his, you know. I made them myself. A child shod in badger skin shoes will always grow up to be a great horseman. Now, once you've got them, I can follow you anywhere, just as that pushy merchant followed your Psalter right here to my lovely chapel."

"But—but—"

"Don't you 'but' me. Don't you know you shouldn't annoy ghosts? I might do something nasty. But instead, I'll do something nice, to convince you I mean business. You know that big snake you've got? Oh, don't look surprised. I saw it. I had one, too, when my sister married a great lord of Brabant. Oh, he was learned, pious, and good. His wealth came in stacks, and my sister dressed in silk and never had to lift her hand. Then I found out he was hunchbacked, and made friends with her again. After all, family is family—you can't do without. I heard none of her children had normal bones. 'Too bad,' I wrote her, 'but at least they've normal brains, which is more than I can say for mine.' So—suppose I take away the snake. Then will you take me?"

"If you can, I will." The thing had begun to stir again, and the pain alone would kill me if I didn't rid myself of it soon.

"You follow me and listen," said the Weeping Lady. I felt my way in the dark after the soft swishing noise she made, to the door of the room next to the chapel. The great room of the Sieur de Vilers, now inhabited by Sir Hugo and his bride. Through the door I could hear muffled sounds.

"Put your ear to it—after all, you can't go through it, as I can. Don't worry, I'll keep watch—you won't be caught," said the Weeping Lady.

This is what I heard.

"Wake up, wake up—I want it again."

"Mmm. No. You've hurt me," a pouting voice responded. "I won't be able to go hunting for a month."

"You should be proud: when they display the sheets tomorrow everyone will praise you."

"Proud of what? Giving up everything for this shabby little house? You swore we'd live in London."

"And so we shall—"

"Ow! Ow! You get off! I tell you, I'm not one of your peasant wenches." There was the sound of flesh hitting flesh.

"You little bitch—that's what you get for clawing me. Try that again and I'll break your nose. Then you won't be so popular in town."

"You touch me again and I'll go home to father. You deceived him. Your manor's a hovel, and your father is nowhere as near death as you let on."

"Talk like that and I'll break every bone in your body. You aren't going anywhere—but—here."

There was the sound of screaming muffled under a pillow. At last came panting, and a thin gasp. "My father will have you murdered for this."

"Not for taking my marital rights, he won't—he'll just want to hear the details." There was a nasty chuckle, followed by a half sob.

"You'll talk differently when he finds out you won't be Lord of Brokesford before Christmas, as you promised, and you haven't yet got full claim to your brother's property," came a voice full of injury.

"Tell him that, and you ruin yourself as well as me. Neither you nor your dear papa want to be a laughing stock, do you? It's too late to be unmarried, so make up your mind to be a dutiful wife and bear my sons, and you'll be living in luxury in London yet."

"Then get rid of that whey-faced widow. I can't stand her. Lock her up somewhere—the cellar, a convent—just so I don't ever see her again. Or those nasty brats. Promise me that, and do it right away, and I'll know you mean what you say."

"Those nasty brats are worth good cash. But it's my business when and where I get rid of them."

"Promise me soon, and I'll be sweet, dear lord." I could hear the whining, wheedling tones of a conniving infant.

"That's more like what I want to hear from you."

"Tomorrow?" The tone suddenly became sharp and commanding.

"You force me? I tell you, unless you understand that I make all decisions, I'll beat you until your father doesn't recognize you—"

"A happy couple, aren't they?" whispered the Weeping Lady rather maliciously. "How's your snake?" I felt my belly. It didn't hurt at all.

"Gone," I said.

"I thought so. And now you'll take me. You're very wise to escape. But you'll have to sneak away. They don't like you, but they don't want anyone else to have you, either. That would spoil their property claim. Yes, you must be either dead, locked up, or forced to enter a convent. I know all about that. I had a cousin once forced to take the veil. And the convent they put her in was no better than a prison. All her lovely hair shaved off. I myself would never have wanted my hair shaved off, annoying as it sometimes was. But then, it's all your fault anyway, for marrying a rich man and outliving him. How on earth did that dreadful old merchant pile up more than a knight? Trade's such a despicable way to make money."

"Instead of stealing it, like a gentleman?"

"Exactly," said the Weeping Lady.

∘ ∘ ∘

As the first pink of dawn shone through the high solar windows, I complied with the Weeping Lady's wishes, and folded up the little shoes tight and stuffed them into an oblong reliquary on a chain and hung them about my neck beneath my surcoat. But the cock had barely finished crowing when the girls came howling to find me, followed by Mother Sarah.

"Mama, mama, she *hit* Alison for no reason at all," cried Cecily.

"And, mistress, when I tried to stop her, she beat me with the riding whip she carries. Said I didn't know my place," and the formidable Mother Sarah sniffed up a tear.

"She is mistress now, and there's nothing I can do. Just stay out of her way, until I think of something," I said.

But later I heard Mother Sarah grumbling to Broad Wat, behind the screen in the hall, as Wat sponged off the old lord's face. "She's too young to be a mistress, that vicious little cat. May the Devil fly off with her."

"Make up your mind to it, Sarah. She is mistress," responded Broad Wat. "But"—and I could hear the old lord groan as Wat lifted his head to assist him to drink—"she's not master . . . nor is *he*."

"The children, Mother Sarah, where are they?" I broke in upon the little scene behind the screen. Wat was straightening the pillows and pulling up the covers to make the old lord more comfortable; he had followed him faithfully through every campaign, and now even into his campaign with Death. He'd never doubted me once he'd seen the changes I'd brought about, but had questioned me closely to learn all that I knew that would assist his master. Now we looked at each other and we understood each other without speaking. We'd both been in hard places, and knew what must be done. Mother Sarah was watching him, wringing her hands. I could see now that one of the cuts had brought blood where it touched the unclad skin of her hand. She'd saved her face with her arms. She was still so distraught, I didn't have it in me to be hard.

146

"Mother Sarah, the girls?"

"Oh, mistress, right there in the corner, playing with dolls."

"I don't see them."

"Oh, my good mistress, they're gone!" And so we hunted high and low, but without success until the forenoon. As the trestle tables were being laid out for dinner, I found them upstairs, strangely well washed on the hands and face. The front of Alison's dress was sopping wet.

"What on earth are you doing? Where have you been?"

"Washing," said Cecily. "Alison's dress was all sticky, so we washed it."

"Yes—icky, icky, sticky. All washed now," chanted Alison.

"And just what *made* it that way?" But I had only just asked when three blasts from the horn at the gate announced a visitor —a visitor of high degree.

"Oh, mama, let's see!" cried Cecily, rather as if to distract me, as I recalled later. And since I no longer needed to rush to the hall door to greet visitors, we all hastened to the window seats above the main entrance to peek out.

It was an astonishing procession that crossed the courtyard. Foreigners—wealthy pilgrims, I imagine, on the way from one of the northern ports to Canterbury, which is where all the foreign pilgrims want to go. There were twenty outriders, all in the same scale mail and black and silver surcoats, embroidered with a device no one recognized. The first two carried black pennons, with three swans worked on them in silver. In the midst of the riders was a beautiful wagon, such as a queen might ride in, pulled by four black horses, two of them ridden by boys in the same black livery. The wheels, the body, and the broad hoops that held the stretched hide cover, now partially rolled back to admit the golden autumn sun, were all elaborately carved and brightly painted with flowers and vines. Beside the wagon rode a Dominican on a little bay cob, his hood thrown back to reveal his aquiline features and tonsured skull.

But in the wagon, that was the amazing sight. Four women were seated on a pair of high benches behind the driver and grooms. Two of them were very elegant, in a foreign sort of way, dressed in strangely cut gowns of gray and black, all trimmed with something that seemed to shine in the distance, and only a bit dusty from the trip. Their high headdresses bobbed as they gossiped with one another, not paying the slightest attention to their surroundings. But on the foremost seat, that was the strangest sight of all. The first woman, from her simple clothes, was a nursemaid, who held on her lap a little black-haired child, possibly two years old, with a fat face, all swathed in a black and silver embroidered garment such as I have never yet seen on a child. But the other woman, she was enough to make your mouth fall open with astonishment. She was dressed all in black, from her head to her toes. Black, with the swans all worked in silver on her bosom, and a black foreign headdress from which a black silk veil enveloped her head and shoulders, and floated behind her too. Even seen from the upper window, the color of her face was unusual. White, white as milk against all that blackness. And beautiful. Perfect and all frozen still, like the face of an ancient statue. She sat as straight as a swordblade on that bench, looking neither left nor right. A queen. She must be a foreign queen, and those her ladies.

We didn't want to miss a thing, so we hurried downstairs to see her enter and be greeted by the new mistress. Lady Petronilla bowed low before her as she offered the hospitality of the house.

"Welcome to the hospitality of Brokesford Manor, great lady. We are honored by your presence. My husband and lord, Sir Hugo de Vilers, is out hunting, but will be back very soon to greet you in the manner deserved by your high degree." Lady Petronilla's French was not her strong point. It was harshly accented and mixed with many English words, for she had not been raised at court or tutored abroad or in a convent.

"Sir Hugo de Vilers? Your husband?" the lady said blandly, without changing her expression in the least.

"Yes, we were wed this week past."

"Just this week past? My, such a little time," and I sensed the strangeness in her even tone.

She wrinkled up her nose as she stepped from the bright sun into the shadowy hall. She rolled her great brown eyes when she saw the hams and sides of venison hanging from the rafters in the smoke from the fire in the center of the Great Hall.

"English," I could hear her say softly to herself in French, in a soft, rolling accent I couldn't quite place. I was nearly behind her, crowded out and unnoticed in the little ceremony. "Savages all," she whispered as she smiled at her hostess, showing her lovely even little white teeth, like a baby's set in pink gums. Lady Petronilla simpered at her, suddenly looking coarse and luridly colored beside the dark stranger. The dark lady took a step—and the fabulously jeweled and worked silver and gold necklaces and bracelets she wore tinkled like little bells.

"My father-in-law is convalescing from a wound and could not stand to greet you, but I will present you to him now," said Lady Petronilla, and took the dark lady behind the screen, where I could not see what was going on. When the two ladies emerged, the stranger was offered the seat of honor, which she took.

"I will await Sir Hugo here," she said in her strange accent, with perfect calm and self-possession. The nurse sat on a nearby bench, while the fat baby sucked contentedly on a sugar-tit. Every so often the nurse would grab the ragged end of the sugar-tit to keep him from swallowing it entirely. He was an unusual-looking child—vast and peaceful, with rolls of fat around his wrists and his little bare ankles. He had thick, raven black hair like his mother, and milky white skin and great brown eyes, bigger than a calf's, it seemed to me. When he crowed, you could see lovely light pink gums, and a set of four tiny, pearly little teeth. He was as indulged as the prince of Perse, and looked benignly at the world as his nurse chucked his fat chins and jiggled him about, constantly murmuring a stream of endearments to him in a foreign tongue. He even had on a tiny necklace and locket and little tinkling bracelets of his own, and it pleased him to wave them and hear the sound.

"Mama, we want a baby like that," whispered Cecily. "All fat and beautiful." The dark lady overheard her whisper, and turned and nodded graciously to Cecily, never losing for a moment her erect and queenly posture.

The sound of the hounds, the clatter of hooves, and the jingle of harness announced Sir Hugo's return, even before a huge buck, legs tied to a pole and head dangling, was brought into the hall for display. Hugo came bounding up the steps and through the door at the head of his companions, only to stop dead at the sight of the dark lady seated at the center of the hall. He staggered slightly, and turned white as a fair linen napkin, before his wife addressed him and he recovered himself.

"My lord husband, a noble visitor is come within our gates; the lady Giuseppina, Marquesa di Montesarchio, who is mistress of wide estates in far places," she said in French, with her nose all pinched. Without a sign of agitation, Sir Hugo offered her the hospitality of the house once again, and enquired her business.

"I travel to fulfill a most sacred vow of pilgrimage made by my late uncle on behalf of my father in his last illness. I have already prostrated myself before the holy martyr on his behalf, and for the soul of my lord and husband so recently deceased. But as for the rest of my business, that, you know full well," responded the lady very formally, in her sweet-sounding, rolling, accented French. She looked as if she were an empress, there in the Sieur de Vilers's great chair, and Sir Hugo a petitioning peasant.

"But I have come too late, it seems, to remind you of your betrothal vows." There was shock and agitation in the hall. Lady Petronilla's eyes opened wide in shock, and she put her hand to her face. After all, betrothal is as serious as marriage—it takes an act of the Church to undo, even if it's only a few words spoken in private, as a prelude to a conquest. Two betrothals, and one not undone? Lady Petronilla's marriage might well be judged a bigamous union—invalid. Sir Hugo was stock-still, but his eyes searched the assembled faces rapidly, and caught the look on his bride's face.

"Lady," said Sir Hugo coolly, "great as you are, you appear to have made a mistake. I do not know you. I have never had the pleasure of intimate acquaintance with any foreign Marquesa."

"Then you deny that this child is your son?"

"Absolutely—why, look at how dark he is. He certainly isn't one of ours. Why, for all I know, he isn't even a boy, with those big eyes, all swaddled up like that. I cannot imagine your reason for so disturbing my bride, most exalted lady, but that child is certainly none of my getting."

The lady's eyes narrowed, almost imperceptibly, but the iron control of her beautiful white face never slipped.

From behind the screen there was groaning, as the old lord heard the exchange of words and asked to see what was going on. Four men moved the huge carved wooden screen, and pulled back the bed curtains to reveal the skeletal figure of the old lord, dressed only in the napkin wrapped around his head and heaped with fur coverlets.

"Ask them to strip the child and bring it here," whispered the old lord to Broad Wat, who repeated it aloud. The dark lady raised a finger, and the nurse removed several layers of embroidered garments. The baby acted pleased to have them gone, and waved his fat arms and legs, crowing with joy. You could see he was most certainly a boy. And he had an odd dark birthmark just below the navel.

"A fine boy, madame," whispered the old lord as the child was displayed to him. "One that could be nourished with honor in any knight's house." The words were repeated to the dark lady, who nodded in acknowledgment. "Ask Hugo," he whispered in English to Broad Wat, "if he still denies all, having seen the birthmark." The old man was so weak, his lips barely moved.

"Why, father," replied Hugo in that language, so the dark

lady would not understand, "how could you? Of course I do! When would I have ever stooped to betrothal to get any woman I wanted into my bed? I've never seen this woman. And as for the birthmark, there's lots of those in the world. A woman eats some tainted meat, or too many dried mushrooms, or gets a fright while carrying the child, and there it is. She ate too much —that's why it's got the mark, and is so fat. And besides, women have no seed, so the child takes the father's image— and look at that child. Its father was a dark man, as you can plainly see." He spoke rapidly, nervously—as much to his bride as to his father.

The dark lady, never rising from her seat, inspected the little scene from a distance. Then, as if she had made up her mind about something, she spoke suddenly, in a clear, strong voice. All heads turned her way.

"Are you prepared to swear, Sir Hugo de Vilers, that this child is none of yours, and that you were never betrothed to me?"

"Why—why, yes," said Hugo, looking around the room like a trapped hare.

"Good," she said. "You have settled everything. Fra Antonio, bring the box and the paper." She stood up and bowed before a little gold reliquary with a peaked roof, all richly decorated, that the Dominican had produced. Then she kissed it and took it from his hands, extending it toward Hugo.

"Put your hand on this, and swear what you have said before these people."

Sir Hugo's knees trembled slightly, and his voice shook as he placed his hand on the little box, and Fra Antonio, seated at the unset table dormant, took down his words on the paper.

"I, Sir Hugo de Vilers," he said in a voice higher than usual, "have never sworn betrothal with this strange lady, the lady Giuseppina who is Marquesa di Montesarchio, and I deny that I am the father of the child that she brings with her and calls her son."

"Good," the lady said. "Have him sign and seal it with his

ring, Fra Antonio. Witnesses?" And two of her men, still in armor, stepped forward to make their marks beneath Fra Antonio's neat signature. Everyone in the room was as still as death.

"The box, good lady," asked the lady Petronilla. "Just what was in it?"

"A splinter of the True Cross, Madame de Vilers," said the dark lady, as she signaled her men to prepare to leave. Lady Petronilla smirked, then begged to be allowed to kiss the box.

"Of course, dear lady," said the marquesa. "Sir Hugo," she announced to the stricken-looking knight. "You have freed me. I go now to unite my lands and life with a greater lord than you will ever be. Remember, in the future, that fate does not always scorn a woman without fortune." She turned to address the company.

"We will not stay the night here. We go to the hospitality of the Austins at Wymondley and then home. I will never again set foot on this miserable, barbaric island." Her men and priest assembled, she walked to the door, her jewels tinkling, followed by the nurse and the baby. Then she turned suddenly, and stretched out a hand. I was beginning to understand that the dark lady was a mistress of the dramatic gesture, so I knew what was coming. So did everybody else.

"And you, Sir Hugo de Vilers," she said, pointing her finger at him, "take my curse with you to the grave: May your marriage bed be forever filled with abominations." And she departed, as folk clustered at the door to see the rattling wagon disappear on the dusty road.

As for me, as I watched the folk all standing and staring, I knew suddenly what I had to do. As quietly as could be I slipped away from the commotion, leading my girls by the hand upstairs, where I grabbed our cloaks and put a few things in the bosom of my gown. Then, swiftly and silently, we made our way down the rickety wooden stairs from the back of the tower and through the unattended sally port, to hurry across the meadow to meet the dark lady on her way to the Augustinians at Wymondley.

If we had not known the short way to meet her at a bend in the road by Sir John's woods, we would have had to tramp all day to the monastery. Of course, even with the short walk, Cecily got a stone in her shoe, and Alison whined to be carried, though she is much too large. Then she fell to exaggerated limping, in imitation of her sister, and groaning—although I have seen her run all day in play, and never sit down once. Luckily it was not long before we had cut ahead of the road, and scrambled down a steep incline just in time to meet the dark lady's slow-moving outriders and wagon. They halted, and I ran up to the wagon and begged her: "For the love of our Blessed Mother, good lady, take us with you as far as London."

"I saw you in the same sty with that God-accursed family. Why should I do anything for you?"

"For your revenge, lady," I gasped, my mind working quickly for a reason. "If I escape from them, almost all their fortune, which comes to them through me, will vanish like snow before the sun."

"And who are you, that you were there with them?"

"I am Margaret de Vilers, the widow of Sir Hugo's younger brother."

"Ah—" said the lady, and smiled her lovely smile, showing all her pretty, white little teeth. "Then get in with me, all you three. You can't go alone, with all the brigands there are about in this wild place." So her ladies assisted us to climb into the back of the wagon, where we settled down miserably amidst the baggage. The whole thing jolted and joggled so that I knew I'd be a mass of bruises by evening. It just goes to show that splendor can be very tiresome; it's better to walk than ride in misery. But I was so tired, I was soon overtaken by a fit of weeping. Thinking to distract me, Cecily began to chatter. She is in many ways older than her years, and sometimes sounds so quaint, particularly when she's speaking French, that it always amuses me.

"Mama, what's an abom—abomination?" she asked.

"Silly, that's what the priest does, if you've been bad," answered Alison.

"No, that's absolution, dummy," answered Cecily.

"An abomination," I answered, drying my eyes, "that's something disgusting, like—like devils, or something smelly."

"Do toads count?" asked Cecily.

"Yes; toads are ugly, and witches make poison from them. Though I suppose hanged men's fingerbones are worse." I was beginning to cheer up.

"Oh," said Cecily, disappointed. "Too bad we couldn't get the fingerbones."

"Yes, they wouldn't have been all icky, icky, sticky," said Alison.

"What do you mean?" I asked her, suddenly suspicious.

"Well, they made my skirt *all* icky, carrying those toads for Cecily."

"Mama, are we really going home to London? To our real house?" Cecily interrupted quickly, to change the subject.

"Of course we are," I answered.

"But it's not the same; papa's dead and those bad men will find us."

"I'll think of something, I swear I will."

As we had been speaking in French, the dark lady had been listening but pretending not to. Now she turned her head to look into the back of the wagon and addressed Cecily: "So, little redheaded savage, what did you do with the toads?" Cecily was silent and looked embarrassed.

"We put them in Lady Petronilla's bed," chirped Alison, "because she's a mean lady. We don't like her, Cecily and I."

"You, you Cecilia," said the dark lady, looking at Cecily from under half-closed lids, a lazy, amused little smile parting her lips. "How many?"

"Oh, lots and lots—it took two trips. There's heaps of them down in the mud by the moat. She'll get warts, which is just what she deserves."

"I told you, Fra Antonio, my curses always work," said the

dark lady to the Dominican, who was riding directly beside where she sat in the wagon. She spoke to him briefly in her own language. The Dominican chuckled. So did her ladies, who had been silent during this interchange. Then she turned back to Cecily.

"Little savage, I like you, so I will give you a gift." The girls perked up.

"Sweets?" asked Alison hopefully.

"No, your lives. I intended to have your throats cut secretly before we reached the monastery at Wymondley, so we could throw out the bodies before we left this forest. Or maybe poison—no, too slow." She looked speculatively up at the masses of gold and russet leaves that towered above us on each side of the rutted, narrow road. "Yes, better to cut your throats. So many bandits here . . ."

"Not much of a present with no sweets," grumbled Alison. Then the dark lady turned to look at me and smiled that lovely, innocent baby's smile at me.

"You were foolish to tell me you carry the only de Vilers heir," she said.

"But I didn't—" I said, stifling my growing horror.

"You think, perhaps, I am stupid?" she inquired, lifting her chin. "You bring the money; the brother dies, the older brother inherits. If you die, you can't go and remarry someone who'll try to claim the money. If you live, he puts you in a convent. But if you're pregnant with an heir, he'd be better off killing you both, otherwise he loses the money. So you run off. It's simple. I know a lot about inheritance. That's why I'm a marquesa today. That, and aconite."

Good Lord. Foreigners do things differently than we do.

"You're shocked? Don't think I did all the poisoning myself. No—they poisoned each other, except for one or two—then it fell in my lap." She raised upturned palms above her lap and gazed upward, as if about to receive a gift from heaven. Her heavy jeweled silver earrings swayed and glittered.

"Why," she said, looking at me again, where even the shadow

of the wagon's hide cover did not conceal my wide and horrified eyes, "even my poor little husband didn't last more than a year—just long enough to give my precious here his name. So young he was, only seventeen, and so impetuous and incautious." She looked briefly sentimental, then smiled and wrinkled up her powdered nose as she gazed into the distance. "Sometimes when the storms come at home, it's best to leave the country for a time. A holy pilgrimage—so pious, so blameless—then, when we come home, the sun is shining again. Politics—men's politics. Like a little black cloud, don't you think? Only the most foolish of young men stay around to pick quarrels."

She paused and looked back at me again with new interest, as if she'd seen a gnat on my nose. "By the way, take my advice and be sure to use a taster at meals. It's not only elegant, but practical. If you can't afford one, or go and lose too many, cats will always do. Just feed them under the table. Everyone will just think you're eccentric. I always keep a lot of cats. That's why I've done so well." She nodded cheerfully, and her jewelry tinkled. I must say, when people like that get talkative, it makes me nervous. The baby crowed, and the nurse produced a rattle and began to hum a wordless song to him. Her ladies joined in, singing words I could not understand. I could hear a buck crashing through the underbrush; the men's heads turned, and I could see the look of watchfulness turn to regret as they realized what it was.

"Is he really Hugo's?" I asked, just to be tactful.

"Oh, that, of course. Mama's lovely baby. Too bad he didn't acknowledge him—he'll never have another. I'll see to that. I know just the proper *strega* to see when I get home to have the spell cast. I always take complete vengeance. It leaves so much less mess. Why I don't kill Hugo, I don't know. I suppose I could send someone to do it, if I chose. Ah well, if he lives, he'll suffer more. Was the younger brother like Sir Hugo? If so, you're lucky to be rid of him."

"He wasn't at all like him. Not in the least. He was dark and scholarly, and couldn't stand Sir Hugo. He said—said Hugo was immoral, and, and—oh, he was everything that is good and kind, and—" I began to weep dreadfully, thinking of how I loved Gregory. She turned and translated for her ladies, who appeared most interested, shedding a tear or two by way of sympathy.

"Ah, I see you loved him. That was foolish of you. A woman should never marry the man she loves, or love the man she marries. It clouds the mind. I loved only once, but it was a sickness that passes. Imagine, me—a new widow, grieving over my first husband's tomb. And such a nice statue I had ordered, too. It was very tragic. And there *he* came, the foreign adventurer, and rolled his ardent blue eyes heavenward, pledging eternal love and service before God. I looked up from the tear-drenched stone—his profile, gazing upward, was the picture of manly devotion. Love, stupid and stupefying love, smote me down right there, like an enemy's sword." The dark lady looked most dramatic. She clenched her fist and beat it on her breast in imitation of a sword striking home, to accompany this speech. "Now I have suffered much and traveled far for my love, and it is a great relief to be rid of it. It was growing to be a ridiculous burden. Now I will join my lands in a powerful alliance and keep cats." Then she peered at me suddenly and said, "But did he love you in return for all this foolish love of yours?"

"At first I thought he didn't, then I knew he did—he was writing this when he was—lost." And I took the paper out of my bosom. Why I was so honest, I don't know. But I couldn't think of any other way to be with a person who was so complicated and more than a little frightening. The ladies leaned forward to peer at the paper, jostling together as the wagon hit a particularly savage rut. Then they returned to gossiping among themselves.

"A poem—or part of one. How sweet. The queen of his heart. Must be he was in love too. Your hands aren't *that* white, you know. And you don't wear enough rings to make them really beautiful. You look as if you do a lot of work with them."

158

"I know. It's just the way he saw them."

"Besotted," she pronounced. Then she looked at me closely. What's she thinking? I wondered. I hope it's not something new and bad.

"But the bosom of your gown is rather lumpy. What else have you got in there?"

"My Psalter," I said, reaching it out from under my surcoat.

"Ah," she said. "So that's why I couldn't kill you." She fumbled around in a little coffer at her feet and pulled out a tiny box.

"Mother of savages, I have a present for you too. I meant it for Hugo. What possessed me not to give it to him, I do not know. A betrothal ring. But after he had damned his soul to hell by swearing falsely on the True Cross, I thought I'd done enough. Did you see how he writhed? As if in hell's fires already." Looking very satisfied, she opened the little box. Inside lay a fabulously worked gold and silver ring, set with jewels and made in the form of a snake swallowing its tail.

"Don't touch—it's poisoned. One of the greatest poisoners in Rome made it for me. You may need it to get rid of a husband someday. Or escape the world yourself. Just put it on. It works very quickly, and is painless, though it leaves a very ugly corpse. I myself keep something like it always about me. We can never tell when life will catch up with us. Have I ever told you about my grandmother's cousin? Burned alive with her daughters, and her male children flayed to death before her eyes. Where I come from, we exterminate enemies root and branch—then there's no one to come after you for vengeance. Oh yes, a ring like this, it can be no end useful."

I shuddered and took the box, thanking her as best I could. She wasn't the sort of hostess one wanted to offend. That evening at the monastery we were housed in luxury and ate at the right hand of the Abbot himself. But all the while, my heart was singing, "London, London and freedom."

159

"The bitch has fled!" cried Sir Hugo when the searchers reported to him in the hall. "So much the better. They'll be killed on the road, and that ends all claim to every penny. I should give a feast of celebration." Those of the household who had placed their bets on Hugo's ascendancy growled and cheered in agreement. But behind the screen, those who had tied their fortunes to the old lord's recovery clustered about him. Propped up on pillows, he smiled a faded version of his once wolfish smile.

"The child is safe, Wat," he whispered. "This begins to get interesting. I think I wish to recover. Bring me spiced wine—but feed a little to one of those pups, first. I don't like the looks of that nurse Dame Petronilla brought with her."

And so things stood for the next several days, until the horn at the gate blew for distinguished company, and Sir William Beaufoy, accompanied by a dozen armed men, was admitted with a message sealed with the Duke of Lancaster's own seal. It was court day in the hall, and the crowd of peasants cleared a path for the splendid company, who came straight to the dais where Sir Hugo was dispensing judgment in his father's place. With great formality, Sir William had the clerk that accompanied him step forward and read the letter to the assembled company. The news made Sir Hugo turn pale. It seemed that Sir Gilbert de Vilers, before leaving for Normandy, had made a will leaving everything to his widow, and left it in the safekeeping of the Duke's household in England. And now, in the firm tones of a lord to a very minor vassal, the Duke reminded Sir Hubert and his eldest son that he, the Duke, was the sworn protector of widows and orphans. At the pain of his great displeasure, they were to send the widow and her daughters to Kenilworth, where they would be housed in luxury until the Duke should arrange a suitable marriage for her with one of his own good knights.

"I can't," said Sir Hugo, turning pale. "She's fled." The

curse, he thought. It's the curse working. First the toads, then this. To the death, she said.

"Fled?" replied Sir William. "Then if I were you, I'd go in search of her and not return until I'd found her—and in good health too. The Duke's displeasure is not a thing I'd want to risk." And, satisfied with the flurry of orders Sir Hugo gave to organize the search party, Sir William concentrated his attention on consoling his old comrade-in-arms, Sir Hubert, on his deathbed.

"So," whispered Sir Hubert on the great bed behind the screen, "the big fish swallows the little fish." He had been seeing things more clearly since his mortal illness. The surface look of the world had faded, and the bare bones of events had become visible.

"Fish? What do you mean?" said Sir William, who was sitting on the edge of the bed beside his dying friend.

"Oh, nothing. The fish in my pond, back before we ate them at Lent," and the sardonic tone in the old man's voice was unmistakable. "Things become interesting now. I intend to get well. I want to see how it turns out."

But Sir William feared that all this talk of fish meant that Sir Hubert's mind had begun to wander, as it so often does before the end. Trying to console me by hiding it all. Gallant fellow. A pity, a terrible pity, Sir William thought. And as he offered up a choice morsel of court gossip to his old friend, he reminded himself that he must tell his wife to mend his black hose.

CHAPTER
6

Things always seem to happen on a long journey. At Wymondley, we were joined by a group of merchants with laden mules, who were so impressed by the Marquesa's armed guard that they put themselves under her protection for the journey to London. She did not, of course, lower herself to speak to them, since she had particular tastes in these matters. Instead, she used Fra Antonio as a sort of go-between. But the merchants offered Cecily and Alison a ride on top of their wool-packs, to vary the bruising ride in the wagon, and the girls did chatter. So it was not long before one of them, a tall, homely, honest-looking fellow, rode his big roan mule up beside the back of the wagon and addressed me in English, which the Marquesa did not understand.

"Is it true, as they say, that you're Roger Kendall's widow?"

"Did you know him?" I asked hopefully, for I still, to this day, love talking about him.

"No, but I wish I had. Who hasn't heard of him? A legend, even in our part of the country, far as it is from London. Yes—

I've heard a lot." He rode awhile in silence, and then he blushed. The dark lady feigned complete inattention, and waved a silver rattle at her baby, who was fussing on the nurse's lap. "Tell me," he went on, "what are you doing here—and where's the—um—handsome—ah—"

"You mean, the 'bold young squire, in guise of a friar'?" I asked. I'd heard the song for the first time at the monastery guesthouse, being sung outside our window by some rowdy carters who stayed up late drinking and annoying everyone.

"I really didn't mean to, um—"

"It wasn't at all true, you know," I said, "though it makes a better story that way."

"Oh, of course I knew right away it wasn't true, not true at all, but—"

"If you must know, he's in France, given up for dead. But I'd appreciate it if you didn't tell anyone you'd seen me—my girls talk too much."

"Oh, I see, I see. Well, if you ever need another husband, I've got a very fine establishment in Colchester. I have a house with fifty women who spin on the ground floor, and above it, very comfortable quarters for a family. My wife is dead these three years in childbirth, and I'd treat your daughters as my own—"

I was about to thank him when the dark lady broke in, in her heavily accented French.

"What is he talking about with you?" she asked. The wool merchant looked curiously at her—it was clear he didn't understand a word of French.

"Actually, I believe he's proposing marriage," I answered in that language. The dark lady's eyes glittered with amusement.

"Oh," she said, "you must have quite a bit more property attached to you than I'd thought."

I thanked the merchant, and we talked of this and that until we stopped to water the horses at a little brook. As the girls happily dabbled their feet in the water, and that fat baby crowed at the yellow leaves that floated from the tree, trying to catch one as it drifted before his face, another of the merchants —a short, plump, balding fellow—approached me.

"Madame," he said, "if you will pardon my boldness, I'll say that you are still a young and lovely woman. Life in Colchester is very dull. Now I'm a man that loves festivities and merriment, myself. And I can tell you'd love the dancing and mirth in a much larger, finer place, such as my own home in York. We have wonderful plays and pageants there, and a great cathedral second to none. I have a very fine house in the best part of town and a greatly respected social position. My wife was carried off by a fever only last Michaelmas"—and here he crossed himself in her remembrance—"and I'd treat those two charming little girls exactly as if they were my own—"

The lady Giuseppina looked up from a conversation with Fra Antonio. "What does that fellow want? Is he proposing marriage too?" she asked, somewhat tartly.

"Yes," I answered, and she smiled her lovely pink and white smile. By the time that we resumed our journey, Cecily and Alison had collected several handfuls of the last of the sturdy little daisies, called marguerites, that still grew in the grass. They occupied themselves in the back of the wagon by weaving a chaplet for the baby, who seemed enchanted by their presence and attention. But the idyllic moment was rudely disturbed by the sound of galloping hooves and unsheathed steel, as the dark lady's guard formed a ring about the wagon at the command of her captain. It was fortunate we were in the back, beneath the shady cover where the Marquesa and her ladies had retired to preserve their complexions.

The Marquesa moved forward and stood up behind her driver, shouting imperiously through the circle of guards to the heavily armed mounted men who had caught up with our party: "Who are you, and how dare you disturb my journey?"

"We are from Brokesford Manor, and seek a woman with two little girls who has fled. Have you seen her anywhere on the road?" I recognized the sour voice of Sir Hubert's steward.

"Of course not," said the dark lady.

"Hide," I whispered to the girls, and threw my cloak over us all as we crouched in the back of the wagon, trying very hard to resemble lumpy luggage.

"Who is it?" whispered Alison.

"Your wicked uncle Hugo, looking for us, so shush," I whispered back, and she was deathly silent.

"How do we know she isn't in the wagon with your ladies?" came the shout.

"My child is in this wagon, and your master has every reason to wish him ill. My men will defend me to the death. Move off." She sounded cold and imperious. I could hear a growling and the clatter of harness.

"It looks like there's nothing in there but foreign women and baggage anyway," a voice said. We could hear the clatter as they turned their horses to address the company of merchants. "Have any of you seen a woman on the road—about twenty-three, pretty, with two redheaded girls? She's wearing mourning—you couldn't mistake her. There's a reward if you spot her for us." Not a sound came from the wool merchants. In the silence, I could hear the horses champing on their bits, and the heavy breathing of the guard.

"Looks hopeless," I heard them say. "We'll try the other road." And they departed at a trot, with a jingle of harness. We crouched there a long time before Fra Antonio, riding beside the wagon, gave the all clear by whispering in French through the canvas.

"They are loyal, your merchant friends," said the dark lady when we emerged.

"They offered a reward," I said, somewhat horrified. "Hugo must have planned something very horrible."

"A reward, eh? Then you do have a great deal of property. That proves it. Better only a chance of marrying you and getting hold of it, think these men here, than a sure reward. But then, knowing Hugo, how sure is the reward, anyway? Perhaps he has a reputation," she speculated aloud.

"People in this country aren't that mercenary; these are good men. They knew of my former husband."

"Nonsense. But I am delighted to be causing that wretched Hugo so much trouble. It's my curse working. My curses always work." She looked pleased with herself. Then she glanced at me again, looking me over as if calculating something. "What's that bit of gold chain on your neck there? When I didn't see any rings, I thought you were poor. I don't like poor people much. But I missed the gold thing you're hiding under your surcoat. What is it under there? Pull it out and let me see."

As I've said, she wasn't the type of woman I wanted to offend. To oblige her, I pulled out my cross from its hiding place between my surcoat and kirtle. As I held it out, her eyes grew huge, and she drew back slightly and crossed herself.

"Holy Virgin, no wonder I couldn't tell them you were here. You wear *that*."

"You know it?" I asked.

"I saw it when I was a little girl, hanging in a shrine in a church in Milan. It disappeared during a sack of the city. They say when Lodrisio Visconti seized it, it seared him to the bone; the next day he was captured at the battle of Parabiago. I've heard of it several times since then. That accursed German mercenary captain Werner von Urslingen is said to have refused to touch it when it was cut off the steaming corpse of a peasant looter. 'I know that thing,' he said, 'I don't need talismans to tell me what I announce to the world.' Then he beat on his breastplate and shouted, 'I am von Urslingen, enemy of God and of compassion. Take it away—no, sell it to some sentimental Italian.' When Fra Moriale, despite his great army, was taken and executed, they say that it was found among his possessions. Now it seems to have made its way to England. How did you get it, and why doesn't it burn you?"

"It was given to me for a good deed."

"Oh—that explains everything. Did you know, it can't be bought or sold or stolen, for it destroys whoever gets it?"

"That's a bit exaggerated, I think, but it does raise a welt occasionally."

"Not on *me*," said Cecily, and put her hand on it.

"Cecily! You stop that!" I was so annoyed. Cecily needs to be trained out of interrupting adults.

"Cecily's a show-off," said Alison, putting her hand on it too.

The dark lady surveyed our three faces very carefully.

"I think I shall be glad to be rid of you three," she said thoughtfully. "London can't come soon enough."

But after several hours of deep silence, she became bored and started talking again. We had joined the great road south, which, unlike other roads, is paved in great stones left either by giants or by Romans, depending on your point of view. As we clattered over the rutted, weedy pavement, she looked back at me with renewed interest.

"Your problem is, you have not studied human nature," she announced. "Now I, I know everything, because I understand that humans all have fixed paths, just as the wandering stars have their epicycles. So if you have studied these paths, you know where everything will come out. For example, you. Your husband is dead, so his older brother inherits. He will lock you up so you can't marry, and put your daughters in a convent, where they can't inherit, so that he can collect everything. But you escape—that's dangerous. He's best off having you killed on the road and pretending it's brigands. However, I have now discovered you have too much money. That means your husband's lord will be interested. Since he has the right to give you in marriage, you will be a rich reward for some follower. So, my conclusion is this: Sir Hugo is searching for you under pain of grievous displeasure from a great lord. My curse is working better than ever, don't you think? Just imagine him, whining and pleading for more time. The great lord will probably have him killed. Hmm, I wonder. Strangled or poisoned? Or maybe he'll just put out his eyes and lock him up forever. Ah, what a splendid curse."

"I don't think so at all. That's not how it's done here. The

Duke is very honorable, my husband said so." I could feel this woman's cynical reasoning poisoning me to the bone. A few more days of this, and I'd never trust anyone again.

"Of course," she went on cheerfully, "this Duke of his may want you for himself—"

Suddenly, I thought of a horrible thing: the go-between who had arrived at Master Kendall's house long ago, with a gift from the Duke, which I'd sent back.

"—and then there's the possibility that he sent your husband to some dangerous place on purpose, just like King David when he coveted Bathsheba . . ." she chattered on.

My God! Could such a thing be possible? Now I had two powerful men to avoid. And of the two, Sir Hugo was my least problem, for the Duke had people everywhere. If they found me, I'd no rights of my own, being husbandless, and the very best that could happen was that I'd be married off by force. How could I hide? What could I do? I clung like a drowning woman to Gregory's praise of the Duke. If he said he was great and honorable, then wasn't he? But suppose Gregory were deceived? Had the dark lady twisted my mind, or was it all really true?

"—of course, it would be natural. You aren't what I call beautiful—you wear too few jewels, for one thing, and for another, you don't use rice powder on your face, so your cheeks look rather garishly pink. But you *are* pretty in a barbaric sort of way, and these English savages have no taste." She shook her head and muttered, "Damn that Sir Hugo to hell." Then she looked me in the face. We were approaching St. Alban's, and there, across the river Ver, I could make out the tower of the abbey, hidden among the trees. Not far, not far now, my heart sang.

But the dark lady had no eyes for the pretty sight; she was intent on explaining her philosophy: "Only one thing disturbs the epicycles. Remember that. That thing is love. It doesn't follow the rules. I made that mistake once, but never again. I followed my love to the ends of the earth. It wasn't logical. But *he* was logical, and so I'm saved. What would I have done with an English pig for a husband, anyway? Now I can resume my proper path. Don't come to visit me, little barbarian, for I may change my mind about you at any time."

I tell you, London couldn't come soon enough.

They left us at Ludgate, and she went off down Fleet Street toward the palaces on the Strand. For she was staying with great acquaintances until she heard whether her "little black trouble cloud" of foreign politics had blown away and it was safe to go home again. We passed through the gate, mingling with the crowds dispersing from Mass at St. Martin's church, which stands immediately within the gate.

Ahead of us loomed the massive bulk and great spire of St. Paul's. I couldn't help pausing as a wave of remembrance passed over me. That was where I'd first seen him, in the nave, my Gregory. We hadn't liked each other at all. I'd been looking for a copyist, and he'd just found the contemplation business inadequate to support him. He announced he was too busy seeking God to write nonsense for a conceited, stubborn woman, and I said to myself: a lot he knows about stubborn! That's the most arrogant man who ever donned a habit. And when he finally took the job, he announced it was because God wished to test his Humility. It seems some spiritual adviser had told him he needed more Humility to see God, so he was out collecting it as if it were a stack of florins. Ten pounds' worth of Humility, God. Now reveal Yourself; may I have a receipt? Men! They're all alike—they get everything backward. But that's the way it is with us women. Fools work their way into our hearts, in spite of all our good sense.

We turned left, passing the Bishop's palace, which to this day fills me with a sort of horrid, prickery feeling, and turned into the Shambles toward the Cheap. Chickens and geese were hanging by their feet in the poulterers' shops, and we had to step carefully to avoid the heaps of butchers' offal.

"Mama, this isn't the way home, is it?" asked Cecily as she

and her sister toiled along beside me. Alison tugged at my hand before a display of ribbons laid out on a market woman's shawl in the Cheap. "Pretty, mama. Buy me that red one." I shook my head.

"No, Cecily, we're not going home. If I were Hugo, that's the first place I'd look. We're going to Mother Hilde's. Hugo has no idea who she is, and he'll never find us there. Besides, she can help me think of what to do."

"Mother Hilde has sweets!" announced Alison joyfully, and the girls began to skip along the street, leaping over the gutters with joy at the thought of it. I only wished I could renew my energy the way that they did. But I always get tired quickly in the first months of making a baby.

But as we turned down Cornhill and the houses got shabbier, my heart started to beat faster and hope began to sing within me. Mother Hilde can fix anything! She'll see it in a dream, or she knows someone who did just the same, only better. A broken heart's nothing to Mother Hilde, she can mend anything! I'll tell her about Gregory's horrible family, and she'll cluck and say, "My, my! That's bad, but I've known worse! Do stir up the fire for me, dear, and pour yourself another mug of ale. Have your babies seen how to make dolls out of a dried apple yet? Let me sing them a song I know about the grasshopper and the ant." Wherever Mother Hilde is, that's better than home.

We were almost at the place; the narrow opening of St. Katherine's Street, which is really rather a grand name for an overgrown gutter, was almost obscured by the displays that street vendors had hung up. Nothing matched: a cup, some spoons, a hood, a pair of well-used gloves, some battered-looking pots. Most people call St. Katherine's Street "Thieves' Alley," because if you're looking for ruffians, or a place to sell stolen goods secretly, it's one of the best. But the rents are cheap, and most of the folk there have honest occupations, despite the name.

A man on the street brushed me, then opened his cloak to show me a polished silver mirror and a comb.

"For you, such a bargain!" he said. I shook my head and smiled. Stolen, of course. I certainly was near home.

"A widow needs to make herself pretty to catch another man. Think it over—I'll be here the rest of the afternoon, if you change your mind." Here? Yes, here—at the opening between two sagging tenements. A woman selling sour milk from a bucket, two lounging apprentices negotiating with an old lady for one of her store of greasy and no longer hot pies. Laundry hanging like pennants from second story to second story. "Thieves' Alley," Mother Hilde, and home, thank the Blessed Lord.

We carefully skirted a massive pig enjoying himself in the oozing muck in the center of the alley, and passed beneath the overhanging second stories of the tenements, where women leaned from between their open shutters to gather in laundry and shout gossip across the narrow way. A bird in a cage chirped somewhere above, and an old yellow dog raised his sleepy head from his paws and barked at us from a doorstep. Midway down the alley we stopped before an old two-story house that seemed to lean drunkenly against its neighbors. The front room on the second floor, seemingly added as an after-thought, was built so far into the street that it cast the front door into perpetual shadow, and prevented a mounted man from riding the length of the alley.

The door had a new knocker on it, made of iron but brightly painted, in the shape of a monkey's face. Above us, marigolds in a second-story window box caught the sun, and the timbers at the house front shone with new color. Mother Hilde's prospering, I thought. I remember when we first came here, there were holes in the roof. I lifted the knocker. It won't be Brother Malachi who answers, I said to myself. The weather's still good, and he never gives up his summer business until the weather shifts. He'll be on the road, selling things. Mother Hilde lives with Brother Malachi, who's nobody's brother, but I think he was a monk once, before he took up his trade of forging indulgences. He sells relics, too, which he makes himself out of bits

171

of this and that. He says you shouldn't consider that he sells false goods because he sells very genuine goods—faith and hope—and that paper and pig bones are simply methods of conveying them to others. Besides, he gives good bargains. At least, that's what he says.

In the winter Brother Malachi stays home and works on his true profession, which is finding the Philosopher's Stone. This takes up the entire back room of the house, for the Philosopher's Stone cannot be found without a lot of strange equipment and positive clouds of bad smells. When I lived here last, he had a boy named Sim, whom we'd found in the street, to pump the bellows and build up the fires and run errands for him. Perhaps Sim would answer my knock.

But I was stopped short when a strange woman opened the door. She was a bit taller than I, with a strong, rawboned face and fading, darkish hair tucked beneath a simple kerchief. Behind her in the room I could see a girl of about twelve, who had left off sweeping the hearth with a twig broom, and turned to see who was at the door. But it was the room itself, Mother Hilde's cramped little hall, that looked strangest of all. True, the fire still leapt on the hearth, and the boiling kettle's lid still clattered, as they had in the old days, but everything else was different: the low rafters had been painted bright red, and the ceiling between them was now dark blue, like the night sky, with the constellations picked out on it in bright flecks of gold. At the center of each a fanciful depiction of the proper sign of the zodiac was painted in bright colors. The twins, entirely nude but for two large fig leaves, the scorpion with his poisonous tail, Capricorn the goat with his little beard and curling horns. The walls beneath the crimson beams were painted as green as a new leaf. New paint, not yet begrimed by the smoke of candles.

I was suddenly terrified and speechless. Who on earth could be living here now? Had Mother Hilde died?

"Were you looking for a midwife?" said the woman, not unkindly, as she surveyed my frightened face and the two little girls clinging to my skirts.

"We've come for Mother Hilde," Alison spoke up from her safe place behind me. "She has sweets." The woman smiled.

"She is here, isn't she?" I asked, my voice rather shaky.

"Why, yes—who shall I say is calling?"

"Tell her it's Margaret, and I need her dreadfully."

"Oh, *Margaret*," responded the woman, as if she'd heard of me. "Of course, she's in back—go right through."

As we passed, the girl tugged at my sleeve and said shyly, "I'm Bet; that's my mother. She's learning from Mother Hilde now too."

And Cecily, turning her wide eyes on her asked, "If you live at Mother Hilde's, do you eat sweets every day?"

"Of course," said Bet, leaning on her broom. "It's what we have for meals instead of vegetables." And before her mother could stop her, she'd launched on such a ridiculous tale that we both had to laugh.

"Tell us more," said Cecily, and she and Alison sat down on the bench and tucked their feet up underneath them to listen, as I passed through the back room to find Mother Hilde in the garden behind the house. In Brother Malachi's dark and shadowy room, I could see his things were neatly packed, all except for the athanor, which is bulky. My eye caught the little crucifix in his oratory corner, and I crossed myself, thinking again of all the mornings—or even the dead of night—when I'd seen him there, praying by the light of a single candle to purify himself before a particularly difficult experiment.

God, I wish I could see his round figure now, turning around to shush me: "Margaret! I suppose by that infernal thumping you think you're sneaking by on little mouse feet! Don't you know better than to disturb me at a time like this? There's no reason, absolutely no reason at all, to come through this room when I'm working! How many times do I have to tell you to go out the front door and around by the side gate? Is there no respect, absolutely none left in the world, for a man in search

173

of Truth? Unless, of course—ah! Is that food you've brought? Set it down on the bench. I'd quite forgotten I was hungry—" Malachi would have choice words about Hugo, and say something humorous that would mend everything, if only he were here.

For a moment the light at the back door dazzled me, and then I could make out Mother Hilde in the yellow autumn sun. She was spreading chicken manure around her cabbages with a rake, and as she raked she leaned over to speak personally to each cabbage head. She didn't have to lean very far, not only because she's not very tall, but because her cabbages are immense—vast green globes all beskirted with great ruffled leaves that stand well over knee height. Everyone thinks it's the seeds, which she saves especially each year from the biggest ones, but I know the secret's not in the seeds, but in what she says to them.

"You're looking a little yellowish and pale today," she'll say, and then cock her kerchiefed head as if she's listening to it. Then she'll fetch it a bucket of water from the well, or dig around its roots, until it's straightened up. That's how she made roses climb all over the donkey shed, where nothing but weeds grew before. And her herbs, all growing higgledy-piggledy here and there in the garden, have a sharp, wild scent as if they grew in the country.

"They're like people, Margaret, you have to put them where they like the company," she'd say, setting a little marigold among the carrots, or moving a new sprout of fennel to a sunny spot by the shed wall. "Now you must know parsnips don't need company, Margaret, they're like contemplatives; they grow by themselves and nobody bothers them. But lettuces, oh, they're social. And frail. And the minute it gets warm, they're so frivolous, they just go to seed." Her bean poles, like little tents, stood among the roses. They'd be needing picking soon. Above this little kingdom, Mother Hilde's big rooster, as vain a creature as ever lived, postured and strutted on the donkey shed roof, surveying his hens behind the wattle fence and showing off his tail feathers to the world. Within the shed, I could hear the tuneless humming of Peter, Mother Hilde's last remaining child, who's not right in the head, as he cleaned out the stalls.

Mother Hilde's shapeless gray gown was covered with her big apron—white, like her kerchief, and I could see that she had on her old clogs. Behind her trailed a little dog that looked like a mound of hair very nearly the same at both ends. It was my own dog, who's named "Lion-heart," or Lion, for short, on account of his great deeds. He'd been left behind when I was taken off so suddenly, and he must have run straight to Mother Hilde's, which is what he does whenever he's let out.

"Mother Hilde!" I called, and as she turned, Lion gave a great leap of joy and bounded toward me barking like a crazy thing.

"Why, Margaret!" Mother Hilde exclaimed with delight. "You're back! I knew you'd come. See? I kept Lion for you. He ran directly here when you left so suddenly." With Lion leaping on me and wagging his whole body, we embraced there, among the cabbages, and I began to weep for joy and relief in seeing her face again.

She stepped back at arm's length, to look me over better. Her face grew serious.

"What's wrong, Margaret? You've got something cold and dark all around your shoulders, and your bosom's all lumpy, as if you'd fled with your life's possessions tucked inside. And where's Brother Gregory? I thought you'd gone and married him."

"The Cold Things are ghosts, Mother Hilde, and Brother Gregory's in France, given up for dead."

"Ghosts? Goodness me, that sounds serious. Come inside and let's talk," said Mother Hilde.

"Now, what do you think of our beautiful new hall, Margaret?" asked Mother Hilde as she checked the contents of her kettle and poured me a mug of ale. "Isn't it splendid? Malachi took it in trade."

"In trade for what, Mother Hilde?"

"Oh, the Elixir of Life," said Mother Hilde, giving her kettle a stir. "Sir Humphrey was very happy with it, and sent his own painter all the way from Dorsetshire."

I couldn't help gasping a little, and as my eyes opened wider I put my hand over my mouth, which had dropped open. Selling to the gentry? Malachi was getting bold beyond belief. I could spy Mother Hilde looking up from her kettle with that amused, indulgent look she gets whenever I'm shocked.

"Mother Hilde, what on earth will Baron Humphrey do when he finds out the Elixir doesn't work? He's got one of the nastiest reputations in Christendom."

"Well, first of all, he was visiting and isn't likely to come back for a while, since he's headed abroad. And second, Malachi told him it wasn't proof against weapons—only natural death. Any man who lives as wickedly as Sir Humphrey, he says, is bound to be murdered by his heirs anyway. So, Malachi says, there's no problem at all, as long as he sells the Elixir only to men who aren't likely to die in bed."

"But what was in it, that convinced Sir Humphrey that it worked?"

"Remember the *aqua ardens* he used to make for coughs? It makes a man powerfully drunk in absolutely no time at all."

"Oh, Mother Hilde, there's no stopping Brother Malachi, is there?" I put my hand on her arm.

"That's because he's a genius, my dear," said Mother Hilde with calm pride.

But then I had to tell everything that had happened to me since the day that Sir Hubert and his retainers had burst into our parlor, fully armed, and left my wicked stepsons in pieces on the floor. By the time I had finished my story, dusk was beginning to fall, and the whole household, consisting of the strange woman, her daughter, Peter, and old Hob, the handyman, had gathered silently to listen.

"I need him back, Mother Hilde. I'd give anything to have him back. I know I can find him—find the money—anything—

if I just try hard enough. He loves me, he said so, and I can't let him go. Oh, Hilde, he might die alone, and I'd never see him again—"

And as I wept into the late supper of pottage she had dished from her kettle, she said: "Margaret, after a good night's sleep, we can come up with a plan. You can always make things come out, if you use your wits. And you aren't even empty-handed. What did you bring with you?"

Silently I laid the things out on the table. Gregory's last letter, with the ink splotch, then my little Psalter. I could see them shudder as the Cold Thing expanded in the room.

"What is the cold stuff I feel?" said Mother Hilde calmly, just as she speaks when she attends a bad birth, so that she won't frighten anyone.

"Master Kendall's ghost," I said, "he said he'd come with me to show me how to get money so that I could pay Gregory's ransom and get him back."

"Advice from ghosts? Really, Margaret, and to think you believe talking to plants is odd. It's nothing compared to conversing with ghosts. But then, you always did hear voices. Where is he now?"

"Papa's over by the fire," said Alison, pointing with a chubby finger.

"Yes—he says it's ever so annoying he can't get warm anymore," added Cecily.

"Well, well. Three of you. Goodness, Margaret, you're always full of surprises. I wonder how the new little one will turn out? As fey as these two? Oh, don't start so. You can't hide these things from me—or even Goodwife Clarice, here, who has just begun to learn from me. How many months along, would you say, Clarice?"

The woman responded seriously, as if repeating a lesson. "Two—maybe nearly three, it seems to me, Mother Hilde." I could feel myself blushing.

"Oh, Margaret, my dear Margaret. You know how well I taught you. Now say, just how did you give yourself away?" I looked down—no one could see through the heavy folds of my bulky surcoat and unlaced kirtle. Then I saw how I'd set my hands, right across the top of my belly. "Oh!" I said, and snatched them away. Mother Hilde laughed.

"Yes, it was the hands, Margaret. They tell better than words. Now, show me the next thing."

"There's this," I said, taking out the little casket from the dark lady. "I think maybe I should throw it away. Look." As I opened the little box they gasped. It was beautiful, that ring, all set with stones that glittered in the firelight.

"Hugo's wedding ring—and poisoned with a deadly venom. Don't any of you dare touch it."

"Don't throw it away just yet," said Mother Hilde. "Things like that don't come to a person for no reason at all. Odd, it's beautiful and terrifying all at once."

"That's just what I thought of the dark lady herself."

"Strange, strange," said Mother Hilde, shaking her head. "She must have loved him a great deal once, to risk so much and come so far. Love into hate, all poisoned, like the ring. And yet in the end, she couldn't give it to him. You've given me a puzzle, Margaret, and I don't know what it means. Show me what else you have." I took the reliquary off my neck, and unfolded the tiny pair of shoes.

"Madame Belle-mère followed them," I said. "But she's not here now. She's probably gone off sight-seeing. She gets bored easily and is very snobbish—this neighborhood wouldn't please her." Mother Hilde picked up the little shoes and turned them over in her hands.

"His, I suppose." She put them back on the table. "This is very serious, Margaret. I'll ask for a dream tonight, to show me what it all means. Otherwise, I'll make a divination with hot wax. But the last thing, you don't have to show to me, for I know what it is." A little voice piped up uncertainly. It was Bet, the little girl with the cheerful brown curls and thin, serious face.

"We'd like to see it, please, since we've heard about it."

Without another word, I took out the Burning Cross, which glistened all ruddy in the firelight.

"Oh," the girl sighed. "That's very beautiful. I want to be a midwife someday, just as you were."

"Well, don't be exactly like me, or you'll wind up before the Bishop—and that can be very uncomfortable."

"Tomorrow," said Mother Hilde, "I'll go myself to your house and see if Hugo's been there yet—but now, to bed everyone. Margaret will have plenty of time to answer questions tomorrow." And for want of other space she tucked us all in with her in the big bed in the front upper room that was hers and Malachi's.

It was as she turned back the sheets that Cecily pulled on her apron conspiratorially: "Mother Hilde," she whispered. "Don't let Alison in the bed. She wets."

"I do *not*, it's you!" squeaked Alison indignantly.

"My dear girls, in Mother Hilde's bed, no one wets. You'll sleep on the side with the chamber pot, and remember to wake up. That's how it *always* is in my house." She spoke so assuredly that it simply had to be so, and it was.

"But since papa won't tell us a story tonight, will you?"

"Papa?" Mother Hilde said quizzically, looking at me for an explanation.

"Master Kendall's ghost has been telling them bedtime stories." Mother Hilde nodded.

"It makes sense," she said. "He never had a moment for them when he was alive. My, you must have been having a time, all alone with that strange family in the country." I didn't say anything. Then Mother Hilde began the story of the clever beasts that frightened away the robbers, but before she was half done, the girls were asleep, wrapped in each other's arms. It was lulling, the story. I lay there listening to Mother Hilde's voice, the familiar creaking of the timbers of the old house, and Lion whuffing in his sleep at the foot of the bed. My eyes were just shutting when Mother Hilde said to me: "You love him desperately, don't you?"

"So much my heart's broken with it," I whispered into the dark.

"It's not easy, loving. Malachi's not the first, but he is the greatest of my loves. And the last, before I am buried—I hope by his side. You know, Margaret, I've come with him a long way. To this city, to another way of life. You'll have to face much more to get your Gregory back—you'll have to risk everything."

"I know that, Mother Hilde. I am terrified. But my love drives me on. I can do nothing else."

"Oh, Margaret, it won't be easy for you. A woman who loves must be prepared to go into far places. And not all of them—how would Malachi say it?—geographical."

"But you'll help?"

"Of course, Margaret. I've never turned away love in need yet."

The very next morning, as Mother Hilde went to poke about Margaret's house by the river, to see if the neighborhood was free from mysterious strangers, including Sir Hugo, Margaret went down to the docks with her little girls and her dog trailing behind her. She had in mind to ask what ships had recently come from the Continent and who had ridden through returning from the great ports of Dover and Southampton. For one thing she knew, and that was that sooner or later, news of everything and everyone must pass through London, which is the hub of all gossip in the entire realm of England.

"Oh, look, mama!" Alison's pudgy finger pointed to an interesting sight on the quay. A foreign galley, bobbing gently at anchor, was being loaded. A squalling black horse, blindfolded, struggled in a sling being lowered into the galley's hold by ropes and pulleys. Two strong men held another black horse, the last of the team, on the quay, while a boy finished tying the blindfold. Behind the horse, a lavishly carved and decorated wagon had attracted the attention of a crowd of admiring street urchins and loafers. The captain of the dark lady's guard was shouting orders to the deck crew, as workmen began the task of dismantling the wagon for loading.

"I think we'd better inquire elsewhere," said Margaret, hurrying her children away from the docks.

"Hey, you." Someone tugged at Margaret's cloak from behind. "I've seen you hunting up and down. It's news from France you're after, isn't it? Bordeaux?" Margaret turned to see a stout woman in clogs, carrying a basket of fish on her head. With the hand that was not aiding the balance of the fish, she still held tight to Margaret's cloak.

"No, news from Calais—the Duke's army, not the Prince's. But how did you know?"

"There's lots of 'em here—women in black, that haunt the dockside. You're wasting your time here today, mistress. The last ship from Calais came in nearly a week ago, and who knows when there'll be another? You'd be just as well off asking at the Bridge what troops have come overland from Dover. Or—I know, if you're lucky, some of the sailors from the last ship might be still lying drunk at the Golden Horn, where you can make inquiries. Then there's the Keys, where the soldiers stay, but that's a stew, and a decent woman shouldn't be seen there. Or try the Castle. The quality stays there on their way inland from the Cinque Ports. There's lots that ask there. What are you looking for? Father? Brother? Or husband?"

"Husband," answered Margaret, thanking her and starting to leave.

"Then it's not so bad," said the woman, surveying Margaret and her daughters with a knowing eye. "You can't get a new father or a brother, but husbands are a-plenty in this world. Take my advice and get a new man, for the sake of the children." Margaret looked shocked.

"Fool," said the woman, as she watched Margaret hurrying away in the direction of the Golden Horn, a child clutched with each hand and the odd-looking little dog trailing behind.

° ° °

It was a great relief when Mother Hilde told me that Sir Hugo hadn't yet thought of searching the London house for me, or mounting a guard on it to snatch me the moment I arrived. But then, I never thought he was the brainy type.

"Just imagine a dunderhead like Sir Hugo married off to that foreign marquesa. Why, Hilde, she'd be running him about like a lapdog, she's so much cleverer than he is. I wonder what possessed her?"

"Now, Margaret, there's no telling the ways of love. But I don't think it would have lasted long, myself. The first time he managed to figure out that she'd used him, he'd have probably strangled her, or beaten her head in, from what you tell me of his character. No—it doesn't usually work out, matching two minds so unlike. She's probably better off the way she is."

"But tell me, how are things at the house? Is everyone well?"

"Well for now, Margaret, but not for long. Your grooms, the kitchen boy, the steward, the cook and her assistant, have stayed on out of loyalty to you. But the pantrymaid has run off to be married, and the rest are grumbling because those stingy de Vilerses haven't paid their wages. The fare's thin, and you're lucky they haven't pawned the silver. I stopped by Master Wengrave's house next door. Master Kendall's apprentices all look as if they're doing well, though Mistress Wengrave is considerably stricter with them than you ever were. I had a chat with her, Margaret, and told her what's happened. She says you're welcome there, and you'd be safer than in church. They have enough stout fellows to fend off any number of your in-laws, and since Master Wengrave's been made an alderman, no one would dare cross him by carrying you or his goddaughters off secretly. Of course, I should warn you I didn't tell them your suspicions about the Duke. If any of it's true, they couldn't hope to keep you."

"Master Kendall always said he was a good man in a fight. I remember the day he made his will, and named Master Wengrave as Cecily and Alison's guardian. I never understood what he meant then." My eyes felt a little itchy thinking about that day, and I had to wipe them a bit.

"Well, it's been a fight, ever since you were carried off, according to Mistress Wengrave. He filed suit to recover the girls, and he's been hounding them in court ever since. He says it's not proper for Roger Kendall's girls to rot away in the country, or get locked up in a convent to satisfy some grasping stepfather. Mistress Wengrave says he gets quite wrathy about it. He says it's not the money, it's the principle. Something about signaling to the gentry that they can't rob the City with impunity."

"Oh, that sounds like him, all right. That's what they'd talk about, he and Master Kendall, when it wasn't Mercer's Guild business, or the organization of the new wool staple."

"So then, what do you want to do, Margaret?"

"Oh, Mother Hilde, I've walked all over until my feet are sore, and the girls howled. I haven't found out anything except that another convoy of merchant cogs are due soon—they were still loading at the same time as the one that's just arrived. They're carrying wounded and some English knights returning home on parole for their ransoms. I'll meet them when they land, but until then there's nothing I can do—except, maybe, see about the mess at home."

"A half year's wages for a household, Margaret—that's no joke. And you've come away without a penny on you."

"Never mind, Hilde—I'll just ask Master Kendall. And if he's right about the money, then he's right about Gregory, too, and he really is alive. Then I'm not being foolish hunting for news of him. Have I told you, Mother Hilde, how many people have made fun of me today? Even a fishwife! And I've had three proposals of marriage, though the men were drunk and it doesn't really count. And six rowdies at the Unicorn sang a horrible song about how fickle women are, all the while I was talking to some old sergeant. And—Mother Hilde, you haven't heard that horrible song about the merchant's wall was high, high, high, have you?"

"I'm afraid I have, but I wasn't going to mention it."

"They sang that, too, even though they didn't know it was about me, and I've never been so embarrassed in my whole life. It's more than my feet that are bruised, Mother Hilde. I've had a *horrible* day!" And I started to cry. If Mother Hilde hadn't embraced me and said, "There, there!" for some time, I'd be crying there still.

But after dinner, when Hilde and I were washing the dishes, while Bet carried water and Clarice scoured out the kettle with sand, Mother Hilde said thoughtfully, "Margaret—you ought to think of your safety. If any of those relatives of yours remembers about me, then there's not a way on earth we can prevent them retaking you. You should take the precaution of going to Master Wengrave's as soon as you can, before they think to make inquiries in the City." And because I remembered how little they scrupled to leave the bodies of indiscriminately slain commoners behind them, it seemed to me better not to lead them to Mother Hilde's house.

So that is how, in the afternoon, I found myself picking my way around the rubbish in the street, with Cecily, Alison, and Lion at my heels. I had a plan: I'd find out where Gregory was, and when Malachi came home, I'd ask him how to go get him, since Brother Malachi has traveled all over the world in his search for the Philosopher's Stone, and surely that's a much harder thing to find than a man. Worrying along the street with my own thoughts, I hardly noticed that the girls were occupied with a new kind of game: They had decided to follow Lion exactly and inspect everything he did from a dog's-eye point of view, so to speak. Now, let's see, I was thinking to myself—I'll have to inspect the street very carefully, and perhaps go in by the back door, to make sure I'm not seen.

It was a relief that Cecily and Alison weren't pestering me for treats from the street vendors as I worked over everything in my mind, until I overheard a woman say to her little boy: "See that? They've turned into dogs. That's what happens when you don't obey your mother, and you play alone where the bad dogs can bite you. Now come away, or you'll look just like them." And she whisked him around to find all three of them breathing with their tongues hanging out in front of a large rat hole between the stones of the gutter.

"You quit that this instant! You're a disgrace! Can't I go anywhere in public without you embarrassing me?"

"But mama, every place you go is boring," announced Cecily, straightening up.

"Yes, very boring," said Alison. "We need to play." Only Lion looked contrite, and wagged his back end, hoping to be forgiven.

There was a crowd around the Cornhill stocks. A seller of bad meat, who had charged roasted kid prices for roasted lamb by changing the tail on the carcass, had been exposed to the jeers of the passersby. Just so you'd know what he'd done, the kid's tail was nailed to the wood by his head. His worn gown was already daubed with the offal that had been thrown at him, and I caught a glimpse of desperate eyes as a poorly aimed stone thudded against the board by his face.

"Alison, Cecily, don't stare so! It's not good for you! You hurry up!" I pulled Alison's thumb out of her mouth, and dragged her from the comfortable vantage point where she had settled in to inspect the spectacle. It was when I had both children by the wrist, and had looked up to find a way through the crowd, that I thought I saw him. A tall figure, hurrying through the press of people toward the Cheap. I could only see his back, but he was wearing the same familiar, shabby old gray gown in which I'd first seen him. His cowl was up. But his walk, erect and businesslike, as he threaded his way through the crowd of gawkers, was unmistakable. My heart stopped, and I could feel the blood leave my face.

"Gregory," I whispered, and began to follow the hooded figure before I lost it in the crowd.

"But this isn't the way home, mama." I shushed Cecily with a word as I dragged them along behind me. Faster, faster, so I wouldn't lose him. My heart pounding, I was pulled along as if tied to the mysterious figure. Farther, farther he went, until I saw him slow to pass the press of horsemen around a haycart coming in through Aldersgate. I was nearly breathless now.

"Gregory, wait!" I called, but the hooded figure never paused. As I got to the gate I saw him turn and plunge into the twisting alleys of the tenement district just outside the walls. Gasping, I followed, only to find that as I turned the last corner down a narrow alley, hard on his heels, that he'd vanished. I was facing the blank back wall of some kind of warehouse. Hard, hard stone, and not a door in sight.

"Gregory, Gregory, don't leave me, don't leave me alone like this! Come back!" I could hear my voice reverberate as I shouted to the echoing wall. There was not a human sound in response, just my own voice, "Come back, come back!" I banged frantically on the wall, looking for a hidden door that the figure might have passed through. "Gone, oh, gone forever," I whispered to the deaf stones as my knees buckled beneath me. It was then that I heard the terrible cry of a man in mortal agony:

"Margaret!"

CHAPTER
7

When I next opened my eyes I saw a smoky ceiling swaying and shifting overhead, and heard a dog whining, and felt a long, rough wet tongue licking my face. I could hear a voice somewhere in the room saying, "There's no doubt who it is. The book we found beside her proves it: see the initials? M.K.—that's her; even without the redheaded girls and the odd dog, it would be certain."

"Always the searcher of evidence, Robert. Whatever made you leave the law? You've got talent."

"The same old sad story, Nicholas. Lack of money. Talent doesn't take you far without a degree. Besides, God meant me for higher things than growing old over musty lawbooks."

"Growing old in taverns is an improvement, I suppose?"

"It is if someone else is doing the paying. Drink to Sir Edward again, the dear little cockerel, and to his indulgent father's fortune."

"I'll go you better. To the Earl himself!"

"Hip, hip, hurrah!" sounded from many throats, and then

there was the clank and gurgle of ale mugs being emptied. I could hear the faint sound of a woman's raucous laughter from another room. A tavern? If so, not a very nice one.

"Well, I must go, Robert. Unlike you, I have a shop to keep. Let me know if you need help again."

"When have I not needed help, Nicholas? But you'll be repaid a hundredfold by God for casting your bread into an empty wine-tun like me." More clanking and gurgling. Then a lengthy belch.

"Aha, your eyes are open, Mistress Margaret Kendall. See? I know you. It's my powers of observation. I even know there's a reward out for you, thanks to your gabby little girls, who are now snoring, dead drunk, underneath the table. Whatever put a rich, silly woman like yourself into a dangerous neighborhood like this?"

"Gregory. I saw Gregory here. For God's sake, tell me where he's hiding." I was still too weak to rise and look for the source of the voice.

"Brother Gregory? He hasn't been here since he ran off with that rich man's widow he'd been tutoring. You, to be precise. Imagine. Practically a grave robber. What a stroke! Swift! Surgical! He beat out half of London—even my little cockerel—who wanted to get their hands on old Master Kendall's fortune. But did he come back and share with his friends? Buy them a drink or two, by way of celebration of his new fortune? Oh, no, the money made him snobbish so fast that he never came back. I saw him once from a distance, riding on a fine horse near the Inns of Court. All dressed up like a gentleman, he was, riding beside two knights in full regalia—an old one and a young one. Didn't look to left or right, like a man going to an execution. I hailed him, but he didn't hear me. And here we'd been the best of friends, except for his rather addle-brained support of nominalism. How many dinners had I bought him when he was broke, the faithless dog? So I revenged myself. I wrote him up as a scurrilous ballad. It's doubtless dogging his heels at this very moment, embarrassing him. He always had enough dignity for three—I'm sure it's driving him crazy at this very moment."

Suddenly I was so angry, I became strong. I sat up on the bench, and the smoky, low-ceilinged tavern swirled around me. I saw a man with several weaving faces in a well-worn scholar's gown. He was seated at a bench on the other side of a long trestle table that stood beside the bench on which I'd been laid out. A number of other interested faces surrounded his, but I didn't care.

"It's you who did it. You made up all those nasty lies—and about a dead man. You should be ashamed. Ashamed, I say! The only person you've hurt is me—and he never lived to hear your horrid song, you jealous vulture."

"Hey, now, those are strong words for a man who's just picked you out of an alley—*gratis*—and not even stolen all the little gewgaws you had stuffed in your bosom."

"It's just as well you didn't—one of them's poisoned," I muttered as my head slumped onto the table.

"Now, none of this. Rise and have a drink, and tell me how you got here."

"I saw him—Gregory—walking through the City, and followed him here. Then I heard his death cry. It was from far away. It—it was terrible. Now I know it was his ghost I followed, and he's gone forever, and I can't even be buried beside him when my own time comes. And I was so sure he'd come home in time to see his baby. I told them all he wasn't dead and I'd find him. They tried to lock me up, but I ran away. I've looked, I've looked. I've talked to all the shipmasters and the soldiers coming home. Oh, God, how could it all happen this way!" And I put my head down on my arms on the table again, this time to sob until my breath was gone.

"Now, now, you can't cry like that. Not with a baby coming, it's not healthy." They'd formed up in a circle around me, and I could feel someone patting my back clumsily. "Tell us what happened."

"He—he had a chance to write for the Duke of Lancaster. A

—a chronicle. A knighthood. To be in the Duke's own personal retinue—"

I could hear their breaths being sucked in, and someone whistled softly and said, "What patronage! The chance of a lifetime!"

"And chronicles go on forever—not like odes," I could hear the first voice, the balladeer, saying regretfully.

"But he had to go to France to do it—it was the Duke's idea. A new kind of chronicle, written at first hand." I lifted my head up from my arms. "I told him just to collect everybody's boasting afterward, when it was safe, but he wouldn't."

"Hmm. Unwise. Yes. Unhealthful, the climate in France right now—" the men around me muttered.

"You see, he said he had to. The Duke had secured my inheritance for him, and he was obliged. Then there was the law, too—once the income was assured, he had to serve in the military—"

"Well, well. Caught. Netted like a pigeon. That's how they catch scholars these days."

"—Yes, money and obligation—the bait and the lime."

"Who'd have thought it? He was the freest of us all. Money and women trap a man, he always said—and he was right. Oh, pardon, mistress—"

"He disappeared in the siege of Verneuil—" They nodded their heads gravely. "But I had hope. The heralds never found his body. So even though there was no ransom demand, I knew, just knew he was alive—but now—" I wiped my eyes on my sleeve.

"You shouldn't waste your time at the dockside, mistress, with all those other women in black. Do you know where you are?" asked a scholar in a frayed Oxford gown.

"Why, yes, this is the second-best place in all of Europe to make inquiries for a lost man—the first, being in Paris, would be difficult for you to visit just now."

"This is the Boar's Head, Mistress—um—ah, what was Brother Gregory's family name, anyway? Did he have one?"

"I never knew it. Just Brother Gregory, that's what he went under."

"I think maybe it was Scrivener."

"Was there a *de* in it? He did put on airs."

"It was de Vilers," I said.

"Oh, my, an old name. From the Lincolnshire de Vilerses?"

"No, from the cadet branch, in Hertfordshire."

"Well, Mistress—or is it Madame—de Vilers, this is the Boar's Head, center of all that is worthy of gossip in Christendom. See this room? Flemish, Germans, Lombards, Gascons—a regular cacophony of nations—all masters of the shaved pate. You'll hear more Latin than English in this hall, for we are all, before anything else, disciples of Minerva."

"Minerva? She owns this place then?"

"And all of us, all of us too, Mistress Margaret-Who-Foolishly-Wed-a-Scholar. It's not an elegant place, as you see, but the *ambience*—it cannot be equaled. The price of ale here is modest, and the women are not. Who comes? See that fellow over there? A monk, sent to buy wine for his priory at Dunstable. He stops here, learns a new ribald ballad, and leaves us with the information that a two-headed calf has been born at King's Langley. Those fellows over there are jongleurs, fresh from the Continent. Did you know that unfrocked clerics make the best jongleurs? It's the vocal study, you see. Who else sings as sweetly? They have brought us a story of an English mercenary captain, who has taken a castle in Languedoc, married the widow, and Frenchified his name. Those fellows over there, dicing? Scholars from Padua and Montpellier. They're on their way to Oxford, but they stop here first, to catch up on anything they ought to know. Those fellows there, with the long faces and the dark cloud of *ut infras* and *lis jub judices* over them? Lawyers—real ones, not like me. But filthy-minded, or they wouldn't be here. They can't help trading the fine coin of their cases on the exchange here. We heard all about how your father-in-law bribed himself off murder charges for the bodies he left behind when he carried you off. 'Self-defense,' ha! It cost a pretty penny, too—all borrowed from your inheritance. The clerk who drew up the document sups here too."

It was true. The snatch of song, the gabble in the corner—all Latin. And despite the motley of foreign robes, monks' habits, and clerical gowns, every man in the room had one thing in common: a clerical tonsure of one sort or another. A group in one corner had struck up a song in French just brought back from abroad. I could hear bits of it through the clatter and voices:

> Tell me, Lisette, who is the better lover
> The man with sword or him with the pen?
> I'll have the man of the tonsure anytime
> He'll be singing love ballads all night long
> When your soldier's come and gone—

But it was drowned out by rising shouts from the table of dicers in the other corner.

"Pardon me a moment, madame," said my informant, making a flourishing gesture of farewell. "Violence threatens, and that is a friend of mine." And he and several of the fellows with him moved into the whirling circle of controversy. I leaned over to check on my girls. They really were sound asleep on the matted rushes under the table. Lion sat by them, like an anxious nursemaid.

"Loaded dice, by God! You think you can get away with that, you Lombard bastard?" could be distinguished from the rumble of angry voices.

A woman carrying a load of empty mugs sat them down on the table and addressed me.

"They're all right, those little girls. Just drunk. I heard the dog, then saw them howling in the alley. I'd gone out to dump the slops. That's how I found you. I had Robert take some of the boys out and bring you back. The girls were thirsty, and there's only one drink in this place—so there you are: three sips and they're out like snuffed candles."

192

"Are you Minerva?"

"No, I'm Berthe. I own the place. My husband left it to me."

"They said Minerva owned it."

"Oh, them—they're jokers, the lot of them. But harmless, generally. That's more than you can say of most. Say, you're not hungry, are you? I thought maybe you'd fainted from hunger."

"No, I saw a ghost. But I am thirsty."

"A ghost, eh? Lots of them about these days, though I, thank goodness, don't see them. Well, then, on the house, for another widow, I'll send some ale over—wait a moment—" and she hurried off in the direction of the controversy.

"I run a quiet house, I tell you!"

"Loaded dice, the son of a bitch—he cleaned me out."

More shouting in foreign tongues.

"Look at 'em—come up the same side every time."

"Weighted, by the bowels of Christ, and so slyly that you can't even see it."

"Mph, mph, mph!"

"Quit strangling him, I say! I'll not have murder done in my house!"

"I'll put as many holes in him as a dovecote." A knife flashed in someone's hand.

"No, Jankyn, put that knife back, didn't you hear her? No murder." Robert's voice sounded above the hubbub.

"Strip him and pitch him out then!"

"Yes, that's it!"

There was a struggle, with terrible howling, as the Lombard was plucked as clean as a chicken and thrown out the door. Robert came back to where I sat sipping the ale, looking satisfied with himself.

"Not bad," he said, "though it took four men. Now, it's times like these that we miss Brother Gregory. He could have flung the man out single-handed."

"He flung dice-cheaters out of taverns?"

"Oh, yes, that and lots more. Never a dull moment with Brother Gregory. And then he'd quote Aquinas, just to rub salt in the wound. God, I loved that man. Picky, snobbish, righteous bastard." I stared at him. He laid the dice on the table.

"There," he said. "My share of the spoils. Sorry it wasn't money. It's an offering. A token of my apology. I'm sorry about the ballad. I was wrong, and I'll make it up to you. You go home and quit wandering about the docks. I'll make the inquiries. If he's alive or dead, in any Christian country, I'll hear about it. Some men could disappear without a trace, but not a man who turns a verse like Brother Gregory. Be assured; somewhere there's a clerk who'll hear of him, and the news will travel to the Boar's Head. Are we quits, now?"

"We're quits. I accept your apology." I took the dice. There were three of them, identical, all made of bone, for playing Hazard. They looked absolutely honest. You couldn't see a seam or a bulge anywhere. I put them in my purse, which hadn't a penny of money in it.

"Where are you staying? I'll escort you, and get someone to help lug those offspring of yours."

"I was going to Master Wengrave's, my daughters' godfather, before I—I followed the—ghost."

"The Alderman's? That's very far from here. But you shouldn't assume it was Brother Gregory's ghost."

"But, who else would it have been? And why would it come here—where he used to be? At least before, I had hope," and I shuddered with the memory of it, so tall and straight, fading into the wall.

"Now, now, you shouldn't take it that way at all. After all, you've no proof. It could have been an apparition of any kind. Or maybe somebody real that you mistook, because his hood was up. And as for the voice, it could have been a hallucination. Grief makes us all crazy, you know—so you must take it as a good sign, that in some way you were led to us."

It was odd. As I watched his mouth opening and closing, his voice seemed to go far away, and his face seemed to take on a gilded, shadowy look, as if painted with a deep gold light. Rather than being an ordinary sort of thirtyish, clean-shaven face topped with thinning, brownish hair, it took on an interesting, deeply folded appearance, as if a very rich and profound character could be read there. The rest of the room, too, seemed unnaturally still, as if the laughter and clanking sounds were muffled in wool. Even though people were moving and speaking at a regular pace, I seemed to be able to see every fine detail of their movement, as if I were so swift in comprehension that they were immeasurably slow. The other faces, too, were illuminated with the somber gold light. Faces that might pass by on the street unnoticed were made deeply beautiful, unique and fascinating. The stillness in the midst of noise caught me and held me, and I stared at their new-created faces without answering, as they scooped up the girls and we passed into the street. The narrow streets were still, too, as people with strangely illuminated faces passed by: carters and ostlers and marketwomen, apprentices and bakers' boys with loaves on their heads. The tree leaves above the garden walls seemed to shimmer with a quiet ecstasy, and Aldersgate itself, tall and shadowy, shone dully, as if it were still touched by the minds that had built it.

"Crazy," I heard them say softly through wool behind me as I led the way to Thames Street beside Master Robert. "She just stares and doesn't speak."

"Well, it's understandable, considering what's happened."

"You wouldn't find me walking off like that fool Gregory if I had a woman like that. Oh, no, if I married a rich widow, I'd stay at home and drink myself to death on the best French wine."

"Not likely—you'd be back at the Boar's Head, telling lies, in no time at all."

Why were they talking about such unimportant things? Couldn't they see what had happened to the City? It was all painted and modeled with living light, shaking with a dim vibration of joy.

At Master Wengrave's, the alderman's pennants before the house shook and trembled in a wind that wasn't there. Master

Kendall's tall house, mine now, which stood only a back alley and a garden away from it down the street, seemed to pulsate with a strange inner life. The glass at the windows had been stored for safekeeping, but the shutters stood open, and air moved in and out from them as if they were living throats. The leaden gargoyles that were the downspouts from the roof gutters seemed frozen alive, impatient to be freed. As I stared at it Mistress Wengrave came to her door to welcome us in, and I turned to see that her face, too, had the rich golden glow. I watched it, silent and fascinated, as she thanked Master Robert, made over her goddaughters, saw them carried up to bed by two grooms, and gave orders to a kitchen maid who'd come to ask about supper. The kitchen maid's face had that look too —and I'd always thought her a simple girl.

"Margaret, do you need something to eat or drink? You're looking rather strange. Are you ill?" Her voice seemed to be coming from a long way away.

I heard myself saying, "I've come a long way . . . Gilbert de Vilers is dead . . . I need . . . alone . . ."

Mistress Wengrave, who has been my neighbor and my friend for a long time, looked grave, and her florid face paled somewhat beneath the golden sheen.

"Alone?" she said. "You shouldn't be alone. Not at a time like this. Come, we'll pray for him and you'll be at ease," and she put an arm around me to steer me to the household chapel. But she had scarcely shown me in when the smell of burning and a heavy clattering sound signaled a crisis in the kitchen. Mistress Wengrave has a mortal fear of fire. When Master Wengrave rebuilt the upper story of his house and added an oriel, she begged him to build a kitchen separated from the house. But he said that the kitchen she had was good enough, for it was built all in stone, and it was more convenient attached to the house anyway, for his food would get cold being brought from an outside kitchen. So she went on waking up in the night, thinking she smelled smoke, and walking about in the dark to check on her children.

"By our dear Lady! Margaret, forgive!" she cried as she fled. But I hardly noticed. The Wengraves' chapel is a tiny room on the ground floor, barely big enough for the family, and has the only glass window in the house. The rest are waxed linen, set in frames that can be taken down when the weather is good. But the chapel window, set on the eastern side of the house to catch the morning sun, is small, and wasn't as costly to glaze. But now, although it was nearly sunset and the window should have been dark, it glistened as though the new dawn were trapped in it. A pinkish golden light, rolling like steam, was pouring through it. The tiny room was incredibly still; the sound in the surrounding house was separated by a veil—there but not there. The faint sound of a woman screaming, cries for more water buckets, and scurrying footsteps seemed eerily muffled. As I watched the rolling clouds of light, I heard a tiny, quiet voice in my ear. It said, "Margaret," as if it expected me to listen.

I didn't move a muscle, for fear it might vanish.

"Margaret!" the voice said again, a little louder.

"It *is* You. I thought You'd left me."

"Left? I don't leave. After all, I am the Eternal Word. You just weren't listening, that's all. Talking, yes; listening, no."

"I thought You'd left because—because—"

"I know. That's why I'm here."

"Is it a sin to love so much? I mean, just a person, a man, and not something divine? I try to think of heavenly things, but all I can see is his face."

"Margaret, who made love?"

"Why, ah—um—"

"I did, Margaret. All kinds and sorts. Little and big. It's one of My better mysteries."

"Mysteries?"

"Why, yes. The more you give away, the more you have. Unlike water, which I made the ordinary way, so when you pour it out, it's gone. How dull My universe would be, without My mysteries."

"But it hurts so. Did You make it just to amuse Yourself?"

"Margaret, you're questioning Me again. Aren't you ever ashamed of being presumptuous? Most people would be singing praises and thanks for this much enlightenment. But not My stubborn, troublesome Margaret."

"I'm sorry."

"I wanted to show you something. But no one seems to be listening these days—even you."

"I'm truly sorry; I'm listening now."

"As well you ought to be! Look what it took to get your attention! Lights! Clouds! Voices! Next you'll be wanting smells and heavenly choirs! If I didn't love you so much—"

"You do, You really do?"

"You're not supposed to interrupt, Margaret. That's another of your failings."

By this time the fire scare had passed by, and Mistress Wengrave had returned to stand by the door. I could hear, with some outer ear, as she said, "Hsst! There's someone else in there. And lights! Has Margaret let in a burglar? She's much too unsuspecting." And someone answered her—I don't know who.

"Have you ever seen the ocean, Margaret?" the Voice asked.

"No."

"But you can imagine it, can't you?"

"Why, yes; it's lots and lots of water."

"But if you'd never seen a drop of water, could you begin to imagine the ocean?"

"No."

"How, then, if you'd never had a drop of love, could you begin to understand My love for creation?"

"It's all right then? Loving him too much?"

"Love is part of My design, Margaret. Look."

What happened next is very hard to describe. The aching thing you feel when you're in love got bigger and bigger as the room grew larger and more beautiful. Then it fell away entirely into something like an ocean of silvery light, vibrating and trembling, spread all around me as far as I could see. It was the entire universe, the stars and moon and the dust spots and the world and the bits and pieces that make everything, the up and the down and the sideways, all dancing for pure joy. I thought my mind and body would burst with the rapture of seeing it. Then with a *crack* I split into a thousand pieces, crying out as I spread into the dancing universe, until "Margaret" was completely lost in a thousand splinters vibrating with passionate love, and dancing, dancing—eternally dancing.

"What happened, Margaret? There was a dreadful flash, like lightning, and we thought you'd been killed." Mistress Wengrave's anxious voice pulled me back into a single piece again. But I could still feel the light, although I didn't see it anymore, though that sounds odd to say.

"Gregory," I said. "I'll find him."

"Of course you will, dear, of course you will," said Mistress Wengrave in that special, indulgent tone that we reserve for infants and crazy people.

That night, lying awake in bed, I discovered that I could hear everything. I don't mean everything in the room, I mean everything. I could hear my girls breathing, and the uneven gasps of little Walter Wengrave as he had a nightmare in the next room. He was Mistress Wengrave's favorite, as frail children often are, and the many nights she'd sat up with him while he struggled for breath had tied him all the closer to her. Twice I'd saved him, and she'd never forgotten, though we'd hidden it from her chaplain, who was very orthodox, and her husband, who was a model of piety.

But now I could hear the sounds in distant rooms as easily as if they were only a few inches from my ear. I heard insects burrowing in the walls and, at the top of the house, two little apprentice boys whispering in the long room under the eaves where the apprentices and journeymen slept in several big beds. Then I listened more: I could hear next door, in my own house, Cook's powerful snore, which had always been something of a joke. I heard cats treading softly in the street, and rats running along the eaves several streets away. A dog barked; men roistered in taverns in defiance of the curfew; a night-walker was collared by the watch, and voiced his grievances while being hustled off to jail. I could hear couples making love in the dark and horses shifting their feet in their stalls. Even the fish swimming in the river made a soft, sliding sound.

All around me, the night voices of the City whispered in the dark. Could I hear beyond the walls? I listened closer and could hear a fox slipping through the grass, and the wings of night hunting owls. Closer and closer I listened, until I heard it: the deep, almost imperceptible humming sound that the earth itself makes. Something in it caught my mind, and as I listened intently to the humming, I heard the narrow high little note made by my own working soul. It was joined by another, and another, as the sounds of other people and finally the tiny notes of the beasts and fowl, each humming like the ringing after-sound that a bell makes long after it has been struck. So many tones—such a soft ringing in the dark, with the mother-hum beneath it, like the bass note on a great organ. It was music; a great chord that filled the universe. It intensified and diminished, all in unison, like a pulsing song with only one note. But there were little spots that seemed empty of song, places that felt wrong. And it was then, listening, that I heard it far away: a discord in the note, a faint shrieking sound where the song had broken, as if the singers had stopped in horror. And there, in the faraway dark space, I heard what was unmistakably Gregory's voice, like a faint echo from the depths, calling,

"Margaret!"

An icy breeze from the towering granite mountains beyond the castle stirred the tapestries on the walls of the Great Hall. A ring of garlanded maidens rippled silently behind the Sieur Renaud d'Aigremont, Comte de St. Médard, as he took a sheet of begrimed, many times refolded paper from the hand of a kneeling groom.

"So, Pedro, this is what you took from him?"

"Yes, my lord, this was all." The Count looked to the black-hooded Dominican beside the courtier for confirmation. The gray-faced, cold-eyed visage nodded silently.

"No holy relic, you're sure of that?"

"Nothing, my lord count, not a splinter, bone, crucifix, or rosary. We overlooked nothing. Just this paper, worn underneath his shirt."

"It's not a prayer, is it? You know how those things make me uneasy."

"No. Just an ordinary letter. You can read it yourself." The Sieur d'Aigremont crossed to a spot beneath a tall, arched window, where the light was clear, and unfolded the letter. There was a spot of blood on it. He wrinkled his nose in distaste.

"I do hope you haven't damaged him. You know I don't like them damaged first. They don't last as long then; remember that I don't like to be deprived of sport—especially in this case." The Count, looking slightly preoccupied, turned to another kneeling groom and raised his eyebrows slightly, as if he wished to be reminded of the fellow's business.

"The *entremets, mon seigneur,* for the ambassador's feast of welcome—you wished to be consulted—" The groom sounded anxious.

"Twelve gilded youths dancing, and a pastry ship on wheels —didn't I make it clear enough last time? I wish to put Count Gaston's fire-breathing dragon to shame. Dragons, bah—tasteless. How typical of him. Now, get out. You are interrupting me." The kitchen groom left backward, bowing extravagantly and muttering, "Twelve gilded youths. My God, where are twelve youths left? I suppose I should rejoice it wasn't maidens he wanted. Perhaps the chapel choir—"

"My lord, your wishes were obeyed precisely," broke in the first groom. "The stain is just from a bloody nose. It took a half-dozen men to do the job, and one of them ended up with a broken collarbone." The count's face relaxed in anticipation of pleasure.

"He put up quite a struggle, then?"

"Like a tiger."

"Wonderful. The most powerful beasts give the most noble sport—and the most satisfying end." The Count unfolded the stained letter with unusual delicacy for one with such wide hands. But then, he was a connoisseur, and prided himself on the exquisiteness of his sense of touch. Rings, two or three to a finger, made deep grooves in the pallid fat that hid the joints. A sprinkling of coarse hair, like a boar's, across the back of his hands detracted somewhat from the perfection of the glittering jewels. For a moment he admired his hands holding the letter. I'll have them shaved, the thought flitted across his mind. It will set off the stones better. Touch, taste, and sensuality were all linked in him. As he read the letter aloud in French he stroked the ink, and a delicious orgasmic sensation, united with a spasm of the salivary glands, traveled briefly through him.

"Charming," he said.

"I thought you'd like it," said Fray Joaquin.

"And how does he enjoy our oubliette? Has it changed his opinions any?"

"He shouts up through the grille that truth can't be altered, and you can't make it go away by hiding from it."

"Arrogant, arrogant as ever. An arrogance beyond his station. It offends me, Fray Joaquin, have I told you how long it has offended me?"

"Yes, my lord."

" 'Homage to My Lady's Tiny Foot' was one of my best, don't you think?"

"Beautiful. Perfection. Who else could possibly have conceived of something of such refinement?"

"It was when I heard that every student in Paris was singing 'Homage to My Lady's Large Shoe,' that I knew I had an enemy."

"One with no taste."

"An enemy to be bent to my will, and then destroyed." He gazed across the hall, where Europa in silk thread gently swayed atop the great bull. "The Master denies me nothing. I had only to make the request and he fell into my hands—even more easily than the little ones. Lovely. And without a prayer or a relic or even a saint's name in protection. How could I ever doubt that it was the Master's work? What shall I do with him, Fray Joaquin?"

"I have not your brilliance, my lord. Cut out his tongue and feed it to the dogs?"

"Nice, but not nice enough. I want to break his mind first, the mind that mocked me—before I break the rest. And he will need his tongue to confess his abjectness. I want him to tell me my work is brilliant, witty. I want him to search desperately for new adjectives of praise before I begin to finish him off, inch by inch. I am not a crude man—never mistake me for that, Fray Joaquin. No, my vengeance is refined, delicate, sensual—just like this flower." Still holding the letter, he plucked a rose from the brass bowl on the table beneath the window and inhaled the scent.

"A rose—rich and refined. Daisies are scentless and vulgar, don't you think?"

"Of course, my lord."

"Not good for much, except to pull the petals off one by one to discover who loves you."

"I don't understand."

"You will. I want a drawing spell. Like the one I cast for him. Have Messer Guglielmo call it up tonight, without excuses, this time."

"Messer Guglielmo? But he says he is still bruised from the last encounter, and the next may be his last. He says Asmodeus may break loose into this world, uncontrolled."

"It is his own fault. He must choose better assistants. If Arnaut hadn't grown cowardly and recited a Paternoster, he could have kept control of him. As it was, we had to sacrifice a perfectly good groom by pushing him out of the circle. Tonight. You will call Asmodeus and cast a drawing spell for a marguerite."

"For a what?"

"For this humble little flower, here, that hides between the grasses and cannot spell. 'I live for the day of your return . . . I kiss this dear paper, since it will take you my words,'" he recited in a mocking falsetto. "I want this little one, this Margaret. I intend to pluck off her petals one by one before him— 'she loves me, she loves me not'—ah, fitting. Yes, fitting indeed. The sort of idea only a poetic mind might have." The Sieur d'Aigremont began to pull the petals from the rose one by one, sniffing each petal before he discarded it onto the patterned carpet. He composed his features in the expression of bland arrogance he favored for assessing newly purchased works of art.

"It's not easy to draw a person from beyond the sea. Not like getting a choirboy from the next seigneury."

"I want her." The Count's arched black eyebrows drew together in a threatening scowl, and a dangerous crimson began to stain his jowly, coarse face.

"Why, yes, yes, of course. It will be done tonight, exactly as you wish."

"Good. I want it soon. I dislike waiting." All at once he tore the remainder of the petals off the flower, and flung the stem to the floor.

"Soon, Margaret." His heavy, sensual red lips parted in a smile as he carefully crushed the head and stem of the rose beneath his gilded Spanish slipper.

"Mistress, there's two disreputable-looking men asking at the door for Mistress Margaret. Shall I send them away? Suppose they're informers?"

"Just a moment, Kat, did they leave their names?" I leaned forward eagerly from my embroidery frame. I was in the solar with Mistress Wengrave, who was spinning, and her two oldest girls, who were hemming sheets. The day was overcast, but the cool air was crisp and clean, for the strong wind that had brought the clouds had blown away the dank chimney smoke of the City. Through the open shutters, we could hear in the back garden the shrieks of smaller children at play, and, loudest of all, Cecily's voice.

"It's *mine*! You give it back or I won't play!"

"Aw, who made *you* the queen of everything?" a little boy's voice answered. It was Peterkin, Mistress Wengrave's fat little seven-year-old.

"I'm the smartest, and I know all the rules. You can't play without rules."

"Can *so*! Ow! You tell your sister to quit kicking!"

"So, give us back our ball!"

"*Catch* me!" The shrieking and whooping resumed.

"*I* got it for you, Cecily!" Walter's voice. And the rattle of play began again. Mistress Wengrave smiled.

"He's much stronger now, Margaret. It's a pleasure to hear him outdoors, instead of seeing him huddled all day by the fireside."

Kat, waiting by the door, shifted impatiently from foot to foot. "One of the men says he's Robert le Clerc, and he's brought the other to you with news."

"News!" I cried, and the embroidery frame clattered to the floor as I stood up too quickly.

"Now Margaret, remember what Master Wengrave said. Don't you go running to the door unescorted. Kat, I want two armed grooms in the hall beside her when they're shown in." Kat curtseyed and ran off.

When Robert and his friend were brought in, I could see why Kat had hesitated. Robert himself was not so bad, though his gray gown was threadbare and he had a hole in his hose. But the man who was with him was utterly astonishing. His chief garment was a strange, patched and repatched cloak, lined with catskins of every variety, parted to reveal a dark wool gown that looked as if it had once belonged to someone much shorter and fatter. And richer too. Beneath the patches on the filthy gown, you could see, like old crusts, the remnants of embroidery in some fancy foreign pattern. I decided the gown must have been either blue or green originally, though it certainly wasn't even close to either color now. The man's hose were a devastation, ending in feet that were shod in several layers of rags, wrapped about like bandages. In short, he looked as if the moths had been at him.

His face did nothing to improve the impression. A gray beard of varying lengths met the few wisps of white hair that remained growing about the edges of his head. His eyes, light blue, had an odd sparkle, as if he were a little mad. His skin was pink like a baby's. An old, mad baby. Had he really heard news of Gregory?

"You are Dame Margaret de Vilers, wife of Sir Gilbert de Vilers? My message is for no one else." He spoke in French.

"Yes, I am she," I answered in that language. My heart started to pound.

"I saw your husband in a cart with six other English prisoners, being transported through the streets of Orléans. People were throwing things at them, and the guards were striking right and left, shouting, 'Don't spoil their value,' though their hearts weren't in it."

"Go on."

"I was promised a rich reward." He stopped.

"You'll have it when the story's done."

"She's honest," interjected Robert.

"I'd just spotted a good opening, and was about to throw my rock, when I heard one of them—a big villainous-looking dark fellow—reciting in Latin. I knew the passage: Seneca. Well, that's certainly unexpected—especially from an English goddam. 'Hey, brother,' I shouted in Latin, 'what are you doing in a cart, instead of parsing Latin in a cozy schoolroom?'

"The same thing you're doing dressed up in rags and catskins. Scholarship has brought me low, brother." Then, before the guards drove me off, he said to go to London and leave a message at the Kendall House for Margaret de Vilers, saying his ransom had been bought by the Comte de St. Médard, who serves King Charles of Navarre. They were bound for the Comte's chateau in the Pyrenees. Since King Charles is currently allied with the English, he said he expected to be back home on parole eventually, but that I should bring you this message and receive a rich reward. Those were his exact words —'a rich reward.'" He looked expectantly at me.

"Go on."

"Rich, I said to myself. I haven't heard that word in a good long time. So I got passage as a pilgrim and begged my way all the way here from Dover."

Alive! He was alive and coming home!

"How long ago was it that you saw him?"

"Oh, more than a month, just before the Feast of the Assumption. Begging's the slow way to travel. Now, about that reward—"

"More than a month? Then why isn't he home already? Has something happened to him on the way?" I didn't like the look on Robert's face.

"Dame Margaret, I don't think he's on the way."

"What on earth do you mean?" I could feel myself becoming alarmed. So much hope, and now so much fear.

"It's true the Count is a feudatory of King Charles. Have you heard of him? No? I thought so. He's not called Charles the Bad for nothing. He's not a man to put your faith in. But the Count's worse. He's got a reputation among the scholars. A necromancer. An alchemist. People who visit him don't always come away; he's not a man whose hospitality I'd ever seek out, though he has a lordly reputation among the gentry."

"But Gregory can pay ransom. Men of good birth are always ransomed."

"Not by the Count." I put my hand over my heart. Suddenly I was freezing.

"I was promised a rich reward," prompted the man in catskins.

"Of course, you'll have supper," said Mistress Wengrave.

"Don't imagine I've traveled all this way for supper. I'm going to stick like a burr until I get my reward." Robert pulled on his cloak and tried to shush him as he grew more and more agitated.

"Your reward will be a good drubbing unless you mend your manners, you beggar." Mistress Wengrave grew haughty.

"No, no—that's not fair. He's brought good news—wonderful news. If you'll come with me, you'll get your reward. But you'll have to wait. It's in my house, and I have to get it out."

"What do you mean, Margaret? Those de Vilerses haven't left you so much as a pin, and they could be back any time and surprise you there. You know what Master Wengrave said. It's their house now, and the law won't be on our side if they get hold of you. It's not like the girls. He has rights, there. But you're a widow."

"Widow no more; it's Gregory's, and I have rights too."

"None that will withstand a shortsword, Mistress Margaret," pointed out Robert. "But I must say, these relatives of Brother Gregory's sound mercenary. No wonder he avoided them."

"It's them that got him in this fix."

"Nice family."

"That's been my thought too—and I've had more time than you to think it over."

"Enough, enough. I didn't come all this way to hear about families. The reward, you've promised."

"Very well, then. Since you won't wait—" I'd already felt the cold shadow of Master Kendall floating in the room. He always turned up for any conversation that looked interesting. When things got dull around me, that's when he went about town, snooping on his old friends, spying on former business rivals, poking into brothels and stews, inspecting his chantry to see if the priest was being neglectful, and generally being far more meddlesome than he'd ever been in life. Lack of occupation always had sat heavy on him.

"Master Kendall?"

"Over here, Margaret, on the bench by the fire." And I watched as the beloved form, so reassuring, swirled like mist.

"You were right." I could feel the others staring. Kat shuddered and crossed herself, and Mistress Wengrave clasped her hands together in agitation.

"Of course, Margaret. I'd never lie to you. Now, I suppose, you want the money."

"Yes, I need it. Travel money, ransom money. And back wages for the household. And now this fellow."

"Why is she talking into the air?" The scholar drew his cat-skin cloak tighter against the chill.

"Hsst. You shush. Margaret's not like other people. You should have left well enough alone and gone away."

"No, no," I interrupted. "Master Kendall never liked to be stingy. This fellow needs his reward."

But, of course, everyone was astonished. We took two grooms with us to keep watch, as we went out the kitchen door at Mistress Wengrave's. Even though it was midafternoon, the heavy clouds of a gathering storm had suddenly made it dark and dank. Crossing the garden and back alley between the houses, we found that Mistress Wengrave's gardener had put down his hoe and followed the odd procession. Oh, bother, I thought, all this and rain too. I clutched my billowing cloak to me and looked up at the glowering sky, where the black clouds were rolling as if in a boiling cauldron. As they saw the gate of our stableyard opened, our own outside grooms, who had been hurrying under cover, paused to stare and joined us. The low rumble of thunder and first heavy drops sent us all scurrying into our back kitchen door. Cook looked up first in pleasure, then alarm, as she saw the faces of the grooms. Then she silently left her pottage while the kitchen boy abandoned the knives he'd been sharpening to join the eerie, almost ceremonious party.

I paused at the screen that separated the kitchen door from the hall. "Where do we go now, Master Kendall?"

"The hearth first; there's a loose stone."

"The hearth?" The hall looked dark and forlorn. The kitchen boy had run to close the shutters as the wind began to blow gusts of pelting rain through the windows. The smell of damp dust and the rattle of rain on the roof made it seem even more gloomy. How different it had been in the days of Master Kendall's life, all garlanded and filled with feasting and mirth! "We'll need a candle," I said, staring into the sad shadows.

"Mistress, is that the ghost you're talking to?" Cook's voice sounded troubled as she brought the flickering candle, newly lit in the kitchen fire.

"Why, yes, of course. How did you know about him?"

"We thought he was back. We've missed him for some time. It was so reassuring, like, feeling him in the corners, and seeing him pass through the door. He was a good master, and we'd have him back anytime. But we thought you didn't see him. You never gave a sign of it before you left."

"It's different now, look. He says he hid your back wages under a stone in the hearth."

"Oh, then he *has* been gone." Cook shook her head ruefully. "Why, otherwise he'd know those fearsome fellows who carried you off came back and pried up all the hearthstones. 'These rich merchants always have money hidden,' said that fierce old knight. 'Believe me, I haven't burned cities for nothing. They're all alike, French, German, or English: pry up the hearth-stones.'"

I'd never seen Master Kendall's ghost angry before, but at this speech he swirled and crackled almost as fiercely as the Weeping Lady in one of her fits. The stirring wind he made extinguished the candle. Several people who could sense him hid their heads in their arms; Mistress Wengrave recited several Paternosters and the stableman crossed himself. The boy hurried back with the relit candle, and I held it high, peering into the darkened hall. The circle of light glittered on the clustered faces of the watchers.

"He asks you, did they look behind the paneling?"

"No, they never thought of that. When they found the gold, they left, gloating." A rolling peal of thunder and the crash of nearby lightning made me start.

"But—Gregory, did he gloat too?" I could feel my heart hurting. Is this what we must all come to, this dusty darkness?

"Oh, no, mistress. He's not like them at all; he looked as if he were going to a funeral." Cook looked sad at the memory, but then brightened. "But he asked me about my bird; he inquired after my sister's health; he remembered my leche lombard. He said no one could make anything to touch it, not even the Duke's own cook! Why, he remembered everything! So gracious! Who'd take the time to remember someone like me when they've got troubles of their own? Oh, he's a gentleman from top to toe, and inside as well, where it counts! I'll wait forever until you come back with him, good mistress, and so will everyone that's here." Will the steward had joined her, and Bess and Tom and all the others. They all nodded silently in agreement with her. My eyes felt damp. There are plenty of places these days for good people like that. Not many are as fortunate as I am in my household.

"Master Kendall says you can't wait without wages, so we must try the panel." Silently, Robert le Clerc took the candle and held it by the seamless paneled wall as I felt with my hands, listening for the soft sound in the air that was Master Kendall's voice. As he instructed me, I felt along the grooves and carving, while they all watched, awestruck. I tapped and put my ear to hear the hollow space, asking his directions as I maneuvered the intricately carpentered little hidden door open.

"Ah!" A breath passed through the watchers all at once, as the segment of panel came off in my hand, revealing a dark little hole behind it.

"Now, Margaret," Master Kendall's voice sounded calm, though the renewed rattle of rain on the roof made it difficult to hear. "Take the little bag right away without opening it and put it in your bosom. As I recall, there are ten or twelve good gold florins in it, if I'm not mistaken. You'll be needing that yourself, though I fear it's not enough. The larger bag is silver.

211

Open it before the company, and use it to pay my obligations. Even in death, it would shame me to be thought stingy."

So I plunged my hand deep into the hole, oblivious of spiders, and took out the bigger bag. While they were exclaiming, I stowed the little bag unnoticed. But when I'd paid everything, there was nothing but a single silver penny left. It certainly did look small, sitting there in the palm of my hand. Not enough. Not enough with twelve florins, either, even if they are good gold. Why, even if I could ransom him, it wouldn't be for this sum; it was all his own fault for going and getting knighted. It raised his price. I felt annoyed all over again, just thinking about it. And let me tell you how proud knights are of their ransoms. The more you cost, the more honor. And there are knights that set their ransom so high, they can't go home for ages, just so they won't be shamed when they return before their fellows. "I'm a big man, set me high," they say. And then they hunt and wench on parole with their captors, who are really more like hosts, while the folks at home scrimp and borrow. And, of course, folks who are judged not capable of raising ransom are chopped to pieces. So the arrangement, like most such arrangements, benefits the rich and not the poor.

"This won't do; I need an expert in money," I said to myself as I tucked the coin into the purse at my waist.

"Who's that? A banker? Master Wengrave knows of several very reliable ones." When Mistress Wengrave spoke, I realized with a start I'd been talking out loud.

"No," I said. "Bankers make loans, and there's not a one on the face of the earth who'd help me. I need someone who can pull money out of nowhere. I need Brother Malachi."

"This sounds altogether interesting," said Master Kendall's ghost, cheering up. "Margaret, you always were a young woman of infinite resourcefulness."

And so, that very afternoon in the pouring rain, Mistress Wengrave dispatched a boy to Mother Hilde's house to find out if Brother Malachi was home yet. And as the little creature dried himself out before the fire, we all exulted to hear that

Brother Malachi, with his usual cat's instinct for finding comfortable spots, had returned home with Sim just before the bad weather had set in, and was all abubble with good news.

"So you see, Brother Malachi, I have a very large-sized problem." I was seated on a bench by the fire, extending my damp shoes and mud-splashed hem toward the warmth. My muddy pattens stood on the hearthstones; the two grooms from Master Wengrave's were drying themselves off, too, and trying to pretend that they weren't listening. Brother Malachi was comfortably ensconced on a big cushion in the household's only chair; Mother Hilde and little Bet were on the bench beside me, stringing dried apples while Clarice, seated on a stool with a big basket on the floor beside her, finished her mending. In the corner behind the woodpile the cat was nursing a new litter of kittens. Peter and Sim, who were supposedly minding the fire under another one of Brother Malachi's experiments in the back room, had taken advantage of the diversion to stand in the door to listen. In short, the little room Hilde and Malachi called their "hall" was full of people and the smell of damp wool and cooking cabbage, the way it usually is in bad weather.

Brother Malachi was so full of his own good news that he found it difficult to listen. His face was all pink and round with contentment, but he managed to make it look long and sad as I spoke.

"Margaret, how many times have I told you that everything has two sides? I remember when you sat in this very place, weeping because the Bishop had put you out of business. And then what happened? Why, the richest old man in town proposed marriage so you could fix his gout on a permanent basis! You see? Two sides! In every bad thing, a good thing is hidden, if you know how to look."

"But, Brother Malachi, what if in every good thing, a bad thing is hidden? That's two-sided too." Brother Malachi's face clouded over for a moment, but then brightened again.

"It can't possibly be—for then inside the bad thing is hidden

213

another good thing. So you see, the bad things must be taken as opportunities. And where would we all be without opportunities? That is why the world becomes constantly better."

Mother Hilde sighed with pleasure. "Oh, Malachi, I never tire of hearing your philosophy. How fortunate I am to live with the wisest man in the world!" She rose from her work to put another log on the fire under the kettle, while Malachi waved his hands airily to explain his theory further. And as he explained his positives and negatives, rising always to a better state, his arms rose higher and his face grew happier. He hesitated briefly when he reached the point where he would have to choose between the comfort of remaining seated and the pleasure of standing to allow his hands to rise in elaboration of his theory concerning the improvement of the world. He rose but an inch briefly before he decided for comfort, wiggling his fingers toward the shining constellations between the bright, red-painted beams in the low ceiling to depict infinite height, and adding "and so forth and so on" to conclude his discourse as he sank with a satisfied plop back into his chair, which was located exactly beneath Ursa Major. The gaudy red and azure and the incongruous painted stars, more suited to a chapel or some nobleman's bedchamber, made the room somehow seem all cheerful and odd-looking, not unlike Brother Malachi himself.

"I'm afraid I'm too dense for your theory, Brother Malachi. It's all ideas, with no illustrations. Bad things turning into good, improving the world—that's too hard for me," I said.

"Let's take me for an example, then. Here I was, sweating and suffering on the road for an honest penny. The mule had got a stone in his shoe, my feet were sore, and Sim was getting a fever. That's the negative. The positive: We were near Southampton, where my old friend Thomas the Apothocary, who is one of the small circle of true philosophers and seekers, owed me money—so we'd stay with him. Perfect! We got to his house—it was in mourning. He'd died. A tragedy. And what's worse, all his equipment had been sold to pay his debts. Not a trace of his work left. And here he'd let me know he'd got as far as the peacock's tail. Can you imagine how much I wanted to see the work he had left? A tragedy—a tragedy of the first order. That's the negative. But remember the positive. Not only did his widow and daughter entertain us well for old times' sake, but it turned out he'd left me a book in his will. The positive! And wait until you see the book, Margaret. It contains the dream of my life."

"The Secret? He was after it too?" I was astonished. Brother Malachi put his finger across his lips and smiled.

"A wonderful book. He left me a letter. It seems he'd labored in vain over it. He couldn't read a word of it. And so he'd left it to me, the greatest living master of our art, to pay off his debt and to assist me in my search for the Ultimate. Who would have thought it from a sour, envious old tightwad like Thomas? But no, his last illness led him to a higher frame of mind. His wife, whom I last saw laboring in rags, was clad in a new dress, his daughter decently dowered, and even I—once the main object of his envy—had been remembered generously. Ah, thus do we reform when faced with the Infinite." Brother Malachi paused briefly for a pious prayer for Thomas's soul, and then continued. "But—in the positive, another negative. The entire text is unreadable. What, do you say, could be the positive? I plan a splendid and mentally enriching trip abroad in search of a translator."

"But, but—what about Hilde? And your household?"

"Why, that's the most positive of all—if Clarice hadn't come to us in a moment of need, then she would not be here to handle Hilde's business and look after Peter and the household." I looked at Hilde, who seemed very pleased, and Clarice, who nodded as if it had been all arranged. Outside, the rain had stopped, and we could hear the shutters on the second stories bang open, as women leaned out to get a bit of air and shout the most confidential gossip to each other across the muddy alley.

"Now, first, according to my theory, you must inspect your

difficulty from all sides," said Brother Malachi, fixing his eyes on me. He looked completely pleased with himself at the opportunity of demonstrating how his theory worked. Shrill voices rattled among the damp rooftops. Someone's goose was honking in the alley.

I looked at my hands. Gregory's narrow gold ring was on my left hand, and old Master Kendall's elaborate one on my right. "It seems pretty hard to me: my husband's given up for dead, and he may well be if I can't retrieve him. His lord wants to marry me off to someone else, his brother wants to kill me for the money Master Kendall left me, and I haven't the funds to get him back. So where do I begin?"

"It seems to me that there are two ways," said Brother Malachi. "One is easy and the other one difficult. So, let's deal with the easy one first. How do you feel about him, Margaret?"

"What do you mean?" There was a long, uncomfortable silence.

"I mean," Brother Malachi went on, "do you love him? The easiest way, you see, is simply to send a message to the Duke's court, telling them where you can be found." His eyes looked very shrewd, as if he were calculating something.

"Malachi!" Mother Hilde was indignant.

"I don't want another man, if that's what you're thinking about. Everybody seems to think that's all a woman needs. But it's him I love, and I don't want to give him up. Oh, I want him back so badly! I'd give anything to hear him grumping about Aquinas or see him prowling about the kitchen, sniffing in all the pots like a hungry wolf. He went and changed, Malachi—all he did was spout about honor and who sat where and whether he should have his personal coat of arms redone and, and, whether or not he should buy a stupid—pavilion. Can you believe it? And it was all bad for him. Just look how it came out."

"Oh, my. That sounds exactly like him, all right. He always did fling himself into whatever he was doing. Were they versifying in pothouses? Why, then he had to be the best—ha, I remember one time in Paris when he was carried through the streets after some triumph in a tavern poetry contest. Was metaphysics in fashion? Then he was the the most fluent elaborator of the *quattuor causae*. Then he heard about God-seeking. Ha! The most mystical mystic I ever met—until even the Carthusians wouldn't have him. Though why, I don't know. Nobody could outdo him for extravagantly ragged clothing and all-night vigils. Now, I take it, he's doing chivalry." Brother Malachi chuckled. "I imagine he's quite unendurable. He often is, at the height of these fancies. Though I must say, in all our long acquaintance, he never gave the impression that he had a family."

"Long acquaintance? You've known him a long time? I never knew that—he never let on, in all the time I talked about you."

"Talked about me? Oh, yes, the fable of the memoirs. Of all the surprises I've had today, by far the greatest is the possibility that he might have been telling me the truth when he said he met you by copying your memoirs. Really, Margaret, what ever put such a notion in your head? You haven't lived long enough to have anything to say. Imagine. And here I thought he was over there seducing you all this time." Brother Malachi shook his head as if there were no end to the wonders of the world. It annoyed me greatly, and I bit my lip so I wouldn't tell him I thought he was very unfair, and vulgar-minded too. He saw the look and laughed.

"Be fair, Margaret—who else but you would take such a fancy into her head? You have to expect people would believe the worst. Besides, when you told him about me, you probably didn't know I'd changed my name since I'd last seen him. That was quite a while ago, when I had to move on very suddenly—" Sadness crossed Brother Malachi's normally sunshiny face like a cloud, but was soon gone. "But I must say, I was mightily surprised when he turned up to borrow the money to abduct you. Something about hiring a horse. Goodness, I hadn't seen him since Paris, where he went about under the nom de guerre of Gilbert l'Escolier, writing scurrilous theological tracts and satirical verse. A man of singular talents, Margaret, the chief of

217

them being that he is always right and everyone else is wrong. Snobbish, obnoxious, and witty as the Devil—though I never thought he was interested enough in women to make off with you in that way. And half of London in pursuit! That Gilbert's never managed to leave any city without a scandal yet. Did I ever tell you how they burned his book in Paris? The idiot! He told me he had twelve irrefutable theological proofs that they were wrong—so of course he stayed and they caught him. Impractical—yes, eternally impractical and stubborn, is Gilbert the Righteous."

"It seems that we see him about the same way." I sighed. "Now, how do I get him back?" Brother Malachi looked speculatively into the air.

"Well, Margaret—that's the difficult way. It seems to me that we might combine all of our problems into one supreme solution: yes—yes, it makes sense. Of course, there's the expense—but—hmm. How many florins did you say? Ten? Yes. Multiplication is in order, especially if you're to go with us."

"Oh, you can multiply it—I just knew you could. Can you make enough to buy him back?"

"Not from the Comte de St. Médard, Margaret. He's eccentric, and already rich. He probably has some completely superfluous reason for not setting the ransom already. But—and here's the useful part—admit, Margaret, you couldn't do without me—he's well known to us hunters of the Green Lion. So I imagine I might very well be able to work a trade. I'll offer him the one thing he simply can't refuse, and back it up with what's left of my reputation. Did you know I was once celebrated, Margaret? And then, having retrieved Gilbert, it's heigh-ho for the great centers of learning and my translator."

"I don't understand, Brother Malachi. Hunters of the green lion? Trading? And why can't you get a translator in England, anyway?"

"Ah, thrifty, thrifty little Margaret. Your head's transparent, as usual, and I can see all the thoughts in it. You're thinking about the last of your florins, aren't you? Do you think I'd hoodwink you like some foolish bumpkin from the country? Aren't we old enough friends, Margaret, for you to know I don't practice my skills on my own family? Yes—you're a sort of family, just like Clarice and little Bet here. Things haven't changed just because you left for a grander life."

"I'm sorry, Malachi. I guess it was small of me. I've just been around Gregory's relatives too much."

"Very well, apology accepted. Come into my laboratorium; I'll show you my book, and that will convince you of everything." He looked toward the low door to the back room and for the first time noticed Sim. It was odd about Sim; even though it had been several years since I first saw him, he'd never really grown. He was still as short as an eight-year-old, though I'd figure him to be anywhere from twelve to fourteen or so. His head was large and a little misshapen, his teeth had gaps between them when he smiled, and he had the shrewd, dark little eyes of a boy who'd grown up fending for himself on the street. But he'd taken to us like a stray cat when we'd fed him, long ago, and from that day to this, he'd stuck to Brother Malachi like a burr. Sim had been listening, taking in everything on the quiet, the way he always does.

"Sim, you devil! Why aren't you minding the fire? I tell you, if it's gone cold, you've ruined it! Heaven save me from the lazy tricks of apprentices!" Sim scampered into the laboratorium ahead of us and poked up the fire with a great show of energy, while I ducked to follow Brother Malachi through the open door to the back room. Mother Hilde followed us and shut the door, so the grooms wouldn't hear.

"It's not as if I haven't hunted far and wide for a translator here," he said, puffing, as he removed a stack of books from the top of a little chest hidden in the corner of his oratorium. "Pothooks, I said to myself, looks as if it might be Hebrew. I'll take it to the university at Oxford. Seems there was a fellow named Benjamin Magister, a Jew with a license to remain in the kingdom to translate the Old Testament. He was dead. Found some dismal doctor of theology who looked down his

Judith Merkle Riley

nose at me and said since the Old Testament was already translated, there was no need for any more Jews at the university. Phoo! What kind of scholar is that? Made inquiries. Went off on a hunt for one Isaac le Convers, said to be in Sussex somewhere, finally found his elderly daughter—she couldn't read a word."

Malachi lifted the little chest and put it carefully in the middle of his worktable. Then, as he rummaged about for the key, he continued.

"I chased all over the realm, leaving no stone unturned. Finally I was so desperate I came back to London and betook me to the Domus Conversorum, even though everyone knows there hasn't been a convert there for a generation. Once the king had the Jews driven out, there was no need to maintain a house for converts. Except that by then it made a nice income for the Warden of the Domus, renting out the rooms. 'Oh, no,' says the Warden, 'I've done my duty as a Christian—I've got a Spanish sailor here on full allowance who says he's planning to convert.' Ha! What people won't do to keep a position—especially a cushy one like his! So I spent nearly a day with this fellow, who calls himself Janettus of Spain. He really was Jewish. 'Oh, my, this is too difficult for me,' he said. 'I'm a simple man, and only know a few prayers—this is full of arcana. I can't make out a word. You need a great translator and scholar, the greatest in the world. You need Abraham the Jew.' I was all ablaze. 'Where can I find him?' 'Oh, he moves about. When I heard of him he was living in Salamanca—but some say he was invited to Paris by the King of France, others that he went to Montpellier, or perhaps he is at Avignon, by invitation of the Pope.' Hazy he was, entirely hazy. But it's clear. Spain or France. He's somewhere. I'll find him. Take him into my confidence. The Secret—I feel it's so close that I wake up at nights, trembling all over."

Brother Malachi had at last located the key, and opened the little chest, lovingly taking out a packet wrapped in oiled silk. He cleared a space among the jars and odd-looking vessels of smoky, swirly colored glass on his table, and wiped it clean with his sleeve. Then he laid the packet reverently in the space. Hilde and I leaned close to him on the high table, to watch him unfold the silk.

"Now, take a look at this, Margaret, and you'll understand everything—and cease worrying about the fate of your florins. Of course, you'll both have to keep it secret that I'm carrying it —especially when we reach the Count's. He's perfectly capable of making sure I have no more earthly need for it. There are many of us who would do in a brother—to get their hands on this."

"Of us? Surely you wouldn't do such a thing!"

"Oh, not me. But 'by us' I mean the whole alchemical fraternity. You have no idea how frantic some of my brother philosophers can get. They'd sell anything, even their children, drive any bargain—even with the Devil, in some cases—or try any method, no matter how unsavory. You'd be surprised—fetuses, babies' blood, virgin's sweat—you name it, they'll try it! Hmph! Not scientists at all! How do they expect to get results working at random like that? Now, I use the theory of Signs when I search, that, and the guidance of the Ancients, who were so much wiser than us. No, like so many others, the fools among us, too, are driven mad with the pursuit of gold. But even so, we're a tightly knit group. We have to be—when outsiders hear what we're doing, they very often arrange a kidnapping, or a bit of a torture session for information."

"Oh, I never had any idea. I thought it was dangerous because of the heresy in it."

"Oh—that." Brother Malachi waved a hand to dismiss the notion. "Some say it is, some say it isn't. It's quite illegal in some places. In others, like this realm, the king says, 'The more gold, the better; let them work.' There's even a pope was one of us, they say. But there are ruthless, money-hungry people who would do anything at all to get their hands on the secret of Transmutation."

"Well, I must say, I know something about that. Everything

that's happened to me lately is because of money, one way or another. Transmutation is obviously worse."

"Exactly. But we aren't stupid—we put everything in code. Those who aren't adepts can't figure out a word. We have passwords, secret signs of recognition, and a lot of other things I'll never tell you about. And we adepts never refer to what we are doing directly—we use other terms. One of them is 'hunters of the Green Lion.' If you'll open the book, I'll show you why."

Malachi had unwrapped the oiled cloth. Inside it lay an old-looking leather-bound book, with heavy metal clasps, set with semiprecious stones. He opened the book, and the acrid stink of old dust and long-gone workrooms rose from its yellowing parchment pages. Between rows of faded brown unreadable pothooks, the still bright colors of startling illuminations shone in glory.

"Oh!" I was quite taken aback. It was magnificent, glittering and mysterious. I could feel it holding and drawing me, as if it had a secret power of its own.

"Feel it?" Brother Malachi said. "I do too. It's the Book of the Secret. It's in there—I know it—and I can't read a blessed word of it." Brother Malachi's eyes half closed, and he entered a state of reverie most unlike him. "It will bring us our dreams. It will shape our fate," he murmured, passing his hands over the pages, as if the writing itself was so powerful that it gave off the perception of warmth. "Here—the end of my quest. And yours, too, Margaret."

"But if you can't read it, how do you know it's got the Secret?"

"By the illuminations, Margaret. They're code. Alchemists' code. The text, obviously, explains the pictures and gives directions for achieving the various stages of the process. See here—" He opened a page at random near the beginning of the book.

"Brother Malachi! This isn't a book about alchemy at all! It's a book of dirty pictures! For shame!"

"No, no, Margaret. I told you it's code. This is the mystical marriage of Sol and Luna—the Sun and the Moon. You can tell because they're wearing crowns. The Sun is gold, the Moon is silver—just as Mars is iron, Mercury is quicksilver, and each of the seven metals is one of the seven planets. Sol must impregnate Luna in order to get the Stone."

"The Philosopher's Stone? This dirty picture gives you instructions?"

"Well, I need the text too. It's not explicit enough in the picture."

"I should think that's plenty explicit. What about this one, where they're lying naked in the bathtub, hugging each other?"

"That's not a bathtub, that's a tomb."

"Well, it certainly fooled me. They look perfectly content, even if they are bathing with their crowns on."

"You should observe more closely, Margaret. The code is in the details. For example, how many sets of feet do you see?"

"Oh, how nasty! Just one set between them. Ugh!"

"That's because this is a picture of the alchemical death. Sol and Luna must lie together after being wed, and die together, to be reborn as one single person of mingled essences—that's why they're drawn as a hermaphrodite; they're all mixed together, if you look closely. They must perish to be renewed— that bird there, that's the spirit. Then they give birth to the spiritual body, which has mastery over all the elements."

"But there's lots more pictures here—what's this one?"

"If I knew that, I'd be that much closer to the Secret. The Virgin being swallowed up by serpents. That's the trouble with code. It's hard to read. Now this one at the end, after the Peacock's Tail, that's the making of the Red Powder. That's the stuff I'm after."

"Powder? I thought it was a stone."

"Only in a manner of speaking. It's really a red powder, water without being wet. I have other works that are quite explicit about that."

"Oh, look. This one's a dragon."

"That dragon, I have. And it does indeed eat metals. I've got it in that glass jar over there. It would eat its way through anything else."

"It's a liquid?"

"Of course. I told you this is code. The bathtub, as you call it, is my crucible."

"So it's all in here? The secret of making gold?"

"No, Margaret. The secret of Transmutation is a far bigger secret than simply making gold. Though, of course, you can use it to make base metals into gold if you want to—which is why most people want it. Transmutation isn't just for metals."

"You mean, it changes other things too?"

"Yes, all kinds of things into other things."

"But all kinds of things are themselves, not something else. A pot's a pot, and a spoon's a spoon."

"Oh, yes, for now they are. But the pot was clay, and will be powder some day. And the spoon used to be tin, and if you melt it, it's tin again. So by applying heat, you transmute it. But if you keep on heating it and fooling with it, you can get it down to its basic elements, or essence. There are only four essences on earth, four things that never change: earth, air, fire, and water. Everything else is made of them, but mixed together in characteristically different proportions, you understand."

"I think I see—like a cake. You stir the ingredients together differently, and you've got something else."

"Yes, that's it, Margaret." Brother Malachi's face, as he spoke, had changed. He was never a beautiful person. Cheery, but not beautiful. But as he grew serious, explaining the workings of nature, the light of intelligence shone in his face, and the love of the ideas he spoke of made him beautiful. It made me see why Hilde loved him.

"But cakes don't transform. They just rot. You can't make gold from a cake."

"A cake's not metal. The character of metal is not to rot—but it's one of the characteristics of cakes to be transformed in this manner."

"Or to be eaten."

"Oh, yes, to be eaten"—he smiled and patted his stomach—"but that's an entirely different transformation." A singey smell had penetrated the laboratorium.

"Oh, my cakes, they're burning!" Mother Hilde hurriedly took her elbows from the table, where she had been leaning beside us to see the book, and sped to the fireplace in the hall, where she found Clarice had already snatched off the griddle with the cakes. Malachi was entirely unperturbed, as he was in the face of most domestic difficulties.

"Burning is a process that transforms cakes, too—but have you ever wondered *why* things transform? That's what I'm after. Not the what, but the why," he went on.

"Do you know why?"

"We all know why in general, we alchemists, but it's the specifics that have eluded us. You see, there's a fifth essence—another element."

"Another?"

"Yes, but it's not on earth. Haven't you ever wondered what the stars are made of? They never change. The heavens are made of special stuff—celestial stuff that is entirely different than anything on earth. I'm oversimplifying a bit for you, Margaret, so you'll understand, but I know you can—Hilde does. The stuff of the heavens—there's a little tiny bit of it present in every earthly thing. Not much, just like the salt in the cake, or the stew, or whatever. But it's the little bit of the fifth essence—the quintessence, we call it—in a thing that allows it to transform. So, to make a long story short, if I can get the quintessence out of something, I can apply it to any substance, and that will make it transform itself into its higher form."

"I see—so a base metal turns into gold, which is higher."

"Exactly. But, of course, that would be just one very ordinary transformation."

"Oh, yes, I see now. Would it work on people, Brother Malachi?"

"It ought to—haven't you wondered why people decay and die? The Philosopher's Stone I seek would heal the sick, since

225

wellness is the higher state of mankind. It would rejuvenate the old—why, people might be able to live thousands of years!"

"Thousands of years? Wouldn't that get dull?"

"Not if you could transform the mind—the highest state of the mind is wisdom, Margaret. People could become wise—in thousands of years you could find a lot of wisdom."

"Could you make them good, too, Brother Malachi?"

"Why, yes, I suppose, that too."

"So it's not really gold you're after, then. That's just a small thing."

"The smallest in the world, Margaret. Who needs gold? Well —I do, for my experiments, and to buy a pie or a winter cloak, which is why I'll make gold first. But gold isn't really the important thing. No, not in the least."

I turned the pages again, looking at the enigmatic pictures. Very near the end of the book was the strangest picture of all. A lion, all in green, swallowing up the sun.

"Look, Malachi, here's your Green Lion. What's he doing there, swallowing up the sun?"

"The Green Lion. So very near the end. He's the symbol of Transmutation, Margaret. He's very hard to make. I have a bit of him in a flask too. There's a method—the method in here, once I can read it, of getting him to swallow up Sol—now, you should know—who is Sol?"

"Gold, isn't it. So you eat up gold to get gold?"

"The Green Lion is the most powerful of the beasts of transformation—much more powerful than the Dragon. Only he can swallow the sun, the noblest and the only incorruptible metal, to release its quintessence—the Stone, the Red Powder of Transformation. That is the page of the Secret, Margaret. It's there—there with the Green Lion."

I traced the outline of the Green Lion with my finger. There was something oddly compelling about him.

"I have to have him, Margaret, just as you have to have your Gilbert back again. So, if you'll allow me to transform your florins, then we can take you with us. There's a ship leaving for

Bayonne as soon as the master finds enough cargo, which should be before the week's out. That gives me just enough time for the multiplication. Oh, no—I don't need all ten. Take these two, and get yourself a pilgrim's cloak, hat, and staff, and anything else you think you'll need. Oh, yes, you'll be wanting your own pillow and blankets on shipboard, and get some biscuits or something that will keep, so you won't go hungry if there's nothing but salt meat. You do think Master Wengrave will look after your girls, don't you?"

"As if they were his own." I could feel my heart sinking. This was the worst idea I'd ever heard of. Leave my babies? Go someplace horrid and full of foreigners? Well, if I had to, who better with than Malachi and Hilde? Malachi spoke so many languages. Besides, he had a way of always landing on his feet in any strange place that made him the ideal traveling companion. Oh, why couldn't Gregory just bring himself home, like proper people do? A reason—there must be a reason I couldn't go.

"But, but—don't I need travel permission from the Bishop?"

"Of course you do—and you'll have it too. After all, I write indulgences from the Pope every day. A letter from the Bishop is nothing. Why, I've even got a plaster cast of his seal somewhere around here." He rummaged around in a box, and came up with several casts he'd made of official seals, along with the papal seals that he'd had forged in metal abroad. "It will look quite official. Margaret—de Vilers, is it?—permission to go on pilgrimage. Oh, yes, I never travel without a sackful of good-looking documents." Then he caught sight of my face.

"What's wrong, Margaret? Are you frightened? You? I saw you walk on live coals once for far less. Now me—I have a right to be frightened. I'm getting on, you know. I love my ease, and my Hilde, and my cozy house. But if I'm not a fool who's wasted my life, then I'll pursue the Green Lion wherever he leads, even to the end. Now you, you say you love Gilbert and want him back. But if you're too frightened to make the attempt, then say it now, and I'll try myself, for your sake and for the sake of an old friendship. Though I haven't the luck you've got in these matters. Say now—will you stay here?"

My mind was whirling. My head was pounding. Pounding like the hoofbeats of pursuing soldiers. I hesitated. "I—I think —they're safer at Master Wengrave's even without—without me. I could be killed. Or carried off and forced to marry. Then he'd die there. It's me—it's me that heard him calling, not anyone else. No—I need to go. I have to go. It's the only way I see. God forgive me."

Deep within the castle on the crags, in a hidden laboratorium located just above the torture chambers, Messer Guglielmo Petrini, adept of the Great Work, philosopher, alchemist, and sometime conjuror of demons and spirits, was twitching all over with annoyance. "Call Asmodeus again?" his irritated voice shrilled above the steady creaking and puffing of an immense bellows apparatus, worked by a huge mute who heaved upon a rope-and-pulley system. "What does he take me for, a fool? I told him that's positively the last time—the demon grows too strong." The little man's dark, tightly curled hair, bristling eyebrows, and stiff beard all quivered with irritation, as an eyelid twitched in sympathy with the left corner of his scornful upper lip. "I tell you, I deserve respect. If all he wants is back-country spells, he should hire the local wisewoman, not the world's most celebrated alchemist. And if he wants gold in a hurry, he should loosen his purse strings a bit and get me some decent equipment and proper assistants. Six masked mutes! The idea!"

He gestured with disdain at the apparatus that stood about him in the hidden laboratorium. The aludel was aboil atop the athanor, dripping its distillate into a copper vessel. Two cauldrons stood on the open hearth, brewing unspeakable smells. Objects both repulsive and familiar were suspended from the walls and ceiling, and above an assortment of glass and pottery vessels, as if to catch their essence—bat wings, large beetles, and sheets of beaten copper growing green in the fumes of the acid beneath them. Atop the worktable stood an open book, greasy with fingerprints and candle droppings, propped to display a complex drawing of pentacles and overlapping circles. The room was an unusually wide one, hidden behind a tiny iron door in the depths of a great tower. Its floor of black tile glistened with the orange lights of the reflected fires, but the room's low ceiling, supported by massive stone arches, seemed perpetually lost in shadow. Burned-out torches in brackets and the melted ends of candles stuck on top of each other in niches in the wall were testimony that this was a place of much night work.

At this speech, Fray Joaquin shrugged his black-cloaked shoulders. "If he had an endless supply of money, do you think he would have hired you to make gold? You had best hurry it up; his losses supporting King Charles in the north have been immense—to say nothing of his gambling losses, and what he spent on that pageant of the seasons that he wrote."

"Did I tell him he had to be King of the Poets? Visiting foreign courts all smelling like a perfumery, chanting epics and having his rivals strangled! Now tell me, do you think that's a respectable occupation for a warlord? And all the while, I have to do with the most inept glassblower this side of purgatory. And clothing! Look at this! He promised me two new gowns a year, and a fur-lined cloak. Cheap stinking wool cut from dead sheepskins. And I imagine it was used before I got it."

"It was used; he impaled the previous alchemist who wore it. And let me warn you, you've delayed too long. And now you balk at calling Asmodeus again. You won't like it if you anger the Count."

"Anger? Why anger him? Just tell him that we've done the job, but that the demon was slow and cranky. Then send a fast messenger to the man's family with a ransom message, saying that the ransom will only be accepted from the hand of his wife, Margaret. The same thing will happen, and we run no risks. The man's a fool. I've told him often enough, he's thinned the ether here too much with his constant experiments—it's dangerous, playing games with one of the most powerful spirits of the infernal. Next time, it won't just be bruises we'll be getting. Asmodeus may very well break free into the world. Tell me, do you remember where the letter was from?"

"Of course. I wrote it down, just to make no mistake." Fray Joaquin drew a wax tablet from his sleeve.

"Then you thought of doing the same thing yourself?"

"Naturally. I'm not stupid. You think calling up devils gets results? If it did, we'd have gold already. Devils, they live to deceive. What makes him think Asmodeus wouldn't deceive us too? So what have we got? Nothing but stink, mess, and bruises. Sending a messenger is much more likely to do the job."

"It's a long way, practically at the end of the earth," said Messer Guglielmo, scrutinizing the tablet. "What civilized place would be called 'Bruksfurd Manr'?"

"I thought we'd send Fray Raphael. After all, he took a vow of poverty, so it's time he experienced a little hardship."

"But the Sieur d'Aigremont needs him in the secret chamber —he has no excuse for leaving—though I'd love to be rid of him for a while. What a whiner. He comes up here to complain, usually when I'm in the middle of some very difficult experiment, and can't be disturbed. The air's bad down there, he whines. You've got it lucky. Lucky! Slaving all day and all night, sweating in the heat! No ventilation! Horrible smells! Clumsy bumpkins for assistants! No proper food, just a bite on the run! I'm worn to the bone! Just look at me!" He looked down at the offending gown, and saw a gray hair in his long, rough black beard. He plucked it out with an injured look. "Gray! I grow aged in the service of this ungrateful patron!"

"If you knew what went on in the secret chambers, you'd not complain."

"What do I need to know? As long as he gets me the right fixative, it's not my business how he does it. Unless, of course, he ignores my advice and manages to make a hole big enough for Asmodeus to come through. Apart from that, my only concern is my science. Who says wisdom ever comes without a price? And I'm paying it—suffering, suffering."

"You'd do better if you suffered a little more silently, Messer Petrini. If he thinks you know anything at all, you won't go free when the gold's made."

"They go in, they never come out. What do I care? They're only peasant brats. There's too many of them in the world already. They breed like rabbits, these lower orders."

"Well then, I suppose the only likely one to go is me. That's what I feared." Fray Joaquin sighed. "I'll tell him I heard of some pretty blond ones in the north, and I've gone to inquire after them. That's the only kind he wants, anyway, and they've grown rather scarce around here."

That evening, accompanied only by a tall deerhound, Fray Joaquin set off for England on the fastest horse in the stable.

"Mama, that's an ugly cloak. Why didn't you buy a pretty one?" Alison was poking through my purchases as I spread them out on the bed in the upstairs room at the Wengrave house. It was hard to hear her, because she was wearing the hat. It was not only very nearly the width of her outstretched arms, but came down well over her chin. The strings hung to her waist.

"It's a pilgrim's cloak, silly." Cecily was inspecting the money belt and heavy shoes. "It makes you look holy when you're traveling. Then everybody helps you and nobody hurts you."

"Nobody will hurt my mama. She's pretty. Besides, Brother Malachi will touch all the bad people with his magic wand. Poof! Then he'll turn them into frogs."

"Who says?"

"Sim told me. Brother Malachi can do anything."

"Mama, you'll come back soon, won't you?" Cecily's voice was troubled.

"Of course she will," Alison's little voice piped from beneath the hat as she clambered up and plumped herself on the bed. "Mama never forgets us. She'll bring presents and sweets. I want a new white pony and five colors of hair ribbons, mama. Remember I like red and green best. No brown."

"Yes, I'll be back just as soon as ever I can. Remember I'll be thinking of you and praying for you every night, and be good for Mistress Wengrave."

"Not—easy," announced Alison, kicking her plump little feet, shod in quilted wool slippers, on the side of the bed. " 'Stand up! Bow down! Quiet now! *Sof*-ter voice, Alison!' Mistress Wengrave is *ve*-ry bossy! She's the *bossiest*!"

"Not as bossy as step-grandfather. *Nobody's* as bossy as *him*," Cecily corrected her sister.

Was it imagination, or was Alison distinctly pudgier than she'd been a month ago? Cecily was growing again. Her skinny shins were peeping beneath her hem. I need to let it down again, I thought. There's one more turn in it before Alison gets it. Maybe I'll trim it with ribbon when I put the hem up again for Alison. Then it will seem more like a new dress. Oh, God, France is so far away. Suppose I don't live to turn up Alison's hem? Who will remember that she doesn't like hand-me-downs unless they're made pretty for her? No, it can't happen that way. It mustn't happen. I couldn't help the tears that came up in my eyes as I embraced them yet another time and said, "You must never be afraid. God has sent His angels to watch over you while I'm gone."

"Angels? Can they make buns too?" And Alison, ever distractible, sat herself down to play with my beads and sing the baby song about all the things that go in a cake.

"Don't worry, mama. I'm big. I'll look after Alison. I can do anything."

"—and saf-fron, and su-gar—"

"You're mama's brave, big girl. Remember, I rely on you—"

"—I'm big too—and *cin*namon—" Alison went on singing.

"I can do anything a grown-up can do. Even grown-up men were afraid of the big horse. But I wasn't. And *I* rode him. I can do anything." Cecily's eyes were serious. She meant exactly what she said.

"You know that I don't want to leave, don't you?"

"I know you have to. I know why too. I hear them whispering in corners when they think I don't understand. About the convent, and the lawsuit, and the bad people trying to steal away the dowry money our papa left us for marrying. You will come back, won't you? And then it will be all fixed?"

"Of course it will. And Master Wengrave is your godfather and your papa's dear friend. You know you are safe here, and he wants only your good?"

"I know." Cecily rubbed her eyes hard. She had become old —too old for a little girl. But sometimes that's what has to be.

"—and ten-ty, 'leven-ty *pounds* of *rai*-sins," sang Alison. "Not bad. I made that part extra all myself. The cake in the song is *not* good enough the old way."

"Is that all you think about—food?" said Cecily righteously.

"Oh, no. I think about mama coming back. Because she will," said Alison calmly, looking at her sister as if she didn't understand anything at all.

CHAPTER
8

Fray Joaquin arrived at Brokesford Manor mud-stained and infuriated by a lost week of searching for this hole at the end of the earth. The natives were savages: when they spoke French at all, it was some beastly variant of Norman dialect, admixed with the native tongue. Fray Joaquin's rolling Provençal, spiced with the occasional Spanish phrase, went entirely uncomprehended. People poked each other and pointed when he asked directions. Or worse, they'd guffaw rudely. He was tired of picking the bedbugs out of his clothes and pack after a miserable night jostled by filthy strangers in the sagging beds of a series of wretched inns. At last he'd found a village priest with a bit of Latin. Barely enough for the Mass, and to say "yes," "no," and point directions. But it was enough to inform him he was in the correct neighborhood, and Brokesford Manor lay half a day's ride to the north.

As usual, even in this little village, it was his horse that excited admiration, rather than himself. A dappled gray Spanish barb, built for speed, with a dainty, square Arab nose and wide-set brown eyes like a woman's. He'd grown used to seeing a circle of gawkers form around it to comment on its points wherever he left it, and to take extra precautions against its theft. Usually, the bared teeth of the massive deerhound were enough to keep people at a distance. Pigs who rode on nothing better than plowhorses ought to stare when they saw what a real horse looked like. Fray Joaquin, who had supervised the breeding stable of one of the most elegant abbots in Castile before coming into the service of the Sieur d'Aigremont, had a fine eye for breeding stock—almost as fine as his eye for selecting a pretty child. Now these English horses were badly bred—but the children he'd seen were quite attractive. Light-haired and rosy-cheeked, the way his Seigneur preferred them. It was a pity he'd come for a woman, when he could probably pick up several children with much less trouble, but business is business.

As he approached the manor he took note of the heavy horses in the pasture and stallion pens. Not bad, not bad. The man knew what he was doing, but the breed needed more depth in the chest still, and more refinement about the head. A barb stallion was what they needed—the very sort he preferred himself—then you could breed up the size later, when you had the conformation right. A little goose girl with a switch drove her charges beside the road. Barefoot in the freezing autumn mud, she stood barely as tall as the geese. Blond ringlets peeped from beneath her coarse wool hood, and she stared at the strange horse and rider. Fray Joaquin took professional note of her rosy cheeks and wide blue eyes. Yes, it was a pity.

At the manor, his welcome was less than adequate, though, of course, what could be expected from the so-called noblesse of this backward place? The lord of this tumbledown heap of a house appeared to have his bed set up in the hall, like some ancient lord in a centuries-old romance. True, he had the excuse he was dying from wounds and couldn't be carried up the narrow circular stair. But wouldn't it be more dignified to be carried up to die decently than insist on going on living in this squalor? Humph, Fray Joaquin sniffed to himself as he looked at the hams hanging from the ceiling, I'm surprised they don't keep live chickens in this hall. It wouldn't add to the disorder in the least.

Behind the screen, a menagerie of hounds and hawks surrounded the old lord where he lay propped up on pillows to receive the visitor. A bitch had given birth to a new litter of puppies in the straw under the huge bed. True, there was a hollow-cheeked son skulking about somewhere, but he'd been barely civil. He'd sent his garish little wife to the door to greet Fray Joaquin, and she'd snubbed him even before he'd had time to state his mission. They already had noble guests, she'd said, and she hoped he hadn't brought any company with him. Fray Joaquin loved the proper ceremony, and wasn't used to being taken for a wandering friar. As the well-born servant of a great lord, he'd expected at least a foot-bath in welcome. But these people didn't seem like the bathing sort.

Most insulting of all, the old lord did not rise even an inch from where he lay in his bed in greeting, even though it was clear he was not even a knight banneret, and hardly looked that ill anyway. He lacked the scent of death that a man lying so long wounded should have. He was incredibly thin, but his eyes glittered with a somewhat malicious intelligence, and two feverish little spots of pink marked his high cheekbones. And the way he dispatched servants and heard petitioners, undressed save only for a napkin on his head and a vast fur coverlet pulled up to his shoulders, looked entirely too gleeful. A spider in the center of his web, thought Fray Joaquin. This so-called dying man runs everything behind the son's back. And something is wrong with the son; he's all disheveled and looks half mad, with those hollow, burning eyes.

Fray Joaquin, who lived by his talent of instantly discerning the politics of great houses, took in the scene behind the screen in a flash, as he stood waiting to be introduced. And who was the knight in richly embroidered crimson velvet, sitting on the bed? Doubtless the noble visitor. But an old friend—perhaps a companion-in-arms, to judge by the age, and the wolfish grins the two shared, as if they had just finished enjoying a joke.

The knight was in fact Sir William Beaufoy, come from the Duke's household to tell Hugo that his time was up. Since he had not produced Margaret, he must go himself to Sir Geoffrey de Courtenay, the Duke's lieutenant in Lincolnshire, to explain precisely why he had failed to deliver her. The distasteful duty was one made palatable in Sir William's mind by the news that his old friend Sir Hubert still lived, and he might yet comfort him on his deathbed. It had been a shock, but a wonderful one, to see that the gray pallor of death had vanished from his old friend's face, that he sat, ate, and drank, and that his mind was whole again.

"A little spiced wine, a lot of disgusting boiled water with ugly herb leaves floating in it to drink. Smelly poultices, and not a decent roast—just some horrible soup. She left the recipes with Wat before she fled and he's been a tyrant about it. I can't get a soul to bring me a proper bite to eat. But I must admit I'm feeling better."

"We at the Duke's household suspect Hugo of murdering her."

"Murder? Stuff and nonsense. She's hidden herself as I told her to. Hugo's in no shape to do murder just now, anyhow. Look at him! All skin and bones! He's got worries of his own, these days. Marriage worries."

"From what I saw, that woman needs a good hiding."

"Oh, he's in more trouble than that. You should hear him walking about at night like a spook. Sometimes he howls. 'My soul, I've damned my soul!' Pfah! He deserves it all. I always told him a real man can get what he wants without promising anything."

"That aside, Sir Hubert, it's a surprise to see you so much better."

It was then that they glanced up to see the cold, dark eyes of Fray Joaquin assessing them with a detached, analytical look. Something about the man looked sinister. It wasn't just the darkness of the cloaked figure, or the black Dominican hood that shadowed the grayish, drawn face. It was something—perhaps just an illusion—that seemed very odd. The glancing beams of autumn sunlight from the window behind the screen seemed somehow to stop short of him, by just a little, as if the light refused to touch him, before it passed on to make a pale yellow splash on the floor. Both the men noticed it, and Sir Hubert shivered slightly, for he had seen the face of death too closely, and too recently, not to know what it meant.

"I have come with news of your son, Sir Gilbert de Vilers. He is held at the chateau at St. Médard-les-Rochers by the Sieur d'Aigremont, Comte de St. Médard, who has stated that he will accept the ransom only from the hand of the fair Dame Margaret, his wife, in person."

Despite his rolling accent, the two knights comprehended at once his meaning. Sir Hubert's face turned rosy with the unexpected joy. He sat up and leaned forward so suddenly that the covers dropped all the way to his navel.

"Gilbert! Alive! Thank the great God above!"

But Sir William, who had had bitter experience ransoming a son from the French, replied smoothly, "Why does not the great and wealthy Sieur d'Aigremont, to whom the ransom of a simple knight must be as a grain of sand on the seashore, release him on parole, to raise and return his own ransom?"

"Ah, that," replied Fray Joaquin diplomatically. "My most noble lord enjoys his company so much, he hates to let him go. They share in common an interest in poetry."

"Ah, yes," answered Sir William in the same bland tone. "I thought perhaps I recognized the name. Is not the Sieur d'Aigremont that princely soul, as renowned for his lordly hospitality as for his exquisite songs? Is he not called by those of great taste the noble trouvère—or was it the Prince of Poets—if I am not mistaken?"

"I am delighted that his reputation has crossed the sea. He is precisely that lord."

"Gilbert has been living in luxury, harping and singing love ballads, while I worried myself into the grave!" Sir Hubert had become instantly wrathy. Sir William shot him a warning glance. "Don't look at me like that! I know the ungrateful whelp all too well."

"Don't forget, I do too," said Sir William between his teeth. For Gilbert had been his esquire long ago, when he was a daft youth of fourteen, before he'd run off to be a scholar, sending his father a rude letter from the safety of a foreign capital.

"Let me think—hmm. I recall at the court of Flanders, hearing a trouvère sing—um—'Ode to My Lady's Tiny Foot.' That was his, was it not?" Sir William addressed the Count's emissary.

"Homage. It was homage."

"And another—'Song of the Tragic Lovers'? Is my memory correct?"

"Never heard of 'em," grumbled Sir Hubert, and Sir William shot him another warning glance—one not unmissed by Fray Joaquin.

"Very, very exquisite. A man of superb talent. And most noble feeling," Sir William went on.

"Ballad. It was 'Ballad of the Tragic Lovers.' "

"You must forgive me. I am only a simple knight from a harsh, rude land. But I can admire the *gentillesse* that I lack." Sir William suddenly leaned forward and fixed his eyes on Fray Joaquin's cold gray face. "How much?" he asked.

"Thirty-five florins."

"And from the hand of the fair Dame Margaret herself? That's a curious request."

"My lord wishes to see for himself the source and inspiration of so many beautiful songs. He will entertain them both royally."

"Of that I'm sure. It will all be arranged as he wishes. Of course, you must allow us, say, a month to raise the ransom and travel to your lord's court. Will you be staying to return with Dame Margaret and her escort?"

"No, I shall be returning as soon as possible." After a discussion involving the exchange of information about safe routes, Sir William slipped a question into the conversation.

"And just how did my lord of Aigremont, who was nowhere near the front in Normandy, come to entertain Sir Gilbert?"

"My lord, hearing of his reputation as a poet, purchased his ransom, along with that of several other English prisoners."

"Ah, I understand all now."

You don't understand a thing, you stupid English pig, thought Fray Joaquin. If you did, your eyes would start in your head from horror. And I'd love to see it. Especially if your head were on a tray.

When the sinister Dominican was shown out for refreshment, Sir Hubert whispered fiercely, "How in the hell can you promise him Margaret, when you know she's gone?"

"Promise now, deliver later is the rule for negotiations," said Sir William. "Besides, I wouldn't send a bitch-hound I cared for within that man's grasp."

"What do you mean? He's a great lord, renowned for his hospitality. By the rules of chivalry, any gentleman prisoners he's got are living in the lap of luxury. Why, our king even lets his prisoners go hunting—though with an escort."

"We are not speaking of kings here, Sir Hubert. We're speaking of the vainest man in all the kingdoms of Europe."

"What do you mean?"

"He had a jongleur dismembered once for implying he had a fat face. I knew the man. He was Flemish, and a real jester."

"What are you getting at? Gilbert's gently born. What lords do to peasants doesn't matter."

"*Usually* it doesn't matter, Sir Hubert. But have you ever heard 'Homage to My Lady's Tiny Foot'?"

"I don't listen to poetry. Music's just jingle-jangle to me. It's all overrated, this art stuff."

"Maybe it is, but let me tell you this. That fat-faced count hired trouvères to sing that ditty in all the courts of Europe. And what's more, that 'Homage' thing is the most ridiculous set of verses ever sung. It made my stomach churn with embarrassment. I had to pretend I was choking, to avoid laughing out loud in polite company. Now—what do you think Gilbert would do, the first time he heard something like that?"

"Tell him the truth," replied Sir Hubert.

"Exactly."

"I'm afraid he's got hold of trouble by the horns," sighed Sir Hubert.

"So am I. I'm glad we see alike on this. We'll have to move very carefully if we're to get him back in one piece."

"It was easier thinking he was dead, the godforsaken idiot."

"Fascinating. To think that I lived an entire lifetime without seeing this done." I could see Master Kendall's shade swirling directly above Brother Malachi's crucible so he could get the best possible view.

Brother Malachi was all a-bustle, as he is when he is working. "Sim, don't stint now on the bellows, we'll need the fire very hot for this process—and Margaret, could you turn the emeralds again? Use the tongs, now, and don't go touching them, or you'll spoil the finish. Oh—ugh. Margaret, is that Master Kendall's gh—er—manifestation above the crucible? I think I've gone and stepped into him. Do tell him, please, to move back a bit. I'm afraid he might inadvertently cool the process midway. I don't want the gold peeling off prematurely—it might prove embarrassing—"

Master Kendall followed me across the cramped little laboratorium as I took the little tongs from the shelf and opened the vessel full of oil where five matched crystals, all stained nicely green, had been soaking for the last several days. I turned them ever so carefully and replaced the lid. Malachi had made them by soaking them in alum and urine, and then heating them in verdigris until they turned quite as green as real emeralds. Jewels, he said, are often useful to include in a ransom. Just now he was making tawdry copper rings bought in the Cheap and an assortment of old copper pennies into gold.

"Passage money, bribes—oh, yes, two of your florins, reduced to powder and mixed with lead, will make us very wealthy travelers, Margaret. You won't be able to tell these by feel, rubbing, or even with a touchstone. Now we're ready for the first coat. We mix the powder with gum, and coat them all evenly. Watch me, Sim, or you'll never make an alchemist— then the heat drives off the lead, and leaves them quite, ah, golden—"

Master Kendall's ghost had settled in a corner just under the ceiling. His arms were folded, and he was smiling and shaking his head. "Margaret," he was saying, "I must say I'm a good bit less worried about you traveling in the company of this resourceful fellow than I was before. It's only a pity that ghosts can't cross the water, or I'd go along, too, just to see what tricks he'll come up with—"

"*If* you please," a voice hissed from the same corner.

"Madame Belle-mère!" I exclaimed.

"If you must cram yourself into my corner when there are three other ones that could serve you equally well, at least have the decency to dematerialize and quit blocking my view."

"Quiet, quiet, Margaret!" admonished Brother Malachi, looking up from his work. "I'm at a very delicate place in the process—chatter with spirits another time, will you?" So I sat silent on the bench while the smell of hot metal and gum permeated the room, and Master Kendall made a cutting retort to Madame Belle-mère.

"I haven't the time to be arguing with baseborn rogues. Move off, I say," she answered, making herself visible as a long, slim column of mist. Master Kendall swirled with annoyance, and turned all bluish.

"Madame, it would be far more appropriate for you to be off peering in cradles, like the other light-witted specters of your sort, than attempting to understand a complex process that is entirely beyond your comprehension."

"Beyond my comprehension, ha! I know exactly what he is doing. Making false gold rings that turn green after they have been worn a few months. I had an uncle who bought one like that once. He had the merchant's ears cropped. As yours obviously should have been long ago." Master Kendall made a crackling sound, but he didn't move from the corner.

"I tell you, there's one thing I know all about. That's jewelry. I wear a lot of rings myself. It's appropriate for a woman of my rank, even in death," she insisted. "Not that I see you wearing all that many—and that gold chain—it's in bad taste—so impossibly bourgeois."

"My taste is perfect, you ill-mannered provincial. I have supplied the greatest collectors and connoisseurs in the realm." I was itching to say something sharp to the Weeping Lady in defense of Master Kendall, who really does have exquisite taste, but I couldn't rouse up Malachi.

"And let me tell *you*," she said, moving herself out of the corner so she could expand to display her dress and jewelry. She had donned quite elaborate court garb for her appearance in the City. Just how, I wondered, do ghosts change clothes? "I have dozens of ways—no, hundreds—of proving that a woman of my blood is made of better stuff than you common upstart ghosts." I could see her face now. She was looking down her long nose in the most condescending and triumphant way. It seemed somehow familiar, that look, and then I remembered with a start. It was exactly the way Gregory looked when he'd just pounced on someone with a quotation from Aristotle. Gregory! My heart felt all squeezed. But still I couldn't even say a word. Malachi was pottering around the athanor, so intent on his business, he didn't notice Sim starting to slack on the bellows. Master Kendall, who now had exclusive possession of the corner by default, looked content with himself and smiled at the Weeping Lady as if she were a ridiculous child.

"That remains to be demonstrated," he said calmly.

"Not a difficult thing to do with someone of *your* sort," said the Weeping Lady. "What would you say if I told you I have every intention of crossing the water with my daughter-in-law here? After all, she seems to be the only interesting relative I have left." My heart sank. The last thing in the world I'd ever needed on a trip. My mother-in-law's ghost. Why, she wasn't even very likable. Now, if she'd been easy to take, or a pleasant conversationalist, I might have overcome the embarrassment of it all. But even the thought of the possibility of it vexed me beyond all telling. So Master Kendall's words cheered me up considerably.

"Impossible," he said. "It can't be done. Your shade will evaporate just like dew in the midday sun. Everyone knows that. It's the first thing they tell you when you get here."

"Nonsense," she retorted. "I've got a mind, unlike some of the lesser types here, and I have it entirely worked out. After all, the soul is immortal, isn't it? So what matter if the form vanishes? Besides, it might not—none of you *men* has been bold enough to try it. And consider this: How can you see everyone disappearing toward Hades, or whatever that place is, if some of them have died abroad?"

"They can arrange for us to move if they want, but we can't do it ourselves." Master Kendall was getting interested in the argument.

"So—just watch me, and you'll eat all your words, you—and Margaret, I see your face. Don't you think not to take those little shoes on the ship with you, or I'll raise such a row you'll wish you'd never been born—"

"So you really intend to make the trial, eh? Not entirely to spite a former mercer who lives between heaven and earth, I presume?"

"You think I'm sentimental? Nonsense! It's entirely for the pleasure of annoying you, I assure you. So say now, if I succeed, you'll admit that I'm the better. Will you?" She was fully formed now, and she shook her head so that her long earrings and shining necklaces, had they been made of more substantial stuff, would have clattered. A wisp of an unruly curl escaped from her tidy coif, and her translucent eyes shone like a willful child's.

Master Kendall took this all in with that long, slow, appraising gaze of his, and he answered, in a voice not unkind: "Why yes, I'd be forced to admit it, wouldn't I?"

But the eerie whistle of their conversation was interrupted by the homely sound of Brother Malachi plopping himself onto his stool and sighing as he mopped his brow with his sleeve. "Ha! Finishing nicely! Sim, my brain needs nourishment. Go see what Hilde can find me—and some for yourself as well. Phew! What heat!" He turned and spied me, starting as if he'd entirely forgotten I had been there the whole time. "Why, Margaret, you've been as quiet as a mouse over there. And what do you think of my process? Splendid, isn't it? Straight from Pliny, with a few improvements of my own. Goodness, what's wrong? You certainly look odd! I imagine you never dreamed two florins could create all this wealth. Ah, Sim, the perfect mind restorative! And all cool from the cellar, too. And one for Margaret as well! Margaret, restore yourself with some ale—you look all white about the mouth. Just what is it you're worrying about now?"

"Me? Oh nothing, Brother Malachi."

"Good, good. You must trust in my capacious mind to anticipate and solve all problems, Margaret."

Actually, there was something I did want to ask him, but I didn't dare. He'd forgotten his touchy mood, and I didn't need any more sharp words about me at that point. But what I wanted to ask was what he'd done with the rest of Master Kendall's gold florins.

"Turn around again," said the old lord.

The girl, dressed in a simple gray kirtle and blue surcoat from the chest upstairs, her hair hidden under a married woman's white veil and wimple, turned again.

"She'll do," said the old lord, gesturing from the bed.

"The effect seems wrong, somehow. You say these were hers? They look very plain." Sir William lounged on the end of the bed, inspecting the girl with calculating eyes.

"Hmm. You're right. On her, they had an air. Simple but not plain. Plain won't do, even for a knight bachelor's wife."

The girl looked at Sir William.

"Ladies wear jewels," she said.

"Indeed. Yes. That's part of it. She needs some rings. Pity we haven't any in silver gilt. And ours are too large." The trio of men inspected their hands. Even the ring on the old lord's little finger was too large for her thumb. Besides, it was a keepsake. "Yes, rings. Hmm. A necklace, too, preferably with a big crucifix. A set of beads, perhaps, on the belt. It's well for a poetic inspiration to look pious. You'll have to learn not to stare so—remember, too, always look down when you're in male company." Sir William looked over the girl again.

"Start now, or you'll never pass for a lady," snapped Hugo, who was red-eyed and tense as he sat on the big chest at the foot of the bed.

"I know how to be a lady. I've studied them. Ladies wear shining gold embroidery, not plain things." She plucked at the squirrel-lined surcoat. The serene sky-blue made her complexion seem coarse and sallowish. When she looked down, her slight natural squint was hardly noticeable.

"Something darker and more showy, then," said the old lord. "Hugo, see what Lady Petronilla has in her chest. And look through her jewels."

The girl didn't move. But the tiniest shadow of a smile flicked across her face for an instant, and her eyes, still gazing modestly at the floor, blazed in triumph.

"Her hands—you'll have to keep them in gloves till they soften. Remember, don't let her lift a finger on the trip. She has to pass," the old lord admonished Sir Hugo as he turned to mount the stairs.

"What about her speech?" said Sir William.

"Don't worry. None of those Frenchies speak English. Even when they do, they can't tell accents apart."

"Warn her to keep her mouth shut. It looks more modest that way, anyway."

"Pious, modest, quiet, and a lady—all the things you aren't, eh, Cis?" The old lord winked lasciviously at her.

"I am now, my lord," she said, looking at the floor and clasping her hands together in the attitude of prayer.

"*Very* good. I told you she'd do, didn't I? We'll just change the clothes."

There was a screaming sound from the solar above. Hugo had left the doors open on his way up.

"My finest crimson, on that hussy, that whore, that—that *laundress*? I'll go straight to father, see if I won't. He'll cut your head right off your shoulders for it."

"You're going nowhere at all, except to fetch your jewel casket."

"I won't, I tell you!"

"You'll do whatever I want. I've lost my immortal soul for you!"

"Your whoring is no fault of mine—"

There was a terrible crashing sound, followed by screams, and then moaning and sobs.

"You think your precious knight errant will ever look at *you* again? Here, take the mirror, and see what I've done. You certainly don't need jewels to set off that ugly face anymore." A horrible, keening cry echoed and re-echoed down the stairs as Hugo rejoined them with several garments draped over his arm, and bearing a little chest in both hands.

"Broke her nose," announced Hugo.

"About time," said the old lord.

"Earrings," said the girl. "The little gold ones. And the ring with the ruby."

"First put on the dress," ordered Hugo.

"Here?" The girl blushed crimson.

"Now is hardly the time for false modesty. There's no one here but Sir William who doesn't know what every inch of your body looks like. And he ought to. She has the sweetest little bottom this side of London, eh, Sir William?"

Sir William, who was a family man, studiously examined his fingernails and didn't answer.

But when she had pulled the laces tight on the blue kirtle with the golden hem, and dropped the crimson embroidered surcoat over her shoulders, even the old lord said, "By God!"

The bright garments set off her golden blond looks, fading her skin to the snowiest of whites. The gold glittering at her neck and narrow little ears set off the blush of pink that was spreading across her cheeks even as they stared. The modest downcast look, which hid eyes blazing with victory, and the generous bosom, heaving with the emotions engendered by the sudden acquisition of the glorious and long-envied dress, made her seem to the male onlookers all aglow with hidden passion. There was no doubt about it: The girl, properly scrubbed up and dressed, was a stunning beauty.

"Definitely a poetical inspiration," pronounced Sir William. "The French will never believe it isn't Margaret de Vilers."

"It *will* work," said Sir Hugo, with new hope in his eyes. "It must work. Gilbert can save me. He's studied theology. He'll know what to do. When he sees the agony I'm in, he'll tell me how I can be saved. He's a brother—brothers have to help brothers, don't they? My soul! My soul! What money can bring me back my soul? The unpardonable sin—the True Cross, God help me. If I'd only known—I haven't slept a night since that dreadful day. It has to work, before I waste away and die."

The girl pretended that she was as deaf as a piece of furniture, which is exactly how they regarded her anyway. Now, in the glorious garments, was not the time to press her advantage.

"Pilgrim's cloaks," said Sir William. "You'll fare better, once you leave the headquarters of the English army at Bordeaux. No one must suspect you're carrying ransom money. I've known too many perished that way."

"No matter what I'm wearing, it will be a relief to be abroad. It's stifling here, locked in with that barren, complaining stick of a wife." Sir Hugo's look of torment changed to one of profound self-pity.

"Good, then," said the old lord. "It's all settled. We'll be able to keep our word to that Fray Whatshisname. Within the month, that French count will receive Gilbert's ransom from the white hand of the fair Margaret de Vilers." He shook his head. "Interesting man, that. Rather repellent. Nice little stud he was riding. But far too small. Fit for monks and ladies, that breed. But not a man's horse." Then he switched to French, and addressed his son. "Just be sure to leave very quickly," he cautioned. "Remember, he's obviously just after the woman. So as soon as you've got hold of Gilbert, leave by a ruse while the Frenchman's busy with her."

"Of course, father. That's understood," answered Hugo.

"Ah, God, I only wish I were a fly on the wall at that fancy French chateau when you arrive with that wench," said Sir Hubert, and he began to cough, because he was still not strong enough to laugh.

I suppose there are some folk who are born to be on the sea, and that is just as well, for the rest of us could never manage otherwise. I mean, how would we have herring in Lent or bring goods from far lands if some people were not mad enough to prefer a life on the salty waves to all others? Now, as for me, if I had known about the sea before I set out on it, I would have been about as eager as Master Kendall's ghost to make the journey. But, of course, by then it was too late.

Brother Malachi had got us passage on a merchant cog that was carrying goods and the last pilgrims of the season to the English seneschal at Bayonne. But the ship, which looked so large in port, seemed to shrink considerably when it was on the open sea, and bobbed up and down so alarmingly that much of the two weeks I passed aboard it were spent clutching the rail, giving up my meals before I'd hardly had the good of them. All the while, the sailors were climbing up and down the mast and the rigging like squirrels, and, if you can believe it, *singing*. That's what I mean about the sea.

"Come now, Margaret, you are being entirely unfair. The

ocean is the inspiration of poets. And what's more, it's hardly been as difficult as you say. Why, we've had fair winds and a sea as calm as a bathtub the entire way. And you just stay huddled up below decks weeping. Come and smell the sea breeze. Or better, join Hilde and Sim and me tonight and see the stars. They're even more beautiful than on land."

"Stars? Night? It will be dark. Suppose I trip and roll off the edge? Or suppose, because of my sins, a big wave comes in the dark and washes me away? It's all water, water, horrid heaving water, and I can't even swim, and the fishes would eat me all up, and I've left my babies, and—and—it would serve me right, aooo—" And I went on howling even though Malachi was at his most charming and persuasive. Of course, the sea didn't bother him. His face stayed rosy instead of turning green, like mine and the other pilgrims'. And as my supposed confessor, he had great sport offering spiritual advice to everyone on board, whether they wanted it or not. Finally even Mother Hilde had to tell him to quit because it was driving her crazy with the thought that she might burst out laughing and so give him away.

But even I cheered up when the long gray line appeared on the horizon, and the pilgrims lined the ship's rail, cheering. Soon we had entered the mouth of a sluggish, muddy green river and the wild dunes—all lovely, lovely solid land—spread out on either side of us. Making slow progress up the Adour, we rounded a wide bend to spy in the distance the heavy yellow stone walls and glittering spires of a city lying on the river's right bank in the bright autumn sun. Approaching the city port, we could see the squat, menacing towers of the fortress above the city walls, the yellow stone incongruously topped with low pinkish-tiled roofs and the gaudy pennants of the English seneschal and his lieutenants.

"My goodness, it certainly doesn't look like England, Malachi," observed Mother Hilde with a satisfied air.

"Or feel like it either—you wouldn't see sun like this at home in this season," answered Malachi, stretching out his limbs like some happy plant reaching its leaves to the light. But as I watched them tying up the ship, my joy at being on land gave way to a growing sense of gloom that even the sun couldn't dispel. A stagnant little river, smelling of garbage, toiled its way through the city before trying to mingle with the majestic Adour at the dockside. Some of the ships that bobbed beside us looked more like privateers than merchantmen. Dark, savage-looking soldiers on the wharf strode between the crates of geese and bales of merchandise being loaded into some foreign ship, kicking at suspicious objects. I didn't like the way they swarmed onto the ship for the landing fees, eyeing us with the appraising look of bandits. It was pretty clearly a rough place, this sea-capital of the mountains. And if this was the best, what was the worst like?

We struggled up the narrow streets to the cathedral, jostled by the pigs, laden donkeys, and drunken mercenaries that crowded the way. All around us incomprehensible street cries and oaths rattled; people gesticulated; a Gascon, shoved by someone, pulled his long knife. How on earth could I ever find Gregory in a land of hostile strangers like this?

But as I sat miserably on our baggage with Hilde in the little square in front of the cathedral porch, Malachi emerged from the shadowy nave in fine good humor with a little friar in tow. He'd found us a good room in a pilgrim's inn squeezed between the tall houses on the Rue Mayou, and the friar was Brother Anselm, who was traveling on the road to Compostela in the party of the Abbot of Corbigny.

"All our needs are provided for," announced Malachi happily, "and we'll travel with an armed escort too."

"Ten stout armed monks, a half a dozen pilgrims, two of them knights who have joined us on the way," announced Brother Anselm, "with three friars like myself. Though I must say the prayers of the holy are worth more than a hundred swords against these godless Basque robbers, for they swarm without number in their mountains, and would kill a man for half a sou—to say nothing of what they do to women," he said,

251

eyeing me. "Still, your lady mistress will be well served. No matter what happens, her soul is assured of heaven if she achieves martyrdom on the road to Compostela in the company of such holy folk."

Oh, lovely, I thought. Holy martyrdom. The perfect end to this wretched journey. But, of course, it didn't seem to bother Malachi at all, who went off to sell our shipboard gear and buy mules for the long trek into the mountains.

But that evening he returned all dusty and empty-handed to the inn. "Not a mule or donkey is to be had in the entire city," he announced over supper at the long table of the inn's common room. "The sound ones have been taken by the English forces for the campaign, and the unsound ones were all sold off to pilgrims early in the summer. I'm afraid we'll have to walk."

"And thus emulate the example of Our Lord," interrupted Brother Anselm, crossing himself and rolling his eyes up beneath his pale brows, as if he spied heaven just above the low, smoky beams of the ceiling. He sat next to Brother Malachi opposite us at the long trestle table before the fire. Brother Malachi's pious cant had caught his fancy, and he seemed to have attached himself to us permanently. We had already received many confidences: about the boils God had sent him last Martinmas, about the distant highborn cousin he had, who might someday get him a place with the Bishop of Pamiers, as well as about the sins of every abbot from here to Byzantium, of which he had an entire catalogue, most of it too spicy to repeat. He had come via Toulouse from the north, where he had joined the Abbot's party on the pilgrim route into Spain.

Now he leaned toward Brother Malachi conspiratorially and muttered in his high-pitched, spiteful voice, "Now that Abbot of Corbigny, who stays at the chateau like a gentleman, sipping fine wine and eating white bread, and not here at the inn like us humble folk, goes on pilgrimage on a white mule with a crimson saddlecloth and a bridle trimmed with little silver bells. Tinkle, tinkle, tinkle, all the way from Toulouse. Ah, my sore feet. As I limped through the dust behind him, I said to myself, 'A lot of good a pilgrimage to Compostela will do *you*, you hypocrite and publican!' Now, if you only knew what I knew about Corbigny. Why, they claim to have the relics of Saint Léonard, and with the money of the gullible they have built an immense shrine and furnished their table with luxuries, when all the time the genuine bones are at Noblat. Oh, they should blush with shame, those monks of Corbigny! For they have baptized a man a second time, and after he was a corpse, as well!"

"Goodness," said Malachi, "a purveyor of false relics? Who could imagine such a dreadful thing? Ah, God protect us in these wicked times!" And he in turn crossed himself.

I couldn't help listening in, even though Hilde and I were speaking to each other in English, for the little friar's conversation was in clear French, the language of the north, rather than the incomprehensible southern dialects that rattled all around us at the table. Besides the travelers from the ship, there were others from the ports and cities of France, a party of Germans that included an elderly knight and his son, and those who had traveled under the protection of the Abbot and his suite. Among these last were a merchant with a wen, two priests, one of whom, the younger, was under a vow of silence, and several monks of various orders—the last of these being the gossipy Brother Anselm. He had a need to constantly unburden the contents of his mind on whomever he happened to fasten himself, and in the days before our departure we heard all about the barbarous habits of the Navarrais, whose language sounds like the barking of dogs, and who will kill a Frenchman for the clothes on his back.

"Ah, they are a wicked people, these Basques and Navarrais of the mountains," Brother Anselm would say. "The *Liber Sancti Jacobi* does not exaggerate when it calls them ugly and full of malice, dishonest, false, and drunken." I wished heartily he would go away and horrify someone else.

The evening before our departure, I groaned as Brother Anselm found us at table, and joined us without invitation.

"So, Brother Malachi, you shall walk and so shall your good dame and her old nurse, but from Ostabat I will be riding a fine mule into Spain. So think of that again when you boast about who is the cleverest."

"Oh, so? How is that?" Brother Malachi rumbled, his mouth full of food.

Brother Anselm leaned close and whispered, "Those two priests who traveled with us from Toulouse—the one with the vow of silence—I've overheard them talking in secret to each other. And let me tell you—I misdoubt that they're any priests at all, despite that psalm-singing old man. They're wearers of the yellow wheel, who've doffed it for travel. The young one—she's a woman with cropped hair. I imagine his wife. At Ostabat I'll turn them in for the reward, and purchase the mule."

"Why, that is clever of you. I must admit you've got the better of me this time. But we'll match wits again, Brother Anselm. Now, try this riddle. . . ." Brother Malachi's face never lost its geniality as he poured all of his wine into Brother Anselm's cup and allowed him to guess every riddle that he owned. Leaving the chinless little creature snoring on the table, he said to us with a formal flourish, "Good Dame Margaret and Mistress Hilde, it will be an early day tomorrow, I will see you to our room." But at the door he cautioned silence and told us to bar the door. Sometime later when I heard his secret tap in the night, I rose to let him in, for Mother Hilde was fast asleep.

"Brother Malachi, what were you doing out there in the dark? You could have been killed, or picked up by the watch," I whispered fiercely. "Then what would have become of us?"

"They're off, Margaret, and I have new hope. Mule! Ha! That Brother Anselm deserves to walk all the way to Purgatory."

"They? Then they were—"

"Of course. Man and wife, and not a yellow wheel between them. It would have been a nasty reception at Ostabat. But once they believed me, they were a wellspring of information. 'You don't happen to read Hebrew, do you? I'm looking for

Abraham the Jew, the famous scholar, to translate a very—hmm—complex holy work I've acquired.' The man smiled—his first smile of the evening. 'Abraham the Jew? He's very hard to find. You won't find him in France at all. Oh no. Not since the Jews were accused of causing the great pestilence and driven out with fire and sword. And Spain? Not even there, I'm sure. Take my advice and go to Avignon. That is where the last Jews in France have sheltered. Pope Clement himself decreed toleration, and none has revoked it since. Go to the papal university at Avignon and seek out Josceus Magister, who is the greatest Talmudic scholar remaining in this realm. Odd, isn't it? In the shadow of the papal palace stands the last temple in the whole land. If Josceus is no longer living, you will find scholars in plenty. Good luck. Accept my adieux, brother. I fear that Gertelote and I must travel in the dark tonight.' So here am I, fired with new hope. So close! So close! Just a brief detour to fetch Gilbert, and then—the Secret!"

As I lay down again, I could sense that he was not sleeping, but lying wide awake, staring into the dark.

CHAPTER
9

"Show in the emissaries of the Count of Foix." The Sieur d'Aigremont had arranged himself on the dais at the end of his great hall to create the most impressive picture. His heavy cloak was thrown back across the arms of the great thronelike wooden chair in which he sat, revealing at the same time the richness of the miniver that lined the cloak and the exquisite pale blue satin of the gold-embroidered doublet that glistened over the rolling fat of his vast torso. His immense, ring-bedecked, and now hairless hands lay idly on the arms of the chair, as if they had nothing better to do in life than lift a pomander to his nostrils. Yet they also suggested a sort of latent menace and power—as if they might suddenly strangle a full-grown man in a single spasm of rage. The seemingly careless arrangement of hands, cloak, and gown was the result of a careful design, set to frame what he considered his most handsome feature: his muscular legs, the legs of a powerful horseman, hunter, warrior, and dancer, encased in white silk pulled taut across huge thighs with showy gold garters.

It seemed an irony that a body of this unusual height and massiveness should be finished off by a head disproportionately small. But as if to compensate, the jowls had grown large enough to conceal the heavy neck entirely. Were it not for the immense jeweled collar that sat at the hidden seam between body and head, it would have been impossible to discern at what place the body left off and the head began. A wide dark blue velvet cap, heavily embroidered with pearls, shadowed the piggy, calculating little eyes, concealing the full extent of their malevolence from observers.

The ambassadors, two knights still dusty from the road, knelt before him and delivered the message that could not be entrusted to writing.

"Join with him in a treaty of peace with the English, eh? Is he so fearful that this Prince of Wales will march east from Gascony that he will not back France?"

"My lord of Foix says, how well has the King of France served him recently, that he should give his lands over to pillage, without any hope of gain? He rides with his cousin, the Captal de Buch, to join the Teutonic knights in crusade against the pagan Slavs in the east, for the sanctity of his soul. He prays that there be peace between you and himself, and that you join with him on a campaign where there is wealth and glory enough for all."

"And protect his backside from me while he's gone, eh? What makes him think it is likely?"

"Does not the commendable desire for vengeance for Navarre, who lies this day in the King of France's prison, and for the slain Norman lords of the alliance move you? Navarre's allegiance is to the English; a treaty with the English prince at Bordeaux would spare your realm and give evidence of your love for your lord. This alone should dispose you to hear my lord of Foix's words with favor, even without the tokens of his love for you that you have so graciously received."

"How could I ever fail to hear the words of the most noble

young Count of Foix with anything but the highest favor? Stay and partake of my hospitality while I consider his words."

As they were shown out, and before the next petitioners entered, he turned to Fray Joaquin, who stood behind him at his shoulder.

"A loving cousin indeed! Has the message from Navarre been decoded yet?"

"This morning, lord. He says, do not bind yourself to any but him; he expects to escape soon and has laid plans for the recapture of his lands in the north, and yours as well."

"Good. We'll delay, then send a message of our eternal friendship to the lord of Foix. I need time now—time and money—to equip the army I've sworn to raise in my lord's support. Damn that captain of thieves, that wretched English duke! If he weren't squatting on my northern lands like some devil, I'd have the money in my hands already. And now this miserable Count of Foix pesters me! Gaston Phoebus, Gaston Phoebus! Why in hell's name should everyone call him after Apollo just because he's got a pretty profile? It's me that should be called Reynaud Phoebus! Me! Who's the better poet? Who's the greater connoisseur? It's me, not that degenerate lordling. Friendship—ugh—I wish I had him in my hands to show him what I think of him." The fingers of the Sieur d'Aigremont's huge hands clutched convulsively, as if tearing apart a cooked egret's wing. Then he turned again to Fray Joaquin.

"How close is Messer Guglielmo? I'm tired of waiting for the gold. Did you tell him I'll impale him if he doesn't make better speed?"

Fray Joaquin's conspiratorial whisper became even more hushed. "He says he needs more fixative for the quicksilver. The stuff you provided wasn't the right quality. He doesn't dare call Asmodeus again. He's losing control of him; he's become too powerful with the offerings you've made, and may break through into the world."

"Out of control? Messer Guglielmo is a weakling. I won't have it. Does that popinjay Gaston Phoebus have trouble with his Orthon? No, he's got his familiar spirit brought to heel—as obedient as can be. And he hasn't fed Orthon half as well as I've fed Asmodeus. I think Messer Guglielmo is telling tales—he's stalling. And as for fixative, what I've sent him has had the highest aesthetic quality. For example, the last little one, who screamed when I—"

"Not here, my lord, not here. But I think I have found an answer to your needs in this respect." Fray Joaquin saw the blood throbbing in his master's temples with the hungry remembrance of last night's work in the hidden chambers. How the fat old fool lost his mind when desire possessed him. It was the weakness by which Fray Joaquin maintained his control over him.

"An answer?" Spit oozed from the corner of the Count's red lips, and he licked them as if they still tasted of blood.

"To the gold problem. The next petitioners. The pilgrim party. Keep them all here under any pretext. The fat friar among them is the most powerful adept in Europe. You've heard of Theophilus of Rotterdam?"

"Theophilus? The one who was rumored to have obtained the Secret, and then vanished from Paris just before King John tried to arrest him?"

"The very one. He wisely chose to disappear to escape being imprisoned to make gold for the rest of his life."

"Tell him I'll torture him if he doesn't reveal the Secret."

"It's entirely unnecessary. He says he'll trade the Secret for the life of Sir Gilbert de Vilers, also known to you as Gilbert l'Escolier."

"Gilbert l'Escolier? How in the Devil's name did he know he was here?"

"He says the Stone gives the All-Seeing Eye."

"All-Seeing Eye? That's far better than Orthon has ever promised that piddling countlet of Foix. I'd be the most powerful man in the world—no, I'm not letting him go. Theophilus must be made to give up his Secret. And as for that arrogant pseudo poet, I haven't the least intention of giving him up to

Theophilus or anyone else. I haven't even begun to work on him. Do you know what he said today? He's as stubborn as ever. No, no, he promises excellent sport—among the best, and I intend to enjoy every tiny little fragment of a moment of it. Beguile this friar—give him the impression I've agreed, and get hold of the Secret. Then we'll eliminate them both."

"I anticipated your wishes, my lord. I have said nothing, but welcomed the entire party and brought them here for your inspection. Offer them your hospitality for a lengthy stay, and I'll pry the Secret from the man—if not by guile, then by force."

"Do whatever is necessary." The Count waved a hand idly. Fray Joaquin, black cloak rippling behind him like a great shadow, vanished into the long corridor that led to the hidden chambers as the Count of St. Médard greeted the band of pilgrims with a pious quotation.

"He certainly *seems* hospitable, dear Malachi," Mother Hilde said as she slid off her wide pilgrim's hat, now limp with damp, and laid her staff and bundle at the foot of one of the beds in the center of the long, arched "pilgrim's hall" that faced the inner courtyard of the castle. For days we had toiled upward along rushing streams from the autumn-clad foothills into the gray and misty heights. Yesterday we had left the spreading apple orchards of the high valley of St. Médard-en-bas behind us in the morning frost, and by the time we had reached the steep, winding streets of St. Médard-en-haut, the mist had turned into a slushy rain that soaked our shoes through and froze our faces.

"What did I tell you, flower of my life? My old name still works magic among the fraternity," said Malachi, spreading his damp things before the great fire with a self-satisfied air. "Theophilus of Rotterdam does not have to stay at that miserable inn in the village with hoi polloi, but Brother Malachi would have had no other choice."

All about us in the hall, the lesser members of the abbot's

party were settling in. Behind a heavy screen at the end of the hall, pierced only by a low wooden door, lay the accommodation for women pilgrims. The smell of wet wool and the sound of travelers' chatter filled the room, giving it a homely air. As I shook the water off my cloak my stomach kept telling me this was all a dismal mistake. I'd never felt farther from home. I couldn't imagine Gregory was in a place like this. Maybe he'd left. Maybe he'd never been there. Margaret, Margaret, you are a stupid, headstrong woman, and look what it's got you. You're freezing and pregnant and standing in the ugliest rooms in Christendom, and you've left your children and a warm bed to follow dreams and imaginings. Everybody always told you not to be so stubborn, and you should have listened.

"Oh, the courtesy, the condescension of this pious lord d'Aigremont. Did you see his rings? He may well make us a gift to speed us on our way." The talkative Brother Anselm plopped his bundle into the corner. "Of course, more than money, what I would like is a nice, surefooted mule. Oh, the treacherousness of those wicked false priests, slipping off like that! Without a doubt they were in league with the Devil, who tells the people of the yellow wheel how to evade God's justice."

But I had noticed something strange. Ever since we'd entered the huge iron gate of the chateau, I'd heard a thin, angry whine like a trapped wasp issuing from the Burning Cross. When I put my hand on it, it would stop, only to resume when I took my hand off again. In the great audience chamber, I feared the sound would be noticed, but luckily there was enough clatter of people coming and going to conceal it. But now, in the quiet of our rooms, it seemed more noticeable than ever, and I could feel it quivering on my breast as if it were alive, where it lay hidden under my surcoat.

The rooms, composed of a long stone chamber divided in two by a massive, carved wooden screen that reached to the ceiling, were completely open to foot traffic through several passages without doors. They were really more like corridors, except for the simple fur-covered bedsteads and little charcoal braziers that warmed them. Cold drafts blew through the door arches, meeting the breeze from the windows in a way that made the brazier flames dance and flicker. But the rooms were in an honorable location, near the chambers of the lady Iseut, the Count's wife, and his young son and only heir. The location was a little too good for pilgrims, in my opinion, although hardly good enough, in the opinion of the more snobbish members of our party.

"Don't look so glum, Margaret," said Brother Malachi as he looked at my worried face. "Everything will work out—you'll see. It's all meant to be—and soon you'll be joyful again."

"Listen, Malachi, don't you hear it?"

"What?"

"A humming sound, like a fly."

"A fly? In this season? Mighty strange flies they have in this part of the world."

I put my staff and bundle at the foot of one of the beds behind the screen. Now I gestured silently through the low wooden door to Mother Hilde to join me, away from the prying eyes of the men.

"Listen, Mother Hilde," I whispered as I pulled the Burning Cross from its hiding place. As I held it away from my dress, the whining buzz grew louder.

"Dear Holy God," she whispered. "It's buzzing."

"It's all warm too," I whispered back. "It got worse when I was near the Count. It can only be the air, Mother Hilde. Even the air is evil in this place."

"You're right, Margaret." Mother Hilde looked very serious.

"Warn Brother Malachi, Hilde, but don't let that chatterbox Brother Anselm know."

I put it between my cupped hands, and it grew silent and cool.

"So, so, women must have their gossip, even at the cost of supper," announced Brother Anselm in pointed tones as we emerged from the little door.

"So is it always. Ah, why I saddled myself with this obligation, I can't imagine," said Brother Malachi loudly. "But I, for one, am hungry. And I hear that this lord sets an elegant table from no less than Sim, who's already inspected the kitchens while you two have been idling back there."

And sure enough, when we looked around, there was Sim, looking as if he'd popped out of an opening in the earth.

"To supper, all. I fear the mounted ones have preceded us and taken the best places," said Brother Malachi.

But he was wrong. Fine places at a middle table had been saved for us. Places too fine for simple pilgrims, I thought. There was an elegant supper, during which musicians played from a hidden gallery. And because there were ambassadors from some neighboring count there, the *entremets* were truly astonishing. There was an entire ship on wheels, made completely of pastry, and boys painted all in gold, dancing. And after supper, there were Moorish dances, with the dancers all painted dark and savage, dressed in jewels and little bells. Then, with the trestle tables cleared away, the table dormant was re-covered with an elegant red cloth and games set out for the amusement of the high lords of the ambassador's party that were the Count's guests. By the time we left, the sun was already setting, and candles had been brought to the gaming table. The lords were well occupied with dice under the smoking new-lit torches, while the Countess and her ladies and *pucelles* sat to one side playing a game of draughts. At the foot of the table, a harper made the air sweet with a doleful song whose words I did not understand. As we wound our way through the torchlit passages to our rooms, the last notes of the song reverberated in my mind, notes that harmonized with the strange, almost inaudible hum from beneath my surcoat.

The next morning, not long after we had broken our fast, the gray-faced Dominican who seemed to be the lord's chief adviser came to fetch Malachi. They spoke Latin, so I didn't understand a word, but I didn't like the man's tone, though it didn't seem to bother Malachi a bit. But he addressed Malachi as "Theophilus," and acted deferential. And then he stared at

Sim in a way I didn't like, as if pricing a pig, and murmured in some dialect words that sounded to me like "too ugly."

"Malachi, are you going to—" I began in English, but Brother Malachi shushed me with a sharp glance, one that looked so alien, it startled me for a moment. Then he spoke cheerfully, also in English. "Good-bye for the moment, my dears. And whatever you do, *keep Sim with you.*"

"Yes, of course, Malachi," answered Mother Hilde in the calmest voice in the world. It was exactly the same voice she uses to say "the child has stopped breathing." I do admire Mother Hilde. I can imagine her walking straight down into hell and telling the Devil to put out the fire, he was making it entirely too warm above, in that exact same tone. As she always used to tell me when she was my teacher, "Margaret, there are times when *firmness* is everything."

Late in the forenoon Malachi caught us three mingled with a crowd of loafers in the tiltyard, watching the squires drilling on horseback, and said to us in English,

"My dears, let us go and inspect our horses."

"Our horses?" I was puzzled. We hadn't any.

"Yes, Margaret. Our horses, so close by in the stable," he repeated firmly as Mother Hilde gave me a sharp glance. We came away without another word.

"We're less likely to meet with English speakers here," said Brother Malachi, solemnly inspecting the backside of a horse in his stall. "Though with all the mercenaries about, you never know," he added, passing to the next stall. We all stared at the switching tail of the next horse as he spoke.

"They have everything I've ever dreamed of. Beautiful equipment. Their own glassblower. Six assistants. Messer Guglielmo, who has to be the greatest jackass in Europe, has done nothing with it. He's half as far as I am. Doesn't keep records—that's his problem. 'Why write down something that doesn't work?' he asks. The fool! So you don't repeat it, that's why! Besides, you may stumble upon something else and you won't remember how you got it. He's got one process he's been simmering for over a year. And two thousand eggs that he buried for six months before trying to create quintessence of egg. Powerful stuff, if he'd got it. But phew! What a stink! I don't know why you complain of me! But what a laboratorium! Philosopher's eggs, all sizes! Pelicans and cucurbits, all you can ask for! An athanor big enough to roast a whole kid! I could be happy the rest of my life with a laboratorium like that one."

Something was wrong with Brother Malachi. His words were the same as ever, but his voice sounded wrong. We passed to the next stall.

"Books. They've got books I've always wanted. The forbidden works of Arnold of Villanova. Graecus's *Book of Fires*. 'So, you've got the *Mappae Clavicula*,' I said. 'Yes,' said that infernal Dominican. 'If you'd like to stay to copy it, you will be assured of my lord's hospitality.' That's when I knew he had no intention of letting us go." Malachi turned his face toward us. In only a few hours it seemed to have sagged into deep folds. Dark circles had emerged beneath his eyes.

"Then I had a good talk with Messer Guglielmo. Snooped around. Criticized. That's when I knew for sure. It's as I suspected." His voice sounded haunted. *"They're using the wrong fixative.* The one I told you about. There are nasty brown splashes of it everywhere. God only knows where they bury the bones. The black candles, too. They've hidden the rest, but I saw the stub of one in a niche that they'd forgotten. Forgive me, forgive me, Hilde. It all seemed so easy when I first thought it out. I should have made more inquiries. I should have guessed. But now it seems my carelessness has brought us to our doom." He turned his tormented face to her, but her strong heart never faltered as she took his hand.

"My place is always beside you, Malachi. It's what I've chosen. You don't need to be forgiven." He looked at her, as if he were drinking in her strength, and took several great breaths.

"Delay them," she said. "You know how. You're good at it. We'll use the time to find out where Gilbert's hidden. Why"— she chuckled grimly—"Sim can practically walk through walls.

And you—you know all those languages, and will have the run of the place. And Margaret and I—well, God will show us the way. He's done it before. And—Margaret—now that I think of it, give me that box with the ring in it. You haven't got the heart to give it away, and besides, the poison might be bad for the baby. I think I will have plans for it. Fixative indeed! We'll see who needs fixative."

Over the next few days, although we were well treated, we had much cause to repine. Malachi vanished daily to the great hidden laboratorium, and Hilde's worry wouldn't stop until she saw him safe at suppertime. And because we didn't speak the languages we heard rattling all around us, we sometimes felt as close kept as if in prison. Occasionally someone would speak the French of the north, and we could make ourselves understood. But no matter where we went, someone always seemed to be following us.

At length Sim, who was always in search of food, managed to make friends in the kitchen, through the use of sign language and the performance of little useful tasks. We were driven frantic with worry when he would vanish, but then he'd return, usually munching an apple from one of the great storage barrels, and telling us of some new sight he'd seen. It was he who told us about the hidden rooms, and the screams that were sometimes heard at night, just as casually as he'd describe a bearbaiting.

"And then," he said, taking another bite of his apple, "they cross themselves and make a show of putting their finger in front of their lips for silence, and drawing it across their throats, like this—" another bite. "And do you know how he gets them? Ships them in from far away with that gloomy old goat in black, or if he gets short, he goes night hunting, like a ghost, all in black. Knocks on his peasants' doors with the butt of that riding whip he carries—the one with the bone death's-head handle, and then points with it to the child he wants—even the babies in the cradle."

"How did they tell you all that, about the color and the babies, if they can't talk?"

"This way," he said. "They point to something black and do like this," and with a few gestures he depicted a cloaked, booted figure in black from top to toe, riding a glistening white horse, surrounded by outriders.

"Well, why don't they tell the Bishop? He'd bring the Inquisition on them. That many babies can't disappear without someone noticing."

"Everyone's afraid of him. He can cast spells and call devils. And when the moon is full, he rides out like the Devil himself, in search of blood." Sim waved his arms behind him like a flying cloak, and leapt about as if galloping, all the while grinning at the ghoulish vision. "When I get home, I'm going to tell my friends. I'll frighten the growth out of them, and then we'll all stay the same size," he said contentedly, sitting down to finish his apple. You'd never take Sim for anything but a street urchin if you saw him eat an apple. He finishes it all off, even the core and the seeds, down to the little twig that was the stem, just as if he thought he'd never get another.

"Now, Sim, you be careful. I don't want anything nasty happening to you," Mother Hilde cautioned.

"Oh, don't worry about that. I'm too ugly, they say. He likes blond babykins. Besides, I'm quick. Good-bye, I'm off to help pluck chickens."

As for Mother Hilde and I, we walked here and there, especially by open cellar windows, hoping to hear something. A hint, a voice, something. But the most likely place, beneath the great donjon keep of the castle itself, seemed to have no windows at all.

"So, Mother Hilde, what should I do? I can't sing by every window like King Richard's troubador. It would look very suspicious in this season, standing in the mud and singing into cellar windows."

"Something will present itself. By the way, speaking of nosy things, what ever happened to that Weeping Lady you said was attached to the little shoes?"

"She said crossing the sea made her ill, and got all filmy and pale and vanished. When even your spooks leave, Mother Hilde, that's when you know you're really in trouble."

"I suppose you're right, Margaret, though I'd never thought of it that way." But it was at that moment that one of the Countess's ladies-in-waiting, a large, dark-haired lady with a preposterous great two-horned headdress, found us as we stood on the outer steps of the great hall, surveying the mud of the inner bailey.

She spoke to me in clear French, though with an odd accent, and said, "Is that woman with you the celebrated mistress of herbal remedies, *la Mère* Hilde?"

"Why yes," I answered, "but how did you know?"

"We heard from your confessor, the Brother Theophilus, that she is in demand with the *noblesse* of England. He says she has treated the Queen herself. Can you speak to her for us?" Oh, clever Malachi, he's up to something, I thought. And so there ensued a three-sided conversation by which Mother Hilde was told that the Countess had many sicknesses, and her son was unwell, and Mother Hilde was asked to attend.

The next thing we knew, we were shown into a wide circular stone-vaulted room, hung with beautiful silk tapestries. A great fire was burning, and the room was all hot and smoky, for the wood was too damp. A sallow, droopy little boy of ten sat by the fire, all wrapped up in a fur coverlet. A vast fur-lined cap of crimson sat upon his stringy, brownish-yellow hair. His father's strange wide red lips, on him faded to yellowish pink and set in a narrow, sickly little face that reminded me of a bald squirrel, gave him a strange look of degeneracy and decay. And like a squirrel's, his timid little eyes seemed to sit almost on either side of his head. The dismal, narrow, chinless little face was almost a perfect replica of his mother's as she leaned over his chair, watching him as he played a game of chess with his tutor. As she saw us enter she detached herself from the group and gave orders to another lady-in-waiting, with a headdress as ridiculous as the first lady's and her own, to show us to her.

"I need remedies, medicines," she said, and her voice faded into a complaining whine. She touched the jeweled headdress that sat atop her sallow rat's face. "I have headaches, terrible headaches. I go nearly blind with them. You holy pilgrims, you must help me. And my digestion, it's so poor. I suffer in my digestion. Pains, pains, you understand? I'm weak. And my son —look—he needs strengthening. He never leaves this chamber. He can only travel in the heat of summertime. Find him a remedy, or cure him with your prayers, and I'll beg my husband to reward you richly. You'll ride to the Holy Land—no, Compostela, is it?—mounted like queens. Hounds, men at arms, money. I'll get anything, if you make him strong, like other children."

"You know the cause, Mother Hilde?" I asked in English.

"Look at her coat of arms on the wall, Margaret. I can't read arms, but I see at least four quarterings with very much the same emblems. Weak blood is the first cause. Great families can afford to get papal exemptions from the forbidden degrees of kinship in marriage—they marry their own kin too much and weaken their blood while they strengthen their purses. The other cause is the evil of the house. It sucks the strength of these innocents, though they have been kept in ignorance."

"And tell her," whispered the Countess in French to me, so her maids would not overhear, "I cannot get another child. My lord would love me again if I had another child. He loved me once. He gave me gifts and made a poem in my honor before we married. If he loved me again, he wouldn't leave me alone like this. All locked up in these rooms, never going outside. We never travel with him anymore. And when my lord resides in this castle, he never speaks to me, save at the table, when company is present. Always his own business, night after night. No time for me. Not a word, a visit, or a sign of favor. His son —look at him! He sneers at the child. If you cannot mend this one, get me a stronger one, I pray you. I don't care by what means—I must have my lord's favor again."

As I translated, Mother Hilde inspected the child, making clucking noises, as he went on playing chess, appearing not to hear. I suppose people had clucked at him all his life.

"I need to seek the right herbs," said Mother Hilde, "tell her that they don't all grow in her garden, and that we need to go outside the walls into the mountains with a boy to show us the way." The little rat face looked terrorized. But that is how, the very next day, with two armed footmen, we got to wander beyond the walls above the village and into the blustery mountain passes. Mother Hilde brews several wonderful headache remedies, though the best, which requires willow bark, could not be made here for lack of ingredients. We learned the lay of the land, but never got any closer to finding Gregory, though I was sure he was there somewhere.

In the meanwhile, some of the other pilgrims chafed at not being able to cross the mountains before the heavy winter snows set in, and sent a delegation to the Count, who rebuffed them with a brutal hint about how lordly hospitality was far finer than crossing the mountains naked in wintertime.

Malachi returned each evening with more news from the concealed alchemical laboratorium.

"Oh, I cannot tell you how *wearying* it is, doing nothing. *You* have the benefit of fresh air, but I where am I? Underground, trapped with the foulest of stinks, and nothing but that king of fools, Messer Guglielmo, and a bunch of mute dullards, stripped like executioners, for conversation. 'My God,' I tell them, 'how could you possibly undertake the Great Work with copper vessels? They contaminate the Dragon. Throw them out. I want glass, all glass. Yours isn't heavy enough.' Then Messer Guglielmo fusses like an old lady, and the glassblower acts injured, and it takes a couple of days to get the stuff right. Then I took the biggest aludel in the place and made spirits of wine. I got them so drunk they couldn't stand. 'The Elixir of Life,' I said, 'just tell my lord to take a portion of it like this every evening before sleep, and it will prolong his life by one hundred years.' So they did that. He came down to watch me. 'Ugh, impossible equipment,' I tell him. 'I need orpiment; I can't work without it.' He got nasty. I think he must be deep in debt and need the money. 'My equipment is the best in six kingdoms,' he says, shaking those menacing jowls of his at me, 'and as for orpiment, if you can't work without it, I'll pluck your fingernails out one by one until you can.' Ugh. Cultured, ptah!" Brother Malachi spat on the floor. "And at dinner I'm supposed to enjoy my food while those minstrels sing those monstrosities he calls verses. Why, Gilbert dead drunk could turn a better verse than that. Gilbert *asleep* could do it."

"Gregory wrote verses drunk?"

"Of course, silly Margaret. He was the toast of every tavern from Paris to London. He could compose extemporaneously in any style. Rondels, sonnets, anything! He was as full of them as a tun is of wine! And nearly all satirical. By Saint Dunstan's beard, some of them were funny! One time, some highborn troubador sent several hired ruffians to have him horse-whipped, but we snuck him out the back door, where, in the alley, he composed a verse commemorating the event. I hear it's still sung in the lower sort of student places. 'Why Poets Need Winged Feet,' it's called. Then he decided he'd make his mark on scholarship—but as it turned out, scholarship made its mark on him, instead. Finding that discouraging, he decided he was destined to see God, and converted himself into a bore of the first order. Now, how he got involved with you is beyond me—I can't feature any man of sense, let alone him, copying your memoirs for you. I can't imagine, if you'll pardon me, that you'd have any ideas worth writing *about*."

"That's exactly what he said."

"And you, of course, told him he was wrong."

"Yes, naturally."

"Of course, naturally," sighed Brother Malachi. "So it's made in heaven."

"Malachi, when you rattle on like that, you're leading up to something. Just what is it?" Mother Hilde interrupted.

"Well, I don't think he's under the donjon."

"Then you've found him!" My heart leapt with hope.

"Not quite. But I finally got myself under the Old Tower today, and what they've got there is salt meat, mostly, and some other supplies. I told them I needed the mold off cheeses. But then I found they've got another basement under us in the athanor room in the New Tower. It's got—oh, goodness—a torture chamber, I heard some poor wretch screaming is how I found out—and a couple of big cells chock-full with ugly equipment and several nasty little oubliettes. They're set up so that water runs through them constantly, and he breeds toads, scorpions, and that sort of thing inside. They're very deep, with grilles at the top—he just strips his prisoners and dumps them in with the vermin. There's a sort of pulley for that, and, I suppose, getting them out as well, although he doesn't seem to have done that within anyone's memory. They say they're very deep, but not so very wide—perhaps four feet across, according to Messer Guglielmo. I got him drunk, and there was no end to the talking he did. It seems the screams spoil his concentration, and he believes that an artiste such as himself deserves greater consideration and a more salubrious location for his labors."

"Oh, Malachi, you're marvelous; he's found!" exclaimed Mother Hilde. But I started to cry.

"Oh, Malachi, that awful place. And so cold. He must be dead. We've come too late."

"Now, now, Margaret, take heart. That's the part I saved for last. It seems that once a week, Fridays, I hear, the Comte makes him a personal visit to see how he's doing. Dumps things through the grille and shouts insults, I suppose. Goes down all full of airs, sniffing a pomander, and comes back so furious that he screams at Messer Guglielmo on the way up. This past Friday, he threw the pomander at him, and threatened to cut off his hands and feet if he didn't make faster progress."

"Friday? But that's only four days ago."

"Exactly, my dear. But now we must lay plans. I have no idea how to get to him, and I am at the end of all my tricks but one. Once I've made gold, we're doomed unless we are far from here that very night. I'll tell him it needs to be done at the full moon—that will give us light to travel by at night, and put him off a while more."

"Make gold? All these years, Malachi, and you always knew how to make gold anyway?" Mother Hilde was shocked.

"Well, after a fashion, my love. There are always complexities."

"But—when we needed money to mend the roof, and when—"

"Ah, Hilde, my precious. The pursuit of the Green Lion is not for the mere mending of roofs. It is a higher spiritual force."

"A *higher* force?" Mother Hilde spluttered.

"Oh, my love, I'll explain it all to you afterward. It's a great secret I've kept for years, and you certainly deserve to know it. But if I fail—well, I'd rather you retain your faith in my powers."

"Malachi, you're up to something."

"Of course. When have I said I wasn't? Prepare for flight at the full moon, my treasure, even if we have to scale the walls with a grappling hook."

"The full moon, you say? But that's a week away. Messer Guglielmo, do you know anything about this full moon business? I swear he's stalling." The Count's deep voice sounded suspicious. Messer Guglielmo had already abandoned the athanor to the mutes, leaving them to supervise the process of calcination of a batch of duck's eggs while he attended his lord. The fading winter light in the long, tile-floored laboratorium had already been supplemented by smoking torches mounted in iron brackets the length of the bare stone walls. Brother Malachi looked wan as he knelt on the cold floor at the Count's feet. He had been losing weight in Sieur d'Aigremont's hidden alchemical workshop, and it wasn't just because of the smell. Messer Guglielmo's eyes flicked back and forth from his patron to his rival, and he combed his rough, grayish-black beard with his fingers as he weighed what he would say.

"Well, I can't deny he's gotten results. *Preliminary* results, of course. But this method from Leyden, it's very primitive in some ways. He doesn't use the classical method for congealing the dragon's sister to the silver. It seems unsound to me—yes, quite unsound."

"Unsound?"

"Yes. Definitely. He won't use the proper fixative, and the quicksilver stays liquid. And he relies on—hmm—unassisted methods."

"Unassisted? You mean I've let this fool dillydally unassisted? And how, pray tell," he addressed the alchemist at his feet, "do you expect to achieve the Secret without supernatural power? With the puny powers of the human mind?"

"My lord, the powers of observation and rationality, applied to the study of nature, can achieve mighty transformations," Brother Malachi answered simply.

"Ha! So you confess all! You've made no sacrifices! Used no powerful fixatives! Theophilus of Rotterdam, you've been toying with me. I want you to finish the process tonight, moon or no moon, with the correct fixative." The rage in the Count's voice rumbled with menace.

Brother Malachi's eyes were like those of a trapped hare.

"Most high lord, that is poor stuff."

"Poor stuff? Poor? It's the freshest to be had. You squeamish little bastard, I'm going to cut out your tongue for that."

Brother Malachi trembled, but his voice was firm.

"I have the proper fixative with me, but it requires a full moon—"

"Where? Show me." The Count's face loomed over Malachi like the face in a nightmare. Somewhere nearby, he could sense the nervous quiver of Messer Guglielmo's beard, as he pushed his narrow face closer to get a better view. His knees were aching and frozen. You'd think at least they'd let me stand up for a great moment like this, he thought as he opened his pilgrim's wallet to remove a tiny leather sack.

"Don't breathe on it. You mustn't lose a grain. And the heat of your breath may spoil it." Deep within the little sack, an opalescent pinkish powder gleamed.

"My God, he has it. The Red Powder!" Even the waspish Messer Guglielmo was briefly awestruck.

"You've had it all along. Use it tonight, or you'll wish you were dead."

"But my part of the bargain? How do I know you've got him still?"

"Do you doubt my word?"

"Oh, never, never. Me? A poor humble Seeker after Truth, doubt the word of a nobleman? Oh, impossible."

"Don't try me," the Count growled. "I despise humor. And especially satire. The refuge of clowns and human garbage. Want to see what I'll do to you if you're being humorous with me?"

"—um, not just now. Later, perhaps?"

"Now is just right. After all, I have a sense of humor too. The proper kind. I think it will be very funny to see your face." And with a snap of his fingers, he had called two of the huge mute assistants, who grabbed Brother Malachi by both elbows, practically suspending him from the floor.

"Messer Guglielmo, I want you to come too. Let me show you what happens to people who fool with me. It will give wings to your mind." With a gesture, Brother Malachi was frogmarched down a shadowy stone staircase into a realm of perpetual darkness. Two torchbearers lit the way before them, and two more followed the party. Brother Malachi could not help looking up at the smoke-stained ceiling of the narrow passage, and wonder how many trips the dripping soot represented.

The passage soon opened out into a low, vaulted room, lit primarily by the flickering embers that burned perpetually beneath a cauldron of rancid oil. Beside the fire stood a rack of iron implements suitable for heating: pinchers, rods, and branding irons. A little brazier, like a low box on legs about the height of a footstool caught Brother Malachi's eye. That one, he'd seen before. A favorite of the Inquisition. He flinched, almost invisibly.

"Why did you come with women, Theophilus? And you so squeamish." The Count's voice was smooth and menacing. Malachi looked about him at the nasty objects in the room: pulleys on the ceiling, a rack, the boot, and a number of other things whose purpose was all too clear. He'd never felt queasier.

"Yes, squeamish. Take a look at this. Nice and sharp, aren't they?" The Count paused before an open iron maiden, dark with the stains of old blood. "Put his hand on the spikes—not too hard, mind you. He needs it to make gold tonight." Brother Malachi was lugged to the apparatus and his right hand forced onto the spikes. "What do you think of it, you soft, cowardly little worm?"

"It—it would be very bad for my complexion."

"Ah, yes—your tender skin, which you have preserved by wandering all over Europe. Still humorous, aren't you? My Master despises humor. And tonight, you'll make the sacrifice and call him to assist you, won't you?" Brother Malachi turned ashen, and slumped between his captors.

"Fresh eyes and heart, right, Messer Guglielmo? I have a new little one from the last hunt. I've nearly finished playing with it—it bores me now. What are you muttering, Theophilus? Prayers? They don't work here. Oh, yes—your bargain. I'm saving the best for last."

The mutes picked their torches out of the brackets, and the little party wound down a deep passage that seemed hollowed out of the solid rock. Brother Malachi could feel drops of icy water splashing from the ceiling onto his face, and hear them hiss as they touched the torches. The corridor ended in a wide spot. Here they paused before several grilles set into the floor. The stench of decay rose from them. The Count took a torch and walked to the farthest one, holding it down to the grille. With his free hand, he took a pomander from the wallet at his belt and held it to his nose. A hoarse voice rose from the grille.

"Back again, are you, you verse-mangler? What new obscenity have you come with this time?"

"I'm going to recite to you my 'Ode to Summer.' "

"The theme's overworked. Face facts—you have a banal imagination."

"Just say it's good, and you're as free as a bird."

"Impossible. You've never written a line yet that isn't trite."

"Trite? Me? Trite? Do you realize where you are, you verminous street sweeping?"

"How can I forget? In your oubliette—where you come to drop in the contents of your chamber pot or the results of your fits of versification. Pretty much the same stuff—they obviously come from the same end. Pull me out and face me like a man, you coward."

"I'm not pulling you out until you're ready to crawl on your stomach like a worm, and kiss my feet, and weep, and say my verse is the best you've ever heard."

"Pull me up, then. You've got enough equipment up there to make a priest sign himself over to the Devil. Making a poet weep shouldn't be half as hard."

"I want you to say it from the heart."

"Impossible."

"Impossible? I don't think so." Striking out like a snake, the Count gave Brother Malachi an immense backhanded blow across the face. As Brother Malachi cried out, he had him flung onto the grille.

"Who's up there?"

"Gilbert, it's me."

"Theophilus? You? What in the hell are you doing here? You're dripping on me—hmm. Blood."

"Just a nosebleed, Gilbert. Don't worry."

"He's come to buy your freedom. Isn't that thoughtful? But that's not the best part, Gilbert l'Escolier—"

"De Vilers, cucumber head."

"You persist in the masquerade, you villein? That is the worst crime of all—impersonating a gentleman."

"You ought to know." The voice sounded raspier, weaker, but still defiant. The sound of coughing echoed from the pit. In the half dark Brother Malachi could feel the Count's rage growing and swelling like a wave of heat radiating from the huge body.

He whispered despairingly down into the pit: "For God's sake, Gilbert, tell him you like his bloody poetry and get out."

"*Et tu,* Theophilus? But it's not true, and that's why I won't."

"You idiot—I can't believe I'm giving him the Secret of Transmutation in exchange for a hammerhead like you."

"The Philosopher's Stone? Good God, Theophilus, do you want him to take over half of Europe? I thought you had more sense than that."

"No, he didn't," broke in the Count's voice, oily with suppressed rage. "But as I always do, I've saved the best surprise for last. I'm sure your Margaret will convince you to come around to my point of view—bit by bit, if you understand what I mean." Malachi felt his whole body go stiff with horror.

"You haven't got her," came the voice from the pit. "You never will. She's safe at home. There's an ocean between her and this place."

"Not for long, you singing jackdaw. I've cast a drawing spell on her. She'll be here before the next new moon."

"Nonsense."

"Nonsense? We'll see." The Count turned to the mutes. "Take this trembling little alchemist here, and see him upstairs. I want him to begin the process tonight. And lock him in. He's not to set foot out of the hidden chambers until the gold is made. Once he's succeeded, I want him bound and brought to me no matter what time of day or night it is. And—oh, yes. Hood him. I don't want the slightest chance of the Secret being communicated to a soul outside the hidden chambers." Brother Malachi's blood ran cold at these words. Suddenly, he realized that not a living creature in the laboratorium would be allowed to survive the achievement of the Great Work.

As the gate-horn echoed in the stony inner court, the *pucelles* in the Countess's antechamber rushed to hang out the windows. "Visitors, visitors!" they cried. "Oh, let me see!" For after all, visitors always bring hope—a future husband may be among them. Mother Hilde suppressed a smile as she went on compounding herbs for a poultice in her mortar. "What's their degree? Can you make out the arms?" came the excited voices of the maids-in-waiting. "Nothing I've ever seen," came a disappointed voice from the window. "A foreigner—three cockleshells and a dragon—no, a lion."

Three cockleshells! My God! I leapt from the hearth and crowded my way into the window. The sight below froze my heart in a moment. A knight in full armor, visor up, a pilgrim's cloak tied behind his saddle, led the procession that rode from the bailey gate into the inner court. Beside him rode his squire, and behind them were six men at arms escorting a hooded woman on a white palfrey whose rich crimson gown peeped out from beneath her heavy dark cloak. The coat of arms—why there wasn't the slightest doubt about it. Sir Hugo de Vilers had found me at last! And as if that weren't enough, he had brought my haughty and vindictive sister-in-law to witness his triumph. Oh, there was no mistaking it—I'd know that dress anywhere. So very close—and now Gregory was lost forever! I couldn't hide my trembling as I turned back to Mother Hilde.

But now the apartments were in a hubbub, for at the thought of a visit by another gentlewoman, the Countess had roused from her lethargy and begun to dig feverishly in her chests.

"At last, a lady to converse with—tell me, what are those arms? I didn't recognize them." The Countess was querying her attendant, who had gone to take a closer look as the guests were received in the hall.

"English arms, my lady."

"Oh, maybe another ambassador. From the English prince's force, at Bordeaux?"

"That's what he said, my lady."

"Was the lady well dressed? Perhaps she can tell me of the latest fashions. Oh, it's so hard, being buried here away from everyone, to entertain in the latest style."

"She was in crimson, embroidered with gold, my lady."

"Crimson, did you say? Then this old brown velvet will hardly do. It's all worn bald. Look! What a shame my lord never sends me to Orléans to have gowns made, the way he once did when I had his favor. Crimson—oh, not the blue, no—"

"The gold silk, my lady?"

"Oh, yes, that's it. Much nicer than crimson. Yes—the gold silk—tell me, has it creases in it?"

And so it went as Mother Hilde and I crouched at the fireside and whispered, unnoticed in the commotion.

At supper, allowed out of her apartments at last, she glittered brilliantly, seated among her ladies, with the beautiful visitor seated by her side. Sir Hugo, being only a knight, and not even a knight banneret, sat many places down from the noble ambassadors of the Count of Foix. Already, the rumor had swept the tables that the knight was from the English force at Bordeaux, and that the noblewoman was his sister-in-law, whom he had escorted here for the purpose of fulfilling a curious request of the Comte de St. Médard: that he would receive her husband's ransom only from her own hand.

"And imagine," said the gossipy Brother Anselm, who was as at home in the *langue d'oc* as the *langue d'oïl*, "there's not a noble prisoner here, unless he's locked below, which would be a great breach of chivalry. 'It would be most unchivalrous—the Count would be despised throughout Christendom,' said I to the ambassador's groom, and he said to me, 'So says my master, who has warned the Count not to make enemies of the English while they are on his doorstep, especially since he has no way of knowing which way his own king will ally himself. But the

Count just growled that the King of Navarre was seized by a
ruse at a dinner party by the French king, and no one says that
the French king is unchivalrous. But my master said the Count
of Foix cannot be seen to make peace with someone who
makes enemies of the English prince.' So, you see, it's altogether curious. My, just look up there at the dais. What kind of
a wife is that? She's flirting with the ambassador himself."

Even from where I sat, shrinking behind the fattest of the
pilgrims to keep from being recognized, I could see the ambassador, his face red with drink and desire, leering from beneath
his gray moustaches at her. And though she was too far from
him to speak, her eyes sent him messages that could not be
ignored. And who could ignore her? Every man in the place
was drawn to stare at her blazing beauty. Wisps of golden curls
peeped from beneath her pearl-embroidered headdress, as she
blushed prettily and stared demurely down at the table. Amid
these sallow southern complexions, her white and rose English
skin shone like a jewel. And never has a crucifix moved up and
down so suggestively as the one that sat on the immense bosom
revealed by her tightly laced, low-cut crimson gown. I was right
about the gown. I knew it well indeed. But it certainly never
had looked like that on Lady Petronilla. Who was the woman
wearing it? Her eyes were down—I waited until she glanced up
to see. But I stared so hard I nearly choked on the wine I was
drinking. Could it be? It certainly could be no one else. It was
Cis, the laundress! What on earth could have brought her here,
dressed like this?

Cis sat at the dais like a brilliantly colored butterfly at the
very center of the Count's web. She fluttered and glanced
about under her eyelashes as if she didn't even understand that
her feet were firmly glued to the fatal net. Then we could see
the Countess speak to her, and she stared at the trencher and
blushed again, to the admiration of the gentlemen at the table.
The Countess appeared frustrated. She gestured to another
lady and had her speak to the beautiful stranger. Again, a pretty
blush. The ambassador sent his own cup of wine to her, as a

favor, and she gazed through her lashes with a look of grateful adoration. The Count raised an eyebrow at the exchange, and his red lips worked as if he tasted some little disgusting thing. I didn't think the look boded well at all. Then he addressed a remark to his partner on the left. Never have I wished more that I could hear what was going on.

At length, supper was done, though Mother Hilde had barely touched her food, and the tables were cleared away for the evening's entertainment. I mixed in what I hoped was an invisible fashion with the knot of pilgrims trying to improve their view of the entertainment, and edged closer so I could try to hear all that was going on. It was pretty much the usual stuff for the Count's hall, a sort of flamboyant little pageant designed by the lord of St. Médard himself to display his artistry and taste. First the minstrels played and sang. Then there were dancers, this time dressed as "savages" in hairy skins and wolf masks, who made mocking, obscene gestures as they cavorted. Then youths all in silk, representing something very symbolic, vanquished the savages with wands wound with silk ribbons. The ambassador managed to get himself seated next to Cis. She took advantage of the situation to let her hand creep into his lap. His hand, in turn, seemed to vanish somewhere behind her where it couldn't be seen. Then, as pages played trumpets to announce something very special, the Count leaned toward Hugo, where he sat on the other side of Cis, and said loudly, "This next creation is my own; tell me what you think of it."

There followed a very silly song about summer. The words rhymed, after a fashion, but though I know little about poetry, I know that something you sing must go bumpety-bumpety the same way, like a horse's gait, and not go changing around from trot to canter, or as if the horse had suddenly gone lame. And oh, goodness, it had shepherds piping, and lasses dancing, and birds singing, but all somewhat wrong, though it's hard to say why. After the song, there was a polite murmur, since everyone had heard the Count's words.

"Well?" said the Count. Sir Hugo shifted uncomfortably.

"I haven't much of a head for poetry, you know. I'm just a soldier. I like hunting horns—ha! That's music! But it seemed very good to me. Yes, especially that part about the birds singing, 'tirilay, tirilay!' I could imagine myself hunting grouse."

The Count's face relaxed. He knew a heartfelt comment when he heard one.

"You wouldn't, by any chance, consider the subject somewhat . . . used?" he said in a significant tone. Why, I could not imagine.

"Used? Whatever for? Doesn't summer come every year? It can't be used up! Myself, I can't get enough of summer. My favorite season!"

"Spoken like a gentleman!" exclaimed the Count, and then he leaned forward with a blazing look. "But not spoken like any brother of the ill-spoken, villainous rogue I hold in my cellar. Either you are an impostor, Sir Hugo, or the man you've come to ransom is one. I prefer to think the latter."

"An impostor? I've come all this way to ransom an impostor?"

"Do you think I'd keep a gentleman in the cellar? What's your game, Sir Hugo—or better yet, that of your master at Bordeaux? And who is that jingle maker I've got in my cellar?"

"How dare you insult me! I've come on a mission of honor to ransom my long-lost brother, Sir Gilbert de Vilers, whose ransom you purchased after the siege of Verneuil, and whom you are honor bound to allow to be redeemed."

"You wish to challenge me, little English sparrow hawk? I am undefeated in tourney and in battle. Look at me, I am the Count of St. Médard!" And the Count unfolded his huge bulk from the chair and stood towering over Hugo: a full head and a half taller than any man in the room, and twice the weight, all solid muscle beneath the rolls of fat.

"I do not insult you. You insult chivalry," replied Hugo, turning red at the neck. "I say here, in front of these noble guests and witnesses, that I am a man of honor, on a mission of peace." Beside him, the ambassador of the Count of Foix seemed most interestingly intertwined with Cis. Perhaps it was that his beard had accidentally become entangled in the elaborate metalwork of the crucifix, but it was hard to tell.

"Peace? Whose peace? Reveal yourself now, or face me in the tiltyard tomorrow." Everyone was staring at them now. Even the ambassador recovered his lost hand, and paid new attention.

"You sent a messenger to England, to request that my brother's ransom be paid by the white hand of Margaret, his wife. And I sent a return message that we should come to meet your terms by that fellow, there—that Dominican with the gray face—and so, we have arrived. And where is our greeting? Why have you not treated us with honor? Only insults, unworthy of a Christian lord."

"I said that?" The Count turned and gave the sinister creature who stood by his shoulder a suspicious glance.

"A vision, my lord. A hallucination. Part of the drawing spell," hastily mumbled the monk at his elbow.

"Oh. Aha. I see. So, Sir Hugo, this is the beautiful Margaret, poetical inspiration?" He cast his eyes on Cis with renewed interest, then glanced sideways about the room, as if he regretted the presence of so many witnesses.

"Absolutely. Come to pay his ransom personally. And since we've met your terms, you're honor bound to accept."

"Come here." The Count motioned to Cis. She looked down demurely. "She doesn't speak French?" he said curiously to Hugo.

"Not all women do in England," Sir Hugo said boldly.

"But the *noblesse* do. This is curious," answered the Count. "She's brought the money."

"But so pious and shy. Perfect for my purpose."

"Whatever you have in mind, you must redeem my brother."

"Your brother? I have my doubts about that. A tall, dark-headed, bony fellow who writes bad poetry?"

"Poetry? I didn't know he wrote poetry. It sounds like him, except for the poetry. Speculations about God, that sort of thing—but poetry? Well, maybe. He had on a seal ring like this—" Sir Hugo extended his hand.

"Like that? No. He didn't have any ring at all. Probably taken. But would you say he's stubborn?"

"Stubborn as the Devil."

"And has the habit of calling his insults Truth?"

"That's him to the life."

"Then that's who I have. But you can't be brothers. Not unless your lady mother slept with a stable-groom."

"You insult my lady mother! By God, did you hear that, you lords? My lady mother was as pure as the snow!"

"Stay your hand, English popinjay, unless you wish to die tomorrow. The Sieur d'Aigremont will slay you at a blow." The ambassador leaned forward to prevent potentially dangerous bloodshed. The Count leaned back in his chair and watched Sir Hugo with a faint smile, as he might watch a foolish animal sniffing the bait in an unsprung trap.

"Tell the lovely Margaret that I will not agree to kill you yet. First, I wish her to see something. Fray Joaquin, the letter, please." Fray Joaquin pulled a little folded paper packet, the seals broken, from beneath his robe, and handed it to his master, who unfolded it and waved it beneath Sir Hugo's nose.

"Now, what does this mean to you, Sir Hugo?" he asked.

"Me? I don't read. Ask the priest to cypher it."

"Give it to the lady Margaret." Cis took it, held it upside down, and gazed demurely at the floor.

"Ask her to read it, Sir Hugo."

"Read it?" Sir Hugo turned pale. "What's in it?"

"It's a letter carried by your pseudo brother from the real Margaret. It appears that this Margaret can't read it. I believe you have cheated me, Sir Hugo. I want the Margaret who wrote this letter, or you haven't fulfilled my terms, have you?"

"Well, ah—umm—that Margaret—that Margaret is the cousin of this Margaret. And that Margaret—she's very ill. Brokenhearted. Near Death's door. Couldn't travel. So this Margaret said she'd come. They look almost exactly alike, and, um, you just said you wanted a Margaret—so here she is, to meet your demands!"

"So this one's a Margaret too. That accounts for it. The fool didn't specify when he cast it," the Count said to himself, and turned to the Dominican, still bowing at his elbow. "Fray Joaquin," he hissed, "you accursed bumbler, you'll pay for this." Then he turned back to Sir Hugo. "No Margaret, no ransom. Go home and get me the real Margaret, Englishman."

"That's entirely unfair. You've insulted my mother, insulted my Margaret, and you won't ransom my brother. Meet me tomorrow in the tiltyard."

"The tiltyard? Good. Then, with your kind consent, I will kill you in a way that becomes a knight. But it is for your mother that I meet you in the lists. For the affair of the substitute Margaret, I should pick your bones apart in my little chamber below. Now, as for the man you claim as your brother, I propose a little sport. You've had your fun, now I get mine. Let Margaret here—the cousin, or whatever she is, in the absence of the real Margaret, play me for him. Her choice, whatever game is here." He waved a hand in the direction of the games laid out on the red cloth of the table dormant for the evening's amusement. "If she wins, I swear on my honor as a nobleman, before all these witnesses, he'll go free with her. If I win, I keep him, and her as well, for whatever purpose I choose." An unpleasant smile stretched the corners of the Count's lips, and his eyes glittered in the torchlight. The company leaned forward with new interest. Here was royal sport. A life for a woman: the stuff of a *chanson de geste*. The chess pieces stood ready on the silver and ebony board; draughts, backgammon, and other games were waiting beside them. Hugo looked about him at the table. Even he realized the Count was playing with him. Chess? When had Cis ever had time to learn to play noblemen's games like that? And what woman could outplay a man anyway?

"Entirely fair, if rather unorthodox." The ambassador looked again at Cis's pink bosom and smiled somewhat ruefully, his voice sounding regretful. "You've no proof the man's his brother, and not a knave, anyway. You don't have to redeem a base-blooded man. And the woman—charming—"

"Do you swear to that?" said Sir Hugo, very slowly, stalling for time to think.

"I swear," said the Count, putting his hand over his heart. "Bring in the relics." Hugo began to sweat.

"Suppose I don't agree?" he said.

"Not agree? To something entirely fair, in my own house? Then you've insulted me. I dislike being insulted. Who knows what I might do?" And he put his hand casually on the reliquary and swore. He smiled as he watched the sweat pouring down Hugo's neck.

"And now, will the lovely Margaret step forward and choose her game."

"I will," I cried loudly, and stepped forward from the knot of pilgrims in the corner of the hall. Fear had made my mind swift, and I had seen something on the table that made me strong. It was dice: several sets in ebony, ivory, and bone, sitting next to a dice board. The bone ones looked exactly like my own. So I put the dice from my pilgrim's wallet into my sleeve and walked boldly before the great lords. Sir Hugo's jaw dropped, and he stared at me as if he'd seen a ghost. "Margaret," he whispered.

"What's this?" said the Count, raising his eyebrows. "More Margarets? Which one are you?" The Dominican beside him looked strangely relieved, I couldn't imagine why.

"I am Margaret de Vilers, wife to Gilbert de Vilers, come to hold you to your vow."

I could hear murmurs from the company in the hall. "Delightful." "Wonderful entertainment." "Is it a play?" "Perhaps he planned it all in advance. So original."

"Oh, really? He said you looked just alike. Who am I to believe?" I suppose I didn't look as fine as Cis, all in black as I was, with my rusty dark pilgrim's cloak and my wide pilgrim's hat slung behind me on my back. "Suppose I want the other

Margaret?" he went on in that bland, menacing voice. I could see the Count of Foix's ambassador purse his lips with annoyance.

"She isn't the proper Margaret at all, and she's not married to anyone, let alone Gilbert de Vilers, so your vow would be broken if she played. Play me." The ambassador regained his contentment.

"If you are indeed the right Margaret."

"I am, and I can prove it. That letter. If it was really his, I'll tell you what's in it. And the seal. It's his. It's from this ring, which he gave me as my wedding ring." I held up my hand.

"And who do you say this is, Sir Hugo?"

"Margaret de Vilers, my brother's wife," he answered wearily.

"The one who was too sick to travel."

"I got well," I said. "Now I want to choose the game."

"Chess, then, little Margaret who cannot spell?" I've never heard a pleasant sentiment sound more threatening.

"I haven't the wit for chess. I'll play dice. Then God's hand will assist me." To think, I once wouldn't have been able to lie this much at all. But then, if God hadn't wanted me to win, He wouldn't have given me the loaded dice, would He?

The Sieur d'Aigremont grinned a strange, triumphant little smile. "Which ones?" he asked.

"Those," I said, pointing to the set of three that looked exactly like my own. He swept away the other sets, and a seat was brought to the table, exactly facing his own across the dice board. As I sat, I could hear the menacing hum of the Burning Cross rise to a higher, more desperate whine.

"What's that noise?" he said.

"A fly, perhaps," I answered. I could feel the press of bodies around us as everyone in the room strained to get a glimpse of the strange game.

"What game do you wish to play? Hazard?"

"I—don't know Hazard. I've never played dice before."

There was a strange sigh from the crowd. "Let's just play for the high number."

"*As plus points?* As you wish, madame. One throw only?"

"All right," I said. It's less risk to change them only once, I thought.

"And we agree before this company that the highest number wins?" His smile was positively wolfish.

"Yes."

He picked up the dice, fingering them elaborately, and then shook them in his cupped hands and dropped them onto the dice board that lay between us on the table.

"Eighteen," he said as they stopped rolling. I could feel the heat of the bodies crowding round us. "You cannot beat that, madame."

"But if it pleases God, I may tie." He picked up the dice with grand flourish and handed them to me. My heart was thumping as if it would leap from my mortal body. Calm, Margaret, calm, I thought to myself. I bowed my head over the dice as if in prayer, and slipped them away for my own, in the way that Master Kendall's shade had shown me the money changers do. I rolled the dice, and watched as they wobbled across the board. The close-crowded watchers breathed in as if they were one person. Eighteen. "A miracle," I heard someone say. "God is on her side."

"A tie," I said. "What now, monsieur?"

"Another match. Agreed?" he said to the company.

"Yes, yes, go on," the murmurs swept around the table. I could feel the faces crowding in on us, and the breath of strangers on my back. Then he put down his hand and swept away my dice. Oh, God, what could I do? I wasn't meant to be a dice cheater after all. It had seemed so easy before—and now, all of a sudden, it wasn't! I could feel the sweat running down my neck and back like a river. I watched his hands. Elaborately, he swept them about. Wait—did I see something? It was my dice, disappearing down his sleeve. I was sure from the angle he held his arm. He'd switched them for his own! They'll come up alike, I thought, and then I'll know. They rattled as they fell: six, another six. The third seemed to catch on the edge of the board, then fell. A four.

"Sixteen," gasped the crowd. And before he could take them to make the pretense of handing them to me while he switched them for the bad ones—or rather, the honest ones—I put my hand on them.

"Now me," I said, snatching them up and rolling them quickly. The cloth seemed to shift beneath the board as they fell.

"Sixteen also," I said, as he turned red in the face.

"We'll go one more round, winner takes all." His face was swollen with rage. But as he looked to the company for approval, I took his loaded dice, and rolled the first pair out of my sleeve in their place.

"Your dice, monsieur." I handed them to him. By now, I was so frightened, I didn't know whether they were a good set or a bad set. But I knew the set I'd just taken from him had to be bad ones, because they'd just rolled high.

"Don't touch those. I'll get them myself," he snapped. Did he suspect something? I opened my eyes very wide and tried to look the picture of injured innocence. "Don't lean against the table. You'll jostle the board," he snapped. He seemed rattled. Then he looked at me through narrowed eyes, and scooped up the dice. This time, I couldn't tell whether he'd switched them with a hidden set or thrown the ones I'd given him. The throw wobbled in a loop, and the first die settled—a six. A moment later, the next two came to rest near the edge of the board, and the crowd around the table let out a sigh. A two. And then a three.

I took the dice from the board. "God save me," I said, and crossed myself. Then, wiping my streaming forehead with my sleeve, I switched the dice again. I've never had such nimble fingers before or since. If you'd ever seen my embroidery, you'd wonder that I ever could have done it. Sometimes I think that only mortal fear makes us perfect. I threw the dice onto the board again. This set has to be his, I thought, and if they are, and he's a cheat, then I'll win, and if he's honest, then—

"Eighteen!" the shout rang through the great hall. "The lady Margaret has ransomed her husband!" "Oh, how like a romance!" someone sighed—I think it was the Countess.

Even the unspeakable Hugo leapt over the table and clapped me on the back. "Well done, Margaret!" he shouted. "Bravely played!"

But the Count was red with rage. His face shook like a rooster's wattles, and he roared like a bull. "Quiet, quiet, or I'll slay you all!" His hand flew to the dagger at his belt.

"How uncouth. Entirely uncouth," murmured the ambassador. "Not at all like my noble master. Gaston Phoebus is a man of honor, especially at the gaming table, as befits a lord."

The Count heard him and his eyes rolled. He turned to spew his rage on Hugo. "You, you English. Don't forget I meet you tomorrow morning. To the death. And you—you've won, Madame de Vilers. But—"

"I want him released now. And two horses. We'll leave in the morning."

His voice softened menacingly. "And just what good is his liberty to you without my letter of safe-conduct?"

I started. What game was he playing now?

"Just how do you expect to get home again? Not by ship. Nothing leaves Bayonne in this season for the north. Or perhaps you expect to cross Aquitaine into Guyenne to the headquarters of the English prince? He has pulled back for the winter, and there are nothing but mercenaries between here and there, and I assure you, they cut the throats of English travelers just as quickly as those of any other nation. No, my dear. There is no escaping it. You must cross my lands and then pass through the neutral countries to the north, by way of Foix, Burgundy, and those other lands as yet untouched by war. I am a powerful man: my letter and seal will carry you to the north in safety. Without them, count yourself dead."

"I—I'd never thought of that." It wasn't an offer he was

making; it was a threat. We'd never pass out of his mountains alive. He'd never sworn to that part, so the witnesses wouldn't fault him for it.

"You must understand, I have no love for your husband. I count him a personal enemy. So let's discuss the terms on which you receive my safe-conduct in my rooms, tonight before midnight. Come alone."

"But—"

"Haven't you figured out yet that he wants to sleep with you? Why else all this charade with the dice? Do it and get the letter, you ninny, and we'll be out of here, as soon as I've met him on the field of honor," Hugo hissed into my ear in English.

"Hugo, you're as filthy-minded as ever. It's indecent. And what's more, he has every intention of killing you. He doesn't want any of us to leave alive—and if he wasn't trying to impress that big ambassador and his friends here, he'd have been a lot more direct about it. Haven't you seen how huge he is? He'll chop you into stewing meat."

"Pfah, you've got it wrong, as usual. He's a knight, and bound by the code of chivalry. Besides, he's older than me and all fat. The big ones are always clumsy—he'll fall like a tower to the sappers. And how do you think he'll be able to sign a letter of safe-conduct after I've defeated him? So which do you prefer? Gilbert the cuckold, or Gilbert the corpse? Besides, you'll like it. Most women do. Tell him yes, you pious little nit." Oh, Hugo infuriated me. As stupid as a brick wall, and as helpful as a cracked jug. Who would help me? I'll stall him. I'll think of something. Maybe I can trick it out of him, or appeal to his mercy. I turned to the Count.

"I want to see this safe-conduct thing first. Then I'll agree to talk, not before." I looked at his billowing face, but could not see past all the debauchery.

"Not bad, not bad. Pity she's not a man. She'd make a good diplomat," I could overhear the ambassador say to one of his companions.

"Why, of course. I'll have it written here. And you shall have it signed and this ring off my finger to go with it, after you have visited my chamber," the Count responded. I didn't like his bland, superior tone.

"And I want it in good plain French—not Latin or something I can't read."

"Sly, sly, that woman," I could hear them saying behind me. "That's how the king sent a death warrant once—death to the bearer, in Latin. Poor bastard never knew."

"Agreed, agreed—" He waved a hand airily. "Fray Joaquin, get pen and paper." As his black-cloaked shadow scurried off, I could feel the Count looking at me, to get my measure. It was a crawly feeling, as if he were imagining me with my clothes off. There wasn't a noise in the room, except the sound of people breathing. It was then, in this horrid stillness, that I felt it. The first ripple from deep within my belly. It was unmistakable. The baby had started to move. Languidly, joyfully, like a swimmer in summer.

How could you be so happy at a time like this? I asked it in my mind.

"Joy," it answered, and rolled over again. Joy, I thought, and I could see the dancing light in the eye of my remembering.

"Joy," repeated the baby, and looped over again. They were droning in the background. Droning French and writing.

Aren't you afraid of dying? We could die, I told it.

"Joy, joy," said the baby, as it rolled.

Mindless thing, you haven't a grain of sense, I scolded.

Someone joggled my arm.

"Your paper, madame, it's done," said Fray Joaquin.

"Give it here. I need to read it."

"Yours, madame," said the Count, pointing to it where it lay on the gaming table. His head was tilted back, making his chins bulge forward, as he looked down his vast wide nose at me. It had black hairs bristling from the inside. Oh, ugly, I thought, and I shuddered as a cold wind passed through me.

"It's worthless without the seal, you know," he added. "I'll seal it and give you this ring after our—private agreement tonight. You understand? When I retire, I expect you there—"

I couldn't bear it. I stuffed the paper into my bosom and bolted through the press of people, weeping.

"Good—it begins," I could hear him say as I fled. The sound of raucous laughter echoed down the corridor after me.

CHAPTER
10

Brother Malachi leaned over the seething mass of molten metal, holding his breath against the hideous fumes rising from the crucible. The firelight glistened on his face, making it all ruddy; sweat ran in great rivulets down his forehead and trickled down his cheeks almost like tears. He was wearing a great leather apron to prevent his gown from going up in flames. Heavy gauntlets, drawn almost to the elbow, protected his hands. His left hand held the leather sack, now open, that contained the Red Powder; his right held his black iron stirring rod.

"Almost ready," he said, pulling his head back from the intense heat.

"Sulfur. You haven't added the sulfur yet. Villanova says it must be at the beginning of the process." The glancing light from the inferno made Messer Guglielmo's eyes blaze unnaturally.

"But Lull says that it can only be now. Unless, of course, you think as little of Lull as you think of Magister Salernus, who says that the process must take place during the full moon, if it is to multiply correctly."

"And where, pray tell, does he say that?" Messer Guglielmo's voice was all sarcasm.

"You think he'd give away a secret like that? It's in the seventh illustration on the twenty-first page. He has them encoded in multiples of seven. It distinctly shows the peacock under the full moon, just after the Green Lion."

"Not in my copy, it doesn't."

"Your copy is corrupted. Did you see the error on the page of the descent of the dove?"

"Well, that I'll grant—but the full moon signifies the presence of silver, whereas carrying out the process under the full moon should be depicted as a pregnant queen, in his system, and I see no such thing."

Even the dumb assistants, taken in by the argument, leaned forward to inspect the process. Brother Malachi ceased stirring, drew the tall stool beside the athanor to the wall, and sat down. He leaned his back against the cool stones and sighed, lifting an arm to wipe the sweat from his forehead with the crook of his elbow, never letting go of the precious little sack. His rod lay across his lap, still clutched in a gauntleted hand.

"Now," the waspish voice of Messer Guglielmo broke in, "you can't go further without the fixative. You must have it prepared before you now, fresh, or you will destroy the process."

"I don't use that fixative. It's not necessary. It's evil. The power that created the universe and transforms it is good. The Red Powder won't work—besides—"

"Excuses again. Cowardly excuses, unfit for a scientist. You can't evade anymore, you overrated excuse for an alchemist. That kind of talk might fool an amateur, but you have to deal with a professional this time. Do you hear?" Messer Guglielmo paced nervously, his voice rising to a raspy screech. Brother Malachi leaned against the wall, drawing long, shaky breaths, his eyes glazed.

"I can't imagine how you ever got as far as you did, without the daring required for true investigation—without the willingness to take risks. It's I who have the Secret almost within my grasp. I didn't need you. But oh, no, the famous Theophilus, or someone who claims he's him, must be given everything." He pulled several hairs from his beard with a nervous gesture as he paced back and forth.

"Tonight is your night, Theophilus, and you cannot dream how greatly I crave your failure. Irritation. Irritation! You infuriate me. Fail, Theophilus, fail! And when Asmodeus has brought me the triumph, I'll have the pleasure of watching you die slowly, slowly—" He looked up with a start. Fray Joaquin, having entered silently, stood before him like a shadow.

"Fail? He's failed?" the Dominican asked with a faint, ghoulish smile.

"The process is at the point of change. The next step is the sulfur, at the peak of the heat. Then, as it changes color, the Red Powder must be added. But I haven't my full moon, so it won't multiply as much as it should—" Brother Malachi explained wearily.

"Do you hear him making excuses already? He's trying to save himself ahead of time. I told you, I know his type."

"You are to call Asmodeus," said the black-cloaked friar.

"Call my Asmodeus to rescue this fool from his mess? Give this amateur here credit for my success? After all I've been through? If I run the risk of calling Asmodeus, it will be for my own triumph."

"You are under orders."

"I haven't the offering. The Count hasn't sent it down yet. Besides, it takes time to lay out the circle. We can't afford to make a mistake with it this time." The memory of the towering demon beating his powerful wings against the frail barrier made even the waspish Messer Guglielmo turn a little pale.

Brother Malachi bowed his head and crossed himself. His lips were moving in silent prayer. The stirring rod lay across his knees.

"Then start laying it out now, you jackass!" Fray Joaquin picked up a large ladle from the broad wooden table in the corner and began to batter the unfortunate Messer Guglielmo about the head. He threw up his hands to protect his head and backed into the corner, crouching until the storm of blows abated.

"But—the sacrifice?"

"You know perfectly well that I don't do them. He always wants to do them himself. He'll be a bit late tonight. You'll have to hold the process until he brings the woman's body down."

"Woman? I thought he had an infant left."

"He does. This is something else. He has a woman in his chambers now, and when his pleasure is done, he'll break her neck and have her brought down with the sacrifice."

"That doesn't sound alchemical. Asmodeus doesn't like women."

"No—he says it's something about art."

Malachi's eyes started, but his body remained slumped against the wall, as if he'd heard nothing. He took a deep breath.

"The time is now," he said, getting up carefully, and making a great show of inspecting the equipment. "The process is ripe. I will produce gold."

"Now?" Fray Joaquin turned on him. "This soon? Take care what you promise." But his eyes were shining with greed.

"He'll fail," snapped Messer Guglielmo. "I'm looking forward to it."

"No I won't," said Brother Malachi, and he leaned over the crucible and emptied the Red Powder into it, stirring it in with the iron rod in the shape of overlapping triangles, the star of Solomon, chanting unintelligibly at each angle the dark rod made in the flaming mass.

"I want him released tonight. Not tomorrow after the joust." My voice sounded firm as I stood a few paces from the open door to the Count's bedchamber, but my knees were shaking and my stomach queasy. Little Brother Anselm had accompanied me to the door, remonstrating the whole while about Ursula and her virgin martyrs.

"The crown of virtue is preferable to the muck of sin," he preached. "Besides, I have come to the considered conclusion that this count is not a trustworthy man. No indeed. He may very well try to trick you, once he has what he wants. After all, he should have brought forth your husband rejoicing, and crowned him with laurel leaves, and had a feast of song. That's what a nobleman would do. But him? He's a poor sport and a bad loser. He makes excuses, he wants jousts. I think he'll cheat you, and then where will you be? Minus your virtue, and minus your husband, too, who will be required by his honor to renounce you, once he hears what's happened."

"I've thought of that already," I told him. God, his chatter was getting tiresome! There's nothing more annoying than someone who's slower than you are to figure out the obvious.

"I tell you, you're a fool. Women are. It's why they should only act with the advice of men."

"Have you ever considered that maybe that's what I'm doing? And you yourself say it's stupid," I turned on him. "So tell me which is right, and then I'll do my duty, eh?"

"Our Lord Jesus Christ," he said, rolling his eyes heavenward and crossing himself.

"Oh! Easy to say!" I turned on my heel in a fury, but he followed me to the threshold anyway. The door was wide open. The room was lit with dozens of flickering candles. There were sconces on the wall, between the perches where his nasty big satin doublet and huge hose with pointed leather soles were hung. A silver candelabrum with a dozen candles sat on a little round table that was covered with an embroidered cloth and set with a jug of wine, a single goblet, and a little rere-supper— a cold fowl in some sort of sauce, a covered dish, and bread. On a vast gilded bed at the center of the room, an immense figure lounged, clad only in the night napkin around his head and a great, fur-lined *robe de chambre* that he had allowed to fall open suggestively.

"I knew you'd come." His deep voice rose from the shadows.

"I want him now, not tomorrow," I said firmly, staying close to the open door.

"I intend to take you to him, once we have finished our little —talk—here—" The figure uncoiled itself from the bed. "Jean, you may go. And close the door after you." The valet left, and the door made a heavy sound as it shut. I felt suddenly cold all over, and shuddered.

"Cold? Perhaps a little wine will warm you." He gestured to the table. Beneath the supper dishes, the gold and silver threads of embroidery on the cloth shone in the candlelight. There was a little bench with a back on it behind the table.

"I'm—not thirsty. I want him back. You've already sworn—"

"Don't be so nervous. You doubt my good faith? Look— here's the ring." He had to twist it to get it off, it was so wedged on. It marred the gesture, which seemed to annoy him briefly. "I put it on the table, so, as a pledge." He moved as carefully and smoothly as a trainer with a wild horse—his eyes never leaving mine, as he set it on the table.

"And the sealing wax too. You see it there?" he said in the soothing voice that animal trainers use. "Sit down, and have some wine."

"It could be poisoned," my mind sang silently in a cool little voice.

"You're afraid of the wine. Look. It's a single cup. The goblet of lovers. Tonight we shall both drink from it. You see? I drink first." He swallowed the wine in a single great gulp and then renewed it from the silver jug.

"The wine already poured was good. Beware the wine in the jug." My mind's silvery trilling seemed to come from far away.

"Now, sit down," he said, in that same even, terrifying tone.

"I'm not tired," I answered. "I came to talk about Gilbert de Vilers. I want horses, I want your ring. I want to be far from here as soon as possible. A gentleman would have offered these things, without all this—charade."

"Sit down!" he roared, and the suddenness of his anger terrified me. I sat.

He crowded himself onto the little bench beside me, and his bulk filled it all up to overflowing. I could feel all those rolls of flesh pressing against me, beneath the robe, which fell open to reveal his curiously hairless chest—no, not hairless. Shaved. Ugh. How revolting. And he smelled of something sickly sweet. What was it? Phew. Lilac water. If I ever get out of this, I thought, I'll never be able to stand lilacs again. Mind, mind—think of something. Make me quick.

"You're not thirsty? Try—a wing of capon." He gouged his fingers into the flesh of the dead bird and came up with a morsel, which he held between his thumb and forefinger near my lips. I could feel my eyes growing wide, and my stomach churning.

"I—I'm not hungry."

"Not hungry?" he said, feeding himself the morsel and wiping his lips on the napkin. "It's delicious." He smacked his curiously red lips. "The sauce—I am a connoisseur of sauces."

"I want Sir Gilbert now."

"Now? That hairy, barbaric ape?" He saw my eyes sneak, with a kind of fascinated horror, to the billowing rolls of naked flesh revealed by the open robe.

"Women tell me it's fascinating," he said, looking at my face. "I am this way all over. You should try it yourself. The pain—is —delicious."

I was so disgusted, I couldn't stop my tongue.

"It's just like a great big ugly baby" popped out of my mouth, and then I shrank back, waiting for the blow.

But he was pleased, and his horrid red lips glistened with spit as he smiled.

"Exactly. A lovely, lovely baby. How would a sweet baby harm you? You will love it entirely. The ultimate moment of your life—"

God assist me, God assist me, I prayed silently. Get me and Gregory out of this in one piece. I didn't know they made people this repulsive in the whole wide world. Time. I need time.

"I—um—thought your 'Ode to Summer' was very beautiful," I ventured. I could feel the odious body relax slightly.

"Which part did you like best?"

"The—ah—summeriness of it. It was so very—summery."

"And—?"

"The birds part—it was very lovely—um, the 'tirilay.' And the flowers. I like flowers." All except lilacs, I thought. I never want to smell one again.

"Flowers—lovely little flowers like marguerites," he said, and he took the pins out of my headdress. I shuddered again as I felt him caress my hair.

"Sip the wine," he said as he offered the goblet with the other hand. "It will take the chill off."

"Do—do you write a lot of poetry? I—I like poetry. Beautiful expression is—ah—very—very nice—in a man. Some say it's—the most attractive thing—"

"Poetry? Has no one told you, I am the greatest trouvère in the history of trouvères, the greatest trouvère that ever lived in six kingdoms? Those formerly accounted great—Count Raymond of Toulouse, Guilhem de Poitou, and the other riffraff—everyone agrees I excel them as the hawk soars above the sparrow. I am called 'The King of Troubadors,' by many. Have you never heard of my 'Ode to My Lady's Tiny Foot'?"

"N-no. I come from a very backward place."

"That you do, let me assure you." He was beginning to be distracted. Now, if I could just get him deep in this poetry thing.

"You have a very tiny foot, I imagine." He was looking at my neck. It made it feel all itchy.

"Well, not *so* tiny."

"You must imagine that I wrote it especially for your lovely little foot. I would have, if I had seen it."

"I'd—really like to hear it."

"Ah, my lovely little flower, only if you promise to bare your precious little white foot for me as my reward."

This was getting more disgusting with every moment that passed. "Time, take time," sang the sweet little voice within.

"Maybe I'll drop him the foot first," I could hear him mutter to himself. "It would be appropriate."

"Your beautiful ode?" I prompted him.

"Oh? Oh, yes." He cleared his throat and began. Midway I interrupted him, by way of encouragement.

"That bit about the pearly toenails, that's very nice," I said. Stupidest verse I could ever have imagined, I thought.

"Now, we mustn't interrupt, must we?" He wagged his finger at me. He's getting mellow, I thought. A little more of this and maybe I can talk him out of his dirty little plan, and get Gregory back. "Never interrupt an artist," he went on, in a special rolling tone that he appeared to reserve solely for reciting verse. But it was all too soon he finished the ridiculous thing.

"And now, your promise."

"It's very crowded sitting here. It's hard to get to—if you just moved away a bit—"

"It will be much easier, I assure you, on the bed."

Oh, my, so much for poetry. I'm worse off than ever.

"The bed? I haven't finished eating yet." I stuffed some bread into my mouth. It was as dry as dust.

"Have a little wine to wash it down. Lovely spiced wine."

Again the wine! The back of my head hurt as he grabbed it to force the cup to my lips. The wine had an odd smell. That certainly isn't a spice, I thought. But I know it from somewhere. What is it?

"Drink," he said, and pressed the cup hard against my clenched teeth.

There was a banging at the sealed door.

"Go away!" he shouted. "I'm busy, and not to be disturbed."

"My lord, my lord. Fray Joaquin sends a message, 'He's done

it,' he says. You told him to notify you, no matter what else you were doing."

"Done it! By Fortuna!" He let me go as he leapt up to the door and shouted through it. The moment he turned his head, I splashed the wine into the corner and set the goblet back on the table.

"Bring him here—hooded. I want no one to recognize him, and above all—not to hear the slightest word from him." He turned back to me, rubbing his hands. "My double triumph, all in one night. Thus does the Black Master keep his bargains."

Black Master? No wonder the Burning Cross buzzed so. I'd wrapped it up in a cloth to muffle the sound. As I watched his figure stride back to the table, I seemed to see its outlines fade and shrivel, and a shapeless mass, stinking of sulfur mingled with the sickly odor of lilacs, took its place. The world seemed to slide away, and I could see it there very clearly, hiding beneath the ordinary surface of human flesh. Evil. Consummate evil. The visitors in the hall had never dreamed what lay beneath the everyday shining facade. They saw the surface—the banners, the gilded roast peacocks, the lordly life—and I suppose if they were worldly, they assumed he had a little vice or two on the side. What lord doesn't, after all? But who, who on earth, could even guess the unspeakable thing that lay beneath this wicked man's foolish pretenses? And then I knew that it wasn't love the Count was after, or even the shabby travesty of love. It was my life, and my soul. Mine, Gregory's, Malachi's, everybody's. His own was long gone, if he'd ever had one, and he wouldn't rest until he could suck away the soul of every decent person who came within his reach.

"Ah, you've drunk the wine. Good." And to my surprise, he poured the rest of the jug into the goblet and tossed it off.

"Enough of poetry. Are you feeling hot yet? No? A little warm in the face, perhaps?"

"What on earth was in that wine?" I asked, standing up in alarm.

"Enough cantharides to put an entire kennelful of bitches in heat. Come here." So that's what it was! I'd seen the stuff in my father-in-law's house. He used it for breeding hunting hounds. I ran behind the bed as nimbly as a deer. He followed, blundering, but even so, he was faster than I was. I leapt back across the bed—he leapt after me. I grabbed the candelabrum from the table and held it, flaming, before me.

"Back, Satan, or I'll set you on fire!" I cried.

He laughed and swatted the thing out of my hand with a single blow from his great paw. The candles spluttered and went out as he kicked it into a corner.

"Not—hot—yet?" He was panting. His face had gone all red. He stumbled and I leapt past him, racing around the bed to the window.

"Threatening to jump?" His breath was coming hard—too hard. The stuff he'd drunk was working. The napkin was all askew on his head. I clambered onto the windowsill.

"You haven't got the bowels for it," he gloated, doubled over to recover his breath. I looked down. Endless miles it seemed, down into the dark, with nothing but the sharp rocks of the mountainside below. A wave of pure fear rippled through me. I must. I have to, I thought. My mind was racing. But that look below had cost me my chance. He grabbed my foot and I toppled down hard into the room, shrieking and bruised. I kicked and tore at him with my fingernails, screaming horribly as he scooped me up and flung me onto the bed.

"Lovely—" he gasped. "Just the way I like them—" but he could hardly speak. His whole body had gone all crimson and blotchy. Let him die, God, let him choke and die on the damned stuff, I prayed. He paused and bent over, breathless and retching for a moment, and I thought my prayers had been answered. I jumped from the bed and raced to unbar the door, but he was on me like a wild beast. He didn't even feel me batter at him with the door bar as he began to tear at my clothes.

But he was slowing. I could feel his breath coming in great gasps, like air from a bellows, as he pinned me to the floor. The odor of lilacs mingled with that of vomit as he suddenly rolled off, all huddled over, and shudderingly gave up the witches' brew he'd drunk.

"He'll never make it," my mind's voice sang. I'll be wanting a new dress after this, I thought. He raised his ugly head and stared into the corner. He seemed suddenly paralyzed, his head frozen and staring into the dark. "You'll get out of this one, Margaret. Aren't you the lucky one?" chirped the little voice. Lucky? I'll have to burn this dress as soon as possible.

"In the corner. There—" he said, and his voice was full of horror.

And a bath. I'll be wanting a nice bath. I crawled away from the door. My hair was all unbound, and my clothes hung about me in tatters. I felt myself. Bruised here and there, but substantially unhurt. No damage, really. The baby started to roll again. We're both fine, I thought. That's got to mean something good. "Joy," sang the baby, as it rolled and rippled. You foolish little thing, I told it in my mind. Don't you ever understand when you're in trouble? And we're not half out yet. But I loved it suddenly so much, with a fierceness that claimed me totally.

The Count let out a horrible scream. What on earth was wrong with him? Why didn't God just strike him with lightning and get it over with? You'd think He'd know how to do it right.

It was then that I saw it, standing in the corner. A child. A pretty blond child, just as real as could be, standing there and pointing at him with an accusing finger. She was unclothed, and eyeless, and her little chest gaped open, where the heart was gone.

"I didn't do it," the Count said. "I had to—they made me." The child was joined by another, a little boy, similarly marred, and then another, who held a mangled head in his arms. "It wasn't me, Fray Joaquin, you want him. He did it. He told me how, and once I called Asmodeus, he wanted more, more. You see? It wasn't my fault, not mine at all. They forced me to do it—" He was crouching, now, retreating from the little figures that were crowding around each other, multiplying in the corner. He tried to smile convincingly as he argued with them, but his mouth twisted grotesquely, and his eyes were full of terror. But the little creatures never answered. Oh, even now I can't bear to tell it all, it was so frightful. One by one, the silent specters filled the room around him, deathly quiet, pointing, while he crawled about the floor with excuses, excuses. . . .

He was screaming and gurgling now. "Not me, not me!" he shrieked as he picked himself up and dashed to the door to escape them. But his way was barred by a fierce, whistling cloud like a storm cloud, a seething mass of poison. He rolled his eyes like a frightened horse as he prepared to try to dash through it.

"Why do you wait, little ones?" A ferocious woman's voice could be heard through the stormy mass. "Destroy him now. He is the one." My breath turned cold and stopped in my chest as I stared up at the raging, billowing cloud. It was the Weeping Lady!

"To me, to me!" the Count cried, and with the answering rattle and crash at the door, I scuttled under the bed. I could hear the fierce whistling, and something like chattering from all sides of the room as the Count thrashed on the floor, as if under attack by invisible hands. I could see the booted feet of his guards, and hands trying to pick him up as he writhed and fought away from them, gripped by some invisible force. I saw him roll and scream on the floor so close by my hiding place that I could have almost reached out and touched him. And the most curious thing was that his naked body was mottled with thousands of tiny welts, exactly like the marks of babies' teeth. . . .

"Help me, get them off!" he shrieked, and I heard his feet race to the window, a horrible prolonged scream, followed by the faint sound of a thud on the rocks below. There were curses and the clatter of feet as the men raced out the door and down to the sharp crags beneath the window.

"Well done, my little ones." The sighing mass of the fast dissipating cloud drifted across the room. I poked my head out from under the bed in the abandoned room to hear a ferocious whisper in my ear.

"I've found there are worse things than marrying beneath oneself."

"Yes, Madame Belle-mère," I answered, still breathing hard against the cold stone floor.

"He wants you." Fray Joaquin stood at the door and looked about the laboratorium. Everything seemed unchanged. Messer Guglielmo was still bristling with irritation and envy as he inspected the metallic stuff in the crucible, while Brother Malachi, still pale with fatigue, was sitting on the stool against the wall with his feet tucked up, looking more like a sack of turnips than a Master of the Great Work.

"Wants me? Whatever for?" Brother Malachi feigned surprise. He was slumped against the wall, grateful for its cool stones, and mopped his brow with his sleeve. The gauntlets and rod lay forgotten in a corner.

"That's what I say too." Messer Guglielmo's testy voice was heard from among the heads crowded around the rapidly cooling crucible. "It's damned little gold you got, after all the bother you've made for me."

"It is gold, though, and the best quality. That's better than you've done with your quintessence of two thousand eggs. You're a parasite, and he's genuine," snapped Fray Joaquin.

"There'd have been more, if we'd had the full moon," Malachi added in a complaining voice. "The moon expands the action of the powder."

"Well, *I've* certainly never heard of that. It's not in Geber, it's not in Villanova. And as for Magister Salernus—"

"Your Geber has never made you so much as a dot of gold." Already Fray Joaquin's mind was racing. Why give this valuable fellow to the Count? It's a long way from the cellar to the tower bedroom. If I can get rid of this blabbermouth Messer Guglielmo and his worthless devils, I can just bundle this Theophilus down to the stables and be off. I've done enough secret business for the Count so that no one will suspect a thing until it's too late. I can sell him practically anywhere for a tidy sum—or no, better yet, find somewhere I can put him to work myself. Quick, decisive. That's the way.

"Tie him up. Hood him. The Count awaits."

"Really, hooded? Isn't that a bit melodramatic? Besides, I might trip and injure my brain. My brain is sensitive, like a delicate plant—"

"The mutes will hold you up. It's orders. That way you can't divulge the Secret to anyone en route." Or see where you're going, either, when I take you off with me. What a good idea.

He'll probably kill me, thought Brother Malachi, as soon as he thinks he's got the recipe. At least I've bought Margaret some time. Now I think I need some myself. A good thing Messer Guglielmo doesn't write down his experiments.

"You've—ah—memorized the steps?" asked Brother Malachi as the mutes tied his hands behind him.

"Of course I have. Do you think I'd trust an important secret like this to writing?" I'll leave in the morning, Messer Guglielmo was thinking. Someone else will pay a lot better than the Count for this secret. Why, he might even kill me once he knows it. Perhaps I'd better just leave tonight, as soon as this Theophilus fellow is taken to the Count.

"Now you remember that you add the sulfur exactly at the point that the struggle of the red dragons becomes visible."

"Nonsense. I distinctly saw you wait until the second color change of the lion."

"You have it wrong. Didn't you see? Do I have to teach lessons to babies?" Malachi drew himself up to his full height between the two mutes. His voice dripped with arrogance.

"Do you think I'm a fool? I know the red dragon when I see it."

"Shut the man up," Fray Joaquin addressed the mutes. "I must speak to Messer Guglielmo alone." Brother Malachi bowed his head as an ox does for slaughter while they finished the job.

Fray Joaquin drew the rageful alchemist into the dark little inner chamber where the familiars were summoned. "Are you sure you've memorized the formula?" he asked.

"Of course," responded Messer Guglielmo.

"Absolutely? This man's a trickster. You heard him trying to mix you up. The Count must have a reserve, in case this weakling gives up the ghost under questioning."

"Understood."

"Good," said Fray Joaquin, and plunged the wicked little stiletto, as sharp as a needle, in between Messer Guglielmo's ribs.

And as the alchemist lay on the floor, the blood bubbling in a bright pink froth through his lips, Fray Joaquin addressed the new-made corpse: "Now only one man has the Secret." Utterly calmly, he wiped his stiletto off and replaced it, stepping out into the workshop.

Brother Anselm had made himself as small as possible outside the door of the Count's chamber. He'd done his duty: he'd remonstrated with the woman. Now he was debating with himself which was the most reasonable course of action: go to bed, or wait to see what happened? There was a third course, the most dramatic, perhaps, but unwise. He could burst in on the scene, brandishing a cross in the air, loudly denouncing their sin like an Old Testament prophet. Of course, it would mean sure death, but it would be a glorious one. Why, one might even go directly to heaven, like a blessed martyr—briefly, he toyed with the idea. One of the guards at the door glared evilly at him, and he thought better of it right away. After all, he hadn't seen Compostela yet, and it would be very sad indeed to have come this far to miss out on the best part. If they could just leave this place, it was only a day's march to Port de Cize, that extraordinary mountain covered with thousands of pilgrim crosses, the gate to Spain and first station on the road to Compostela itself. It was counted a very blessed thing even to get just that far, if one had the misfortune of dying before reaching the ultimate shrine.

He shrank back into the shadows. It was then that he spied another figure lurking about the door. The old nurse-companion who'd come with the widow—the one who was too friendly with the widow's confessor—it *was* her, hiding behind a bend in the corridor in the dark. And was there someone else with her? The ill-favored little boy?

Not long after, he heard a woman's terrible shrieks, and the sound of a scuffle inside. It seemed wiser not to make inquiries. After all, she should have known better. The guards chuckled and looked at each other. Then there was the Count's frightened voice, crying, *"à moi, à moi!"* and the two guards sprang into action, battering open the door with a single heavy blow, and rushing inside to try to grab hold of the Count's thrashing, convulsing body, as he appeared to have a bout of the falling sickness. Brother Anselm found himself drawn to watch. Two figures stood silently behind him in the dark. Then the Count dove out of the window with a terrible cry, as if pursued by something invisible and demonic. The figures at the door prudently withdrew as the guards turned from staring out the window to raise the alarm and gather searchers to go out into the dark after the body.

The old woman peered into the room. "Margaret? Margaret?" he could hear her saying, and a muffled voice from under the bed responded in that barbaric, incomprehensible tongue. The woman scurried into the room, with the boy behind her. Margaret emerged from under the bed, her dress torn and her hair all exposed, without any proper head covering. Brother Anselm averted his eyes from the indecency of spying her long, half-unraveled braids.

"Get thee behind me, Satan," he muttered. Perhaps now was the time to burst in and remonstrate, since they appeared to be rifling the room.

"Get the seal ring from the table, Mother Hilde, and the

sealing wax too." Margaret was going through the garments on the perches systematically.

"What are you doing there, Margaret?"

"I'm going in search of Gregory, and I know he'll be cold down there."

"Hungry too," said Sim, who tied the capon and the bread up in a napkin. And if he isn't, I'll eat it later myself, he added silently in his mind.

"Humph. Look at all this gaudy stuff." Margaret wrinkled up her nose. "And most of it stinks of lilac water. Oh, here's something nice—Sim, do you know where Malachi is?"

"Course I do. I followed him to the door."

Margaret took the candelabrum from the floor, and refitted it with lit candles from the wall sconces. With the clothes heaped over one arm, and the candelabrum held high, she marched to the door. There, she was stopped by the little figure of Brother Anselm, puffed up to its maximum height. He had one hand upraised.

"Stop!" he cried in French. "Consider your sins, and repent!"

"Oh, bother," said Margaret in English, and then spoke firmly in French to the little friar. "Come with us." Something about her eyes convinced Brother Anselm to comply. It was the way they flashed in the light of the upraised candelabrum in her hand, exactly like a falcon's on the hunt.

As they wound down the stairs toward the hidden chambers, the spreading sound of scurry and bustle as servants were awakened, and the first keening wail of mourning echoed through the dark corridors of the chateau.

"Good riddance," said Margaret as she set her jaw stubbornly and redoubled her pace. At the end of a long, open stair set down the inner wall of the so-called New Tower, which was only newer than the Old Tower, she came to a low iron door cast with the figures of monsters on it. Mother Hilde pulled at her sleeve, but she hardly noticed it.

"Margaret, be careful. Remember that Malachi said the

place is full of sinister folk," Mother Hilde cautioned. "Don't rile them up. Suppose they harm him because you've angered them."

But Margaret was so enraged, she pounded on the door without a thought for the consequences.

Inside, Fray Joaquin was wondering just how to keep the mutes from getting suspicious when they found they were headed for the stables and not the Count's chambers. They'll know it's not right, and they might just strangle me. I'll take the alchemist by myself. A ruse may be needed to escape them. I'll tell them I don't want to share the honor with them. . . .

"Open, open right away, Brother Malachi. The Count is dead." He heard a woman's voice crying at the door in English. Now, he didn't really understand English, but he knew the words for *death* and *money* in more than a dozen languages. And he heard *Count* and *dead* and the sound made his heart leap with hope. Perfect, perfect. His fondest wish come true, and at the perfect moment. But suppose he'd heard wrong? He pulled his stiletto and opened the door.

"Count—dead?" he asked, but the sight at the door stopped him short, and his voice faltered. There in the open door stood a woman holding a candelabrum. The light from a dozen candles glittered in her wild eyes and caught the silky river of her unbound hair. The white flesh of a bare shoulder glistened through her torn gown. He could see nothing more. Women. Yes. It was women he'd have with the gold. He'd been deprived too long. He'd change his name—dress like a lord. Live among dozens of perfumed, bare-breasted women . . .

"Malachi. I want Malachi—Theophilus, you call him."

Devil take that little man. Maybe he'd summoned the woman, all undressed like this, with the magic that made the gold. He recognized her with a start. It was the little English widow, all transformed and shining with madness. He must do it often, cast this terrifying spell to bring women to his bed and men to do his bidding. That's why he's been so docile. He's been planning to bewitch me. Power—power is more than gold. He'd known it all along, the dangerous little man. No wonder he was so careless with the gold secret. He had a greater one in reserve.

Margaret saw the knife. She also saw the look in Fray Joaquin's eyes, and knew that in his madness, he could strike without warning. How was she to get past him?

"The ring.". Mother Hilde's voice was softer than a whisper in Margaret's ear. "Get him to take the ring."

Margaret chose her words carefully.

"Theophilus—requires me—to bring his ring—his secret ring—the ring of power."

It was clear she was under a spell. The way she spoke, each word so careful and so slow. He would deceive her.

"Theophilus wishes me to take the ring," he said softly and persuasively. Women under spells are stupefied, and easily taken in. "Do you have it?"

Margaret saw that the knife still glinted wickedly in his hand. If she said she had it, he might well stab her and search her. She answered, in what she hoped was a mystical-sounding fashion, "It is with me and not with me. Call Theophilus."

"Theophilus is engaged right now. Give me the ring and I'll take it to him."

"No one but Theophilus must wear the ring." Margaret spoke in an oracular voice. She was warming to her task. The man was a first-rate ass. "Now, let us see if we can get him to put it on," the silvery little voice of her working mind hummed in her head.

"The-power-is-too-great. No one else must hold it. He—who —puts—it—on—and—turns—three—times—will—"

"Yes, yes?" He couldn't restrain himself.

"Rule—the—world." She watched his eyes light up with greed. And if you thought it worked, why don't you imagine I'd put it on myself and rule the world, you stupid man, you, she thought. Why is it that women always have to lug around magic rings and guard magic springs and sacred books of wisdom, and all the rest of that silly stuff, and never get the good of it for themselves? Bite, bite, you bloody, blind, ridiculous ghoul.

"Give it to me," he whispered.

"Prepare—yourself—master," Margaret said portentously. Fray Joaquin tucked his knife up his sleeve.

"The box." Margaret gestured magisterially to Hilde. Hilde, her face perfectly blank, took out the box, opened the lid, and extended it to him. The jewels on the ring glittered in the flickering light.

"Ourabourous. The snake swallowing its tail. The universe—master." With trembling hands, he seized the ring and put it on his middle finger and turned it three times.

"Bow—to the—Master of the Ring," said Margaret, and knelt upon one knee, as if for a king. Work, work, you beastly ring. Or did the Dark Lady fool me? Mother Hilde and Sim were quick to follow Margaret's example.

"What is your command, O Master of the Ring?" Margaret couldn't resist laying it on thicker and thicker. It just came over her. "This is what they all want," the little voice sang. "Give him his fill of it."

"Women—" he whispered. "First, I want you—and then bring more." No, first he'd better kill Theophilus, who knew the secret. He turned from the kneeling women in the direction of the bound alchemist. No—wait, wasn't he master of everybody now? Theophilus could be his slave, and make gold day and night. Why should he get himself all hot and singed? He was going to live like a lord—lords don't toil in laboratoria. No, no, he shouldn't kill a valuable slave. But suppose the ring worked only on women? He looked out the open door. He hadn't even heard Sim whisper fiercely to Brother Anselm, "Kneel, you nit," as he gave him a vicious kick in the shins so that he'd understand the English. Brother Anselm, who was so quick at responses in the choir, saw that kneeling was the thing to do. Perhaps there was a relic of great power in the little box. He joined the kneeling figures.

Fray Joaquin addressed Margaret hoarsely: "The ring—commands everyone?"

"Everyone," said Margaret. How long is this going to take? "Theophilus too?"

"His power is gone—he does not have the ring."

"Stay right there—I must see—"

"Yes, O Master."

Fray Joaquin turned and went into the laboratorium, and for the first time the watchers at the door could make out the bound figure of Brother Malachi, in the light from behind the grating of the tall brick athanor, standing between two muscular, black-clad figures. They watched as the black-cloaked Dominican cut the ropes and removed the hood. I do hope he's heard everything, thought Margaret. As Fray Joaquin finished loosing Brother Malachi, Margaret intoned, just to be on the safe side, "Bow to the Master of the Ring."

"Master of the wha—?" said Malachi, blinking, but stopped when he saw the ring on the hand that Fray Joaquin extended before him.

"O Master, I surrender," said Malachi, kneeling extravagantly.

"You are my slave, Theophilus." Oh, good grief, what next? thought Malachi.

"Kiss the hem of my garment." I suppose I've done worse, thought Brother Malachi to himself. But when he gingerly lifted the hem of Fray Joaquin's rather grimy black cloak to the vicinity of his lips, the garment was tugged from his hand as Fray Joaquin fell to his knees.

"Sick—sick," he gasped.

"Hmm. Powerful ring," said Brother Malachi, arising. Indeed, a powerful transformation was taking place in Fray Joaquin. His limbs were rigidly extended, he was shaking all over, and his face—pulled into a hideous grimace—had turned all dark.

"Oh, Malachi," said Margaret, "that's horrible stuff."

"It was entirely too good for him," said Brother Malachi

316

bitterly. "Did you know that he was the procurer of the little ones that were used in his master's Devil worship?"

"What's happened, what's happened?" Brother Anselm's querulous voice broke in.

"The ring of power—I'm afraid it was too strong for him," said Brother Malachi lightly. "It takes years of purification with the proper prayers to wear it without danger." He nudged the corpse with his toe, to assure himself it was really dead. "Let that be a lesson to you on the vanity of human wishes," he couldn't resist adding rather sententiously.

"All is vanity," agreed Brother Anselm as he crossed himself. "Malachi, where is my Gregory? Can you take me to him?"

"Nothing easier. But it's damp and slippery. We'll need torchbearers. We'll have to ask these mutes to help out." He glanced about him. The mutes were squatting on the floor in a circle. In the center was Mother Hilde, sitting on her heels. They were all rapidly gesturing with their hands. Malachi noticed one of them make a strangling motion about his neck, and then a little house with his hands, and fingers walking like little feet.

"Hmm," said Brother Malachi. "They don't understand a word of English and dear Hilde there can't pronounce a syllable of any foreign language, but they all seem to be communicating quite well without that."

"Devil's symbols," said Brother Anselm nervously. "I saw the Sign of the Devil."

"Nonsense, they're talking. Hilde, dear, what are they saying?"

"This one says it's no fun being a mute and living in the dark down here and strangling people. He wants to go home to his uncle's farm where there's a nice apple orchard."

"He said all that?"

"Of course. The other one says the fellows here were all as mean as the Devil, except you. He wants to know where we come from."

Brother Malachi smiled. He made ocean waves with his

hands, then a little boat, and then what he thought looked like an island.

The mutes threw back their heads and shook, as if they were laughing. One of them even made a sort of little barking cough.

"They say you have a terrible accent, Malachi," said Hilde.

"Tell them the Count's dead, and they can quit and go home if they like. Ask them if they will help us get Gilbert out of the oubliette first."

"They say nobody ever comes out of the oubliettes, at least not in their time here. They're too deep. They lower them in, then cut the rope. Then the man's in forever."

"Tell them, what goes in must come out."

"They're dubious, but they say they'll go with us."

"He's dead? Really dead?" I asked, surveying the black-clad figure stretched out on the tiles of the hidden alchemical workshop. I could feel the rage leaving me and a strange light-headed giddiness taking its place.

"Most assuredly, Margaret. The final transformation but one. With him the last, which is decay, does not concern me." Brother Malachi spoke lightly, so as not to frighten me, I'm sure. But his face was still haggard and stubbly from his imprisonment and from whatever he'd seen going on in that room. Even Mother Hilde's passionate embrace and tears of joy had not totally erased the unmistakably ravaged look of a person who has stared directly at the true face of evil.

"Gregory? You're sure he's down there?" I asked, pointing to the open door into the darkness below.

"Yes, he's there." Brother Malachi detached an arm from around Mother Hilde and gestured with it to the mutes, who lit new torches from those in the wall brackets for the descent.

I don't think I'll write about everything I saw down in the horrible cellars beneath the laboratorium because it was altogether too morbid and depressing. It reminded me of the inside of the Count's head—or at least the gruesomer parts of his imagination that he reserved for special occasions. Really, you can never be too careful in examining ahead of time the character of those you stay with as houseguests. But, of course, the place made my heart pound for fear we had come too late for Gregory.

As we approached the great pits, the mutes put the torches in the brackets above the last of them and pointed to the pulley above the grating. At the first flicker of light, I could hear a voice reverberating from down below. Tired and hoarse, but his.

"What is it this time? Heroic couplets? Yours should be called cowardly couplets, you perfumed baboon." The familiar sound made my heart leap.

"Gregory!" I flung myself on the grating. "It's me, it's me! We've come for you." My joyful shout echoed and vanished into the deep stone pit.

"Oh, Jesu," I heard the hollow mutter from below. "I'm hallucinating again. The end can't be far."

"It's Margaret! Answer me! How deep is it to the bottom? We need to get a rope long enough to get you out."

"Oh, Margaret, how many times I've called to you in the dark. And I heard you answer too. But this is the first time we've carried on such a complex conversation. I suppose it's a mercy my mind is going at last." The voice seemed to fade as it came up from the dark.

"For God's sake, I'm real, Gregory. Give me the depth."

"Between three and four times the height of a man, Margaret." He sounded lost, as if he were in a dream.

"If we lower a rope, can you climb up it?"

"I don't think so, Margaret. It's—rather cramped down here at the bottom. I've lacked my usual exercise, I fear: my arms and legs are quite numb. I haven't the strength."

"Then tie it about you, and we'll use the pulley to haul you up." I stood and the mutes loosened the grate and heaved it aside with a practiced gesture.

As it was removed, I heard him say: "If it's not real, it's

certainly the best one so far." But as the rope reached him, he gave a cry of despair.

"What's wrong?" I called down to him.

"Blasted cold—can't get my fingers to work—can't tie it properly." His voice was lost in the dull, echoing sound of racking coughing that rose from the pit.

I knelt by the hole as one of the mutes held a torch for me to see. Sim, who loved all things lurid and gruesome, had tired of inspecting the apparatus in the Count's torture chamber and had come to kneel beside me to peer in.

"Phew. Stinks down there, don't it? Hey, what's that stuff down there? Bones?" Sim sounded pleased.

Gregory was curled at the bottom of the hole, without even a shirt to keep him warm. I could just barely make out his figure in the dim, flickering light.

"Of course it's bones. What d'you think's down here? Roses?" The waspish tone in his voice renewed my hope.

"Any skulls?"

"Several."

"I sure could use one of them."

"Sim! You're horrid! We're supposed to be getting him out— not collecting souvenirs."

"Use your thinker, Margaret. You just lower me down on the rope—I tie it under his arms—then I get my skull and ride up on the rope with him. It's easy. Wimmen!" He snorted in imitation of a grown-up male.

It was not long before we heard Sim's voice echoing up from the pit, alternating with inarticulate spluttering noises from the object of his attention.

"Move yer arm, will you? My goodness, you've got a long beard! —How long did it take you to grow it that way? —Hey, look, I didn't mean to pinch—quit grumping. —So why'd Margaret ever go and marry *you*? —What do you think of *this* one? The jaw's still on it, but it ain't got many teeth. —No, this one's better. Maybe I'll take both. —You'll hold 'em for me, won't you? I'll need at least one hand for the rope. —Come on, be a sport and help me out. —Hey, Margaret! Grab my skulls as he comes up before he rolls on 'em and smashes 'em!"

Soon enough, Gregory was gasping above ground beside the grated holes like a newly landed fish, and Sim was happily polishing his acquisitions with his sleeve. Gregory seemed as weak as a kitten as I wrapped him in the Count's big fur-lined cloak and rubbed his hands between my own to warm them.

"Oh, Margaret, it really is you," he said, but his voice sounded terrifyingly frail. "I thought of you—I saw you—I heard you calling." His skin was stretched tight across his bones like parchment. I've never imagined that anyone alive could be so thin. But the eyes that stared out of the tangle of long hair and beard were blazing and alive. I could see him staring at me, looking, looking, as if he could not get enough. Then a lazy half smile crossed his lips. And that old look, half tenderness and half mischief, glinted in his eyes.

"Why, Margaret," he said mildly. "You've been putting on weight."

"Me? I have not!"

"Come now, you can't deny you're rather thick in the waist. You've been living well since I left."

"Living well! I've been pining away! Pining away and making your baby! Do you think that's easy? I got seasick! I walked and walked! I had to trick that horrible man! At the very least, you might have considered telling him you liked his blasted poetry and sparing yourself and me all this trouble!"

He slumped on his back and his smile was weak, but triumphant.

"I've got standards, Margaret."

"Carry him up!" I told the mutes. And two of them gave their torches to Brother Malachi and Brother Anselm, taking Gregory up and swinging him between them as easily as if he were a sackful of cabbages.

Laid out on a bench in the alchemical workshop, he scarcely protested as I washed his face and trimmed his hair and beard. I could see his eyes travel from my face to my spreading waistline, back and forth, and a look of wonder growing on his face. It was as if the idea couldn't get through his head that there would soon enough be three of us.

"You shouldn't be so hard on him," I could hear Mother Hilde saying behind me. But I just said, "I'm not being hard at all!" and went on clipping silently. Then I passed to bandaging his open sores, and wanted to weep. But I certainly wasn't going to let *him* know that.

"I suppose you told him you loved his poetry," he said. His voice was terribly weak, and he ended with a spasm of coughing that squeezed my heart.

"Of course I did. What else? And let me tell you, it wasn't easy." The remembrance of lilac water made my stomach all queasy.

"He recited 'Ode to Summer' to you, I suppose." I went on sponging him off and began dressing him. He was too weak even to assist putting his arms into the sleeves of the heavy tunic.

"Oh, yes. That horrid one with the birds and plants. The man knew nothing about summer. He hadn't an ounce of feeling in him."

Gregory smiled, and coughed again. Then an odd look crossed his face.

"Hadn't? He's dead?"

"Yes, of course. Why else do you think I'm here? He had nasty designs on me, but when I went to see him about you, he jumped out the window."

"Oh, really? You pushed him?"

"No. *I* didn't. He drank too much aphrodisiac and turned all purple—and then, well, then he jumped. I was very relieved, you may imagine." I sat back on my heels to drink him in with my eyes.

"I'm relieved too. But you still have a sin on your conscience."

"I do *not*!" I was indignant. But he doubled over coughing, and I could see that he was laughing.

322

"You told him you liked 'Ode to Summer.' And that, Margaret, was a lie."

"At least I know how to stay out of trouble."

"You think I'd have got out if I told him I liked his preposterous versification? Oh no. The moment I agreed with him, I would have been a dead man. I worked on my insults, Margaret. They kept him coming back. And as long as he came back, they kept me alive. The minute he lost interest, it would have been over. I had plenty of time to think up good ones—but I was wearing down some. I couldn't have kept it up much longer."

"Bless you, you'll never change." I knelt down and put my arms around him. But it was when I put my head on his chest that I could hear the rattle with each breath that he drew. God in heaven, I wept to myself. The Gift is too weak to help him. Spare him. I've suffered too much.

"Sim," I could hear Brother Malachi's voice intoning behind me, "it strikes me that for my pains I am owed—now—hmm—Marcus Graecus, *The Book of Fires*, that looks nice, I've always wanted that one. Aristotle's *De lapidibus*—I have that, and this one's ill copied. Goodness, yes, the *Mappae Clavicula*—I've never had more than an excerpt. And a most satisfying copy—with illuminations, too. Arnoldus Villanova, of course I'll have that. *Opus de chemia,* lovely, lovely. Now—this thing—hmm. 'On the Secret Art of Calling Devils'—I'll leave that for the Inquisition, which will probably be called in to clean up this mess. Geber, the *Summa Perfectionis*, rather spotty from use, but better than my copy. I'll have that. Yes, this is just about right." I turned in the direction of the sound to see several volumes disappearing into the bosom of Brother Malachi's capacious gown. Gregory's eyes followed mine. He could barely turn his head.

"Theophilus. It really is you there, after all. I thought I'd imagined you. What stupidity led you into this hellhole?"

"Me?" said Brother Malachi. "I'm traveling in search of a

323

translator for a rare work I've acquired. And, incidentally, help-ing out Margaret here."

"Theophilus, you old rascal. I didn't think you liked me."

"I don't, Gilbert, I don't. You are a hopeless, bad-tempered, thorny-tongued, arrogant young troublemaker. Wherever you go, disasters occur, despite my frequently offered—and en-tirely ignored—wise advice. Most days, I simply can't abide even the thought of you. Today, however, I like you. You are in a state too weak to annoy me. And then there was the day you composed 'Ode to My Lady's Large Shoe,' and I laughed until I wept. That day I liked you too. And, of course, the day you gave me your last sou so that I might flee from Paris, and as you turned to go back out into the snow, I saw that you had sold your cloak. That day, Gilbert, I loved you, and I wept as I tucked my manuscripts into my pack. But on the whole, you are unendurable."

"I suppose now I'll have to say I like your poetry too." Greg-ory's voice was reduced to a whisper.

"How typical of your promises, Gilbert, since you know I don't write any." Brother Malachi paused to look regretfully about the laboratorium. He shook his head. "What I'd like to take with me is the glassware. Do you know how hard it is to get a proper philosopher's egg made in London?"

"Who's the dead man, Theophilus?"

"That, Gilbert? Just another monster who wanted to rule the world—he is no loss, no loss at all. Now, where's my rod?"

As Brother Malachi knelt, puffing, beneath the wide table full of curious glass and copper vessels, Mother Hilde re-marked, "We really ought to be going, Malachi, dear. The morning light will be here soon, and I, for one, have never wanted to be out of a place more."

"Morning!" I exclaimed. "Good heavens! Hugo probably still thinks he's meeting the Count in single combat! Knowing him, he's slept like a log through all of this. Someone really ought to go and let him know." How easy it was to forget Hugo. And what a pleasure.

"Hugo who?"

"Hugo your brother."

"Hugo meet the Count? He wouldn't last a minute. The man's twice his size, and a better swordsman to boot."

"Was."

"Oh, yes—was. But Hugo, here? In mortal combat with the Count? Not on my account, surely."

"Not directly, no. It's over an insult to his blood. But he did come here for you."

"For me? He must have gone soft in the head."

"I suppose he did. But he probably wants to talk to you about that himself."

"In my current state, Margaret, Hugo is very nearly the last person in the world I want to see." He curled over, convulsed with coughing. "The absolutely last is father. Stay with me, Margaret, your hands are nice and warm."

"You were always the one with warm hands."

"Not anymore."

"I'll never leave you; you know that, don't you?" I knelt next to him and pulled the Count's heavy cloak around him as I embraced him. He reached out a hand and pulled mine to him beneath the cloak as he closed his eyes. In the warmth of the dying fire in the athanor, he fell asleep, his breath coming in long, rattling sighs.

It was long before matins. The stars were still brightly shining when Hugo got up in the night. Traveling had been good to him; he'd ceased his agonized night wanderings and had his first real sleep in months. But now he'd had nightmares of the vast bulk of the Sieur d'Aigremont coming at him in the lists. Just as the Count had unhorsed him and dismounted to finish him off, he woke with a horrible start: he remembered he was a man under a curse. He was stained with a horrible sin—God could not favor him on the morrow, even if he was so clearly the better man in every other respect. "The curse, the curse," he mumbled as he paced the floor among the straw palliasses where his men slumbered contentedly. Robert, his squire, turned on the mattress at the foot of the bed. He was snoring. "God, even to be a man at arms—a nobody—with an unstained heart," Hugo whispered enviously. "Save me, Lord, save me. Forgive me. I'll reform. I swear. Gilbert can tell me how to do it, to break this curse. There's a holy man somewhere he knows about. Maybe there's a shrine for the accursed—some saint. I'll do a penance, God. Anything." Prayers. Maybe prayers would do it. Beads, that was it. But who had any? Cis, that was who. "Damned slut! What does she need them for?" he muttered as he leaned to stare out the window at the dark dome of the sky. She'd vanished with that old dandy, the Sieur de Soule, the so-called ambassador. Snuck off without a hint of gratitude or loyalty. Who did she think she was anyway?

The cold night wind pushed banks of icy clouds across the face of the waxing moon. Come out of the sky, God! cried Hugo in his mind. Show Yourself and tell me that You hear me. . . .

There was a clattering in the courtyard below. Hugo looked down and saw a familiar figure, huge and menacing, in the moonlight, mounted on a tall black horse. He was entirely enveloped in an immense black cloak that fell on either side of the saddle and whipped about his horse's legs in the icy night wind. Hugo heard his deep voice calling,

"Come! I hunt tonight." And from the shadows, two more cloaked horsemen joined him. One had a tightly curling black beard and immense eyebrows. The other Hugo recognized as the friar who had leaned against the Count's great chair to whisper in his ear the night before. They pulled their little black cobs in behind the Count's immense stallion. As Hugo watched, a parade of solemn figures on tall black palfreys, black without even a patch of white on them, seemed to emerge from nowhere to escort the first three figures. They, too, were cloaked in black, but their hoods were up so that their faces could not be seen—that is, if they had any faces at all. As they rode slowly to the inner bailey gate, Hugo noted with a start that there were thirteen of them.

"Open!" the Count's deep voice cried, and the bailey gate swung wide without the aid of a gatekeeper.

"Coward!" shouted Hugo from the tower window. "Coward! You're running out on me!" And those who were roused to look out the windows by his cries all saw the Count raise his blood-less face to the tower window and stare long, long, up at Hugo before he turned wordlessly to ride out of the gate.

"You damned coward, come back!" Hugo was racing down the stairs in a rage, all wrapped in his bed quilt, his night-napkin still on his head. Below, he saw unaccustomed lights, and heard sounds from the chapel. He heard chanting and, without a thought for his state of disattire, followed the rising swell of the notes. He paused at the door, which was already flung open, and shrank back in horror. There, on a high black-draped bier before the altar, lay the mangled body of the Comte de St. Médard.

Not a soul who saw the black cavalcade on that icy Saint Crispin's night ever doubted that it was the shade of the Count himself, on his last ride to the gates of hell.

CHAPTER
11

"I tell you, brother, I saw him, just as plain as day, riding out the gate, but the body was lying in state all along." Hugo shuddered and crossed himself.

Gregory was lying on a narrow bed in the pilgrim's hall, pulled as close as possible to the blazing fire. He was half propped up, heaped with blankets topped off by a vast wolf fur robe big enough to be a carpet, and Margaret was spooning soup into his mouth. Even though his eyes were open, he was having an unpleasant dream. He was dreaming that his brother Hugo had somehow appeared and was telling him ghost stories while Margaret tried to choke him with soup.

"Stop," he said to no one in particular, and the soup spoon went away, while he doubled over to cough blood into the towel Margaret held before his face. He could feel her arms around him, holding him while he gasped for breath.

"It's a sign, don't you think? Brother, I may be spared after all. The curse may be lifted. The proper prayers. A pilgrimage perhaps. Brother, you must help me. I've sinned."

"Oh, really? Who would have expected it." Gregory rolled back and closed his eyes. His brother shook him by the shoulder.

"Open your eyes, Gilbert. You have to listen to me."

"So what is it this time?" Gregory's voice was barely audible. "Murder? Fornication? The razing of cottages containing widows and orphans? The torture of old men for hidden gold? How is that different from what any other soldier does? Get Father Three Aves to fix it for you. I'm not a specialist in these matters."

"You don't understand." Hugo's voice was desperate as he shouted into Gregory's ear. "This is *real* sin. I've sworn falsely on the True Cross and signed a paper. I'm doomed. A terrible curse is on me."

"False swearing? For you, nothing. Buy an indulgence. But the paper—that's serious." Sweat was rolling off Gregory's grayish, pallid skin. His eyes were half closed, and he spoke in between labored breaths. Hugo's face was twisted with anxiety. Margaret wanted nothing better than to strangle him for harassing Gregory, but there wasn't a thing she could do.

The dream had gotten worse. His brother was shaking him, and Margaret had taken away the soup.

"What's the paper about? Money? Land?"

"A promise of betrothal."

Gregory turned his head to one side, and clutched his chest as his breath came in short gusts. Margaret picked up another towel. But no, he wasn't coughing this time. He was laughing.

"I never thought you'd be caught in that trap, brother," he whispered. "Only the Pope can get you off that one."

Hugo clutched Gregory's shoulder desperately.

"The Pope? You say the Pope can do it?"

"Of course," said Gregory as he lost consciousness. Hugo stood up abruptly, and began to walk around the room wringing his hands. "The Pope," he muttered. "The Pope. Connections—money—how on earth—? Somehow. Yes. That's how—"

Brother Malachi was sitting on the large bed in the corner by the screen, while Hilde packed his things.

"Hilde, my love, do you think I'd look more dignified with a long beard?"

"Very distinguished, Malachi, especially with the gray that's in it now. Otherwise it would be entirely too gingery for distinction."

"Good. I'm glad you think it's attractive. For you, attractive, for others, distractive."

"What do you mean, Malachi? You've a plan?"

"Yes, of course. I fear that to accomplish my task, I must visit old haunts. Haunts where my—um—clerical attire may still be remembered. I cannot decide whether I would look better as a merchant of hides or perhaps of—say, something nicer. Flemish cloth, perhaps? English wool?" He took several seashells, wrapped up in a napkin, from his capacious purse. "Would you be so kind, my precious love, as to sew these on our cloaks? We will be returning from Compostela the easy way—without having been there." He rummaged some more, and took out another, tightly bundled napkin that he spread before him. "Good—the green's not faded yet. Best batch I ever made. Hmm. The rings are as good as new. Yes, our finances are in order."

"Surely," broke in Margaret, "we're not leaving soon. Gregory is in no condition to be moved, especially through these mountains."

"We may be moving sooner than you think. Have you noticed that the talkative Brother Anselm is missing? I fear he went to the Bishop to unburden himself of all that he saw last night. Sorcery, murder, suicide, alchemy—yes, without a doubt the Bishop will be here. If he's honest, to clean up. If he's sticky-fingered—well, the goods of a heretic, even one condemned postmortem, are forfeit. This place is rather a large and tempting prize. To tell the truth, I'd not be surprised at all if we had quite a few visitors soon. Nosy visitors, who will do a lot of questioning—with the aid of—oh, well, why burden you."

"But look there, Malachi," pointed out Mother Hilde reasonably enough, "he really can't be moved. Even you can see that." She pointed to Gregory where he lay, a living skeleton, with another of Margaret's towels, this one wrung out in cold water, across his feverish forehead. "He'll die, Malachi."

"Oh, Hilde," said Brother Malachi, and the sadness washed across his face again. "It's far easier to die by God's hand than in the hands of the Inquisition."

That night the fever soared, and Margaret sat sleepless by the banked fire, watching and waiting. When the racking chills began shortly after midnight, she climbed in underneath the covers beside him to warm him with her own body. She was so exhausted, she fell asleep almost immediately, one arm thrown protectively over his skeletal ribs.

When she next awoke, the cold gray light of the mountains had already illuminated the room for many hours. The fire had been rekindled. Lazily she opened her eyes, and as she did, she felt that the grayish penumbra of death had faded around Gregory. She herself could hardly move; her bones felt bruised, as if she had wrestled with grim Death himself, all that past night. She turned her head. Hilde was by the fire, where she had warmed a posset for them.

"Is he still living?" Hilde asked gently.

"Yes, Mother Hilde. Hear him breathing?" Margaret whispered. She felt as weak as a kitten. Sure enough, Mother Hilde could make out the harsh rattle of his breath, coming evenly now.

"Where's Malachi?" Margaret asked.

"Gone to explain to the Countess the predicament she's in. He's arranged with her physician to swear that the Count had an epileptic fit—that he had them all the time—and he fell out of the window by accident. That way she can bury him in the family tomb, instead of on unconsecrated ground. He's proposing that she provide us with money and horses and a guide to take us out through the mountains in a way that avoids the main road. That way we can't be questioned. Her own people she can rely on for silence. It must be working—I've already seen a team of workmen on their way to the secret chambers to demolish the evidence. Surely he'll be back soon. Would you like this posset? You look completely drained."

"That's how I feel, Mother Hilde. I feel as if I wrestled all night with Death." Margaret sat up and wrapped her hands around the warm goblet, as if she were too weak to lift it to her mouth, and could somehow take the warmth into her body through her hands to restore herself. Mother Hilde saw her hesitate, and came and tilted the goblet to Margaret's mouth with her own hands.

"Knowing you, Margaret, that's probably exactly what you were doing."

I have never felt less like getting out of bed than the morning when Brother Malachi came to announce that we were leaving the chateau immediately. Now if he'd been lugubrious, I might have borne it, but it was his infernal cheerfulness that made the thing so hateful.

"Why don't you just go away and leave us here?" I grumbled at him, burying my head under the big wolf fur robe. We could just lie here, Gregory and I, until spring, when it was fit to travel. Excellent idea.

"Nonsense, nonsense. It's all arranged, my dears." I could hear his optimistic flutter even under the robe, so I poked just my eyes out to see what he was doing. He'd evidently made a detour via the kitchen, for he had a jug of applejack in one hand, and in the other, a large piece of boiled salt beef, wrapped up in a soggy napkin. Under one elbow he clutched an immense long loaf of bread. His new beard was growing out helter-skelter in every direction, and he looked so comic, I couldn't help smiling.

"And now, to tempt Margaret the lazybones out of bed," he announced. And putting down his load, he bowed before the bed and with an extravagant flourish produced an immense boiled goose egg from the bosom of his gown. "See that? Not an eye on it, and still warm. Consider the advantages of breakfast before travel, and favor us with the sunshine of your regard." I poked my nose out from under the robe. "Better, better," he said. "But I suggest you cannot eat breakfast with your nose. Besides, you need to sit up to properly appreciate my tale." I put my whole head out. Certain now of his success, he turned and put the egg with the other things he'd brought, and uncorked the jug.

I could feel Gregory shift in his sleep; his breathing sounded much better. So, Margaret, it can't be all bad, I thought to myself. Maybe it will all work out after all. I suppose you ought to get out of bed. When I sat up I couldn't help looking down at my crumpled clothes, now not only torn and devastated, but slept in. Margaret, you're a mess, I thought. It's a good thing Gregory can't see you now, or he wouldn't have you. But, of course, when Malachi is set on telling a story about himself, everyone must listen, or he becomes morose and says he feels unappreciated. Besides, the breakfast he'd brought looked good.

"Oh, it's a wonderful thing, to discuss matters of importance with a woman who can deal with logic," he was rattling on, as he laid out the beef and took out his knife. "She hesitated. She looked at her ladies and the captain of her guard. 'Why needlessly deprive your son of his inheritance just because your husband was a tiny bit more sinful than most?' I asked. 'Besides, it isn't as if you knew about it all. You yourself are as innocent as a newborn lamb. And surely, you may now be one of the greatest ladies in France. You could travel—go to Orléans, Paris, mingle with the most elegant elements of society. Consider: There is nothing sadder than a widow without property, and no one happier than a widow with a fortune. It all hinges on your quick, decisive action.' So she gave orders—and whoosh!—it was all done." Brother Malachi finished cutting up the bread and beef while the jug made the rounds.

"Now, I'll tell you, it was no such easy matter convincing that thickheaded brother of Gilbert," Brother Malachi went on, after licking his fingers. "What a mutton brain! 'I see no reason to leave now,' he says. 'I'll just tell them the truth.' 'What truth is that?' I ask. 'Oh, that he was so frightened of meeting me on the field of honor in single combat in the morning that he jumped out of the window.' I racked my brains. How to get through? Then I hit on it. 'Surely, you wouldn't deprive a widow of her last solace. If he can't be buried in the family tomb, she will waste away with grief, and then you'll have another sin on your conscience. Honor requires that you remain forever silent about his death.' 'Sin,' he says, and gets all panicky-looking. 'Sin. I've got to see the Pope.' 'What better time than now?' I say. Goodness, he does hold on to an idea, once it's finally penetrated whatever mind resides in that thick skull. So now he's off at the stables, getting things ready. Though how he expects to see the Pope, short of months spent waiting and bribing people, I do not know. He seems to think all he has to do is arrive, and he'll be shown right in. Humph! Well, we must allow for the possibility of enlightenment before he gets there."

It was not long before the Countess's men had come with a stretcher to take Gregory to the waiting horse litter in the inner bailey. He stirred and groaned, but did not waken as he was wrapped in fur robes and loaded onto the litter with a stone that had been heated in the fire at his feet. I was beginning to feel restored not only by Malachi's breakfast but by the new kirtle and surcoat provided by the Countess. They were quite foreign in cut, and large, to allow for my expanding condition. The kirtle was heavy dark green wool, suitable for the winter, with wide sleeves. The surcoat was embroidered brown velvet, grown as bald as a baby's bottom with age and wear, but still redolent of a certain faded elegance. I'd unwrapped the Burning Cross when the buzzing had stopped, and it shone resplendently against its handsome background. She'd pronounced the effect attractive, but seemed shocked when I declined the offer of a proper tall French headdress. 'What? No hennin?' she cried. 'You might as well be seen naked.' But I convinced her that as a foreigner, I wasn't used to such tall headgear, and might be at risk of my neck if I caught it in an overhanging branch while riding. It was all very friendly, if a bit hasty, and we all swore silence on a book of the Gospels that she had.

So very soon we were beyond the postern gate, headed to the main road by a roundabout way through the mountains. I was mounted on a little rough-gaited dun mare, and Brother Malachi on a rangy roan with Mother Hilde on the crupper behind him. The horse litter was slung between the mounts of two of Sir Hugo's men, with Sim perched up behind the latter of the two. Sir Hugo, of course, was glorious in newly shined armor, with his pennant flying from his lance tip. Robert, his squire, rode beside him, carrying his shield, helm, and great sword. Hugo always liked to see things done right, and did not believe in slinking out by back ways in disguise. At the end of the party were Hugo's sumpter mules. We were certainly leaving in better style than we came. There was, however, one of the Brokesford party missing. Cis, the false lady Margaret, had refused to be roused from the ambassador's quarters, and the doors remained firmly barred while Hugo thumped and shouted insults in English outside.

"You shush," I'd told him when he came back to see to Gregory's removal, swearing and threatening to get her back at any cost.

"Dammit, she's from my estate; she's my *laundress*, the little slut. And she's palming herself off as gentry."

"It's nothing you didn't start. And look here, Hugo, she's beyond you now. She could be a king's mistress someday, the way she's going. There may come a time you'll be grateful that you know her and can ask her intervention. So leave her alone; she's chosen her way. And let us choose ours, and quickly too."

"At the very least, you should be ashamed she's using your name, you foolish little nit."

I bit my tongue to keep from telling him what I thought of him, and said: "It doesn't bother me in the least. I wish her good fortune with it."

So Hugo, grumbling and storming, had gone about his business, and we had departed, leaving Cis to the life she had chosen. But I did worry about her, all alone with strangers, and not speaking a word of the language.

High on the mountain, the track our guide showed us doubled back over a promontory that gave a view of the entire valley below. At his frantic signing we dismounted and held the horses out of sight.

"Look," whispered Brother Malachi, pointing to the road below, which led to the castle gate. "Not a moment too soon." There on the road was an armed party, banners flying. At the head rode a broad-looking man in full armor, his bascinet glistening in the sun and a mace at his saddlebow. Beside him rode his squire with his shield and great helm. Only his episcopal arms distinguished him from some great secular lord. Behind him clattered a party of armed knights of the bishopric, escorting a company of well-mounted priests and heavily laden pack mules. We could see the inquisitioners draw up at the far side of the raised drawbridge.

"Hmm. Tough-looking fellow," said Brother Malachi. "I hear he says Mass with his helm on the altar. I'm glad I didn't have any explaining to do to him. Something tells me he is not amenable to logic."

The bridge was lowered, and we could hear the faint echo of the sounding horn among the rocks as the party entered the open gates.

"What are you mumbling about, Margaret?" asked Brother Malachi.

"I'm praying for the Countess's good fortune," I answered.

With the Bishop's party safely inside, we resumed our trek, rejoining the main road to Bayonne as it wandered below St. Médard-en-bas. When the Countess's guide had safely left us, Malachi entered into negotiations with an old man to show us through the mountains in the opposite direction. So we proceeded by winding tracks through the mountains on the way to rejoin the high road to Pau. But once among the high rocks and windy peaks, the jostling wakened Gregory, who had lain unconscious this while, and he stared up glassy-eyed, as if unsure where he was. A hawk wheeled high above, and I could see his eye following it. His lips moved, and I could see what he was saying, though I couldn't hear him, even riding as close behind him as I was.

"The sky. I thought I'd never see it again. Where am I?"

"Where are you?" I called out, echoing his question. "You're on your way home." My heart gave a leap and I was so happy I could hardly hear the baby singing, "Joy! joy!" as it turned.

Rolling dark clouds massed across the broad sky, the grayish brown remnants of the summer's grass on either side of the road flattened beneath a sudden gust of cold wind. For days now they had wound their way through perilous mountain roads and villages without names, filled with savages who provided food and shelter only at the menacing rattle of Sir Hugo's sword in its sheath. And even now that they had rejoined the high road, Margaret had never felt herself farther from home. Even the baby's cheerful turning and Malachi's chatter couldn't convince her that things would turn out well anymore. But the longer on the road, the more cheerful grew Hugo. He stood up in the saddle, his cloak whipping around him, and lifted a hand up to feel for the first icy drops from the ominous sky. Ahead of them the descending curves of the foothills of the Pyrenees stretched like the waves of a vast rocky ocean toward the horizon.

"Hmm. Looks like a storm. But we may be able to beat it to Pau with any luck." And he signaled to those behind him to speed to the fastest walk that could be managed. "Well, well. Wish it were summer. Of course, not too hot a summer. Now, how did that nice summery poem go? Humty, tumty, tumptity something, youths in hats sing virelays, birds in trees cry 'tiri-lay!' Something like that. Clever rhymes that fella had."

The pace had shaken Gregory awake. There was a groan from the litter. Hugo dropped back in the line of march to lean down from his horse with newfound concern and catch the words he could barely make out.

"If I ever hear you speak one word from that wretched 'Ode to Summer' again, I'll strangle you, Hugo, I swear. Live or dead. I'll rise from the grave, if necessary."

"What's wrong with it? I thought you liked poetry, Gilbert."

"That poem's a sore spot with me, Hugo. Don't mention it again. Remember, from the grave." There was a movement under the furs as Gilbert clutched his ribs to stay the pain of coughing. Hugo wasn't bothered in the least. Sick people are all like that. After all, father had whispered imprecations all the way from Calais to Brokesford Manor, and it hadn't meant a thing.

"Why, look, I do believe that's Pau I see ahead," cried out Hugo, and trotted up ahead to see if it really was the spires of the town that he'd spied in the gray distance.

We stayed only one night at a shabby little inn called La Couronne, where the beds were full of bugs. There at the long table before the fire, Malachi and Robert, between bites of a dreadful-smelling ragout, loudly discussed our plans to go west to Orthez and the coast. But before dawn we rose and headed east toward Tarbes by starlight, to avoid any chance of pursuit by the unsavory folk we'd seen at the inn.

But bad weather held us at Tarbes three days, with Hugo pacing and fuming, while Robert cleaned his armor and joined his men in dicing and chasing the women at the inn. One night, as the icy rain rattled at the shutters, Hugo came from sheer boredom to pick a quarrel with Malachi. Gregory lay propped up in bed, too weak to eat, but drinking hot wine in little sips from the cup I held. Hilde and Malachi sat by the brazier, inspecting his new books by the light of the glowing coals. Hilde couldn't read a word, and the books were in Latin anyway, but Malachi was explaining the pictures. Hilde's shrewd comments showed how wide was her understanding of natural things. Sim peeped over her shoulder while he finished off an immense sausage he'd purloined from somewhere.

"Now this one, Hilde, is the mystic marriage of Sol and

Luna. You can tell by the crowns; it means to mingle melted gold and silver together to extract the quintessence—how many times must I remind you, Sim, not to risk dropping grease on the pages?—while *this* depicts—"

The door slammed open.

"How can any man with a particle of wit waste his time reading books? What use are they? All that stuff rots the mind of an active man and turns him into an idle daydreamer." Hugo stood fuming on the threshold, eager to offend someone.

On the bed, Gregory spluttered. Ordinarily, he'd have heaved a bench at Hugo, thus splintering the rainy day dullness into a thousand pieces. But as he was too weak to lift his head, he merely growled menacingly.

"This one you'd find interesting," remarked Malachi, completely unperturbed. "It's Graecus's *De igniis*."

"What's that? Some priestly nonsense?"

"No, a book on fires, and the various ways to start them. here, for example, is the recipe for Greek Fire—quite useful for you active sorts in defending against a siege."

Hugo edged closer. "Now, what's that picture of the naked man and woman there?" he interrupted, his arrogance unabated. "Is it a book of filthy stories? Now, *that's* a reason for books—"

"It's a book of alchemy."

"Alchemy with dirty pictures, eh? Now I know what keeps those fellas warm at night. Pity there isn't anything to the gold-making part. Now, if I owned a book, it would be all dirty pictures and no gibberish—say, what's that dragon doing? And that lion with the spangles, in green?" I looked from where I was sitting on the bed, and even at that distance, I could see another Green Lion on the page of Malachi's new book. This one was thinner, and had a row of stars down his sides. But he was the same creature, and had in his jaws a sun with a smiling face and rays like waving arms.

"The Green Dragon and the Green Lion have the power of transforming the most perfect and unchangeable metals. They are the subject of the quest. Only through them can one obtain the Red Powder that is, of course, what every alchemist wants."

"So where's the gold?"

"There, in the book"—and Malachi pointed to the golden sun in the lion's mouth—"and here." He tapped his head.

"Then you've got it? The Secret?"

"Not quite, but very soon." Hugo made the same face he does when a Gascon in his cups tells him he's undefeated in battle. Malachi saw it, and gave an aggrieved sniff. "I was quite close before I left London, I'll have you know. I had approached the Phoenix, but in so doing I broke several rather costly vessels, and was unable to repeat the experiment. But I expect that what I learn when I get my book translated will enable me to complete my lifetime's quest." He closed the book and put it back in its wrapping without even a glance at Hugo's stolid, doltish face. Sometimes that man had all the illumination of the back side of a brick wall. "Interesting, isn't it?" Malachi went on in his cheerful voice. "You seek pardon in Avignon, and I seek enlightenment there. That is, should we evade the hairy fellow in the stable I overheard discussing plans to have us ambushed and robbed on the way to Toulouse."

"Toulouse? But we're not going to Toulouse," said Hugo.

"Exactly," replied Malachi. "But they somehow got the impression that we are, thanks to the loose tongue of a certain Flemish wool merchant. I suggest that when the weather breaks we leave early."

Hugo looked at Brother Malachi suddenly; then he grinned. "So be it, Old Fox," he answered, and bidding farewell to us all, left for bed in a changed humor.

And so we set out in more cheerful fashion through the wintry hills for Foix, where we were certain of a good welcome, for we had a letter of introduction from Count Gaston's ambassador.

As it turned out, we had little need for the letter, for the Count's ambassador, the Sieur de Soule, had stayed at St.

Médard barely long enough to kiss the Bishop's ring before he was off like the wind with his entourage. Not only was he among those who believe it more comfortable to be far from the Inquisition, but he now had urgent news to send to his master. For not only was his old rival and enemy unexpectedly dead, but on his flank, in place of a mighty warlord, was an heir in his minority and a marriageable widow—things that make for very interesting politics indeed. Indeed, as we approached the city, we had seen the figures of fast horseman disappearing to the east—as it turned out, messengers sent to the Slavic lands to inform the Count of Foix and the Captal de Buch of the happenings at St. Médard-les-Rochers.

So even though Gaston Phoebus, the young count celebrated for his beauty, munificence, and ferocity, was not there, we had a most lordly reception from his constable and the hospitality of his house. But not only had the ambassador preceded us, so had the scandal of the dice game, and even a fragment of the tale had made us curiosities of the first order. So nothing would do but that I should sit on the right hand of the constable himself during supper, all crimson with embarrassment, as he quizzed me about the entire affair, and I answered as little as possible about the whole disgraceful business. But through flattery and wine he managed to worm out more than I'd intended to tell, and soon all the tables were abuzz with the rumor that the Count of Foix's old enemy had killed himself by an accidental overindulgence in dogs' aphrodisiacs. Then the constable smiled most strangely indeed and announced that God was on the side of the virtuous, and Hugo, his face all red with too much wine, shouted affirmation. I wished that I could hide under the table. I tell you, Gregory had the easy part of that visit, all tucked up in a big featherbed upstairs, being made much of and waited on hand and foot. They even sent a harper to make music for him, and his color began to get better, though he was still too weak to sit up.

As my fears for Gregory faded, other fears took their place. For one thing, the Weeping Lady was making herself felt as she snooped through the house, setting the dogs howling and making the back of people's necks prickle. And since she enjoyed offering her comments on the domestic arrangements, I feared being overheard in my nighttime conversations with her. Still, it would have been rude to remain silent, considering what she'd done. And having expended the greater part of her chronic wrath in the affair with the Count, she had fallen to being a cheerfully malicious gossip instead.

"Madame Belle-mère, if you'll graciously pardon me for saying so, I fear that if you frighten the horses again that way, they'll call in an exorcist."

"Exorcist?" she'd sniff. "Phoo! I don't give a fig for exorcists. After all, I've crossed the water—" But, of course, she'd never tell me how. "If you can't understand it, and you a mother, then you never will," she'd say, drifting off to inspect the Countess's jewels and frighten the waiting-ladies.

Another great fear, that Hugo would make some ungodly row over Cis, had been forestalled by the Sieur de Soule's sudden departure in a grand cavalcade but a day after we arrived. Some said he had new business for his master with the Pope, having something to do with the Church and the campaign against the pagan Slavs, and others that he had to attend to his neglected lands in the south. I have no idea whether any of it was so or not.

But Hugo contrived to make a scene anyway, since he was never happy if he wasn't the object of everyone's interest. This time, it was all over his Unspeakable Sin, as he called it, which of course made everyone terribly fascinated by it—much more so than they would have been over the speakable sort. Knights interested in some new sort of scandal would take him aside, and I'd hear him say, "Never—it's too horrible. It's unspeakable. I couldn't burden you with it." And they'd depart, shaking their heads, each secretly rejoicing he'd never done anything *that* unspeakable himself.

Each day he announced some new plan—to walk to Avignon barefoot, for example—and then he would beat his breast and shed tears and let himself be seen all prostrated before the chapel altar until absolutely everyone agreed he was the very model of holy repentance.

"Tell me," he'd say, cozying up to some priest or other, "should I arrange to be scourged all the way to Avignon? Or would a procession of monks, chanting, be better? Should I enter the town gate in my shirt?—Oh, I see. Yes. Gray friars might well be best —Oh, the sin of it, how it stains me! The Curse, the terrible Curse!" And, of course, the fact that some romantic-minded demoiselle was usually nearby to overhear didn't hurt matters any. They loved consoling him, and drying his tears and offering him holy medallions and other tokens for his trip. In fact, his repentance soon caused dark circles to appear under his eyes, for in going from bed to bed all night long he never had a moment's sleep.

But at last the trip could be put off no longer. A little page, one of Hugo's paid informants, let him know that he was soon to be sent on pilgrimage to the next world by several aggrieved gentlemen of the court if he did not continue on his way to Avignon. Gregory was well enough to eat now, and to be propped half sitting in the litter, though the fever still came and went. And most convenient of all, we got news that the Bishop of Pamiers was dispatching a heavily guarded party to Avignon, and was well disposed to allowing pilgrims to travel in their company. We might perhaps have hesitated had we known that it was a gold shipment, and they might have hesitated had they known we were English. But once there, Malachi pleaded our case in Latin, rolling his eyes heavenward and crossing himself frequently while he explained our need to visit the holy places of Avignon for restoration of soul and body. Then it was all settled by the captain of the guard, who said, looking over our straggling party, that it might be just as well in case we met up with any English mercenary captains to have someone who could speak their language, though he himself found that tongue difficult to distinguish from the barking of dogs.

In this way we found ourselves crossing the devastated lands to the east, then following the banks of the Aude north to Carcassonne. There, our welcome was not entirely hospitable, for only recently had the lower city beneath the walls been burned by the English prince, on one of his forays from Bordeaux. But in general it is well to travel with an ecclesiastical party, for they get good accommodations at the monasteries, and in those times of trouble, often only the church had anything to spare for visitors. Then there were the disadvantages, too, for convents, churches, and the comfortable sort of traveling clerics were special targets for the raiders and marauders.

And then, naturally, there was the endless number of beggars and wanderers maimed and made homeless by the continual warfare. These our guard drove off without much trouble, shouting that their lords should take care of them. But of course their lords were off raiding, too, since it was good ready money. Anyway, those beggars couldn't go home even if they had one left, since they hadn't been forgiven their taxes, which you'd think any sensible lord would do, given the state of the fields. When we heard later that these same peasants had risen, and roasted and eaten their lords into the bargain, it certainly came as no surprise to me, for I have seen the tithe barns burned in England for far less. Why wouldn't these hardened people meet such ferocity with equal ferocity?

At every place we stopped, the captains of our party made inquiries about the whereabouts of the local raiders, *écorcheurs*, mercenaries, and Free Companies. Then we'd halt, or change routes, according to the news. Most of all, our captains sought news of the "Archpriest," the monstrous renegade priest turned mercenary commander whose immense traveling army, called the "Society of Acquisition," was said to be somewhere between us and the papal city of Avignon. Cities and fortresses had fallen to him, and should we have the misfortune to cross his path, we had heard he'd more than likely drink our blood from the chalices of the churches he'd burned.

But God was with us; we avoided the *écorcheurs* and arrived eventually at Avignon having lost only one man, and that one a frail old clerk, to a fever in Narbonne. And we saw many curious sights along the way: some nasty, such as skinned or dismembered corpses, and some beautiful, such as ancient shrines and the ruins of shining buildings left by the pagan Romans. But the white gravelly roads across the dry hills, and the bleak rolling dunes and stunted pines by the alien ocean, made me weep for the comfortable green of England.

At Montpellier, where there is a university, we were greeted outside the walls by a ferocious crowd, shouting and pelting a man in a scholar's robe, tied backward on a donkey. Malachi, who had been there long ago, told us that is how they drive out those who practice medicine without a degree in that city.

"After all," he said, "there's a celebrated medical faculty here, and they have to keep control of trade."

"Well, it's just as well they don't have that idea in England, or there wouldn't be a donkey left in London," I replied. "It would be much more sensible to drive off the doctors who kill people, and just keep the ones that make folks better."

"Ha," he said. "Then there wouldn't be a donkey left in all of Christendom."

"But Malachi, surely it is a terrible thing to drive a man out of the city walls in times like these," Mother Hilde worried as we sat on our horses outside the city gate, waiting for the crowd to thin out so we could enter. The donkey was driven some distance beyond us down the road before its passenger was forcibly dismounted and abandoned there in the deep mud, the donkey being led back by the thrifty citizens of the town.

"Not entirely, my dear. Consider the good that is hidden within the situation. In times of peace, no city would have him, and he would wander homeless and without a trade. But in these times of trouble, he will soon have employment with the *écorcheurs,* if he has the slightest sense," responded Malachi, as we dismounted to enter the city gate.

"But what will this poor country do if everyone becomes an *écorcheur*?" I asked.

"Margaret," responded Malachi firmly, "thinking about big

problems that you cannot solve will bring you nothing but grief. Do as I do and think about the small problems that are easily resolved. That is how God sends us nothing but joy. For example, I am currently pondering the wonderful fact that in the bosom of this extraordinary university may well reside the translator whom I seek. While you do nothing but fret, my next few hours will be full of happiness, the eagerness of the hunt, and the exquisite pleasure of anticipation. Think of that, and mend your ways."

But after making inquiries, Malachi came back very discouraged, for the pestilence and the wars had shriveled the university to only a poor shadow of its former self—just a few hundred students and a handful of masters. He'd found three converts, several people who had claimed they had once known a Jew, a lunatic master who had told him that God had given him the power to read Hebrew scriptures in a dream, and an elderly doctor of theology who told him to go to Avignon. And no one, no one at all, was interested in his book full of strange pothooks.

Only Hugo found profit in our brief stay there. In the cold of the evening, when the winter rain had broken and the wind had pushed the dark clouds away from the moon, we heard the voices of students in the alley behind our lodgings. Their song echoed plaintively against the rain-slick stone walls, and we could hear the splash and clatter of their footsteps on the wet, uneven cobblestones. I opened the shutters to let the music in. There in the damp and moonlight, three young men, the one in the center with a beribboned lute, were strolling and singing together, as students have always done and always will do, in spite of war or plague, until the end of time. They paused at the end of the alley and began another song—one of the strange, lovely winding melodies of the south. Another pair of shutters opened, and a girl's head peeped out in the shadows. Her heavy dark braids brushed the sill, and I could hear her laugh.

"Let me see," said Hugo, pushing in behind me—for all of us were staying in the same room, even the squires and the grooms, who slept on the floor on straw mattresses at the foot of Hugo's bed. And I could hear him mutter as I pulled my head in, "—A lute, yes. Just the thing. More romantic—"

It was at just that moment that I heard an older woman's voice scolding and the shutters down the alley slam shut with a crash that ended the music. But the seed had been planted, and Sir Hugo's baggage, when we left a day later, included a lute made in the Saracen style in strips of light and dark wood and with a sound-hole covered with a filigree of carved ivory.

"Quite a lute," said Gregory, and a shadow of his old, ironic smile crossed his ravaged face. "It will be interesting to watch him learn to play it. Hugo as troubador. To think I had always underestimated his artistic side—" But then his head fell back against the pillow from the effort of speech, and he was silent all the way to the tomb of the blessed Saint Gilles, which gives great virtue to all those who visit it, for it contains the entire body of the holy confessor, except for one armbone, which was stolen to make a shrine elsewhere.

Menacing black clouds were rolling overhead, and the first big drops of rain had begun to fall as we reached the great bridge that leads to the papal city of Avignon. The yellow-white stone of the span and of the domes and turrets that rise on the hill within the city's massive walls, all shining with the damp, glistened like gold against the seething black of the sky. The river here runs swift and green, too wide and dangerous to bridge except by a miracle. But indeed there was one, for God Himself gave orders that the bridge be built, and told a little shepherd boy named Bénézet how to do it. Of course, the bishop threatened to cut off Bénézet's hands and feet for proposing it to him. But once this difficulty was past, Bénézet became a saint, which is what happens if you can survive the instruction of heavenly voices. The bridge is very fine and fair, with a chapel in the middle, just like we have on London Bridge at home, which I must say I consider to be far finer, even though it wasn't designed by heavenly instruction. But God did not warn Bénézet about how slippery it would be for horses to make the roadway of such fine white close-set stone. So everyone must dismount and lead their animals across by the bridle, if they do not wish to risk injury. Of course, this may have been God's way of humbling everybody equally and reminding them that Our Savior did a lot of walking.

But Malachi said that was the sort of thing I would say, and went on counting. "One, two—yes, there's one," as if he'd finally lost his mind. And then he explained to me that there's an old saying that you can't cross the bridge at Avignon without meeting two monks, two donkeys, and two whores, and he thought if it came true, he'd have good fortune in Avignon. It turned out the donkeys were the most difficult to come by, for in a city populated by churchmen and students it turns out that there are an extraordinary number of the other sort of person.

The rain began to fall in earnest as we clustered with the other marketwomen and pilgrims, waiting for the bishop's armed party to be admitted and pass through the town gate. I paused to pull the furs over Gregory's face before Robert helped me to remount. Gregory's breath was wheezing, and his eyes looked all glassy, as if his mind were wandering again. I wished we were all inside; watching the strangers hurry by us in the street as they dashed for cover, all with someplace of their own to go, made me feel desperately homeless.

By the time we'd ridden into the courtyard of the first inn we found inside the wall, the downpour had turned the dust to heavy mud that caked our horses' feet. The rolling thunderclouds had darkened the sky even before the sun had set, and we were soaked through. As we tried to huddle in the shelter of the overhanging second story, Hugo reached up from horseback and rapped on the closed shutters of the room above the arched entrance to the inn's courtyard.

A woman's head popped out, addressed us briefly in an incomprehensible language, disappeared, and reappeared with another woman—the firm, matronly sort. The new woman, obviously the mistress, shouted in French with a rolling southern accent: "You want places? Who are you?"

"Foreigners of high degree in need of shelter, good woman," shouted Sir Hugo over the thunder.

"What's that you've got there? A corpse? I run a good house. No corpses," shouted the woman.

"It's a wounded knight," shouted Hugo, taking some license.

"Wounded? Ha. Probably sick. And catching. You think I need sick foreigners? Go away!" and she started to close the shutters.

"Close those shutters and I'll burn your house down!" shouted Hugo, and Robert shouted a fierce second.

"Talk, talk, talk," said the woman. "Go to the *quartier des soldats* and ask at the Moor's Head. She'll take anyone. A proper case of plague would do her good." So we waited, drenched and freezing, for a break in the pounding rain, Hugo's men growling as their horses shifted and whinnied under the overhang.

By the time we reached the Tête du Maure, it was dark and I was shivering, and praying that we would not lose Gregory to the soaking rain. But with the litter laid out by the great fire in the room downstairs, and with everyone drying and regaining warmth, it soon became apparent why we'd been sent there. Women were playing dice with drunken soldiers, women were drinking with elderly priests, women were fondling tipsy students in corners. There were old women and young women, fat women and thin women, light women and dark women. They looked at us curiously for a moment, and then resumed their business. A very large woman, with a vast tissue-thin headdress that revealed mountainous braids of false black hair and immense tinkling silver combs and earrings, approached us. Her face was unusually red and white, with rolls of rice powder settled in all the creases. Just now, the creases were smiling. She spoke to Hugo, who was shaking the water out of his hair like a dog, making little *splut-splut* noises as the drops hit the fire.

"What's your pleasure?" she asked. "I'm Jeannot the Fat, and I'm known as the 'Abbess' here in Avignon. You won't find a better place in town."

"By the bowels of God!" Hugo exclaimed, grinning and looking about eagerly. "I've died and gone to Mussulman heaven!"

The Tête du Maure was a house of ill repute.

By the time the sun had come out the next day, it had become clear how the Moor's Head was run. The first floor was the public floor, a tavern with two great wide fireplaces, narrow little barred windows, and a large number of alcoves, many curtained. The second floor was where the women lived, with rooms that were, shall we say, let by the night. On the uppermost floor, served by a rickety outside staircase, were a few rooms under the leaky eaves, let at long term to the most dubious of travelers.

In the center of the house was a wide courtyard, which you could see from our little window. Open staircases led from the courtyard to the rooms on each floor. And when the weather was good, the court was filled with travelers in strange costumes, Jews with their yellow badges opening their packs to display colorful wares, groups of students jesting in Latin, and women all finely dressed, with tinkling jewelry, tall headdresses, and high pattens, coming and going on mysterious business. All of it was a hint of the vibrant life of the streets and buildings beyond, a life I craved to go and see for myself. But most of the time I couldn't even leave the little room, for someone had to be with Gregory, who was still too weak to be out of bed. And besides, I couldn't go through town without a man to escort me, and Hugo and Malachi and the others all had business of their own. How I wished with all my heart that a miracle would happen and Gregory would sit up one day with his old energy renewed, all curious to see the new places! Then he would take me everywhere on his strong arm, and we could see everything together, and talk all about it, just as in the old days: the Turkish ambassadors in their strange turbans, the swarthy foreigners with the talking birds on their shoulders, the shops, the peddlers, the shrines, and the wonderful churches full of incense and chanting.

Instead, I had to content myself with hearing all about it at second hand. Malachi told me all about the streets in which he wandered daily, and Hugo told me about the palaces of the great, where he loitered for hours, hoping for audiences with someone who might help him get the Pope's intercession. Even Hilde had got one of Hugo's attendants to take her about to various shrines, and though she did try to stay with me, I could see the holy places tugging at her heart, and told her to go and pray for Gregory there, if she wished to help me.

One day Hugo came in all cross, followed by Robert carrying his lute.

"Throw the damned thing in the fire, Robert. The man who sold it to me cheated me: the neck's too narrow for a man's fingers."

"My lord, I beg you—it's too valuable for firewood. Give it to me, instead."

"You? You heard the man. You strive to outdo me?"

"Me? Oh, no, not at all. After all, it's the verse that's the higher thing. The music is only accompaniment. The work of the mind is proper to the lord, the job of noisemaker should be left to his squire."

Hugo turned to inspect Robert's face. His mind appeared to be working, although with Hugo you can never be sure.

"The damned little bitch laughed at me. You heard her. And that preposterous little fellow who calls himself a master of music says I need to perfect myself. Perfect myself! I'm perfect already!"

"Yes, my lord," responded Robert without the slightest hint of sarcasm in his voice. He really wants that lute, I thought. He must have found an entirely different woman to court, and doesn't want Hugo to know about it.

"Very well, Robert. You play it. I think I'll go enhance my talents with that little dark fellow we met in the cardinal's ante-chamber. He seemed to know quite a lot about that sort of thing. Yes, in this town poetry's the lure that catches the most dear little fishes. Who'd have thought it? Usually they're content with a handsome face and well-turned figure. Well, everyplace is different. Did you see that sweet little thing that lives upstairs in the Street of the Painters, Robert?"

"The one with the mole?"

"Quite right. And she's got another on her—"

"Sir Hugo," I interrupted. "How can you go to see the Pope when you live worse and worse every day?" He looked puzzled.

"Worse? I've never been so holy. I'm practically halfway into heaven these days. Haven't killed any begging burghers for months, haven't had a woman I haven't paid for. Why, at home I was only shriven once a year at Easter, and, of course, before going into battle. Now, I'm shriven every week. Bleached almost as white as snow. Found a priest at St. Agricol who doesn't speak a word of English. I tell him everything. He nods. I beat my breast and weep. He absolves me. I make an offering. I tell you, I'm living a new life. Ah, God, it's the sacredness of this place. It rubs off, even on a sinner like me." He rolled his eyes heavenward, and clasped his hands, and it was clear that being the knothead that he was, he was perfectly sincere. "At times—at times I feel myself—surrounded by saints here. Elevated. The golden halls! The incense! The magnificence! God must live this way! It's just like heaven!" And he hurried off to the second floor.

Brother Malachi, of course, was equally busy. He spent his days searching for his translator, and his evenings complaining. Weary and footsore, he'd return from scouring the shabby streets of the Jewish quarter, and grumble as he sat on the bed: "That ghastly sailor, Jannetus, that wretch at Montpellier, they've deceived me! Do you know how many men in the Jewish quarter are named Abraham? Only those who aren't named David or Isaac. And surnames! I swear, I've been misled on purpose! Of course, in any Christian city, anyone who's Jewish is given "the Jew" as his surname. So, from all over Christendom, Abraham the Jews have poured into Avignon. It's like looking for John the Smith or William the Cook in London."

"But what about the university? I thought there were people there who could read Hebrew. Didn't you say so yourself?"

"They refuse to translate anything but Scripture. It seems tolerance doesn't stretch too far, even in Avignon. I inquired after that fellow Josceus Magister. Well, at least he was real. But he was dead too—several years ago from plague. So I found his successor, a Jewish professor, a very learned man. 'Is it sacred?' he said. 'Surely, you understand I'd lose my post if I got involved in anything shady. Go find someone who won't be dismissed for doing your translation.' So I told him about Abraham the Jew. 'Oh, yes, him. Perfect. Go get him to do it. Goodbye.'"

"Well, surely among all those Abrahams, you'll find the wise one you heard about very soon."

"The wise one? They're all wise—wise to me, that's what. I go to Abraham the money changer. 'What's this?' he says. 'A book? My, how I'd love to help you, but I don't read a word of Hebrew. Try Abraham the goldsmith.' So I go to the goldsmith's. 'A book?' he says. 'Oh, it's the tragedy of my life I don't read Hebrew,' and he even manages to look as if he's wiping away a tear. A tear as dubious as some of the saints' tears I've sold. Ha! They just don't *want* to read my book, that's what, and I've come to the conclusion they're playing a game with me."

"But Malachi, you yourself have often said that alchemy can be a dangerous business. Look at what happened with the Count of St. Médard. They may fear the risk you put them at—and it seems entirely fair to me," Mother Hilde broke in. She had put down her mending and had gone to get the flask to renew Malachi's glass.

"But Hilde, my love, Avignon is a hotbed of alchemy. It's unlike any other place in Christendom that way. People who already have a lot of gold can always use more. I thought I'd told you that even a pope was one of us. That's what made me

353

so sure I'd find my translator here. There's probably dozens of them somewhere, laboring away in cellars, translating arcana. Why not mine? Oh, the injustice of it all. Think, think—I must think."

On the litter, propped across benches in the corner, Gregory groaned and stirred.

"Not now, Gilbert, not now. Can you never understand when it is inappropriate to interrupt my delicate thought processes? It's like breathing into my vessels, just when the process must not be disturbed—a sin to which your curiosity led you often in the old days. Consideration! Consideration! Think of my delicate brain, and be silent!"

"Noisy yourself" was the sound that seemed to come from the litter as Gregory pulled the covers over his head.

"A pope an alchemist, Malachi? Which one?" I was very curious.

"They say, the last Pope John. The twenty-second of that name, I believe. He certainly left enough gold in the treasury. But I don't think he found the Secret, even though it's rumored. It was probably through the sale of indulgences, it seems to me. But then, that's a kind of alchemy, turning paper into gold. I've practiced a little of that sort myself, and ought to know."

"Speaking of alchemy, Malachi," began Hilde, pouring wine into his cup to make him mellow, "I'm still waiting to hear how you made the gold for that count, when you've never made any for me, even when the roof needed fixing."

"Me?" Malachi looked around him in feigned surprise. Then he looked at Hilde, and sighed. "I suppose it's only fair. You'd think the less of me if I didn't tell. Hilde, queen of my heart, haven't I sworn that the first gold I make after I get the Secret will be used to crown you for your years of patience?" Hilde smiled indulgently. But she didn't quit looking as if she were waiting for an answer. "I'd planned a ruse, my treasure, as you must have suspected all along. The secret's in my rod. The gold was Margaret's florins, melted down."

"Malachi, you mean you offered the Count a false Secret as ransom? I swear, I'd have died of fear if I'd known you were just planning another of your tricks," I broke in.

"And so I thought myself, Margaret. So of course you didn't know. I thought the man would be gullible. What I didn't suspect was that he was evil, as well."

"Malachi, stick to the point. I'm waiting to hear how you did it," said Hilde.

"Very simple. The oldest trick there is. The rod was hollow, stopped up with black wax. The gold was inside. The heat melts the wax, and there it is! The gold tumbles out. The rest consists of mystic hand-waving, strange chants, and other acts of my constantly creative imagination. They swallowed it all. Desire made them blind. It often does."

Hilde sat down and shook her head wonderingly. "Oh, Malachi, dear Malachi," she said. He looked at her as if he suddenly feared she might say something sharp for taking such a risk. But she saw the look, and smiled, and said, "Oh, Malachi. You're such a philosopher." And he beamed in response.

I waited for the precious moment to pass, and then broke in with something that had been bothering me.

"Malachi," I asked, "have you told them it's an alchemical text? Maybe you should make the agreement before you show them."

"I haven't shown it yet, but they always seem to know. And then it's 'try down the street.'"

"Well, suppose they know you have the Secret. Then they'll think that if they translate it, you might not want them to know it too—"

"Yes, sensible, sensible. If I were a man like the Count, I might just send an assassin after them. An accident in the street, a fire— No, suppose I were fearful they'd told? I might just get rid of the lot. Yes. It's clear. No wonder nobody reads Hebrew. I'll have to give guarantees—prove my sincerity—" and he was off again, thinking of fanciful schemes.

"Malachi, you must press on," said Hilde. "We can't stay

much longer. Did you know that Hugo was here trying to borrow money? We think he must have spent the passage money back. Margaret questioned him, and he got very annoyed. 'I'm the heir of Brokesford, and need to live like a knight. You don't want me to live like a peasant, do you?' He hasn't paid his men, and two of them have vanished. They say they've run off to join the Archpriest. The rest are loyal, at least for now. But the sooner we leave, the better."

"That wretched cabbage brain! I can't believe he's any relative of Gilbert's. I imagine he put the passage money on the gaming table. He hasn't got the sense of a cooked carrot! He's probably counting on getting home by hiring out to a party traveling in the right direction. Armed men are at a shortage now, and he can name his price. But us—we've got no such recourse. I wouldn't put it past him to leave without us."

Now Malachi had a second preoccupation. In the night, when I'd get up to attend to Gregory, whose fever waxed and waned without reason, I'd hear him muttering.

"Money, money. I need money. Think, brain, think. For God's sake, Gilbert, stop that moaning and gibberish. You're interfering with my mental processes." Then I'd hear the bed creak and know that he'd sat up, to stare into the dark for hours.

Abraham the tailor was nobody's fool. He knew how to smell things coming in the air. That is why he was already packed and on the road when they'd fired the Jewish quarter in Marseilles. He himself had led the mule laden with his wife, his goods, and two little babies in the panniers all night beneath the unseeing stars. He'd never turned his face back once on the road to Avignon, even on the rise of ground just beyond the city, when he heard the faint echo of distant cries behind him. His oldest son, a little boy just ten, who walked beside him with a tall stick and a pack exactly like his own, had turned and cried, "Oh, look, father," pausing to stare at the column of flames climbing into the night sky. But even then, the old man had only hunched his back and turned his face like iron to the road ahead.

Now he was confronted with a stranger who wanted a book translated. Looking the man over carefully, he went through his mental checklist. Not armed; not evil; not crazy; and not a Flemish wool merchant. No matter what he claimed, the man lacked the countinghouse eyes and ponderous mind of the merchant of the north. He checked the hands as the man held out the book for him to inspect. Acid-stained. And the sleeves —marred by tiny little burn holes, as if from flying sparks. Oh, God, not another alchemist, thought Abraham. What have I done to deserve this? Still, it was tempting. His wife was wanting a new pair of shoes, and his oldest boy had just outgrown his gown, which was ready, even in its patched condition, to be passed to the next child.

"These are indeed Hebrew letters," said Abraham. "But I will need to be paid in advance."

"I can't let the book go. Will you translate it in my presence?" Brother Malachi's voice was unusually controlled, considering the state of high excitement he was in.

Abraham the tailor took the book and they sat together at the broad table on which he did his cutting.

"Let me see—hmm." He turned the pages carefully. He sighed. He looked again. He sighed another time, a long, resigned sigh.

"In my opinion, this book is a fraud," he said.

"What do you mean, a fraud?" Brother Malachi was agitated.

"Whoever wrote it didn't know any Hebrew. They just put down letters any way it suited them." He looked at Brother Malachi's face. The man looked as if he'd been struck by lightning. "Still, the illuminations are very nicely done," he added consolingly.

"But—but couldn't it be a corrupted text—or perhaps a code —a cypher?" Brother Malachi's world was dissolving around him.

"A corrupted text would have meaningless words that had

been miscopied mixed in among words with meaning. Here, there is not a syllable of meaning anywhere." Abraham pointed with a callused finger to the rows of letters on the page. His eyes missed nothing as he watched grief and shock alternate on Brother Malachi's face.

"But a cypher?" Malachi scrabbled for a last word of hope.

"Well, who knows? Perhaps it is. But large numbers of letters aren't even correctly written. See this one here? It's as if you wrote an *m* with five humps—and over there, three, and then again four. This leads me to think that the person who wrote it didn't know what he was doing."

"But the diagrams—the squares, the pentacles?" Brother Malachi sounded desperate now. They all do, thought Abraham. It's so sad, letting them down gently. No wonder no one but me is willing to do it. I'm becoming a specialist in the art.

"I will transliterate the letters. Perhaps then you will find a clue to another language—one which I do not know."

Brother Malachi put his elbows on the table; he buried his face in his hands.

"A fake—a fraud. Who would have thought it? Me, of all people, taken in by a fraudulent bunch of paper. Still, it has a kind of justice in it. God must have willed it."

"Why do you say that?" asked Abraham, who had rarely seen any of them take the news this calmly. So many of them became dangerous at this point.

"Because of my business—hm—my former business, I mean, before I became a wool merchant, that is."

"And what was that?"

"I sold indulgences," said Brother Malachi, and then he looked at the beautiful book and began to laugh. Abraham's eyes glittered with the irony of it, and he began to laugh too.

Malachi laughed even harder, until the tears stood in his eyes and his breath came in sobs. It felt almost like crying, but of course it was much better than weeping. And as Malachi laughed, Abraham laughed harder too. Life had not been all that easy for him in Avignon either.

"Thank you," said Brother Malachi as he wiped his eyes.

"Thank you," said Abraham the tailor, doing the same. "Do you want the transliteration now?"

"Can I come back tomorrow? I need to walk about and think a bit," said Brother Malachi.

"Of course," said Abraham. But the false wool merchant had already tucked the volume into his bosom and left with his head bowed down.

"Too bad," said Abraham the Jew. "There must be hundreds of those things floating about the world, and somehow they all end up here."

The pseudo wool merchant, hands behind his back and head sunk low, wandered for a considerable time until he emerged from the maze of narrow alleys into the tiny, cobblestoned square before the massive Gothic portals of the church of St. Pierre. There in the jostling crowd emerging from the dark interior of the church, he saw a comfortable-looking older woman in pilgrim's garb, escorted by a bored-looking little boy. Even from the back, the figure was familiar.

"Hilde, Hilde, wait!" called the wool merchant, and she turned. She had spent the morning walking all over town; she had visited six churches as well as the cave where the most blessed Saint Martha, hostess of Our Lord, had dwelt with her servant Marcella when she preached the Gospel and conquered the dragon with holy water. She was still in a dazzle with the grandeur, the gold and incense, the high shadowy vaults where God so obviously dwelt, and the multitude of enshrined relics. Kneebones, fingerbones, skulls, fragments of cloth and vials of blood—even the very girdle with which Saint Martha had bound the dragon—they'd all moved her to tears. She'd had such a lovely time envisioning the martyrs they'd belonged to and dabbing at her eyes, her heart was all full of it. It had been an absolutely ecstatic morning, one of the few she'd treated herself to in many days of being shut inside helping Margaret.

At the cry, she looked up and waved. Then she said something to the restive little boy, and he sped off in the opposite direction more swiftly than a bolt sent from a crossbow.

"Hilde, I've been gulled." Brother Malachi was puffing as he caught up with her. "Can you believe it? Me? Of all people."

"Surely not, Malachi, you're very clever."

"Not this time. I tell you, that Thomas always had it in for me. Jealous, he was, because I was farther along than he was. He'd never even got as far as the dragon. I told him he was going in the wrong direction, and he said I was trying to trick him into failure, so I could keep the gold for myself. I imagine he died laughing, after he'd signed the will leaving me this thing. 'If I can't have it, neither can he—I'll send him off on a hunt he won't come back from.' I'm just lucky he didn't make it up in Egyptian, I suppose."

"He may have been a friend, Malachi, and been fooled himself."

"Him? Not likely. Did I tell you about the time he visited my laboratorium and dropped some powder out of his sleeve into all my experimental vessels? Turned everything green—ruined six months of work. And to top it off, he confided he'd seen the Peacock's Tail, which was entirely untrue. Made me morose for weeks."

"Morose? Oh, Malachi, you're not morose. It's not in your character."

"Not since I found you, O Jewel of My Existence. It is impossible to be morose in the presence of your lovely self and that marvelous onion pie that only you can make so well."

"Oh, Malachi, you are so brilliant and genial." Mother Hilde took the wool merchant's arm as they strolled beneath the new-leafed trees. "I'm very lucky that some other woman didn't make you onion pie first."

"It would have been imperfect, Hilde. No, I was looking for the perfect onion pie and the perfect woman. With whom else could I share my life? Still, I am very sorry to have brought you on this wild-goose chase."

"Sorry? Malachi, I've always wanted to travel. Without you, where would I have ever been, except the village where I was born? And now—why, we live in London! I've met princes, dukes, counts—even though that last one wasn't much, I must say. And look in here—" She opened her pilgrim's wallet. It was full of pressed tin pilgrim's badges from the shrines she'd visited. There were pebbles and little pottery vials of this and that, all stoppered with wax. "See those? When I was a girl, Malachi, I'd see the pilgrims ride by, with their badges on their hats, and I'd be envious. They've *been* somewhere, I'd say to myself. Now I've been somewhere too. How amazing. After enough life for two women, I have another. A life of travel and adventure with the cleverest man in the whole world. I don't understand why you're sorry about that."

As she spoke Brother Malachi's face began to relax. It regained its normal pinkness, and the deep lines started to fade away.

"Hilde, I'll make it all up to you. We'll go back. I've learned a lot on this trip, though not from that wretched book. I've a new idea I'll set to work on. You'll see. Someday, I'll make you rich beyond your dreams."

"Malachi," she said, smiling at the everlasting optimism that always made him seem so eternally youthful, "I already am that way."

CHAPTER 12

"**H**e's feeling low, Malachi, I can tell." I'd been hanging out the window, trying to catch the spring sun on my face. The heat had come early, making the room under the eaves stifling. I was crazy with being inside too long, doing little but listening to Gregory's gasping breath, or the strange words he said when his mind was wandering. So when I saw Malachi puffing up the outside stair to the garret room, I was ready to burst for wanting to tell him my idea.

"Low?" Even Malachi had to duck when he crossed the threshold to the little room. "You're worried about him feeling low? He's alive! If that isn't sufficient cause for rejoicing, I don't know what is!" He glanced briefly at the sleeping figure on the bed. "In the meanwhile, I worry about serious things, such as the fact we haven't money or means to get home again. But am I low? No! My brain is churning with plans. I occupy myself with useful thoughts. And it's me that ought to be low! I deserve to be low, and lie in bed all day with people worrying about me and offering me wine and fruit. My book, my wonderful treasure that sent me off on this foolish chase, is a worthless forgery. Just tell me what else could make a sensitive soul like mine lower?"

There's no dealing with Brother Malachi in a mood like this, you just have to distract him.

"Brother Malachi, I need your help. Hilde and I had an idea, and we're going shopping. But we need an expert like you to assist us."

"Don't think to distract me with that sly, flattering tone, Margaret. Where did you get any money, besides what you gave over to me?"

"I sold a few things I didn't want."

"What—?" He scrutinized me closely, to see what was missing.

"I want to buy him a present. He needs a book."

"Margaret, I see your hood's missing, but that won't buy a book."

"It's summer. We'll be leaving soon, and I don't need it."

"What else, you foolish woman?"

"Those nasty mourning clothes. I mended them and sold them. Everyone needs mourning clothes, it's the plague season. Everybody except me. I'm not sad anymore. They fetched a good price—that horrible lilac water smell made them seem more genteel. Ugh. Lilac water." I couldn't help shuddering.

"Tsk, tsk. You're shuddering, Margaret," Malachi remarked. "You've been rather hasty in divesting yourself of clothing, I fear. But I can tell from your face you've gone behind my back. What else did you sell?"

"Just the horse litter."

"Just the—what? And, pray, how do you think to get him home again without it?"

"He'll ride when we leave, Malachi, because he'll be well. Once he gets his spirits back, he won't do anything *but* ride."

Brother Malachi shook his head. "Margaret, you are a hopeless dreamer and a madwoman. The fever comes and goes; he still hallucinates, and when he's himself, he's become so morose, he doesn't speak. So with the harebrained notion you'll cure him with a book, you have stripped yourself of your last worldly goods. Consider this: You have grown as large as a small mountain. Shouldn't you have better bought a cradle and swaddling clothes?"

"That's why I need you to help me find the book. It has to be just right. See? Here's Hilde back again, so we can go." Indeed, Mother Hilde had returned with a bucket of water. Setting it beside the bed, she felt Gregory's forehead where he slept, his eyes all sunken in, and wrung out a towel in the cold water. Laying it across his forehead, she motioned Sim to sit with him and renew the towel when it was needed. Sim nodded, but I could see he took it ill that we were going out when he had to stay.

The wonderful early April sunshine brightened the whole world. Spring comes so soon in the south. It's really more like summer with us. High white clouds floated in the blue sky. The towers of the papal palace shone like the blessed Jerusalem itself. Below it, the narrow streets were crowded with fruit and flower vendors, strollers, and the grandees with which this town abounds.

"Oh, Malachi, look," cried Mother Hilde. "Who is that? The Pope?" A score of outriders were pushing aside the crowds to make room for an elaborate gilded horse litter to pass. In it sat an elderly gentleman, all dressed in silk like the King of Heaven, sniffing at a pomander to keep the street smell from him. From the hounds and horses and members of his household in livery that accompanied him, he looked like a very great lord indeed. Behind his mounted escort came a half-dozen heavily draped mule litters, and a train of sumpter mules and attendants of all description, on foot and mounted. It was a most sumptuous procession; everyone had stopped to gawk.

"No, it's a cardinal," said Brother Malachi. "You can tell by the coat of arms. He must be removing his household to his summer palace in the Venaissin, now that heat has brought the season of illness to the town."

"Malachi, look at the women."

"Margaret, I thought you knew enough not to be shocked by a little thing like—oh, my goodness—" Brother Malachi had seen what I had seen. Riding in the gay cavalcade in a covered mule litter with the cardinal's coat of arms displayed in the gilt carving was a woman. The curtains of the litter had been tied back to give her air. She was all blond and white, glittering with jewels and clutching two tiny white lapdogs. Behind her ran two little black boys in turbans and a half-dozen liveried footmen. I stared like a fool, then smiled and waved, because I just couldn't help it. She turned her head—she'd seen me, but she didn't nod in acknowledgment. She'd fixed her gaze straight ahead, so that everyone could admire her profile and jeweled headdress. It was Cis.

"Well, well," said Brother Malachi. "Isn't the world full of strange things? Here, Margaret. Take my arm over these cobblestones—you must admit you've become totally unwieldy lately. Who'd have ever thought that a slender young thing such as you used to be would become unable to see her own toes?"

"That is the usual occurrence in this state, Malachi dear," observed Mother Hilde. "Your mind has been just too occupied to notice before."

"Indeed, Hilde, I defer to your greater wisdom in this area of expertise. Do they all get as large as Margaret here?"

"Larger," she answered.

A woman pressed by us with a large basket of strawberries on her head.

"Oh, strawberries," I cried. "Where on earth did she get them in this season? I could eat the whole basket. I must have some."

"First garlic, then dandelion greens, and now there's no end to it. Oh, the ceaseless demands of women! Margaret, you must restrain these mad appetites, or you'll give the baby a birthmark."

"Malachi—" Mother Hilde pulled at his sleeve. "I'd like some too. It's been so long—" So while we waited in the shade of the cool stone arch of a long arcade, Brother Malachi pursued the woman, returning, all out of breath, with the entire basket.

"I hope this satisfies you greedy ladies; now we'll all be covered with blotches."

But soon enough, strawberries and all, he had brought us to the Street of Studies, where stood the shop of one of the numerous literary entrepreneurs of Avignon. This one was the best and the largest, he'd explained. The proprietor had his own scriptorum, and rented books to the masters of the university, as well as providing for sale fair copies of all the most fashionable and scholarly works, both newly made and previously owned. The presence of the papacy had made Avignon the most cultured city in Christendom, full of illuminators, painters, and masters of fair writing of every sort. We passed the rows of desks for the full-time copyists of the scriptorum, the displays of pens and paper, and stood before the wide, slanted shelves on which the finished books were laid flat for display. The man took no chances; the precious things were chained to the shelves. Many were too wide and heavy for me to lift anyway; some were fabulously bound and decorated. Too expensive, I thought, and looked for the plainer ones. The proprietor, sensing our lack of respectability from the basket of strawberries, hovered immediately behind us.

"You wished?" he said in Latin to Brother Malachi. He had dark, close-trimmed hair with a scholar's tonsure, and a long, expressive olive-skinned face.

"I want to buy a book." I spoke to him directly in the French of the north. Switching to that language, he addressed Brother Malachi in response.

"You want to buy a book?"

"She wants to buy a book," responded Brother Malachi. "I am merely here to help."

"I want to buy a book for a present," I said to the man.

"She wishes to buy a book for a present?" the man asked Brother Malachi, as if he were a translator, and women's words needed to be decoded by him before they could be understood by another man. I was surveying the books. The fatter ones, even plainly bound, looked too expensive. I'd try the thin ones that looked well thumbed. The first was in Latin.

"That's a theological tract about damnation, Margaret," said Brother Malachi in English. "I don't think he'd like it." I looked at another. The undecorated calfskin binding looked well worn. The lines inside were short, as if they were poetry. It wasn't Latin.

"This one's poetry?" I asked. It was the thinnest of all. Sold from an estate, perhaps, or by a student who needed passage money home. I might get a bargain. Besides, Gregory liked poetry, or at least he had liked poetry.

The man burst into a flood of Latin at Brother Malachi. He waved his arms. He rolled his eyes.

"The man says, Margaret, that this is the work of the divine Petrarch, whom he knows personally. He himself is a passionate devotee of the muses, and has captured the most subtle sensations of passion in his own poetry, which was nurtured and encouraged by the great Petrarch himself, at whose feet he sat. He says if you like Petrarch's sonnets, you'll adore his, which he'll sell us even cheaper." Brother Malachi spoke the French of the north, so that all parties in the negotiation would be aware of what he said.

"Ask him," I answered in that same language, "just how long he sat at the feet of this Petrarch." Though the man heard everything, Brother Malachi again had to translate from the female. At length the man responded to Brother Malachi, waving his arms and gesticulating passionately.

"I pursued him. Like the shy roe deer, he vanished. At his inn, surrounded by worshipers, he disappeared out the back door. 'My poems!' I cried as he lowered himself secretly from the back window at midnight, 'you must read them! Tell me, great master, should I pursue my course?' 'Pursue!' he cried as he fled on horseback. So I pursued. Soon I had several slim volumes. My love poetry. My odes. My epic, on the taking of

Constantinople. And I knew where to find him. He'd hidden in Vaucluse. I made a pilgrimage to his shrine. What divine simplicity! Like the ancient Romans! He lived alone with a dog. I knocked at the door. 'My God, not you again!' he cried. That is how I knew the light of my rising sun had dazzled him beyond measure. 'My poetry,' I cried. 'Read my poetry. You must tell me what you think of it.' He had to read, though I could see how it pained him to see how he'd been surpassed. 'These love poems,' he admitted grudgingly, 'they're—unique.' 'My odes?' I queried. 'Even more unique.' Ah! Even the greatest minds must wrestle with the serpent of jealousy. But he, the great man, the genius, overcame it! 'And my epic?' I asked. 'The most unique of all.' 'Bless you, bless you, maestro!' I kissed his hands and feet. I fled in rapture, taking my poems with me, so that he could not steal the ideas."

"How can you sit at feet that are running, Malachi?" I asked in English.

"Now, Margaret. Don't be saucy," answered Brother Malachi in that same language.

"Ask him, Brother Malachi," I resumed in French, "whether, since Petrarch has been surpassed by himself, wouldn't he give me a bargain on this outmoded old fellow—say, less than his own book, which is so much better?"

"Margaret—" Brother Malachi cautioned. "You go too far."

The man rolled his eyes up to heaven. Tears appeared in them. "Tell her," he said, "it is the greatest tragedy of my life that my poetry is not more widely recognized. If I were not trying to build my world renown, I would not be offering it to foreigners at a discount."

"Tell him," I said as I dabbed artistically at my eyes with my sleeve, "that my poor husband lies so ill that only poetry can console him, but that he is so weak that if he reads the most powerful poetry first, he might be carried off by emotions. However, if he begins with the feebler verse, he can build his strength to the point that he can absorb the greater work without danger. So he should sell me the Petrarch for less, so I can return for his own work later."

"Tell her I'll give it at the same price, no less." Brother Malachi, of course, had no time to tell anybody anything.

"Done," I said. And the man said to Brother Malachi, "Tell her I'm a fool, and my tiny babies will starve."

"Tell him the tiny babies of a great soul never starve."

"Hilde, Margaret." Brother Malachi turned to us, and his face was shining. "I've just thought of how we can get home."

Sim had every intention of staying at first. Even though it was disgusting how Margaret made over this worthless fellow, he had gone and given his promise to her. The man had done nothing but lie around for weeks, unutterably dull, doing little more than breathing. Some nights he would rouse with a start, open his eyes, and scream as if he saw horrible things; then he was at least interesting, if somewhat dangerous, since he might start trying to fight off the things or claw them off himself, leaving his own skin bleeding. But awake, that was the worst of all. The fellow was a veritable cloud of gloom. He didn't even take pleasure in Sim's lovely new acquisitions, which lay, with shining crowns and hollow eye-sockets, all well polished upon the long bench with which the room was furnished.

"I've seen enough of you old fellows," Gregory would mutter when he opened his eyes and spied the skulls there. "It's poor conversationalists you've been all these weeks. Must you follow me about, staring so? I'll be in your company soon enough." Trapped all afternoon with this bore, Sim thought, as he went to look out the window.

Three floors below, in the courtyard of the Tête du Maure, he spied something wonderful. There, right at the stable door, was a man putting away his horse. Behind him were two greyhounds. And at his side, on a leash connected to a collar with little bells, was an ape. A real Barbary ape with a hairy body and long leathery hands and feet.

"Where's he *from*?" Sim's voice was full of admiration as he prepared to rush down to the courtyard. Then he remembered his promise. "Look after" doesn't mean "look at," now, does it? he reasoned to himself. They'll be mad if he charges around and breaks things, thought Sim. So he changed the towel as insurance against that unlikely event, and then tied the sleeping figure's hands stoutly together with the rope from the packsaddles, knotting the loose ends to the bed frame.

"With any luck, you won't wake up," he addressed the sleeping body. "And if you do, you won't be running around and getting hurt. And I'll be back long before then, anyway. They'll never know. So we're square, aren't we? I've looked after you fine, Sir Gloomy." And he sped downstairs in great bounds like a hare.

Gregory might not have awakened if a devil had not chosen to sit on his chest. It was big and gray and shapeless, and so heavy, he couldn't breathe very well. Get off, he said in his mind, but the thing wouldn't budge, even when he tried desperately to suck in air. It smelled bad, too, like rotten grave clothes. He tried to push it off, but found his hands were paralyzed. He began to scream and writhe, but he couldn't move. He opened his eyes wide and looked all about the room for help. Not a soul there. Margaret had left him. He always knew that she would. And the devil; it was so heavy, crushing his life out.

"So be it," he whispered, and turned his face to the wall. But even as he did it he could hear the click of the latch and the sound of the door swinging open. Curiosity had always been the most powerful impulse within him. "I'll die later," he murmured to himself. "First I'll see who it is." The devil seemed rather translucent; he could see right through it now, and as he watched the figure come through the door, the gray thing seemed to fade and go, as if it had never been there at all. The air felt good. He took big breaths as he stared at the stranger who'd entered.

The man seemed a pleasant enough sort of fellow, not that much older than Gregory, with a beard trimmed short and hair he'd let go a bit too long—probably to save money, judging by his clothes. He had on a physician's gown and hat, but both were rather too well worn. Gregory could detect several very neatly made patches, almost invisible, on the most threadbare stretches of the gown. He smiled. Without a doubt, someone Margaret had found. She hadn't left him after all. She'd gone to get a doctor. She did have a gift for making friends of the shabbier sort. She'd probably traded something, or begged him to come. She didn't have the money for a successful doctor. He could sense the stranger inspecting him with his dark, whimsical eyes.

"Margaret sent you, didn't she?" Gregory asked.

"Well, she asked me to come, yes—but I really came because you called. You needed me to come." He sat down on the bed, as if he were already an old acquaintance.

"I'm sorry I can't rise to greet you. Look what they've done to me."

"They were just afraid you'd hurt yourself," said the stranger, "but I know you won't." His fingers were busy with Sim's crude knots.

"I've been crazy," said Gregory. "But I haven't hurt anyone, have I?" The stranger finished up and took up Gregory's wrist to feel his pulse.

"Not really," he said. "Not yet."

"That's a nasty mark you've got on your hand. I didn't do that, did I?"

"Well, in a manner of speaking, you did. But it's not important just now."

"I'm very sorry. You've been here before?"

"All along."

"Then I really have been off my head, haven't I—I don't remember you at all."

The physician sighed. "You're not alone in that. Most people don't."

"I'm very sorry about that. I take it business hasn't been good for you here? You should take heart. I had a time in my life like that. Popular to have around when everyone was having a good time, but no real employment. Even my father didn't like me."

"Oh, I know all about that. But you see I've done especially poorly in this city, even though I inherited my father's business."

Gregory felt much better. He sat up.

"It's all the quacks, you know. People like a big show. Doctors should make pronouncements in Latin over your urine in a glass vessel, and give vile, expensive medicines that poison your body, and do painful things like bleeding and cupping."

"Are you telling me my business?" The physician looked straight-faced, but his eyes were dancing with the joke of it.

"Oh, no, I didn't mean it that way at all. But an honest doctor like you, who hasn't got any tricks—for example, look how much better I feel already and you haven't even bled me —well, you're not going to get as many paying clients when you're in competition with—ah—showmen. You'll be reduced to treating the riffraff for free."

"Oh really, the riffraff—like you?"

"Exactly, like me." Gregory looked very sad for a minute. Then he leaned forward. "Tell me, how did she convince you to come? You know we can't pay you."

"Oh, you can repay me. Just tell Margaret that you love her. I want to see her face when you do."

"I can't do that. Besides, she knows how I feel. I don't have to tell her."

"Why can't you tell her?"

"It's wrong, all wrong, you know. I shouldn't really have married her at all. I—I had a vocation, you know." Gregory sounded embarrassed.

"Oh, really, a vocation? What sort?"

"You know, the real kind. Serving God."

"Oh, I see. Other vocations don't serve God. And if you serve God, you can't love anything He made. So to prove you still love God, you won't tell Margaret that you love her, even though you do."

"Well, put that way, it does sound rather confused and narrow-minded, I suppose."

"You said it, not I."

As Gregory thought this over, his face became worried. "But she might leave me—go away, or—or die. That's why men should put no store by earthly things, and only love something more—well, *substantial*, like God," said Gregory.

"Tell me," said the physician, "have you ever observed how Margaret loves?"

"How she—what do you mean?"

"How she throws her heart into the balance, without ever counting the cost? Do you think she is so foolish that she doesn't know that a baby's smile, or a man's life, is the most transitory thing on earth? Who do you think taught her to love like that?"

Gregory was silent a long time. The physician watched him as he thought.

"Doesn't God Himself love unreservedly? Even those who might be lost to Him?" The physician looked at Gregory's troubled face. Gregory turned his dark eyes on him and looked long and hard. "Isn't it rather presumptuous of you to think you can love perfectly, without risks?" The questioner's voice was not unkind.

"But my heart might hurt," said Gregory, in a burst of honesty.

"It's hurting now," the physician answered.

Gregory bowed his head.

After a long silence, during which Gregory seemed to be thinking very hard, he began to cough again. As he doubled over, the physician steadied him. Then the stranger got up and rummaged about the room just as if it were his own, until he found the half-empty jug of wine. A moment later, Gregory found he was holding a cup between his hands and being assisted to drink.

"Drink something, and the cough will pass." The physician was being as pushy as Margaret. Gregory finished drinking.

"I should have died there in Normandy, you know. It would have been better. You know what the poet says: 'A man is worth more dead than alive and beaten.'"

"Which poet is that?" asked the physician, putting away the cup.

"Bertran de Born—one of the few my father ever liked. Say, the cough is better. Whatever did you do with that devil? It was too big to be hiding in the room." Gregory looked around, but every corner of the room was full of sunshine.

"Oh, I got rid of it. As devils go, it wasn't all that big. What makes you think nobody wants you back? Look at the trouble Margaret went to: pregnant women should be able to sit at home, making little clothes and eating fruit. Here she walked through the mountains, mended a hole in My creation, and fetched you out, at no end of trouble."

"She's been doing your mending? So that's how she got you here. What a disgrace. Taking in mending in a strange city. Did I tell you how rich she was when I met her? Her last husband gave her an easy life, and I've given her nothing but trouble. But even so, she didn't stick at disgrace to pay a doctor's fee and fetch you here. It's a shame. A knight's wife, to take in mending. Even if it was only a purchased knighthood." Gregory shook his head. The physician took the cup back and put it away. "I can't believe I've been so hardhearted, not telling her what she wanted to hear. After all, I did marry her, so the sin's mine."

The physician sat down once more, and then took his pulse again. "Much better," he said.

"I've been ungracious. Yes, that's it," Gregory went on earnestly, as if arguing with an invisible scholastic. "After all, consider what she's done. That's really unusual, even if she weren't a woman. Now Blondel had a ballad written about him, when he rescued King Richard. Nobody said King Richard was better off dead; they were glad to have him back."

The physician looked at Gregory with a long, shrewd look. "You haven't got it all straight, but you seem to be working in the right direction now. Feeling better? Any more questions?"

"Just one, I suppose. I've been having nightmares—hallucinations about my brother Hugo. They're so real, he almost seems to be here. I hear dreadful music, and then his face appears, quoting horrible poetry. Is there any significance to that? Is it an augury?"

"Actually, he *is* here. Your father sent him after you, and he caught up with Margaret after she found you. Being what he is, he is under the delusion that it is he who rescued you, though he is as yet unsure about the means. As for the poetry, I can do nothing about it. People have free will, even to embrace bad poetry. And now, good-bye."

"Hugo? And father sent him?" Gregory's voice was full of wonder. "Don't go—please stay longer."

"I have others I have to see." The physician smiled, and stood up, leaving a rumpled place on the bedclothes.

"But you'll be back?"

"Whenever you ask."

"But is there anything else? Something I should take? Nasty medicine? Clysters? Steam baths? An unpleasant diet?"

"Anything else?" The physician turned back, his hand still resting on the door latch. "Yes, there is. I know two lonely little girls who need a flesh-and-blood father. Give your mind to it when you return. There will be days you'll yearn for bitter medicine instead. On those days, think of it as a penance, and remember I asked it of you."

As the physician stooped to step over the threshold of the low doorway, Gregory smiled and shook his head. Where on earth had Margaret managed to find a physician who was such a business failure? He hadn't even thought of a single way to inflate the charge, though he'd had plenty of opportunity. And as he opened the door, it was possible for Gregory to see that below the frayed hem of his gown, he was barefoot as a peasant on a weekday.

◦ ◦ ◦

In the courtyard of the inn I thought I caught a glimpse of someone very like Sim, slipping away in another direction. Of course, if I'd seen the ape, I would have known for sure it was Sim, since he was never a boy to miss out on any rare sight.

"Oh, that boy," said Mother Hilde, shifting the basket from one hip to another. Malachi, his purchases tucked safely in his bosom, had been following her, picking strawberries out of the basket. Now he took a last one, plucked it bare of leaves, and popped it into his mouth.

"Malachi," laughed Mother Hilde, looking at the way we had come, "if an enemy were pursuing us, he would have only to follow the trail you've laid down." We looked back and saw the telltale green leaves lying at intervals all the way down the dusty street.

"And you said *we'd* get blotches!" I exclaimed.

"Only a few," he answered guiltily, his mouth still full. "To see if they were sweet enough for you. Unripe strawberries are unhealthful. We couldn't have you ill, you know."

"Oh, Brother Malachi," I said, in a tone of exaggerated earnestness. "It's so good of you to take the risk."

"Thank you," he answered, swallowing as we mounted the outside stair. "I knew you'd appreciate my efforts."

I was first to open the door. I was afraid and hopeful all at once of what I'd see. But I wanted to be the first. Maybe he'd be sleeping easily. Maybe he'd be seeing things again, his eyes darting back and forth like a madman's. But instead, it was something wonderful. Gregory was sitting up in bed. The grayish color had left his face and the circles around his eyes were gone. He was still as thin as a ghost, but at last he looked as if he were mending. His eyes lit up when he saw me. He was speaking, too, as if his mind were working again.

"Margaret?" he said, almost tentatively. "You did come back, didn't you?"

"Gregory, what's happened? You look so much better! See

here, I've brought you a present. You must have known ahead of time. I *told* them you'd be better soon!"

"I suppose you'll be wanting blotches too," complained Brother Malachi, but his voice sounded relieved. "It's just as well I bought the whole basket."

"What's that, strawberries? It's strawberry season already?"

"It comes sooner here, Gregory. It isn't even June yet. Here, let me take the leaves off for you."

"You think I can't even take my own leaves off? Margaret, I've been eating strawberries much longer than you."

"Why, this is worth a celebration!" exclaimed Hilde. Malachi drew the bench closer so we could all sit near Gregory and around the basket.

"If you're celebrating, then you aren't mad at me?" Sim's voice sounded very small in the doorway behind us.

"Not if you go downstairs and fetch up supper from the kitchen for us," said Brother Malachi without even looking up.

"You know that woman shouts. Even though I don't know the words, it's bad. She wants the bill paid."

"Well, then, I'll go with you and swear to her she'll be paid before the week is up. I've had a brilliant idea." And with that, he took a farewell handful of strawberries and departed downstairs, sharing them with Sim.

"Hey, don't eat them all before I'm back," Sim shouted back up the stairs.

"Now let me show you what I've brought," I said, wiping my hands. "It will make you all well. It's a book."

"A book?" he said, curiosity and pleasure lighting his eyes. "What kind of book?"

"Why, it's poetry."

"Poetry?" He looked horrified. "Is it good poetry?"

"Why, the best. It's by some man called Francesco Petrarca, who used to live here. Everybody's still talking about him." Gregory looked at me intently.

"Petrarch? The greatest living poet in the world? Tell me,

Margaret, did you get the book because you knew it was good, or because it was very thin and you thought you'd get it at a bargain?"

Mother Hilde covered her face with her hands, but I could hear her splutter anyway.

"How did you know I'd got a bargain?"

"Margaret, you forget how well I know you. You've never been able to resist a bargain. Even me. Remember when we met? I was one of your bargains too."

"I bargain very well, Gregory. I get only the best. Admit it," I said, handing him the book. He wiped his hands in turn, and took the little book, turning it over and over tenderly, looking at the cover.

"Oh, Margaret, do you know what you've bought?" he asked.

"Well—not quite. I can't read a word. But Brother Malachi says you can read it. And I know books make you happier than just about anything."

"Margaret, it's love poetry. Petrarch's sonnets to his Laura." He looked down at his hands and blushed. The pink color made him look ever so much better.

"And Margaret, there's something I've been needing to tell you for a long time. I love you, Margaret. I've always loved you, but I didn't know it myself at first. Then I did, but I didn't know how to say it. I thought if I did great things, then you'd know it without me saying it. I guess I was afraid I'd seem silly if I just told you. Or that maybe you wouldn't love me back."

I couldn't help it; I burst into tears.

"Margaret, have I said it wrong? I haven't made you angry, have I?"

"Oh, no, Gregory, you just don't understand. I always knew everything would come out right if you'd say it. And now you have, and I know everything will all work out." As he put the book on his lap and leaned forward to embrace me, I couldn't help noticing that Mother Hilde had tactfully removed herself from the bench and was across the room, staring out the window. I think I cried for a long time, clutching him very tight, as he consoled me. Still, he seemed so puzzled and taken aback. At last he said, very mildly, "He certainly never said this is what would happen. I guess I'll never understand women."

"He? Who's he?" I asked, looking up at his face.

"The physician you sent, Margaret."

"I never sent a physician, Gregory. They're much too expensive. Also, they usually kill people. Why pay money to be killed?"

"He said you did some mending for him."

"Mending? I didn't do that. You must have had another of your hallucinations."

"That's odd. He seemed real enough. He was very pleasant. Not snobbish at all. But then, how could he be? He was the poorest-looking physician I've ever seen. That's why I thought you'd sent him. You know, another bargain. Why, he was even going barefoot like a peasant, to save his shoes. Who would have ever thought of such a thing? But when he made things clear to me, then I started feeling well. He couldn't stay, though. He had a lot of visits to make. He went out the door just before you came back."

"Well, we certainly didn't see anyone coming down the stairs," I said, looking at the door as if it could tell me something.

"No, not at all," said Mother Hilde at the window.

"Gregory, read us from the book, Hilde and me," I said. "We want to hear what everyone's carrying on about so much in town."

"How do you want it? Shall I turn it into English for you?"

"First in Italian, so we can hear the music of it, and then in English, so we understand. Hilde and I, we know a lot about love, and we want to hear what the poet says." Gregory read in his lovely strong voice first the rolling sounds of the Italian. Then he paused, and slowly pieced the thing into English, pausing between the harder words and phrases.

Judith Merkle Riley

> " 'Trovommi Amor del tutto disarmato
> et aperta la via per gli occhi al core,
> che di lagrime son fatti uscio e varco.' "

His voice caught, and it seemed very beautiful, the way it sounded, even before he said what it meant. "Love found me—altogether disarmed," he translated, and his face looked so grave and luminous with love that I felt my own heart totally disarmed too. "And the way open through my eyes to my heart, —um—which are now the portal and passageway of tears." Oh, yes. This was very different. This poet knew all about love.

"This Laura—did she love him back?"

"Well, only in a spiritual sense. She visited him in a dream."

"But she did give him a token, didn't she?"

"There was her glove—she dropped it and he picked it up. But then she grabbed it back."

"So—she took back her glove, got mad when he surprised her bathing, and never did more than smile at him—at least, he thinks she did, for twenty-one years? I think he should have found another lady—one who loved him back."

"Margaret, you just don't understand higher, spiritual love."

"*Higher* love? If a man followed me for twenty-one years, always trying to run into me on the street, snooping to see if he could see me bathing, trying to steal my gloves or anything else I put down just for the moment, when I hadn't given him the slightest encouragement, do you know what I'd call it? Puppy love, that's what! He's behaving like a silly boy, playing the lute all night at the window of a married woman with six children who's already gone to sleep."

"That's *ideal* love, unmarked by low carnality—and you call it puppy love?" Gregory sounded indignant.

"Well, if it's so ideal, I suppose he never loved anyone else?"

"Ah—um—he did have a mistress and children."

"And he didn't love them, and went trailing after this woman who didn't love him? That's crazy!"

380

"You're calling the greatest poet alive in the world today crazy? You have a hopelessly bourgeois mind!"

"Well, *I* say he's crazy, if he spends his life running after someone who doesn't love him back. It's not grown-up at all. What do you think, Mother Hilde?"

"I think you are both feeling ever so much better, because you are quarreling."

"Quarreling? I'm not quarreling at all. I'm right. Italians are crazy." I was very indignant. Mother Hilde should have taken my side.

"You're trying to shift ground, Margaret. That's what you always do when you're wrong." Gregory sounded pompous. "You just don't want to admit that *I'm* right." I looked at his face. Hilde was right. The argument had made his eyes bright. His color was up. His dear, familiar old arrogance was back. He was as wrong as could be. Most men are, about important things like love. I laughed at him.

"And now you laugh. Never was a woman so arrogant as to set herself up against the greatest love poet in the world. One, I might add, whose work she can't even read!"

"This Laura—I imagine she was a blonde, wasn't she?"

"Of course. That's what it says here: 'i cape' d'oro fin'—' That means hair of fine gold."

"Well then, that explains everything."

"And, pray tell, how is that? There's no logic in that statement at all! Women!"

It was a lucky thing that at that very moment we heard steps on the stairs and a pounding at the door.

"Open, open! Supper's here, and it's hot!"

"Why, Malachi," exclaimed Hilde, throwing open the door. "How did you get so much?"

There at the door stood Brother Malachi, holding with two hands a big iron stewpot by its towel-wrapped handle. A bottle of wine could be seen peeping from the bosom of his gown. Sim clutched a vast loaf of bread, a wedge of cheese, and the long green ends of two big onions that hung almost to his knees. On his head, carefully balanced, was a stack of wooden bowls.

"My silver tongue, love. And when she looked skeptical, I revealed to her the rare alchemical work I shall soon be selling at a fabulous sum."

"Malachi, you're selling your book?" asked Mother Hilde, tears running down her face as she sliced the onions.

"Oh, not at all. This one's the model. I intend to make several. With Gilbert's help, I can make even more. Everywhere, there are adepts in search of the Secret. Each would be willing to part with no small sum for this precious work. And because it contains the Secret of the Universe, none will reveal to a mortal soul that they have it. Except, of course, to Abraham or his equivalent. And when he tells them it's worthless, they'll simply believe it's in a deeper code, beyond his powers of translation. The most brilliant idea of my life—no one pursuing the honest craftsman with pitchforks and torches, demanding his skin. No. They will all hide their shame, as I have hidden mine. And we shall go home in style, selling a book in each city at which we stop. And now, supper. We must build Gilbert's strength so we can begin our great work."

As supper vanished, Gregory looked up from eating, and said, "Theophilus, you old rascal, which part of you is honest?"

"All parts, all parts, Gilbert, you sour and doubting young man. I sell happiness and hope—and at much lower prices than certain large religious institutions I could name. It's because I have less overhead. Always travel light, I say—'Light feet and light hands,' that's my motto."

"Oh, Malachi, you have such a generous spirit!" exclaimed Mother Hilde.

"If there were more generous spirits here, they'd have left me better than half a dozen strawberries, and those the greenest of the lot," grumped Sim.

"Now, Sim," Brother Malachi intoned, "there is the affair of the Barbary ape, for which we have not yet taken you to task. Best to leave well enough alone."

"I'm not sharing my skulls, then. And don't you think you're selling them for relics, either."

"Relics? My dear child. A dangerous and unsavory business. I have found a higher calling. —Gilbert, as I recall, you always were good at drawing. I will need allegorical pictures for this effort. Nicely colored ones. I still remember the excellent rendering you did of the rector long ago—the one depicting him with an ass's head, as I recall."

"You have colors?" Gregory said cheerfully.

"Just three, plus black and white. It's all I could afford. No gold leaf. You can mix them, can't you? I need quality work."

"Do I get to make up the allegories myself?"

"Now, now—don't get fancy on me. Just follow the models in the book here."

"Show me."

Until the light failed, Gregory and Brother Malachi conferred happily on the new merchandise.

"That's a lot of copying."

"Well, you don't have to be precise."

"It would be easier if you put some Latin in somewhere. How about a curse?"

"A curse? A master stroke, Gilbert. 'Curses on anyone who reveals the secret of this work.' Marvelous. Adds tone."

"You could split up the pages, too—cryptic groups. Seven times three, things like that. And put in more diagrams between. That takes up space."

"Oh, excellent. I'll do the diagrams. I'm well acquainted with the sort needed."

"This one's nice. The Green Lion. If I get home in one piece, I'll add it to my coat of arms."

"Gilbert, restrain yourself. Someone might prosecute you. Stick to red lions and assorted implements of death. Alchemy goes in and out of fashion with the *noblesse*."

"Again, Malachi, you're cautioning me. Must you always be such a fussy old nursemaid?"

"Only when you're a troublesome young jackanapes."

"What are you doing, Mother Hilde?" I asked as Mother Hilde knelt at the threshold with a bit of rag.

"Malachi's slopped something, coming in, and I'm going to wipe it up before it hardens. I don't want foreigners to say that we are dirty—oh!"

She sat back on her heels for a moment, looking at the spot. My eyes followed her gaze. No one else but us noticed. It wasn't spilled gravy that stained the threshold. It was a bloody mark left by a bare foot. As I watched, Mother Hilde wiped it up carefully, folded the still damp rag, and put it in her pilgrim's wallet.

CHAPTER
13

"This set's dry, Gilbert—or should I call you Gregory, as Margaret does?" Mother Hilde removed several colorful manuscript pages from the windowsill, where they had been weighted down with old wine bottles to dry in the sun. Below the windowsill, on a rope stretched from the bedpost inside to the great timber supporting the stair outside, the travelers' laundry flapped like a string of pennants. The sun and the blue sky, almost entirely too gaudy for good taste, as they so often are in the south, had brightened the cramped little room and chased away the stale scent of illness.

"Oh, good, then stack them away with the others," replied Gregory, who was hard at work, bent over a colorful depiction of a woman in a field of snakes. "I've never been able to break Margaret of the habit—hmm, that has the makings of a pun there, if I redo it—having left the habit, I can't break her of it. No, better yet, I've left off the habit, but she hasn't. See? My wits are mending, albeit slowly. But you may call me what you wish, Mother Hilde."

"Then I'll call you Gilbert, as Malachi does. He says that's what he knew you as back when you were studying in Paris."

"Now, that's not entirely fair, I'd say, since I've been very careful not to slip and call him Theophilus." Gregory's voice took on an exaggerated tone of injury. Then he turned to where Margaret labored with her pen, copying the rows of squiggles from a page of Malachi's book. "Margaret, have you got the next set of pages ready? This picture's almost done."

Margaret picked up the page, and held it this way and that to the light, to admire the effect. It looked altogether mystical, and seemed most admirably like the original, give or take a few little things.

"Here they are," she announced cheerfully. She was filled with the contentment that accompanies advancing pregnancy. The baby had ceased to roll—there was too little room for that anymore. But she could watch her immense stomach ripple up and down under her gown, as the baby wriggled in pleasure when she told it in her mind, baby, we're going home. And in style, too, thanks to Brother Malachi's clever mind. "Look at this. Don't they look nice? How many books' worth do we have now?"

"Six," said Mother Hilde, counting the pages as a mother hen would gloat over the eggs in her nest. "We're going for seven. That's a lucky number." She peeked out the window again. "Why, not only is the laundry dry, but there's Malachi and Sim coming into the courtyard below, and they look quite pleased with themselves. My, isn't it wonderful how quickly the hot sun dries linen in this blessed climate? How will I ever manage in the damp and cold again?"

"Best of news!" Brother Malachi burst through the door into the busy book manufactory. "I've a client lined up already. I was masterful. I shed a tear, which I wiped away secretly. 'My chief treasure,' I said. 'I wouldn't part with it, but for this terrible necessity.' Oh, I was good. Sim played my son. The boy has talent. Yes, talent! Oh, if I'd only had the good start that he's been given, who knows how great I could have become? So, we must have at least one of them ready by tonight." He·drifted to the window and inspected the pages weighted down on the sill. "Lovely," he said, nodding his head approvingly. "If I bind it tonight—I will need help on the stitchery, ladies—then we can toast it by the fire tomorrow morning. Gilbert—was it you that did bookbinding, or Aimery?"

Gregory blew on a damp spot on his drawing, where the red ink on a snake's head had not yet dried. He answered without looking up.

"Aimery—you have us mixed up because he wrote drinking songs too."

"Then I suppose I'll have to show you how—we have a vast amount of work to do to get them ready in time. We leave day after tomorrow. That's the other part of my good news. A convoy of armed merchants is leaving up the Rhône for Lyons. They've hired guards, and merged forces with a papal ambassador's party going to Paris. Another one of those entreaties to the French and English kings to make peace. We'll be as safe as in church traveling in their company. We can toast the rest of the books en route."

"But Malachi, dear, why toast them? You'll spoil the pretty pictures. Everything will turn all brown."

"Exactly, my dear treasure. You foresee my purpose. Who buys a new alchemical book? No one. By tomorrow, one of them at least will be ancient. Besides, the heat will drive off the smell of the new glue." Brother Malachi was rubbing his hands in anticipation.

"Yes, yes. That's it. The next big sale we'll make is in Lyons. There used to be hunters of the Green Lion in plenty there. Surely even war has not diminished their numbers excessively." He sat down on the bed, arranging dried pages around him, and began to hum.

But Margaret, who entertained a sensible skepticism about all of Brother Malachi's schemes, broke off her busy scribbling. "But Malachi," she asked, "what about Hugo and the last of the Brokesford men? He's been as silly as a goose since he came out of that last audience, and I think he's run through every penny he brought, celebrating his shining new self, including the ransom money."

"Haven't I told you that great minds think of everything? I hired him out to the merchants, and then told him about it. He was, at the time, as they say, *in flagrante delicto*, but he seemed to take the news well enough. So cease worrying, Margaret. My vast and capacious mind has left no detail unhandled." He went on arranging pages, and added words to his hum. It was "Angelus ad Virginem."

Margaret went back to her writing, her brow wrinkled, only to look up with surprise when another voice joined Malachi's. It was a sound she'd never heard before. Gregory's rolling baritone had added the bass line, and he was singing the words of the angel in Latin. In all the time she'd known him, she'd never suspected he could sing. Though, of course, it made sense, clerics mostly do. She didn't understand the words, but naturally she knew the song well, for it was a great favorite in English, too, being all about the Angel Gabriel.

"No fair, no fair, Gilbert. Now I shall have to do the treble," and Brother Malachi switched to a high falsetto to sing the Virgin's response.

Margaret couldn't help it: at the chorus, she added the descant, her bright English sounding above the sonorous Latin. After all, it wasn't at all proper to let men go on thinking that they could sing higher than a woman. As the sweet harmony floated out the window into the bright foreign sky, a set of quarreling voices in the courtyard stopped abruptly, as if someone had turned to listen.

"Why, Margaret, I didn't know you could sing so well." Gregory looked up at Margaret with pleased surprise.

"Aha!" broke in Brother Malachi. "That proves it. If you had indeed copied Margaret's memoirs from dictation—which, by the way, is the most pitifully feeble story I've ever heard you come up with, Gilbert—then you would have known she can sing, and very well, too. *Quod erat demonstrandum*—you were up to no good when you used to hang around Margaret's house."

"Malachi, you're wrong. I was as pure as the driven snow. Just because I *copied* didn't mean I *listened*."

"Now that, I admit, sounds more like you, Gilbert—but it's still weak, weak indeed."

"Malachi," Margaret broke in, "you may as well put a stop to malicious speculation. I'll show you my book when we get home. I even wrote the last chapter all by myself, after Gregory gave me reading and writing lessons."

"You disappoint me, Margaret. I'd hoped for a more lurid story. But I must admit, you're handy with a pen now, and you were totally unlettered when I first knew you. Teaching women, Gilbert. Look where it's brought you."

"Yes—to forging alchemical works in the garret of a foreign whorehouse. It's exactly the sort of end my father always predicted for me," said Gregory, with some acid in his voice, which led Brother Malachi to change the subject.

The morning of our departure dawned clear and bright. It was barely past mid-April, but there was already a promise of summer heat in the morning air, and I began to hope that the way would be shady. Great barges were bobbing at the river's edge, being laden with goods. The teams of oxen that would pull against the river's powerful current were already hitched, the boys who were to drive them lounging about on the bank with their long whips in their hands. Hugo had never looked more resplendent, with Robert mounted at his side, and both in full harness. Hugo's armor was shining white, the product of Robert's last-minute nocturnal labors, and the Brokesford pennant never fluttered more gaily. The waiting mercenaries cheered a welcome, while the papal knights and their retainers made a grave formal salutation. I've never felt more out of place than in this company, so unwieldy that I could barely sit a horse, and Hilde and I the only women in the whole great party. Curiosity seekers, relatives, and ragamuffins had crowded around to watch the immense procession depart.

Then there was a murmur in the crowd of watchers as a mule litter with a cardinal's crest, its curtains closed, approached the quay. Six footmen in livery followed it, and two boys ran before, to clear the way. The litter drew alongside Hilde and me and halted, and I could feel stares as the curtain was parted by the heavily beringed hand of a beautiful woman.

"Lady Margaret," the familiar voice with the coarse accent sounded in English, "I've come to say good-bye." I could see Cis wedged in the uncomfortable darkened confines of the litter, the folds of her rich gown heaped about her. She was in bright violet silk today. Silk and cloth of gold. She leaned her head forward to speak, and the gawkers strained for a sight of the rich headdress set with pearls and cunningly arranged clasps that daringly revealed the curling golden hair at her brow, and the little wisps of hair that escaped from the shining coils of her braids. On her lap was tucked a tiny white dog with a gilded leather collar.

"Na Margaret," I said (for *Na* is what they call ladies in that country, and *En* means lord), "wear my name well, and God bless you."

"You were always kind, lady. Not like the others. But I'm saying good-bye to them all, even Sir Hugo, if he's civil. *He* never even thanked me for the audience I got him—just grumbled that it wasn't personal, and he should have known I would make him rub shoulders with a lot of garlicky nobodies. But I got the message of thanks you sent by that little boy, so I came. I—I doubt if I'll ever hear English spoken again. But tell my friends, will you, that I live like a queen. No—better than a queen. No queen in England ever dreamed of the wealth that I've seen here. Tell them I'm a lady, and I've got chests, and servants, and a lapdog."

"You had better be careful." How strange her face looked now, set in these sumptuous surroundings. "You've risen fast on men's favors, and I've heard the women here are poisoners. You should keep cats, like that dark lady."

"Cats?" She laughed, and the sound drew more stares from the uncomprehending crowd. "Those are for witches. I've got my little dogs. This is the third, already. We may not be as sly as these foreigners, lady, but we English village girls are shrewd —and fast learners."

"We? You knew then?"

"Always. I could tell by the slips you used to make that you didn't start your life where you are now. That, and by your heart. You were my inspiration. I'm not suffering for nothing, I used to say to myself. I'm going to *get* something for all of this. But you have the better man. Here," she said, fumbling among her clothes. "It's a gift. For luck on your trip. I had it blessed by the Pope, and my cardinal too, for good measure." She extended a little silver-gilt medallion on a chain, and watched my face as I thanked her. Already, I thought, she's getting new habits from playing this dangerous game among strangers. And she and I both knew that she was saying good-bye to more than us. Someday, maybe soon, she'd no longer be able to afford the luxury of a straight heart. "I knew you wouldn't scorn it," she said as I took it in my hand. "Think of me, sometimes." And she gave the signal to her men to move on, closing the curtains once more. I saw the litter pause again before Hugo's mount. The curtains opened briefly, and she nodded like a *grande dame,* leaving Hugo crimson and spluttering as she departed.

"Now, who would have ever thought it?" Gregory followed her progress with his eyes while he pushed his nag closer to me. He was mounted on one litter horse, and leading the other. They were a sight, the three of them, for they were all equally bony. And the Comte de St. Médard's vast velvet doublet and woolen hose swam on him. If it hadn't been for the lordly way he sat on the nag, you'd have thought he was a jongleur dressed in his master's castoffs.

"She's given us a present. Put it on for me, will you? I've

already got a talisman, and I feel like a fool in too many necklaces."

"Hmm. The Holy Virgin. Considering the source, it must mean something, but I'm not quite sure what," he said, arching a dark eyebrow. "Still, I'm not one to scorn a blessing. Heaven knows, I've been offered few enough." He hung the little medallion about his neck.

We made slow progress that day, limited as we were by the speed of the barges. The party spread out before and after the ox teams on the bank, armed guards before, after, and flanking the high dignitaries. As the sun beat down on us, even Hilde's and my big straw hats were little protection. I could see Gregory looking at me with new concern.

"The sweat's running in rivers down your face, Margaret, and you're all red. You should be riding in the barge, and not on horseback like this."

"It doesn't mean a thing, Gregory—women always feel the heat more when they're with child. But—you don't see any freckles, do you?" He inspected carefully.

"Just a few. They've come out on your nose."

"Oh, blessed Mary, not many, are they?"

"Why, thousands and thousands, Margaret. But don't worry, they're very nice ones."

"I must say, that's mean. I'm going to ask Hilde how many freckles I've got. It shows you just can't trust men about anything really important."

"Oh, yes, you can, and just to show you I mean it, I'm going to speak to Messer Pietro and get you off that horse and onto the lead barge at the next stop."

"Don't you dare bother with that. I'm doing very well just as I am. Besides, I told you I get seasick easily. The rolling might affect me." The truth was, he still looked pallid and frail to me, and I had no intention of leaving his side. Like someone who's found a valuable ring that she's lost, I didn't want him out of my sight again. But I guess my excuse sounded a little farfetched. First he looked at the barges, being hauled along so steadily on the rushing waters of the Rhône. Then he inspected my face intently, a long, amused look, and a strange little smile flitted across his face. Oh, caught again, I thought.

"I need to see your face," I confessed, looking again at his profile, as if I could fix it in my mind forever that way. "I've missed it too long."

"Have I told you today that you're a silly woman, but very precious?" he asked with a smile.

"Not today. Yesterday. And, I hope, tomorrow."

But several days on horseback, even at this slow pace, took their toll on him. I could see the gray lines of fatigue in Gregory's face, so I hid from him the news that the baby, now tightly folded in my immense stomach, was moving in that strange, impatient way that signaled that it wished to be born. Brother Malachi could see our strain, and tried to lighten our trip by telling stories of other trips he'd taken, mostly either in search of the Secret, or to evade people who wanted the Secret from him. It was all very entrancing, for he knew about the long apples of Egypt that when cut have the sign of the cross in them, and of the deadly serpent called the crocodile, which can swallow a man in one gulp, and also of the geese that grow on trees in the countries of the far north, and so are fitting food for Lent.

"Isn't there anyplace you've never been, Malachi?" I asked.

"Why, Tartary and the Indies—lots of places. Africa—I'd like to see that. And Cathay, too, though some say it's a myth. There's wisdom in those places. Things that might lead me to the Secret."

Mother Hilde nodded happily from the pillion seat behind him.

"If you go to those places, Malachi, I'll go too. For I've found travel agrees with me. Have you seen all of my seeds, Margaret? I've some real curiosities. Some of them may even grow in England." At every stop, until the winter winds had knocked the last rattling, dry plants bare of seeds, Mother Hilde had searched for seeds. You could see her beam as she found a

393

plant she liked the look of, and tapped the seeds off into a little bit of colored rag. And her memory was so good that she'd describe the look of each of the plants by looking at the seeds alone, though sometimes if they resembled each other too much, she'd make a little stitch or two—parallel or crossed—to mark off the packet as different. Then she rolled up all her little bundles at the end of the day in a big napkin, which she sometimes opened on gloomy days to count over her treasures like a miser. And once the season of green had come upon us, she had with equal fervor made forays to the local wisewomen, where, gesticulating and miming, she contrived to work trades for even more seeds with which to extend her collection.

"The world is so full of things to learn about," she'd say dreamily. "It wouldn't be so bad if Malachi did find the Secret. If we lived longer, we could go to all those places, and just *think* of the seeds I'd have then! But it's a great pity it's too cold to grow oranges at home. Now, if you could think of a way to keep them warm in winter, it would be very fine to have an orange tree in the back of our house . . ." And she'd be off, as full of fancies as a child. It's odd, how close wisdom and childhood are together, and Mother Hilde, who is the wisest woman I've ever known, is a good example.

"In a few days, we'll be at Vienne. Then to Lyons, it's hardly anything. These merchant folk will unload their goods and return downriver. We'll sell another book—and what a stroke of fortune it was to sell two already!—then hey, ho, in style to Paris in the company of the papal grandees! Good fortune is smiling on us, my dears! Gilbert, you've not congratulated me even once on my clever planning. You should be thanking God for the powerful mind that's made our return so comfortable. Ah, my! It's a lovely day! I feel all brain—just pure intelligence, soaring into the ether! Could it be you're not anxious to see Paris again? Never fear, you've changed entirely since then. They'll never recognize you, I guarantee it entirely. Just keep your hood up and don't trim your beard. Yes, yes. You look entirely different. Don't look to tomorrow for trouble, I always say, the troubles of today are usually enough."

This thing about the troubles of today being sufficient—I don't like it at all. I'd prefer no troubles today at all, but that's not how it works most of the time. We were still far from anyplace at all when I felt something unmistakable. "Gregory, help me," I hissed between my teeth, for the waves of pain could not be taken for anything else. "The baby's coming."

"It can't be," he said. "We aren't home yet."

"For God's sake, whoever gave you the idea it wouldn't come until we're home? It's coming now."

"Are you sure?"

"Gregory, I've had two already. I'm sure, I'm sure as can be. Now please tell Malachi and Hilde," and he turned and rode ahead to where Malachi was telling Hilde all about Hippocrates' daughter, who was changed into the form of a hideous dragon by enchantment, and lives on the isle of Langos near Greece, waiting for a knight brave enough to kiss her and change her back again. I was now bent over in the saddle, my hands clasping the sides of my immense belly as if that would somehow slow it all down. The reins slid onto the horse's neck, and the little mare, sensing that something had gone wrong, picked up her head and began to amble away. The jarring made it worse. I could sense Gregory as he rode in close and grabbed the mare's reins.

"Hide me, oh, please. Don't make me have it in front of all these people," I wept. Wordlessly, he signaled, and Malachi and Hilde followed. Behind, Hugo broke from the line of march behind us and cantered forward.

"She's having the baby," Gregory told him.

"Oh, can't do that. Very risky to leave the line of march just now. Say, Margaret, can't you just tell it to wait until later?"

"It's not waiting," I said, my face all red and the tears running from my eyes.

"Well, brother, I never thought I'd do a thing this stupid for you," said Hugo as he rode ahead to the captain of the mercenaries, and then signaled his men to follow us off the road. There, in a copse of trees that hid the blackened ruins of what had once been a little village, they spread out on guard as Gregory pulled me, gasping, from my little mare. I caught a glimpse of his horrified face as I bent to my work. Somebody had spread his cloak underneath me.

"Don't look, don't look," I panted. "It's not decent."

"It's not a question of decency at this point, Margaret," said Hilde. "The head's already showing. Now don't make a peep. Heaven only knows who might hear it here. Bite on this if you feel like screaming." It was a belt, the one Gregory had been wearing. Thank the Holy Virgin for Mother Hilde! If one must go traveling while pregnant, it is always a good thing if you can have the best midwife in London with you. It was as I felt her hands, so steady and sure, that I knew all at once she had come along for more than Malachi's sake. The most generous friend in the world had followed me on a crackpot scheme, because she knew all along I couldn't manage.

"Keep pushing, Margaret. We've almost got the head. Gilbert! Could you kindly avert your eyes? This is women's business. It's not for husbands to see. If you are curious, go look in a book." The effort was big, bigger than I remembered somehow, for God always hides the difficulties from our memory each time, so we won't be afraid of the next. And to keep silence the while—it was agonizing. It was then I felt a hand holding mine. His hand. It was wrong, I know, and not proper at all. How many times had Hilde and I barred husbands from the labor room? Everyone knows if a husband sees his wife at this time, he won't love her anymore.

"That's it—if you must be here, sit beside her so you're facing the other way. It's not proper to be watching every move I make," Mother Hilde scolded. He rearranged himself, never letting go of my hand. I could see his face against the sky, all shadowy with worry, his dark hair blowing against the aureole of the sun. He was watching my own face intently. Then he leaned over me and took my other hand too. I grabbed them both and heaved.

"We've got it," Mother Hilde said. "Keep at it." Gregory's face looked so shocked, I was about to say something altogether snippy about the male half of the human race, until I realized suddenly what was wrong. He was afraid I'd die.

"Hold my hand tighter, Gregory. —This is how it always is. —Don't worry. —I'm strong. —I'll be fine—" I found myself reassuring him in between gasps and groans. He never said a word, but held on with all the strength that was in him, as if he could give it to me. And it did strengthen me. I could feel it renewing me with each great labor pain.

"I'm sorry," I whispered, the sweat matting my hair to my face, all decency long forgotten. "Now you won't think I'm pretty anymore."

He found his voice. "I'll always love you, Margaret. Always. No matter what. And—and you're still pretty." Gallant liar, I thought.

"Why, goodness, Margaret. Who'd have thought it? You've got a boy this time. Sir Gilbert, it's a son and heir. The very first try too. You're a lucky man." Hilde held the baby up by the heels until its mewling told her it was breathing well. Gregory turned his head so he could see it. I've never seen him look more horrified.

"That—?" he stammered. "Is it *supposed* to look that way? It's not abnormal, is it?"

"Of course not. You looked exactly the same when you were born." Mother Hilde was wiping the baby off the best she could with a cloth dampened from her water flask. She delivered the afterbirth and cut the cord. Gregory looked paralyzed.

"Now, just look at *that*, will you, Margaret?" said Mother Hilde as she held the naked baby out to me. Its skinny red arms and legs wheeled uselessly. I saw right away what she meant. Dried off, the fuzzy hair looked all brownish, and stood up straight out every whichaway, like the homely fluff on a baby swan. The baby had the most shocked expression on its face. Its mouth worked up and down, and its eyes were wide open, as if with amazement. Without a doubt, it was the oddest, funniest-looking face I'd ever seen on a baby. I loved it immensely.

"You shouldn't act so surprised. You're the one who had the idea of being born," I scolded it. Then Mother Hilde held it up face-to-face with Gregory, so he could see it better. I could see its eyes as it caught sight of Gregory's face. I know some people think new babies are blind, like kittens, but if they are, then why don't their eyes stick shut, like kittens'? I think they see, because I watch them see, and because even little babies aren't stupid. The two of them stared at each other, father and son, their faces mirror images of utter astonishment. Both sets of eyes widened, both jaws dropped in exactly the same way. I've never seen anything so droll in my life. I couldn't help it. No matter how much it hurt, I had to laugh. I tried to stop, and made a weak coughing sound that shook the poor, loose muscles of my belly like the waves in the ocean.

"You're *laughing*?" Gregory couldn't believe it. "At your own son?" There was something infinitely touching in the way that he rushed to defend the tiny creature against the imagined slight.

"I've never seen such a funny-looking baby in my life. Give him to me, Mother Hilde, so I can feed him before he starts peeping." And when the baby started to suck, making such vast gulping and smacking sounds that I had to laugh again, Gregory, taken aback, stared and said, "It's *greedy*."

"You should know," I said drowsily, for I was very tired now. "You're something of a trencherman yourself."

"Not like *that*," he said, as the baby fell asleep after an immense belch.

"Margaret, he needs to be baptized," Mother Hilde prompted.

"I'll do that," Gregory answered, looking suddenly pleased with himself. "I've just thought of a good name."

"You know the form for emergency baptism?" Hilde was

always careful. It won't do to make a mistake at a time like this with something as important as somebody's soul.

"Of course. I used to be something of a specialist, as you may recall," said Gregory. And before I'd really had time to think about it, he'd collected his brother and Malachi to be witnesses, and splashed water on the sleeping infant's head from the leather water bag at his saddle.

"Peregrinus, I baptize thee in the name of the Father, and of the Son, and of the Holy Ghost. Amen."

My eyes opened wide with shock, but they were already reciting the Paternoster. It was already done.

"What have you named my baby?" I said, with rising suspicion.

"A perfect name, considering the circumstances. Peregrine." Gregory looked benignant, as if he'd done the baby a great favor.

"Peregrine? What saint is that?" I was appalled. At the very least, he could have asked me first.

"It means pilgrim—traveler—or wanderer in Latin," said Brother Malachi, as if he considered the name perfect himself.

"Peregrine? You named my beautiful baby *Peregrine*? Instead of for an evangelist or a saint, or even just a holy martyr?"

"Why, Margaret, it's just perfect." Gregory beamed. "You have to admit not many babies have done so much traveling before they were born—or need to do so much before they get home."

"It's not bad," opined Hugo. "Not bad at all, except it might have been better to name him for a hero—say, Oliver or Floris, or maybe Gawain."

"Oh, worse and worse. Your whole family is the same. A saint's name is best." A conspiracy, that's what it was. A conspiracy of men.

"Well, best or worst, we'd better get out of here. We have some catching up to do."

"Catching up? Hugo? Do you honestly think I can ride in

this state? It's like sitting on a boil. Besides, I'm monstrously tired."

"Sir Hugo, you can't move a woman in this condition. She'll bleed too heavily."

"We'll all bleed too heavily if we don't catch up. But I'll leave her until tomorrow. We'll post a watch and camp here without a fire. But tomorrow she's sitting a horse, whatever condition she's in." I hardly cared. Tomorrow was a long way away. I fell asleep with the baby in my arms, and never even knew who lifted me onto a bed of boughs in the night. Sometime in the dark, I woke to hear the baby stirring, and fed him again as I looked at the stars. I thought I heard something in the distance. A din. Something bad. But it could have been just imagining.

In the morning, we were ready to move by dawn. A debris-filled well had yielded enough water for washing up most of the mess of the night before, and I saw that a wet cloak hung behind Gregory's saddle as he lifted me onto the little mare and handed up Peregrine. I was too exhausted and sore even to care about the shameful state of my dress, as we rode silently to rejoin the road at the riverbank. But there, at the river's edge, a horrible sight met our eyes. The blazing ruin of one of the barges that had gone ahead of us was drifting downriver with the current. Caught in the eddies, it hung for a brief moment on an outcropping of rock and then slid beyond view. But in that moment, we had all seen more than anyone ought to see. Hacked-up bits of stripped bodies, arranged in obscene ways I won't even bother to tell you about, could be glimpsed in the charred wreckage. And on the prow of the barge, a severed head had been placed as a kind of hideous travesty of a figure-head. The features were unrecognizable. It was decorated with a sort of imitation of a bishop's mitre fashioned of parchment. Splashed with water, it had somehow escaped catching fire, but the ink had run in great black trickles down the man's face. A seal dangled like a blood clot against the temple of the ghastly head. The papal ambassador. If not for Peregrine, it would have been us drifting unburied in the rushing green waters.

"Ordinarily, I'd think it was English forces," Gregory remarked calmly to his brother.

"You're right. This one, we didn't do. Our people would never waste a barge like that. It's not Hawkwood or the Gascons: they wouldn't have set up the hat."

"And none of them would have sacrificed the ransom of a man as high ranking as a papal ambassador."

"They're probably still drunk, celebrating upstream," said Hugo, as unperturbed as if he were discussing fishing.

And that is how we learned that the Archpriest, with an army of three thousand mercenary adventurers, had begun his march down the Rhône valley toward the richest prize in Christendom: the papal city of Avignon.

I will not write of the days that followed, for they are all mixed up in my mind as if they were one day or a hundred—I really can't remember, though afterward they told me it was seven days' march. We left the banks of the river and wandered far into the shattered countryside, evading the forces of the dreadful army of brigands. We did not see them, except once we spied a column of smoke in the distance. But we saw their handiwork everywhere: burned orchards slashed to the ground, or the blasted ruins of convents, villages, and churches. In this dead land, there was nothing, nothing at all. When one of the horses grew lame, the men were so hungry that after they had cut its throat they stripped the flesh from it and ate it raw, for fear of making a fire. When my arms grew weak, I strapped the baby to me. And when I could no longer sit, they tied me in the saddle. But always beside me rode Gregory, silent and straight, leading the mare. It was now that I borrowed the will from him to go on; my husband, my strength and my shield.

At night he slept beside us, the little pilgrim and I, with his sword drawn. We learned to talk without words, then, for what I thought, he thought, and what he thought, I thought, and we could act together without a single sound passing between us. One night I woke at the sound of a brief, strangled cry to find myself alone in our blankets. Gregory had surprised a straggler from the Archpriest's army, and, circling around behind him as he crept toward our camp, lopped off his head before his brother had even drawn his sword. The loot the man was laden with was enough to buy a knight's freedom, but the man had babies' hands on a string, which they buried quickly in hopes of keeping it from me. But, of course, nothing went on that I didn't know about sooner or later, for unseen to them, the Weeping Lady was still with us, much depleted, drifting formlessly nearby. Every so often I'd hear her whispering in the darkness, offering her opinions and commenting on what she'd seen. But she wasn't much use; she had even less idea of where we were than anyone else.

After that, they decided that we must leave all sight of the river, and go into the mountains, following the sun and stars north. Malachi made it sound easy, since he said he'd followed the route before, and it was a positive shortcut to Paris, and Hugo laughed and slapped him on the back, which was the last laughing anyone did for quite a while. But when we found inhabited villages, the sullen folk in them would give no directions worth having, and I began to fear we were hopelessly lost. But Malachi said he knew exactly where he was, and acted so confident that we forded rivers and clambered through rocky passes at his direction without ever a question being asked. But through all these trials, by day and by night, the Holy Virgin sustained me so that my milk did not dry up, and the little wanderer continued to live.

When at length we emerged from the mountains and saw a rich, cultivated valley spread before us, we knew we were beyond the path of the madman. At a bend of the green, rushing river that wound through the valley we could see the walls and towers of a prosperous city. No—it was not a city. As we followed the sound of bells rolling across the fields, we spied above the walls the spires and domes of an immense monastery, looking as welcome as the Holy City itself. We rode through the little village and halted at the great gate, all filthy and tattered as we were, and Hugo, in battered and blackened armor, leaned from the saddle to bang on the grille and announce our presence. The grille opened, and part of a suspicious-looking face peered out.

"Who are you?" a voice asked in French. It was heavily accented, but the *langue d'oïl*. Surely, I thought, we must have come a long way, all the way to the north again.

"We are from the party of the papal ambassador that was destroyed on the way to Paris by the Archpriest. In the name of God, we beg your mercy." From behind the gate, voices conferred in Latin. I thought I could hear the words *Norman— English* or something very like them, before the first voice called through the grille.

"You must vow to disarm before you enter our holy precincts." Once agreed, we entered and dismounted in the outer courtyard, in the shadow of the immense wall, where Gregory pulled me and the baby from the blood-drenched saddle before surrendering his weapon with the others. Even the eating knives were taken. Monks could afford to take no chances in these perilous times, even with their hospitality. As the horses were taken to the stables, lay Brothers showed us to a low stone house huddled just within the outer walls in the shadow of the gatehouse. It had a decidedly humble look, this pilgrims' guesthouse, with its thatched roof and narrow, unshuttered windows. So did the people lounging about it in the sunny dust at the doorway: an old soldier with a leg gone, gossiping with a pair of ancient fellows whose only pilgrimage was probably from free lodging to free lodging.

"I say, what's this? Beggars' quarters? See here, my men, you have mistaken my quality. Where is your house for noble guests?" Hugo's voice had risen with indignation. When he turned to spy a velvet-clad lord with long-toed shoes delicately picking his way from the stables to an elegant-looking guesthouse near the church, you could see the veins in his neck throbbing.

The Brothers escorting us looked at the guesthouse for the

nobility. Then they looked up and down at Hugo. Their noses wrinkled the way Frenchmen's do when the sauce is too salty or the wine is full of cork bits. "Your quality?" said one of them, in a tone too close to sarcasm to mistake. Unshaven and grimy in the padded, rust-stained tunic that had underlain his breast-plate, Hugo looked like nothing better than a cobbler's son turned mercenary. He'd lost weight, too, and the tunic fitted him as if he had taken it off a corpse. The rest of us were, if anything, worse.

"Hugo, don't rile them," Gregory hissed between his teeth, but Hugo was beyond caution.

"My quality, you base-blooded French psalm-singer! You insult a lord, the heir of Brokesford!" His face turned red and swelled up, and he grabbed for the place his sword hilt should have been. Gregory and Malachi grabbed his arms to restrain him, but he puffed up like a wrathful gander, and their pleas to calm himself only made him louder.

As the commotion increased a number of other Brothers arrived on the scene to confer. Suddenly, at a gesture from one of them who looked to be important, the two lay Brothers with the group broke away to show us to our quarters. The building was divided by an interior wall into two large bare-looking halls, each with a separate door. Evidently one hall was for women, the other for men. As Hilde and I stood in the low stone doorway, surveying the plain, whitewashed walls of the hall, furnished only with a bench, a row of straw beds, and an old blind woman humming and rocking like a bundle in the corner, we could hear Hugo still shouting on the other side of the building.

"You thickheaded numskulls, you have no idea how a man of great blood should be treated! You deserve nothing better than to have this whole place burned down around you! I deserve a special place, I tell you, and not this hovel!"

"A special place?" I heard them answer as the shouting subsided. "Yes, my lord, you are right. We've made a mistake.

You'll have a special place. Let us escort you there, most noble guests."

But I was so tired that even a straw bed in a bare hall looked good. It was not until we awoke hours later that we found that the door had been sealed from the outside.

"Brother, I am sorry," said Gregory. The chains rattled as he stretched out his long legs on the stone floor of the Abbot's prison. A thread of light found its way through the narrow slit above them and made a long streak of light on the heavy studded door. Gregory was feeling very gloomy. He'd been listening to the Latin outside the door, and it did not bode well. What he'd overheard was a discussion of how the Abbot couldn't decide whether to flay them alive or merely behead them before he hung them from the walls as a warning to other mercenaries. So this was where it all ended. It seemed altogether depressing. Still, Hugo was happy. So why spoil his last minutes on earth by telling him? He owed him that much, at least.

"Nonsense, nonsense," Hugo said cheerfully. "It's all a mistake. It'll soon be settled. I'll just talk to the Abbot here and get it cleared up. That's all. I probably set them off by insulting their rather shabby hospitality. You know these foreign monks. Touchy, all of them. It will be set right in a trice, as soon as I apologize. We deserved better places, and we'll get them as soon as he hears. After all, we were traveling under a papal safe-conduct. He owes us consideration."

"Hugo, the papal safe-conduct is floating downstream on the ambassador's head. You can't prove a thing; we can't even prove we're not mercenaries. There's not a chance, without the paper."

"Gloom and doom, Gilbert. You're still sick, that's what. I've got better ways to occupy my time. I think I'll make a prison song. They're all the rage now; it may very well make my reputation. Let's see—a noble soul's too great for walls of stone—that's me, of course. And then there should be birds flying free.

That's the symbolism. I took three lessons on symbolism, did I tell you? The trick is to get the symbols to rhyme. I should have stayed for a few more lessons, I think. Did I tell you he'd sat at the feet of Petrarch?"

"Several times, Hugo." Grief was giving way to profound irritation. Hugo, eternally Hugo, to the end.

"Let's see—tumpty, tumpty—ta—hmm. First I must get my meter. Have I told you that poems need meter?" Gregory ground his teeth.

"Brother, I am trying to clear my soul of a lifetime of sin by confessing to you. Can't the poem wait?"

"Confession? Whatever for? You're acting like a condemned man. Let's see—what rhymes with *oiseau*?"

The listeners at the aperture leaned forward. Almost invisible, the narrow air shaft penetrated the cell so that every word a prisoner spoke could be heard in the tiny room beyond.

"Hst! He's about to confess!"

"But do we have to take down the poem?"

"The Abbot said put them together after the first questioning, and then take down everything. He has to be sure. You take the poem, I'll take the confession."

"You always do this to me—the poem is dreadful."

"That's not my fault, now, is it?" And two styluses hovered above wax tablets as Hugo, having switched *oiseau* for *hirondelle*, tried again.

"Brother, I envied you for being first. I crave your forgiveness." Gregory's voice was grave. He'd agonized a whole month over this point, and examined the sin of it in several different ways, all of them theologically interesting.

"First? Of course you envied me. Why not? It's only proper. I get the title, you get nothing. That's how it is. That's how it always will be. You never did know how to accept the obvious. I, on the other hand, learned to do it long ago, and put envy aside."

"Envy? You, envious?" Gregory's gloom shifted to shock.

"Of course. I envied you your freedom. Do you think it's a

pleasure, playing handmaid to a stingy old tyrant like father? And when you got all that money without even going to war for it, I went absolutely crazy with it. Luckily, it passed like a disease. And now, of course, I've found the Muse—which muse did you say poetry was?"

"For your kind of poetry? Erato, I suppose."

"Yes, that muse. Tell me, since *hirondelle* doesn't seem to be creating any inspiration, I need another French bird. What do you think of *alouette*?"

"So, have they revealed anything?" a patrician voice sounded behind the listeners.

"My lord abbot!" The listeners whirled about. It was indeed Abbot Thibault himself in full hunting garb, a pomander in one gloved hand to ward off the smell of the place. His other hand grasped a leash that restrained a pair of mastiffs on a hunting couple. Behind him pattered his favorite greyhound and his private secretary, Frère Guillaume. The newcomers, man and beast, filled the narrow room behind the wall to bursting.

"One of them—the dark one—is trying to confess, but the other persists in interrupting him with a poem he's making."

"A poem? By God, the man has sangfroid. Take the coward first. We need to speed things up." The Abbot made a languid circular motion with the pomander hand. "We need to find out who they are spying for before their confederates are on us. I wouldn't be surprised if it were the Archpriest himself, his war chest renewed with the Holy Father's bribe. Sparing Avignon will have left him hungry." He paused to inspect the clerk's notes, then turned toward his secretary. "It is just as well that boastful fellow let their plans slip like that. I do like to have warning when I prepare a defense against siege engines. Frère Guillaume, you've told them to double the watch?"

"Yes, of course, my lord abbot." Frère Guillaume bowed as he spoke, though sadly hampered by the number of bodies in the room.

When the heavy door swung open, Gregory was not surprised that it was him that they wanted. Last to be born, first to be skinned, he thought. That's how it's always gone in this family. When they went through the ritual of showing him the instruments, he said sarcastically, "Certainly. What would you like confessed?"

"The truth," said the Abbot, handing the leash to Frère Guillaume and sniffing his pomander.

"I can do that without all this trash," said Gregory, waving a hand at the Abbot's modest but very modern collection of truth extractors. The Abbot spoke to his monks in Latin.

"I thought you said he was the cowardly one." Gregory's ears burned, but he said nothing.

"I think you don't take us seriously," said the Abbot, returning to face Gregory.

"On the contrary, I take you very seriously indeed," replied Gregory.

"Then tell us how you got here."

"I've told you already. We escaped the Archpriest on the Rhône above Avignon."

"Now I know you are lying. No one escapes the Archpriest," replied the Abbot as he gave the signal for the next stage in the process. Gregory was a bit too long for the rack bed, so it took a while to adjust things properly.

"My, he's bony," remarked one of the laboring Brothers in Latin, surveying the stripped figure in front of him.

"A regular starveling," agreed his colleague. "You can always tell these peasant robbers—haven't a muscle on them. Now the other one's much sturdier-looking. I wouldn't be surprised if that one turned out to really be of the *noblesse*." A livid stain of rage rose up Gregory's neck and flushed his face. If there was one thing he was touchy about, it was about bloodlines and the clear visibility of the proper order of the universe.

"Why, look," said Frère Guillaume to his master, "I believe the fellow understands Latin." The Abbot's eyes flicked across Gregory's crimson face.

"This makes it interesting indeed," the Abbot said, sniffing his pomander once more. "A renegade priest, perhaps. All sorts of riffraff are joining the *écorcheurs* these days." He crossed the room and leaned close to Gregory's face, speaking in Latin.

"Tell me who your master is." He gestured absentmindedly with a gloved hand, and the slack was taken up on the infernal machine.

"The Duke of Lancaster."

"Aha. That's better. The English duke. So what are you doing here, so far from Normandy? And why should we not turn you over to the authorities in Dijon for that alone?"

"Because we travel under a papal safe-conduct. Besides, why Dijon? Isn't Paris closer?"

"Paris? Do you know where you are?"

"Not really. We could not keep up with the party when my lady wife's time came most inconveniently upon her. We hid long enough for her to give birth, then traveled roundabout to avoid the *écorcheurs*. We thought we'd traveled northwest."

"You are at St. Michel Archange in Burgundy."

"Burgundy? My God. That damned Malachi. He said he knew the country." A glitter caught the Abbot's eye. A silver-gilt medallion of little value, lying on the *écorcheur's* bony torso. He recognized it—one of the thousands blessed annually at the Holy See. A pilgrim's souvenir. There were several exactly like it at the abbey.

"From whom did you steal this?"

"Didn't—steal—it. Given—for good luck—on the trip. Good luck—hah." The Abbot looked up from his work at a discreet cough from behind him. A lay Brother with a message had come in and spoke to him in low tones. Gregory could catch a few words: *confession, woman,* and the Abbot saying, somewhat louder, "a curious name, that. Not the sort they're partial to. You'd expect a saint's name—" He felt his breath freeze. Margaret. They'd hurt her. The Abbot returned to his business.

"You are the English duke's spy."

"No—what spy—takes along his pregnant—wife?"

"What are you then?"

"His chronicler." The gloved hand signaled once more.

o o o

"His *chronicler*?" Brother Malachi's mouth was full of capon as he spoke. He was pouring another cup of wine from one of several full jugs that graced the well-set table in the comfortable house established for guests of the higher sort that sat in the very shadow of the immense, arched abbey church. Tallow candles fended off the dark, and a cozy fire crackled on the hearth.

"Yes, that's what I told him, and he said, 'Ah, a scholar. That explains why your son is Peregrinus. You should have called him Fortunatus, for he has saved you twice.' Then we were oh, so jovial. 'You wouldn't put anything bad in your chronicle about me, would you?' 'I'm a generous man,' I said. 'I can forgive everything if I'm well treated. My wife, for example, is very tired and hungry, and hasn't a thing to wear.' He looked annoyed. 'I suppose the Duke knows where you are.' 'Of course he does, I send him regular dispatches,' I told him. 'And don't let that unworthy thought I see cross your mind,' I added, 'lords who slay chroniclers live in infamy for eternity. The brotherhood of scholars sees to that. Surely you, an educated man, should understand how that works. Isn't everlasting glory a better alternative?' 'I've got my own chronicler,' he growled. 'Nice for a local reputation,' I said, 'but I'd be surprised if it were even worth a line in one of the really great chronicles. Now, my master the duke is lord in two nations—that's a chronicle worth being mentioned in. I imagine you'd have a whole paragraph.' 'One?' he asked. 'That scarcely does justice to me.' 'The Duke of Burgundy has only two,' I told him. 'That shows you how scarce space is in a truly significant chronicle.' 'Only two?' he said, and his face got all suspicious. 'How many did you give the Abbot of Cluny?' 'The current abbot?' I said, sounding innocent. 'Why, he doesn't have a half a line, and that only in conjunction with the Duke.' His eyes narrowed and he thought for a while, then he said, 'I want three,' and I knew I had him. 'I'm worth a lot more than the Duke of Burgundy, it's my spiritual reputation, you understand—"

"Try this wine, Sir Hugo," interrupted Malachi, taking the bottle away from Sim.

"This pheasant is excellent," pronounced Hugo, wiping his mouth on the tablecloth. "Do take a sample, Old Fox," and Hugo exchanged bird for wine. "It's the sauce, you know. These French certainly do know how to make sauces." He stifled a comfortable belch. "Now I, for my part, offered to write the man an ode of gratitude, but he said he was too modest to accept such tributes, and demanded that Gilbert and I go see his scriptorum. And his library. Absolutely *full* of books—no wonder these foreigners have soft minds. Tomorrow we have to go see his holy spring and collection of shrines, as well as the waterwheel he had built for his mill. Tallest in the region, he says. What a windbag." Robert, who was cheerfully drunk, had given up eating and was lying propped up against the wall, plinking his lute discordantly and singing:

"Byrd one brere, brid, brid, one brere,
Kynd is come of love, love to crave. . . ."

"Let's drink to Clio, the muse of history," proposed Brother Malachi, renewing his cup.

"What about Erato?" Hugo asked almost plaintively.

"Her too," said Gregory, "though she's been a troublesome mistress."

"Mistress? And here I thought you were a tiresomely married man," said Hugo, his voice slurring.

"That I am," responded his brother. "And I wish they'd bring me the news of Margaret that I asked. That's the only problem with this place. They're great sticklers for segregation of the sexes. Did I tell you that tomorrow we'll be dining at the high table at the Abbot's right hand? At least the Latin speakers will. You'll be at the head of the guest table, Hugo. No, no—he doesn't mean to insult you—he says clerical jokes make most noble visitors very bored, even if they aren't in Latin." He broke off at the arrival of two lay Brothers.

411

"Your lady wife does well, my lord chronicler. She is sitting up in bed with her hair all hanging down, giving the baby suck, eating sweetmeats, and complaining. Such is the way of women." Gregory looked at the man's horrified face, and a strange, ironic smile flitted across his own.

"Complaining? What about?"

"She says the featherbed is not soft enough, that the maid we sent from the village is not quick enough, and that the bath we had drawn does not have rose water in it. She says it is a great hardship to bathe without rose water."

"Brother, this does not sound like your wife; it sounds like mine."

"Wait a moment," said Gregory, shushing him. "I want to hear more."

"Oh, how could it ever be doubted that she is a very great lady? She says the linen shift we sent was too coarse, it damages her skin, and she wants new swaddling bands and a basket for the infant to travel in. She says she wishes to be churched, and we must have a feast, or she will always believe we are of little consequence."

"Oh, she is a tyrant, a shrew," muttered the second lay Brother. "The man who marries is a fool, lured by a honeypot into the Devil's own existence." He shook his tonsured head. "And of all women," he went on bitterly, "those of great blood are the worst."

"Have you any idea of what she said to me?" The first turned to his associate for support. "She said I was rude! Imagine! God spare me from the wiles and wickedness of women!" The first lay Brother blessed himself.

"I thank you for your news. Send my lady wife this dish from our table, and assure her that she has my favor." Gregory spoke in the arrogant, reserved tone of a grand seigneur. When they'd left, he laughed. "I needn't worry about Margaret; she's having fun."

"Fun? I say she's become spoiled in an instant. You need to beat her again, brother."

"Whatever for? Didn't you say your wife acts like that? How many months do you think Margaret observed her? You underestimate Margaret, Hugo. She's a grand mimic, and she's having sport. She's convincing them that she's a great lady by behaving exactly as they expect. I think she'll like the dish. It looks to be all vegetables."

Up in the corner, I could see something misty swirling. "That was well done," announced the Weeping Lady. "Yes—I couldn't have done any better myself." The swirling seemed decidedly self-satisfied. "You can always tell a lady by her tantrums." There was a tinge of cheerful arrogance in the spectral voice. She surveyed the elegant little room and nodded approvingly at the comfortable furnishings, the well-set table, the little cradle, and the high, soft featherbed. The guesthouse for women of rank even had a high-walled garden before the front door, so that a duchess or queen might take the air without tempting any of the brethren with her bright garments or flashing eyes.

"What's she saying now, Margaret?" asked Mother Hilde. She was seated in a wonderfully carved little chair, happily counting over the treasures in her pilgrim's wallet. I must say, I've never seen anyone so set on souvenirs as Mother Hilde. Sometimes I think she'd rather have the remembrance than actually be at the place itself. She says that if you've only been somewhere, then it's just in your head, but if you have a souvenir, then everyone else knows you've been there, too, and respects you for it. Of course, I think you could just make up a tall story about any old rock or fingerbone, and get the same effect—and you'd think after all the time she'd lived with Brother Malachi, she'd know that too. But oh, no, she says false things don't light up your memory the same way, and she's surprised at me. So I repeated the Weeping Lady's words to her, since she couldn't hear them as clearly as I can.

The poor silly village girl they'd sent, who spoke heaven knows what kind of dialect, crouched in the opposite corner, as far as possible from the Weeping Lady's damp mist, trembling and weeping. I must say, she was a useless thing. What on earth possessed them to send such a spineless, hopeless creature to assist us, I do not know. And not a word we said seemed to penetrate her head.

"Now, did I understand it right? You're in Burgundy?"

"Yes, Madame Belle-mère." I could see the wall painting—the virtuous maidens with their lamps lit—right through her, she seemed so much less stormy and agitated than before.

"Well then, that is very fortunate. My sister, the one who married so well, lives in Brabant. She has a splendid big house and is always hospitable to relatives. That's where you must go. There's many a messenger to and from the court of Hainault to there, so you can easily return home by that route. You see? It's ever so simple."

It didn't seem all that simple to me, but I never contradict Madame Belle-mère. She seemed content, and went her way, as she always does. Perhaps it was a fancy, but she appeared decidedly *thinner*, or perhaps one should say more vaporous, and hadn't manifested herself half as much since the incident with the dreadful count.

"She's gone, Margaret. Let's try the dish that Gregory sent over. My, weren't those two lay Brothers droll! I imagine they come in pairs to protect each other from us." She held up a little stone, all smooth, with little bits of color in it. "Look at this, Margaret, it's a new one. They've a holy spring within the wall, near the village entrance, with a fine-looking shrine over it, all hung about with crutches from crippled people cured by the waters. Malachi showed it to me this afternoon, when he and those lay Brothers took me to see the relics in the church. 'Well, Malachi,' I said to him, 'when I told you I wanted to travel and see new places and people, I didn't mean this place or these sour-faced Brothers. But since it's turned out all right, I'll have a souvenir.' So I took this little pebble."

I wish I could go out, I thought. They seem to think I need confinement. And I suppose they don't want me walking most places, since I'm unchurched. If I'm kept here much longer, I think I'll have to have another tantrum. They're certainly more satisfying than I ever suspected. I can see why a person would get in the habit of it.

"Just think, Mother Hilde," I observed, "if every pilgrim takes a pebble, in a hundred years, the little spring will be naked." I just couldn't help teasing her a bit.

"Oh, no, Margaret," she assured me. "God will grow new pebbles there so that everybody can have one. Now do try the spiced wine that the Abbot sent over. It will be good for your milk."

"Not as good as ale, Mother Hilde, and you know it too. I wish we were home."

"Oh, I don't know about that," said Mother Hilde with a faraway look in her eye. "Now that everything's fine, I'd like to see a few more new places. And who knows? Maybe someday —Cathay."

"Mother Hilde, you're incorrigible."

"You think I'm bad? Wait until you're this old, Margaret— just you wait."

In the middle of the night I heard a sound just like my dog, Lion, scratching at the door to be let in.

"Lion, go away, I'm sleeping," I muttered, and turned over in the nice soft featherbed Mother Hilde and I were sharing. It was hard to go back to sleep. The village girl, sleeping at the foot of the bed, snored so. And she slept so hard, even the baby's cries couldn't wake her. Exactly the sort of girl monks would find to help a new mother.

"Lion?" I sat up suddenly. "But we're not home yet—who's there?" I whispered. Mother Hilde opened one eye.

"I'd be very surprised if it wasn't your man," she said, taking advantage of my rising to roll up in the entire bed coverlet and go back to sleep.

"Gregory? Is that you?" I whispered.

"Of course. Open the shutters," the whisper came back.

"Why didn't you come sooner?" I asked, opening the tall shutters and peering into the dark. "They told me you were being feted, and didn't want to see me, so I had a tantrum and they brought me all these things. I decided it meant you were well. Come in the door, now, I've missed you." I could just make him out in the shadows, standing between Malachi and Hugo.

"We can't. There's too much moon. We came in the shadow of the church wall so they wouldn't see us. They built the gate in your courtyard wall so that they could see it from the dorter windows. But this window is hidden around the corner in the shadow."

"Then climb in the window."

"Can't. I got racked this afternoon—or at least the beginnings of it. I'm much too sore."

"Oh, those treacherous liars! They told me you were well." Now I could see that Hugo and Brother Malachi weren't standing on either side of him. They were holding him up. "You're drunk, too, aren't you?"

"Drunk as a king—no, drunk as an emperor. It helps a lot. But don't make a fuss, it's supposed to be a secret from you."

"Yes, we had to take an oath," said Hugo. His speech was all slurred. He seemed almost too wobbly to stand, himself.

"Standard procedure with ecclesiastical torture," hiccuped Brother Malachi. "But they've really been quite civil about it, so you can't start carrying on now. There's not many would own up to a mistake like that. Easier to get rid of the evidence."

"Oh, that's horrible, horrible! And I'm supposed to say nothing?"

"Absolutely," Gregory's voice came to me as I leaned out the window.

"Malachi," I whispered down to them in the dark. "You and Hugo boost him through the window right away. My strength is back, and so is the Gift."

"Gift? What gift? Tosh!" I heard Hugo say.

But Malachi just said, "Shut up and push, and you'll see."

He fell through the window in a sort of shapeless, groaning bundle. I straightened him all out and went to work. I ran my hands over his joints, barely touching them. I could feel the warmth that radiates from injury.

"Not too bad," I said to myself.

"Margaret, what are you doing?" he asked as I rubbed my palms together and brought my mind to the place where the Gift begins.

"Fixing your joints, as I used to fix Master Kendall's gout."

"Moonshine," he said, and his voice was all slurred. "If you persist in this fantasy, you'll become altogether crazy, and then what will I do?"

"Shush, you, I'm working." I'd reached the place. The familiar orangish-pink light began to glow in the corners of the room. In the dark, of course, it was very bright. Then it sprang up all around, warm, comforting, healing.

"You're back," I said to it, as the heat coursed up my spine and the lovely presence filled the room. "Thank you." I had a dim perception of Malachi closing the shutters as Hugo muttered something. I could feel Gregory's eyes. All around me the light surged gently. How can I ever doubt the goodness of God when it's with me, folded around me like a living cloak? I put my hands on each of the places, and then sat back on my heels, feeling the light fade away as the sweetness of it softly drained from me.

"Margaret," he said. "It doesn't hurt anymore. You fixed it." I could hear the movement as he felt himself over in the dark. "You fixed it and—and you *took away my drunk*. Do you have any idea how long it took me to get this besotted? Now I'm as sober as a wretched saint, lying here with all my troubles just pounding on me. I tell you, the pain was easier! I liked my pain! And if ever a man deserved to be drunk tonight, it's me! Especially now! After all that has happened to me, I turn out to be married to a woman who glows in the dark, like some phosphorescent old bone! What will father say? What will my friends say, especially the ones who know all about my devotion to

Judith Merkle Riley

Contemplation? They'll hoot! There goes the ex-Brother Gregory, who wanted to see God, but instead he fell from grace with a woman who glows. What's he do now? Why, he bought himself a knighthood and lives on her money! How's the holiness business, 'Brother' Gregory? My God! I can't ever go home!"

I grabbed up the decanter of spiced wine from our table. It was nearly full. "Here," I said, shoving it into his hands. "Drink it all now, you ingrate."

He propped his back against the wall and he drank. I could hear him *glug-glug-glug* in the dark.

"Good, but not enough," he said, and I could feel his eyes glaring at me. I whirled across the room and felt about to find two additional jugs, different kinds of red and white wine that Hilde and I hadn't even touched.

"Drink these, too," I whispered, all in a rage. "And when you've done, you just slither back out that window, you snake." There were more drinking sounds, and I heard the sound of a half-filled jug being set down.

"Margaret," he said, and his voice was slurred again, "you look very beautiful when you're glowing." Then there was the sound of him stumbling as he rose. He pushed open the shutters, and I could see his curly head silhouetted against the stars.

"But don't take it for approval," he said as he put his feet over the sill and dropped to the ground.

"Feeling better?" I heard Malachi inquire outside.

"Worse," he said as I closed the shutters.

"Oooooh! Men!" I stamped across the cold floor and popped into bed again.

"What did you expect?" said Mother Hilde.

"You were awake through it all? You heard everything?"

"Of course. How could I not be? Lights! Voices! A dead person couldn't sleep through it. No, I take that back—only that girl who's supposed to help you could."

I was sitting up in bed, all rolled up, clutching my knees and my grievance very tight. "Well, how could he be so awful? You

418

just answer me that! I just can't believe he'd be so horrid!" I'd begun to weep with rage.

"Oh, Margaret, you are so very young," sighed Mother Hilde, patting my shoulder.

"What do you mean? I've done everything for him, suffered everything!" I'd rolled over now, and was soaking the pillow with burning tears.

"Margaret, you silly, silly goose. Can't you understand that he wishes he could glow too?"

CHAPTER
14

We did not depart for three more days, but when we did, it was in style. Our horses were fat and rested, and I not only had a basket with a little canvas sunshade stretched over it strapped behind the saddle, but was mounted on the prettiest little ambling mare you ever did see. All cream-colored, she was, with gaits as smooth as silk, so her going didn't jar the baby. We were newly clad, Gregory and I, though we had paid them for it. A tunic's hard to repair when it has been cut off a person from head to heel, and my gown could never be made decent again. And though I suppose it might have been recut to get rid of the stains, I didn't want to be the one who did it.

Hugo led the party, with Robert beside him, both in full harness, for, after all, who knew what the road might bring? He gave off that air of contentment concerning himself that always settled about him when his armor was new-polished and his pennant fluttering from his lance tip. I couldn't help thinking that being dense has its advantages. Little things could fill Hugo with happiness: the way his feet looked in the stirrup, sporting newly shined sabatons over mail chausses, for example. You could see him stretch them out to admire them as he mounted, and hear him wiggle them just a bit to savor the chink of expensive metal on metal. Or there was his foolish smile at the scent of a posy he'd pass under his nose before he tucked it jauntily behind his ear to go off courting some equally foolish woman. And then there was the way that sometimes the light from a stained-glass window would fall upon his upturned face in prayer, just at the very moment he was praising his Creator for making him the very model of a *preux chevalier*. It was all good, and he never questioned it.

Gregory, who rode just behind them, his buckler and bascinet tied to his pommel, looked pale and morose. He'd been drunk for three days straight, and now even the birds that sang by the road seemed to sense he had a terrible headache, and redoubled their efforts as he passed by, causing him to wince.

"And what do you *expect* when I had to write pages of praise about that damned perfumed psalm-singer?" he'd growled at me that morning as he strapped his gear up behind his saddle. "I certainly couldn't do it sober."

"You've written it already?" I'd asked.

"Of course," he responded, giving his saddle girth such a vicious yank that his horse started, and blew out the immense breath it had swelled itself up with. "That was part of the agreement. I had to swear on a ton of relics, and he'd see the draft before I went. Then he *corrected* it, in the margins, no less. Added a whole bit about how despite his outward splendor, he was a modest and humble man. Phaw! Blessed Jesu, my head—it feels as if it had been chewed on by devils."

"I'm not fixing it."

"I didn't expect you to," he'd snapped, and turned on his heel.

So of course I rode beside Brother Malachi and Mother Hilde, where I could chatter with someone in a better temper.

"That's how it is with people who have minds," I told them. "They have problems thickheaded folks can't even imagine.

Can you imagine Hugo worried about 'historical accuracy'? Why, he hasn't even got to 'artistic veracity' yet!" I rolled Gregory's long words out of my mouth just as he'd say them himself. Malachi laughed.

"I always thought Gilbert had met his match when he tangled with you, Margaret" was his cheerful pronouncement.

"One thing puzzles me, Malachi. Why did the Abbot trade me this nice ambler for that rough-gaited little dun? I don't believe for a minute all the high-flown things he said."

"Oh, I don't know," answered Brother Malachi, looking into the distance. Mother Hilde, who rode behind him with her arms about his waist, stifled a smile. But it was too late, I'd seen it.

"Mother Hilde, you know, don't you!" I accused her.

"It's for Malachi to tell, or not at all," she answered, looking very pleased with herself.

"Oh, all right." His grumpy reticence was all pretense. It was clear he was dying to expand himself. "Well, Margaret, my dear," he rumbled happily. "It seems a certain holy confessor of yours was so overwhelmed by the Abbot's good works and manifest devotion, that he felt that the monastery of St. Michel Archange was the only appropriate place to deposit a rare treasure he'd been given in deepest trust."

"And just what treasure was that?" The germ of suspicion had already stirred in me.

"Five great perfectly matched emeralds from the crown of the Queen of Sheba herself, entrusted to me on his deathbed by one Abraham the Jew—in return, of course, for my instructing him in the Christian faith—in which faith he died. May angels sing him to his rest. Alleluia! I gather they are planning a very splendid shrine."

The audacity of it, even for Brother Malachi, caught me by surprise. My eyes opened wide and one hand flew to my open mouth. He looked supremely pleased with himself. Then I thought a bit.

"But, Brother Malachi, what will those monks do when they fade?"

"Why, find another alchemist to dip them again, if they have any sense. By that time they'll have probably made back the price of the mare in increased offerings. And remember, she *was* a trade. Oh, yes—my value's always fair. Besides, it was in a good cause."

"I hear you laughing back there. You're talking about me. Just quit it, will you? I've had entirely enough of this." Gregory had turned in his saddle to shout back at us. Of course, it didn't faze Hugo up ahead. He was singing one of his own creations as gaily as a lark. I suppose I haven't mentioned it before, but Hugo doesn't sing in tune either.

"As the wise Cato says, the suspicious man thinks everyone is talking about him, Gilbert," Brother Malachi shouted back.

"I don't think, I know. You're all laughing at me." He put his hand on his head to stop the pounding his shouting had made.

"When next we water the horses, Margaret, you absolutely must fix Gilbert's headache. I require it of you; I beg it. He has grown altogether waspish," Malachi addressed me in a loud tone of exaggerated confidence.

"You see? I said you were talking about me," came the pained voice from in front of us.

"I was indeed talking about you, Gilbert. I was saying, you are the most hardheaded young person I have ever met—even harder-headed than Margaret here." Gregory turned his head slightly to catch the sound in his ear, but refused to look back at us. "Who else would," Brother Malachi went on, "after saving us all at the price of his intellectual honor, ride ahead of us in a veritable cloud of stubborn arrogance and self-pity, spurning the possibility of riding among us and basking in our admiration and gratitude?" Gregory's horse began to slow. As we caught up with him, Malachi said firmly: "Gilbert, you will allow Margaret to fix your head and you will return to the human race."

Ahead, Hugo burst into a joyful exclamation. He had finally managed to rhyme *hirondelle* with *immortelle*.

◦ ◦ ◦

It was not as easy coming into Brabant as the Weeping Lady had suggested, but then it was not much harder either. And we did indeed have a hearty welcome from Dame Bertrande's sister. When she heard who it was that was at the gate, she ran all the way out to the gatehouse herself, so that she might greet us and exclaim over us. After she had ordered our horses led away, she paused to survey us all, her hands raised in wonder and joy.

"Why! This magnificent knight is tiny baby Hugo, whom I've only seen once before! How grand you've grown! The very picture of a *preux chevalier*!" Hugo set his chin forward so he would look more rugged. "And this beautiful young man is your squire? Have a care, sirrah, I have many charming *pucelles*, and you are not to break their hearts!" Robert blushed becomingly. You couldn't mistake her. She looked rather like her sister, only shorter and plumper. And, of course, much older, for Madame Belle-mère had died many years before. But when she got to Gregory, she burst into tears.

"Her nose! Yes! It is her nose. I never thought I'd see it again." Gregory looked taken aback, and unconsciously put his hand over the offending feature. "To think, the son I've never seen, and there it is, her nose, to the life. My poor dear dead sister!" And taking up the tip of the long sleeve of her kirtle, she delicately dabbed at her eyes, sniffing. "You've got her hair too. It never would lie smooth. She hated it." Gregory took his hand from his nose and put it on his wild curls, and, leaning over to me as she turned her gaze elsewhere, said in a puzzled fashion, his voice low, "I thought my hair was all right, Margaret."

"It's most becoming, Gregory. You wouldn't be half as handsome with different hair," I whispered back.

"And this is your wife, and your precious baby! You must all come at once to meet the Sieur Bernard de Martensburg, my husband."

Leading the way into her hall, she cautioned us, "Now, don't be offended if he does not get up to greet you, for his bones are twisted, and he is confined to a chair. But when you speak to him, you will find he is a man of great wit. Oh, yes. Very admirable. And for this I count myself fortunate in all ways." And she swirled busily through her front door in the center of a swarm of *pucelles,* pages, guests, grooms, dogs, and a half-dozen grimy-faced, naked little peasant babies that she had somehow acquired in her trip across the inner bailey. That is how it always was with her, for she was the source of all good things, and whether you wanted thread, a muffin, an oxcart, a feast for five hundred, or a funeral with sixty hired mourners, it was always "see Madame." Thus hopeful creatures of all sorts were perpetually crowded around her, and she was ever busy.

The hall was wide and fair, built of light-colored stone, with high, columned windows. At the table dormant, all covered with a fine, rich cloth, we were brought to meet the Lord of Martensburg, where he worked at papers laid unrolled and flattened at the corners by books. An astrolabe and other instruments lay to one side, and there were pens and a jar of ink nearby. At a word, one of the two grooms who were his constant companions would pick up or fetch whatever he wanted. His wizened body was seated in a great, cushioned chair, his withered legs hanging uselessly. His back was hunched and his chest caved in; his breath came in wheezes. By contrast to his shriveled frame, the head he raised from his work was massive, with a wide, high forehead and long jaw. The eyes with which he gazed at us were dark, and they were deep with an intelligence that was almost frightening.

"Most gracious lord and husband, these are my sister's sons and their family that have come to us." The swirl of activity paused for a moment and her garments came to rest, as it were, while she knelt briefly before him and then, rising, introduced us all. When the groom bearing the basket presented the baby for his inspection, he looked long into his sleeping face. Peregrine was making little eating motions with his mouth as he slept, snoring lustily.

"The child is straight?" he asked.

"Yes, my lord," I answered.

"Then it is *my* blood," he said, as if answering an unspoken question. Then I remembered something Madame Belle-mère had said: The children had bad bones. "You are curious?" He had addressed us all. "You have never seen this before? It is an affliction of God that grows worse over time. When I wed, my legs still carried me, and my good wife said a straight heart was more precious to her than a straight back."

Then Malachi said something about his star charts to distract him from the unpleasant moment. It had to do with the sun entering the Virgin's house, as I recall, though talk about stars is too complicated for me. Sieur Bernard brightened up considerably, and soon the two of them were looking at his calculations. Malachi knows a lot about stars: he needs it for his work in metals. As he once explained it, there are seven wandering stars, corresponding to the seven metals: mercury for quicksilver, and Mars for iron, for example. All the rest are fixed stars and don't go anywhere. Gregory looked, too, as he began to explain his charts, but hardly anyone knows more than Brother Malachi about stars, and this man could see it right away.

From what I heard, I could make out two big problems: The first was that he was engaged in calculating from the stars the exact time of the Second Coming. He would have had it done long ago, but for problems with the calendar caused by the poor quality of previous star charts. There were things wrong— the calculations of movements and the years were not right. His pages of Roman numerals were an attempt to right the mischief, but it was a vast undertaking.

"I'm afraid it is beyond my powers in this life," he sighed. "But there must be a new calendar." Brother Malachi and Gregory nodded. Hugo had assumed the faraway look that he assumes during sermons and discussions of the fluctuations in the price of salt herring during Lent. But even though I don't understand stars, I wanted to know why.

"To put it simply, for a woman's mind, the stars and the

calendar are out of phase, and if it keeps on this way, we shall have summer in January and winter in July."

"Oh!" I was alarmed. "How soon will that be?"

"Not for hundreds and hundreds of years." He smiled wryly at my agitation.

"Well, then, why worry? That's a long time—too long for me to think about," I answered.

"I worry," he responded, "because it confuses my calculation of the time of the Second Coming." He turned his great head to Brother Malachi. "It will be a great effort: the greatest in Christendom, the new calendar. It can only be directed and ordered by the Pope himself. And as yet, these Avignon popes have not seen the need to turn from heresy hunting and palace building to the greatest problem in Christendom. Sometimes I despair: perhaps God has sown this confusion on earth because He does not wish us to know the day of the Second Coming." Again, Brother Malachi and Gregory nodded gravely.

We stayed for some time. I couldn't untwist the bones, but I did take away the pain and renew his breath, so that the Lord of Martensburg could be carried without agony up the long, twisting stairs of the tower to view his beloved stars once again. Many were the nights that we clambered up behind him, to the light of torches, to the platform he had caused to be built on the tower roof as his observatory. There, the torches were extinguished to give a clearer view of the stars in the dark arch of the sky. He and Malachi would talk about things I didn't understand, such as how many heavenly spheres there are, and Malachi would produce dozens of arguments for eight, corresponding to the seven planets and the sphere of the fixed stars, but Sieur Bernard would produce a dozen more for a ninth, beyond the sphere of Saturn. And though they never resolved it, they seemed very content, the both of them, in their complex arguments. Then they would fall to making measurements with the astrolabe, and pointing, and discussing the movement of the celestial houses.

Gregory could not always follow, but I could see his quick

mind absorbing as he took notes behind a hooded candle for the frail lord. I would help, leaning close to the tiny hidden light to sharpen the quills and blot the finished sheets, so that Gregory would not fall behind in his recording of his uncle's observations. The baby, carried up by a footman, lay beside me in his basket, for it is never too soon for a child to see the stars.

But even the best of visits must come to an end. Sieur Bernard had been pleased to discover that Gregory had been commissioned to do a chronicle, and begged him to include his concerns about the calendar in it. "All that and more," Gregory responded graciously. And we left with a letter to the celebrated Jehan le Bel, Canon of Liège, who is a great churchman and one of the most successful chroniclers of our age.

"Just so you have an idea of what glory may be attained in this worldly enterprise, unlike that of watching the stars," said Gregory's uncle with an ironic smile. And of course, Gregory's aunt began to weep a full day in advance of our departure in anticipation of how sad she would be when we left.

"Oh my, oh my, it is almost like losing my dear sister all over again," she sobbed as we sat spinning in her bower. Her youngest daughter, now thirteen and destined for the convent, sat beside us, frail and twisted, but with agile hands that embroidered an altar cloth in elegant, precise stitches. As I admired her work I thought I saw a smoky figure hovering over the embroidery frame, peering at the exquisite design.

"Oh! What's that?" cried the mother as she crossed herself, and the girl glanced up to survey the forming face with interest.

"Tell her I'll stay," said Madame Belle-mère. "I'm not strong enough to cross the water again. Not, of course," she added with hauteur, "that any other spirit has done it even once anyway. Tell her."

"Madame, your sister is here with us in spirit," I said.

"So I see. And she looks so fresh and young too." Madame sighed. The ghost smiled with pleasure, and rearranged her veil so that the dark curls at her forehead would show to advantage.

"She says she's going to stay. She doesn't want to cross with us, and she's missed you."

"Oh, you can *hear* her? How I wish I could! Dear Bertrande, make a sign if you hear me." The ghost raised a vaporous finger.

"Well, if I can speak and you can sign, something can be arranged. I have years' worth of gossip to catch you up on. And you must tell me of yourself. Whatever happened to the little girl you told me of in the letter you had written to me? . . ." And so we left Madame in great contentment, for as she said, a whole ghost is quite as satisfactory as a nose anytime.

A stiff breeze had filled the sail of the little merchant cog and set its pennants flying. It whipped Gregory's cloak about him as he leaned over the rail, peering for the first sign of the familiar white cliffs. It made the penned horses in the hold raise their heads and whinny. Margaret wrapped her cloak tighter around herself and the baby where she stood, several safe feet behind Gregory. It was her theory that people who leaned over ship's rails might tumble off at any time and that you can never be too careful. Only the imminent danger to her husband had brought her this many paces from the mast.

"I'm sure I see it, Margaret," he cried. "And listen to the horses! Even they know we're almost home."

"For the good Lord Jesu's sake, don't lean so far," she cried into the salty wind.

"Margaret? What's happened to you? You're as brave as a tiger on land."

"The ocean is entirely different. It's full of water," she cried in reply. Gregory removed himself from the rail and returned to her side.

"All right, all right. Here I am, and I didn't even fall off. People don't, you know." He put his arm around her and lifted the cloak so he could peek at the baby's sleeping face. He still found it hard to believe that he actually had that commodity most desired by men, a son, and had to check often to make sure that the little creature was still exactly the same.

"They could, they could anytime." Margaret's voice was agitated. He could feel her shiver as she spoke. "And then it's just 'splash'! and the fishes eat them. And what would I do then?"

"What about me? I'm the one that would be eaten by fishes." He lifted a sardonic eyebrow.

"It would be your own fault," she said firmly. "But it would be me who'd be left, and I would suffer more."

"Then I'll not be eaten by fishes; I would never wish you to suffer." He looked out at the ocean, as if dreaming. "Speaking of fishes, what did you think of the one the Canon of Liège served at his banquet?"

"The huge gilded one with the eyes in? Ugh."

"Biggest I ever saw. And the peacocks, and the swan. He certainly lives well."

"I like your uncle's house better."

"He's a cleric, but he dresses like a knight, and has a lady and two handsome grown sons for whom he will buy church benefices."

"Your uncle's house is visited by learned men. His dinner table is full of wise discussion."

"So is the Canon's. And art and music as well. There's no reason a historian should live shabbily, is there? I mean, God's not angry at the Canon for living a worldly life, is He?" Gregory drew his cloak around him as he looked up at the fast-flying clouds.

"He certainly doesn't appear so, does He? Perhaps He favors historians, have you ever thought of that? Did you hear that the Canon always travels with forty armed retainers?" Margaret watched Gregory's face carefully, and didn't miss the look of speculation in his dark eyes.

"Now that's an elegant retinue," mused Gregory. "He goes wherever interests him, seeking out facts for his chronicle, and kings and princes welcome him and seek his counsel." His whole face had relaxed as he thought about this, and the shadow of a smile crossed it.

"They shower him with gold and gifts for his writing," Margaret added helpfully.

"It all goes to show you don't have to join the Fishmonger's Guild, like Sir Thomas, if you want to set a nice table in London." He looked at her.

"You know," she said, cocking her head on one side as if thinking, "once we've set the house to rights and settled our obligations to the neighbors, we should invite your friends to a dinner party. The scholars at the Boar's Head, I mean. I like them. Only they have to promise not to throw the furniture when they're drunk."

"They don't throw the furniture, Margaret. They're civilized. They throw people. Father throws furniture."

"Oh, my goodness. Your father. We'll have to send him a message when we've landed. I wonder how many days of peace we'll have before he figures out another way to interfere with our lives."

When we landed at last, Sir Hugo did not wait the night but set off immediately for his father's house, bearing our news. He had heard at Dover that reinforcements would be soon leaving to join the troops of the Duke in Normandy, and he chafed to be back in action and as far from his wife as possible.

"I'll look in on father, get that woman with child, and then— it's back to France and Fortune. Why leave all the luck to the Prince's followers? They're all coming back from Bordeaux richer than the Devil himself. Well, I say, next time it'll be me!" And off they all went, in a clatter of hoofbeats.

We rode into London from the Southwark side. Even before we'd reached the bridge, people had stopped to gawk and point, for we made an odd sight. Since we had but three horses, Sim rode up behind Gregory, and as little fond as he was of urchins in general, he had become attached, in a sort of horrified and fascinated way, to this urchin in particular. It was hard to say what Gregory looked like, at this point, light-armed and travel stained, his beard untrimmed and his hood rolled around his head like a heathen's turban. Most likely, a mercenary home from a bad campaign. But there was no mistaking Mother Hilde. With her wide straw hat, now quite battered, tied firmly over her veil and wimple, and her pilgrim badges sewn all over her dusty cape, she rode home in triumph behind Brother Malachi.

"Look, look! Pilgrims come from over the sea!" a girl cried, and Mother Hilde beamed.

"Bless us, good mother!" cried a woman in a patched gray surcoat as she ran up to touch Mother Hilde's cloak, as if the goodness of the holy places could be rubbed off it. When a little crowd gathered and followed her all the way past the stews to the bridge, she was transported with joy. I got my share, too, for I could hear people say, "Look! A baby born abroad! Look at the beautiful white horse! She must be a lady!"

There were no new heads on the bridge today, which I counted a mercy, for I wished to leave off seeing heads for a while. Just a single skull, picked dry by ravens and unclaimed by relatives, rattled on its spike in the breeze to greet us. Below, the bridge was aswarm with travelers, for it was a fine day. The shops were open, and tradespeople crying their wares. As we threaded our way past the crowds and laden mules by St. Thomas's chapel, I heard a voice call, "Dame Margaret!" It was Philip, one of Master Kendall's apprentices who had been given over, at his death, to Master Wengrave. He was taller, and his voice was cracking, but I still knew him. I hailed him and he pushed through the noisy crowd close enough to hear me as I leaned down from the saddle.

"Run to Master Wengrave's house as fast as you can, good Philip, and tell him I've returned safe home, with my lord husband who was in France. And bid Mistress Wengrave to tell our steward to ready the house, for we will sleep there this very night." And with a joyful whoop, the boy vanished into the throng.

But, of course, once said, the damage was done. The rumor began to rattle that I had abandoned my husband and married a Frenchman, and by the time we turned down Thames Street a woman cried from a window: "That's him! That's the Frenchman! Shame! Shame!"

"That's London for you, Gregory. Everyone knows everything, and it's wrong. London's not so great as Paris, nor as grand as Rome, but it's still best because it's—"

"Please, God, you weren't going to rhyme *Rome* with *home,* were you?" he interrupted me.

"Why, no, but I was going to *say* 'home'—oh, my goodness—" and I put my hand up to my mouth. "No, I swear to you, Gregory, I haven't contracted the rhyming disease. Well, anyway, not yet."

"If you love me even the tiniest speck or scrap, refrain from becoming infected with it. I fear I have a lifetime of suffering ahead with Hugo."

"Very well." I smiled. "I love you more than a speck."

But we really were home, as Lion's joyful barking attested and the shouts and laughter confirmed, when we rode into the alley that ran between our stableyard and that of the Wengraves'. Every shutter had been thrown open on either side of the street, and all the neighbors had leaned out to huzzah and wave napkins and scarves like banners before they rushed out to crowd about us and hear the news.

But it was Cecily and Alison I was looking for, even before I'd dismounted. They ran from the door of the Wengraves' kitchen ahead of everyone else shouting, "Mama! Mama! Mama's back; I told you she'd come back!" Oh, I was overjoyed.

"My precious babies!" I cried. But when they saw the basket, they stopped short.

"What," said Cecily, pointing her finger, "is that?"

"Not a present," said Alison.

"My dears, this is your new little baby brother, who was born overseas. Would you like to see him?"

"We don't want a baby brother," announced Cecily in a firm little voice.

"No. Boys are dis-gusting," added Alison.

Gregory had dismounted and stood beside me to help me down from the mare.

"*He's* back, too," said Cecily.

"Did you have to bring *him*?" queried Alison.

Gregory had his back to them, and was facing the mare's flank. When he heard what they said, he turned around very slowly to look at them. Then he pulled together his fierce, dark eyebrows in a grim stare of disapproval. Never in his life had he looked more like an *écorcheur,* fresh from the killing fields, all dusty and swarthy from the sun.

"I am not 'him.' Henceforth, you will address me as 'father,'" he stated, very slowly and distinctly. An ordinary child would have quailed.

But the skinny little mophead who had ridden the destrier that had killed a man looked him in the eye and said: "You're not my papa."

"No," he said, and his voice was grave and quiet. "But your papa lives in heaven now, and you need a flesh-and-blood father on this earth, if you are to live to grow up. I am what you have while God wills it. Remember that, and call me father." It seemed like an eternity that Cecily stared at him, turning it over in her mind. Alison stuck her thumb in her mouth, waiting for Cecily's response.

"Yes, father," she said, and, hesitating briefly, curtsied in the fashion she had learned from Mistress Wengrave. A look of disgust crossed Alison's baby face at this betrayal, and she turned on her fat little heel.

"And you," said Gregory. Alison ignored him. "The little one. Alison. Turn 'round." She turned. She ruminated on her thumb awhile, thinking. Then she took it out of her mouth. I know her well. She was calculating her advantage.

"Yes, father," she said. And holding her skirt in both hands, she wobbled a bit in the form of a curtsey.

"Good," he said. "Now I will help your mother down so that you may embrace her." And handing me down, he called a groom to assist him in unfastening the basket, standing guard while the neighbor women swarmed about it crying "Precious! Sweet! How beautiful! How big!" and the horses were led away.

Late in the night, Gregory sat up in bed. It was so silent that even the crickets had stopped chirping in the garden. The newly hung bed curtains were drawn back, but it was impossible to see anything in the dark behind the closed shutters. The chamber was still stark, denuded of its chests and hangings, and the carpet not yet put back, but that didn't account for the strangeness of it. He had never slept there before. And he had never sat at the head of his own table before, giving orders and having the servants bring him the dishes for his approval. And never, in his wildest imaginings, had he dreamed that after supper, sitting by the fire, he would hold two little girls on his lap while reading aloud from the romance of *Ywain, the Knight of the Lion,* which stood on the candle-lit bookstand before him. The entire household had watched silently as Alison had taken him by the hand and pointed to the place he should begin—a beautifully painted bookmark placed there by Master Kendall only two days before his death. They had listened with rapt attention as he began to read in his clear, grave voice, for the story, all written in the common tongue from some Frenchman's tale, is a very good one, and they all had been wondering for some time what had happened after the lion was rescued from the venomous serpent. It was all different. So very different.

Margaret heard him right away, for being a mother, every rustle in the night awakened her.

"Are you up?" she whispered, wrapping the covers around her tighter.

"Of course. What do you think?" he whispered back in the dark.

"You aren't sick, are you?"

"No, I'm thinking."

"Thinking about what?"

"That my life didn't turn out the way I'd expected."

"Nobody's does."

"I guess I'll never see God after all. It seemed very close there, for a while, but then it slipped away."

"Don't worry, God sees you."

"God sees everybody. I wanted to be special. I guess I thought it would be very fine if everybody said, 'There goes Brother Gregory; he may only be a second son, but he's really illuminated. But that just turns out to be Pride." He sighed. "I guess you can't find God by looking."

"I think—I think you can by asking. And—by listening . . ." She curled up in the covers and closed her eyes again. Gregory tucked his knees up, and put his elbows on them. Resting his chin on his cupped hands, he peered into the impenetrable darkness. He listened. First he heard his own breath coming evenly in the quiet, and the soft pulse of Margaret's beside him as she returned to sleep. Then he heard the little uneven puffs of the baby in the cradle, and through the walls the children and old Mother Sarah and Cook and even the neighbors. The little thoughts that cluttered his mind like busy ships moving to and fro in the harbor had been swept away in the listening, and he no longer sensed himself as he listened. He wasn't turning over old sins like moss-covered stones to see what was underneath; he wasn't addressing prayers to the Virgin or imagining the Passion; he wasn't naming the seven virtues or praising the mighty deeds of God. Not a thought of last night's supper or tomorrow's breakfast flitted past like a distracting moth. And still he listened, until he could hear the deep and ageless sound of the earth breathing. And beyond that, nothing. As he entered Nothing, a strange warmth sprang up in his breast, somewhere around the heart. And he didn't say, Aha! this is described in the *Incendium Amoris* but not in the *Scala Claustralium*, but instead, Let it be. It kindled and sprang higher until he was ablaze with it. It reached high up, outward, and inward into the Nothing. Pure love, on fire. It blazed, for a fragment of a moment, all the way to God, like a spark rising in the darkness. And as it died down, he could sense that everything on earth was softly glowing with it.

"Astonishing," said Gregory to himself as it faded and he returned. "I must try this again sometime," he mumbled, as he rolled over and sleep overtook him.

"Let's see—you'll be wanting to invite that Robert le Clerc—" Margaret was all abustle, counting off potential guests on her fingers in order to keep track of the place settings.

"How do you know that old tosspot? He's not the proper sort of person for you to be acquainted with, Margaret." Gregory's voice was not altogether undismayed. It's like uncovering an unconfessed sin, when you discover your wife has made the acquaintance of your old friends from bachelor days.

"I know him from when you were gone."

"Worse and worse. Did he try any of his lecherous tricks?"

"Him? Oh, no," Margaret laughed. "He came to apologize for a filthy song he'd written about you."

"You mean—there's a filthy song about me going the rounds of the City?" Gregory had been enjoying his newfound respectability, wallowing in it, even, and so the thought of the song disturbed him more than usual.

"It's going the rounds of the *realm*, Gregory. So just don't bother yourself about it." He put his hand on his head and groaned.

He was sitting in the room off the hall on the ground floor where Roger Kendall had once done his accounts. The wide oak table and narrow bench were as they ever had been. The glass had been put back in the window. The room looked bigger without the bales and bolts that had been perpetually stacked there, even though it now contained a new piece of furniture—a plain, iron-studded wooden chest containing excerpts from Jehan le Bel's new chronicle, as well as a nicely bound copy of his virelays given as a parting gift. There was also a borrowed copy of the chronicles of Matthew Paris for reference in addition to the untidy stacks and rolls of notes taken abroad.

Above the table, on which quills, knife, sand, and ink were neatly laid out beside the half-written sheet of paper that lay beneath his hand, there was another new thing hanging on the wall halfway between floor and ceiling. It was a crucifix, austere and dark, with the figure of Christ carved in light wood. While the cross itself was ebony, inlaid and beautifully finished, the little figure was unpainted. Gregory, browsing along the street one morning, had seen it in the woodcarver's shop that way. He stopped to watch the man as he sat in the window, finishing it off with delicate strokes, as he prepared it for the lurid coating of gilt, azure, and gore that characterized all of his finer works. Something about the face of the little figure—perhaps it was just the way the light caught it—seemed oddly familiar to Gregory, so he entered into negotiations on the spot out of concern that paint might spoil the illusion.

Now he found there were times it was good to look at it as it hung there, and sit quietly a moment, before beginning again. When the chronicle was going badly or when he'd opened and read a letter from his father, for example, it seemed to calm him. Or then there was the day when a terrified cat, dressed in baby clothes, had leapt through the open door and onto his writing table in a single bound, spilling his ink across an entire page. He'd confronted the creature's clattering little pursuers without even shouting, which was really quite astonishing, all things considered.

"Are you sure?" he asked Margaret, looking again at his crucifix, sighing, and taking his hand off his head.

"Oh, yes. I heard the song on the road from Wymondley last fall. Your only hope is that a worse one about somebody else will supplant it. Now, what about that nice fellow who sells books?"

"Nicholas? You know him too?"

"A bit. Now you be sure to tell them it's an evening dedicated to the muses, so they must each bring some of their work. Cook's planning her finest, and I've already ordered the wine."

"There'll be ale too?"

"Absolute gallons. You know, I've just been thinking. We never had a wedding feast, and we've been married over a year. So this will serve, in a belated sort of way, won't it? Now, how about Master Will?"

"That priest who rants on street corners about the end of the world? Are you sure, Margaret?"

"He's writing a long poem about the sins of the rich, Gregory. Master Kendall supported his efforts for years, and I believe you've inherited him. He stopped by just yesterday for something to keep him in paper."

"Oh, all right, since you insist."

It was the vintner's wife who first discovered that Margaret was having a feast of the muses. She heard of the wine order from one of her husband's journeymen, which led her to consult further through her cook to Margaret's cook to discover the precise nature of the gathering. She then took counsel with Mistress Wengrave, who agreed that it was entirely unfair that old friends should be neglected in an evening that promised to be so interesting, with such unusual and fascinatingly raffish guests—the sort who aroused curiosity precisely because one was not allowed to greet them on the street. It was only a moment's work to convince Margaret to pretend that she had intended for them to come all along and order more wine. It was a much more touchy matter to rouse their husbands from their ledgers and convince them that an evening with the muses would be quite as lovely as an evening spent cultivating business contacts in high places.

"The muses? You mean poetry and singing?" rumbled Master Shadworth, the mercer, who had a very splendid establishment two streets from the tall house on Thames Street. "Surely, this is some unworthy charity of yours, mistress. You don't expect me to greet a woman who ran off with one of her husband's clerks before his corpse was cold, do you?" He paused to weigh the number and force of his wife's words as he would silver in a balance. He never actually listened to what she said, but only measured the amount. A man should never make judgments on his wife's reasoning, since women have no logic to speak of, and one can easily be led into foolish actions by their chatter.

He nodded occasionally, in a neutral sort of way, as one does in this sort of situation. "Of course, we've paid visits before," he broke into the torrent of argumentation with the careful tone one would use to address a mental incompetent. "But that was when Master Kendall lived. You must understand there's a difference now. I've no wish to meet clerks who spout French verse: they'll only want to borrow money." But in the end he was prevailed upon, as was Master Barton the pepperer and even Sir Thomas de Pultney, the fishmonger, or perhaps he might better be called a fish broker, for the only fish he dealt with personally were numbered barrels of salt herring on paper.

Then Margaret had to send another order to the butcher's and the poulterer's and the grocer's, and arrange for the loan of an extra trestle table from Mistress Wengrave.

"Margaret," an appalled Gregory addressed her. "This has gotten entirely out of hand. The disaster I foresee makes me yearn for the monastery. Robert will get drunk and pinch the ladies; Master Will will denounce the rich; the fishmongering knight will deliver his opinion on the lower orders in trade. All that it lacks is my father, denouncing the merchants of the City as money-grubbing parasites bent on consuming the honor of England in their cash boxes. How could you have allowed it to happen?"

"But Gregory, think of it this way. You've never been properly introduced to the neighbors. You can't just slink back into town and pretend nothing's happened, after all. I've doubled the wine order; if they drink enough, it will all work out smoothly—you'll see."

Gregory sighed. "Yes, I imagine I will see. The more they drink, the more they'll fight. Then I shall have to change my name and return to the Continent to hide for the rest of my life. I think I'll organize a Free Company and die in harness. Thus, with one disastrous evening, you'll have accomplished what my father has failed to manage for years." He shoved his thumbs under his belt and went off to walk mournfully about the streets as a way of saying good-bye to the City he loved so.

But Margaret went off to consult with Cook on the *entremets,* for she knew that when something like this happens to a person, the only way out of it is through it, and activity is a great distraction for the troubled mind.

"Now, what more can possibly happen?" said Margaret to herself on the morning of her fete, sitting down to nurse the baby as a way of getting off her feet. The trestle tables were being brought into the hall, the goblets unpacked, and the long unused linens shaken out and aired. Good smells had been coming for days from the kitchen, and Cook had wept into the broth at how it all reminded her of the old days, when good Master Kendall was alive. And all the while for the past several days there had been an ebb and flow of visitors, ostensibly to admire the baby, but also to try to catch a glimpse of that fabulous object of gossip, Margaret's new husband, who was rumored to be—oh, heaven knows what. Possibly a Frenchman, maybe once a monk. Perhaps a French monk or maybe a soldier. Or was it a foreign lord or an English knight? Well, at any rate, he had "Sir" in front of his name, whether it was authentic or not. And he knew the King, or perhaps it was the Duke of Lancaster, or the Prince of Wales, or the Archbishop, or somebody else very interesting on the most intimate of terms. He was a step up or a comedown, but in any event, well worth inspecting. Of course, it was difficult to tell quite what he was, by his grave, polite salutation. And wasn't that an interesting cut of foreign doublet he had on? And the *chaperon*. Quite unusual, and would certainly look quite nice on one's own husband if one could coax him into wearing fancy foreign styles.

Margaret sighed, letting the easy wave of relaxation and pleasure sweep over her body as the milk let down. Her feet were propped on the little stool before her chair, and she half closed her eyes to shut out the booming clatter of the world before looking down to admire the blissful fulfillment on the tiny face working away at her breast. Once again, we two, she thought. A familiar cold, damp feeling caught her at the back of the neck.

"Master Kendall? Are you there? I've missed you; it's been hard."

"Oh, Margaret, you look so contented there. I think he must have said it."

"He did, but it wasn't easy."

"Then you won't be wanting me anymore."

"Yes, I will, I'll always love you."

"Margaret, you have a big heart."

"Always big enough for you."

"But I have news. I've been accepted among the blessed. A very nice location they've reserved too. They said it was an honor I didn't deserve, but they were tired of your bothering them. I thank you, little Margaret."

"Oh, but don't go too soon. Stay for the party, at least. There'll be poetry, and music, and readings. You'll like that."

"I've already got permission to stay for it, Margaret. You know how I've always enjoyed an evening of good conversation." Master Kendall's ghost was formed up now, all filmy in his long merchant's gown.

"You look good," said Margaret. "Not all flimsy like Madame Belle-mère got after crossing the water."

"She actually made it? I've never heard of such a thing." Kendall's head was cocked to one side, and the interest shone in his translucent eyes. He always had loved a good story.

"Stay with me, stay with me, Master Kendall, and hear what happened. Not a living soul wants to hear my side of the story.

442

They're all busy making up their own versions right at this very moment."

"As I recall, that always was one of your problems. Anyway, you know I can't resist a good story. I'll hear it to the end."

"And you'll tell me how it fared with the girls—I worried greatly, you know."

"Of course. But Margaret, you know you can't hold me here forever. I'm required to ascend, once heaven has been opened."

"I know. But can you ask them to let you come back? For special occasions? Perhaps when Cecily and Alison are married?"

"I've put in a request already."

Margaret was so caught up in the comfort and quiet of the moment, and her mind so engaged in pleasant conversation with the long loved voice, that she did not hear the commotion at the front door, the loud voices, and the clatter of spurred feet invading the hall.

"Well, where IS he?" boomed through the parlor door. And before she had time to take her feet from the footstool or the baby from the breast, she was confronted at close range by an unexpected sight. His liripipe was wound all askew; his white beard and hair were flying about like a depiction of Jupiter among the storm clouds. His shaggy eyebrows were restored to their thunderous menace. He was wearing his best red velvet surcoat, the one he saved for weddings, baptisms, and the visits of high dignitaries. My God, he's well, thought Margaret.

"My lord father-in-law," she said, rising to greet him. Clustered at the door she could make out various figures. Hugo. Her husband. Sir William Beaufoy, from the Duke's suite. Sir John, the neighbor from the country. It was exactly as Gregory had foreseen. The final disaster.

"Is this HIM?"

"Yes, my lord father-in-law. It is your grandson." The baby, his peaceful moment broken, looked up at the source of the disturbance in a vaguely annoyed fashion. Milk dribbled down his chin.

Old Sir Hubert took in at a glance the odd, baby swan–colored fuzz, which was beginning to show curls, the watchful, all-absorbing little eyes, and the trickle of white oozing from the corner of a determined little mouth.

"Looks not unlike his father at that age," he said. Then he prowled about a bit, as if to see them, mother and baby, from all angles. "Are his limbs straight? Unwrap him, madame, if you please." Margaret silently removed the swaddling clothes and held the naked baby up to face the old man's inspection. His eyes narrowed, and he peered shrewdly up and down at the tiny body, the way he'd inspect a horse for sale. Something about the waving white beard or glaring blue eye offended the baby. He startled, his tiny limbs suddenly stuck out all stiff and trembling, his minuscule fingers spread wide apart. Almost simultaneously, he turned red all over his body and began to howl. Somehow, his mouth seemed to be by far the largest part of him at this moment—larger than his head, if that were possible.

"*Sounds* not unlike his father at that age," observed the old man.

"Now, now," clucked Margaret, as she wrapped the baby up again and tried to console him.

As the howling subsided into hiccups, the old man said, "He looks as if he's a heavy feeder. Is he a heavy feeder, madame?"

"Yes, my lord."

"His father required two wet nurses." There was a long silence. "His mother was in bed a month." Then he looked again at them both.

"I am told that a day after the birth you rode a full day's march for seven days, and your milk never failed."

"Yes, my lord."

"I chose well. You are a strong woman." Margaret could feel the rage rising in her. If this is what you mean for a compliment, you stingy old thing, you can take it right back home again with you, she thought.

"I am told that you bartered my son's ransom over a game of dice, by wagering your life." She could see Gregory's eyebrows go up in shock. She'd hoped to keep the dice game a secret from him forever, it was so demeaning. God, what a tactless old man. He leaned his face into hers suddenly and growled, "What madness *possessed* you, madame?"

"The dice were loaded, my lord."

"Loaded? Hugo, you never said—" the old man spluttered. "Loaded! HAW! Loaded indeed!" His face turned red with suppressed delight, and his eyes flicked over Margaret as if he suddenly saw her as someone else entirely. "You ARE a de Vilers woman, after all! Come in, my lords, come in, I say, and do honor to the woman who cheated the Devil himself with a set of loaded dice!" And as they poured into the room to do just that, Margaret flushed scarlet with embarrassment.

And, of course, they had to stay for the party, even if they were on their way to Dover, to sail for France again. As Margaret left to order more places laid, she could hear male voices congratulating Gregory on the birth of his son and grumbling, "Imagine! Holding a prisoner of rank without ransom! Dishonorable! Unheard of! And a Devil worshiper, too, they say!" And above it all rose the voice of the old Sieur de Vilers:

"Dammit. You look THIN! I've seen better-fleshed SKELETONS hanging on GIBBETS! You can't go back into the field looking like Death in PERSON!"

"—and John, have Cook send to the bakeshop at the end of the street for absolutely *everything* they have. I don't care if it's an insult to her skill. These people are heavy feeders. I swear, there won't be enough. Oh! The wine! And the tables! Do we need another? How *will* we fit it in?" And Margaret rushed off, full of worries, to inspect the progress being made on rearranging the places in the hall.

With the first course, the neighbors noticed across the potages the fancy French manners Margaret had picked up abroad. Her husband certainly seemed suspiciously deft at table for an Englishman, but then, wasn't he gracious as he offered her the cup and the best bits of the dishes? And didn't she look happy? And one had to admit the company was most distinguished, as well as witty. Nobody had mentioned that there'd be gentry present. That made the evening ever so much more elegant, and one's husband looked mollified already. Why, one had yet to hear a single discussion of accounts receivable.

And while it was really altogether improper that the little Kendall girls had been allowed to be seated at table like adults for the evening, one had to admit they behaved most admirably, even if they had been seen cuffing each other when that old knight's good-looking squire had looked in their direction. But you must credit Mistress Wengrave for the unexpected improvement in their manners, and certainly she is a candidate for sainthood, my dear—oh, you hadn't heard. If you only knew, you would understand—a martyr, yes a martyr, for almost an *entire* year.

With the second course, when the elegantly displayed peacock was brought in and set among the profusion of dishes, it became apparent that the wines were very well chosen, and the air seemed most delightfully warm and rosy in the room. Sir John had begun to form a good opinion of the merchants of the City, who were clearly men of gravity and far sight, not the comfort-seeking, money-hungry, and ignoble parasites that he had been led to believe. A younger son who was a bit on the frail side, like his little Thomas, who wasn't really suited for the clergy, might do very well in a place like this, if he could purchase him an apprenticeship with a respectable-looking fellow such as this Alderman Wengrave, who spoke so intelligently about banking and the new laws concerning coinage.

"Not at all bad for a younger son, is it?" Sir Hubert leaned over to Sir William and whispered in a voice that could have been heard all the way to Dover.

"You certainly seem to have established him well, though I

must say, it wasn't quite the common way of doing so," replied Sir William, noting the way that Sir Hubert's Gilbert and his Margaret seemed to be able to finish off each other's sentences, as if each knew what the other was thinking already. It was a trick he and his good Dame Alys had, but then, they had been betrothed in the cradle and had been raised together with the knowledge that they would wed, if, by God's grace, they lived to grow up.

"I am NEVER common," harrumphed the old lord, looking quite piratical, even in his best clothes.

"That, I would never say, Sir Hubert. But have you noticed how they get on together?"

"Don't think it hasn't escaped my eye. And damned unseemly it is too. A man shouldn't get set on a woman that way. It weakens the fiber."

"You are fortunate in your grandson," said Sir William, tactfully changing the subject. His own Philip had yet to do as well by him.

"Fortune? It's the STRENGTH of the BLOOD!" the old lord announced. "Look over there." Sir Hubert waved a wing of pheasant in the direction of the girls and lowered his voice to a conspiratorial whisper that made the rafters shiver. "The woman's a girl breeder, if I ever saw one. I spotted it right away. 'Fit only for a second son,' I said to myself. 'If there's anything in him, maybe he'll get something worth having.' With a girl breeder, the POWER of the MALE SEED must overcome the FEMALE FLUIDS." It was fortunate that Gregory was in the midst of making a pun in Latin and did not overhear. But Margaret did, and her face turned bright crimson. The old lord paused to consume the pheasant wing, crunching the bones with some relish and swallowing noisily before he continued. "Now, at least, I begin to think some part of the boy's in working order. Who knows? Maybe if he hadn't weakened his mind with too much book-reading, he'd have accomplished something."

As the last remnants of the fruits and confections were removed, and yet more wine brought, there were those who thought the evening might have been a bit too high-flown for them after all, for Robert le Clerc stood and raised his cup for a long-drawn-out toast in Latin. But those who knew the tongue quickly explained to their neighbors that it was an invocation to Bacchus, the god of wine, though they neglected to mention how very pagan it was, for Robert had been much taken, of late, by the more disreputable works of Ovid.

And Bacchus, so handsomely invoked after so many centuries of neglect, spread his blessing on the evening. For when Master Will arose to announce that he would recite in English, he rejoiced all those who had no French. When he denounced the fickle faddism of foreign rhyming and the neglect of the fine old alliterative style, he rejoiced all the old knights, who expected a heroic saga. There was, to be certain, a brief moment of trepidation when he began with a Gospel text: "In quorum manibus iniquitates sunt; dextra eorum repleta est muneribus," that is to say, "In whose hands is mischief, and their right hand is full of bribes." But it dissolved into general hilarity when it transpired that his subject for the evening was lawyers.

"Lawyers?" growled Sir Hubert. "By God, I could tell him a thing or two about lawyers. I think I may like this, after all."

"Lawyers?" Sir Thomas turned to Master Wengrave. "The man can't teach us anything about those rogues. Say on, sirrah!"

"Law is so lordly and loath to make an end / without presents or pence, it pleaseth full few . . ." recited the poet.

"Your contract was voided, then?" inquired Master Wengrave.

"How *did* you guess?" responded Sir Thomas sarcastically. "They'd had a silver cup and a hatful of florins from the other side."

"Tchah. Bitterness will get you nowhere. Just raise your prices."

"Learning and covetousness she coupleth together . . ." the poet was reciting, and Sir Thomas and Master Wengrave turned from their conversation to applaud the man's well-turned phrase.

"Hear, hear! Well said, Master Poet!" Sir Thomas had entirely lost his customary gravity.

"Of course, I mean to revise substantially." He could overhear the poet speaking modestly to the scholars at the lower table, who were applauding too.

"Not a line different, I say!" cried Sir Thomas. "Tell me where you live, fellow. I'll send you a new woolen cloak in the morning!"

"Husband!" his good Dame Emma cautioned him.

"Don't 'husband' me! I tell you, there's something to this stuff," announced Sir Thomas.

After this, there was nothing that could go wrong, even when Robert's witty sonnet to a faithless florin moved Sir Hugo to say, "No money? Why, that's not a topic for a great soul. And the fella hasn't got a single symbol in it!" and clamber up from his seat.

Gregory's face registered horror: the dreaded moment had come. His eyes rolled toward Margaret like those of a startled horse about to bolt, but she put a calming hand on his arm to steady him as he rapidly gulped down the entire contents of the cup. At Sir Hugo's first rhymed couplets, old Sir Hubert gave a cry like a wounded bear.

"Betrayed, by God! It's a disease! What in the HELL did you do to him? Gilbert, I hold this to your account—" Sir William put a firm hand on the old man's arm to keep him from rising to do some act of violence, and handed him a full cup, that he might follow the example set by his second son.

There was great murmur and emotion in the hall as Hugo declaimed the work he had polished to its highest point.

"What is that, what is that, dear Master Barton?"

"Umph. The French is not like that in my contracts—very flowery."

"But he's saying?" persisted Mistress Barton.

"Um—a great—no, truly great soul—cannot be imprisoned within stone walls—"

"Why, it's about his brother! How touching, how noble of him!"

"—and—uh, poetry flies free to heaven, like—um, birds. Something, something—immortal."

"Oh, it's lovely!" cried Mistress Barton, wiping her eyes. Several others followed suit, for the ardent and unselfish tribute of a *preux chevalier* is always so touching.

"Migod, Robert, no wonder Gregory wanted to hide from his family," said Nicholas, still pink, wiping the tears from his eyes.

"To think he's been concealing the presence of a mind like that from us all this time. Damned ungenerous of him," responded Robert, his sides still aching and his head resting on the table.

"There's only one proper thing to do in revenge," announced Jankyn.

"What's that?" chorused the others, secure in the knowledge that Latin had protected this interchange from the company.

"Why, I'll set it to music, and we'll sing it to him if he ever dares set foot in the Boar's Head again," responded Jankyn in high glee. "Won't it be a treat to see his face?"

"Hilde," said Brother Malachi, who had overheard everything. "I think that I had better warn Gilbert that he's in trouble again."

"Any more than usual?" she inquired.

"No, just the same as always," answered Malachi.

But as Hugo surveyed the company, trying to decide whether it was best to leave them weeping or satisfy their taste for more, he overheard behind his back his father's hoarse query: "Tell me, Sir William, do you think it will keep spreading, like the plague?"

"What's that?"

"The disease. The versifying bookworship disease."

"Oh, of course not. It's just a fad, like pointed shoes. It will limit itself. Who knows? Next year, it may just as well be playing at tenetz."

Tennis, thought Sir Hugo as he sat down. Isn't that the game so fashionable with the young French lords? I wonder where I might find lessons.

"I tell you, if it goes on, it will SAP the fiber of the NATION. The king should regulate it." Sir Hubert's voice was rising again. He was poised on the very brink of his famous peroration on fiber, and the causes of its weakening.

"Oh, I'm not too concerned," responded Sir William in his most calming voice. He was already well aware of Sir Hubert's views on fiber, and believed the evening might not be improved by them. "Be realistic. What's a fire without tinder? The cost of copyists and scarcity of paper will keep the thing under control."

With the compliments of the departing guests still ringing in her ears, Margaret turned to her husband.

"So," she queried, "are you still going to change your name and flee to the Continent?"

"Not just yet," he answered, putting an arm around her waist. "I think I can bear up. Besides, I must take into consideration how difficult it is to hide from you."

"I'm giving notice now." She smiled. "I'll pursue you to the ends of the earth. I'm very determined, you know."

"Stubborn is what you mean, Margaret. And it isn't as if I haven't always known it. And what's more, you're so stubborn that you flaunt it, instead of hiding it decently, as a woman should."

"Are you saying I'm not decent?"

"Not at all, Margaret. No. I'm saying you're just right. I really wouldn't want you any other way at all."

451

* * *

And so it was with feasting and mirth that we returned home, and all was mended and put right except for a few tiny things not worth mentioning. The fuss and the food of the round of entertainments in our honor restored Gregory's humor and began to fatten him up until he was very nearly his old size again. Gregory's father sent him a letter from France that wasn't half bad, Hugo renounced the muse, at least for a while, after a disastrous affair, and Peregrine pleased him by growing a tooth, which he showed off in a gummy grin every time he spied his father.

One day I caught Gregory inspecting his face in the little bronze hand-mirror. He held it at arm's length, turning his head first to one side and then the other, to examine the effect.

"Beards are coming into fashion again, Margaret. What would you say if I grew a nice long one? Much more like a paterfamilias, don't you think?"

"You look good in all ways, my lord husband, so grow as long a beard as you please."

"My lady wife, have I informed you lately that sarcasm is my specialty, not yours? What do you have against a long beard?"

"Me? Why, nothing at all, except the risk you run of treading on it."

"Come now, think of how splendid it would look when I sat in my great chair before retiring, and each of my children and grandchildren in turn came to kneel and kiss my hand. 'Blessings on you, my child—blessings on you, daughter—blessings on you, my son—' Not so bad, being a patriarch. Now that I think of it, God probably has the longest beard of all."

"Oh! You! You're teasing me! Besides, how do you know what God looks like?"

"Me?" he said, putting down the mirror. "Why, I always used to think that God looked exactly like my father. But now I'm not so sure that's the case at all."

"Gregory, you dear madman," I said as I embraced him.

"My precious, crazy Margaret," he said, gathering me up and kissing me so that my feet didn't even touch the floor.

It was then that I decided that those foolish writers of romances and ballads don't know what they're talking about. For what is the getting compared with the having? And, after all, my chevalier had never even once played the harp beneath my window, nor have we exchanged any tokens, except our hearts.